INK
AND
BONE

LISA UNGER

SIMON &
SCHUSTER

London · New York · Sydney · Toronto · New Delhi

A CBS COMPANY

First published in the US by Simon & Schuster, Inc., 2016
First published in Great Britain by Simon & Schuster UK Ltd, 2016
A CBS COMPANY

1 3 5 7 9 10 8 6 4 2

Simon & Schuster UK Ltd
1st Floor
Gray's Inn Road
London WC1X 8HB

www.simonandschuster.co.uk

Simon & Schuster Australia, Sydney
Simon & Schuster India, New Delhi

A CIP catalogue record for this book
is available from the British Library

Paperback ISBN: 978-1-4711-5047-0
Trade Paperback ISBN: 978-1-4711-5048-7
eBook ISBN: 978-1-4711-5049-4

Printed and bound by CPI Group (UK) Ltd, Croydon, CR0 4YY

Simon & Schuster UK Ltd are committed to sourcing paper
that is made from wood grown in sustainable forests and support the Forest
Stewardship Council, the leading international forest certification organisation.
Our books displaying the FSC logo are printed on FSC certified paper.

For Tara Popick
Thank you for a lifetime of friendship, laughter, and love.
I can't imagine what this journey would be
without you.

PROLOGUE

Daddy was on the phone, talking soft and low, dropping behind them on the path. Nothing new. He was *always* on the phone—or on the computer. Penny knew that her daddy loved her, but she also knew that he was almost never paying attention. He was "busy, sweetie," or "with a client," or "just a minute, honey, Daddy's talking to someone." He was a good storyteller, a bear-hugger, always opened his arms to her, lifted her high, or took her into his lap while he worked at his desk. Mommy couldn't lift her anymore, but Daddy still could. She loved the feel of him, the smell of him. He was never angry, always funny. But *sometimes* she had to say his name like *one hundred times* before he heard her, even when she was right next to him.

Dad. Dad? Daddy!

Honey, you don't have to yell.

How could you not hear someone who was right next to you?

If Mommy was out and Daddy was in charge, then she and her brother could: eat whatever they wanted (all you had to do was go into the kitchen and take it; he wouldn't even notice); play on the iPad *forever* (he would never suggest that they read a book or play a game together); ride their plasma cars up and down the long hallway from the foyer to the living room. And it was only when they got too loud that he might appear in the doorway to his office and say: "Hey, guys? Keep it down, okay?"

He wasn't even *supposed* to talk on his phone on the hike—which was his idea. As far as she was concerned, hikes were just walks that never seemed to end. A walk with nothing exciting—like ice cream or a movie—at the end of it. It was just so that they could "be in nature"—which was Daddy's favorite place to be. And Mom wasn't there, because it was their time to just "be with Dad."

"Don't tell Mom, okay?" he'd said, as he fished his phone out of his backpack.

She and her brother had exchanged a look. It made her uncomfortable when he asked her to keep things from her mom, because Mommy had made her promise never to keep secrets. She said: "Anyone who asks you to keep a secret from your mom—a teacher, a friend, a stranger, anyone—is not looking out for you. No good person would ever ask you to do that."

She knew that her mom was talking about stranger danger and how people weren't allowed to touch her body (ew!) or "push drugs" at her. Mommy hadn't said *anything* about Daddy. She very badly wanted to ask: "What if Daddy asks me to keep a secret?" But she had a feeling that wouldn't be a good idea.

So she and her brother walked ahead on the shady path, leaving Daddy trailing behind talking in a soft voice to someone. She couldn't hear him and didn't care anyway. When grown-ups talked to each other it was *so* boring. She didn't understand their words, their tones, why—out of nowhere—they got angry at each other, started yelling. Or worse, got suddenly really quiet, not talking at all. Talking to each other in fake voices, then changing back to normal voices for her and her brother. Weird.

"Look, *what* do you want me to do?" Daddy said, his voice suddenly growing louder.

When she looked back at him, he glanced up at her quickly, then down at the ground again.

"Come on," said her brother.

He took her by the hand, and they ran up the path. All around them the trees were thick and tall, the air clean and fresh. There were no horns and sirens, just the sweet songs of birds in the branches. The crunching dirt path beneath her sneakers felt so different than concrete. The ground was wobbly and soft; she had to watch her step. But the air filled her lungs. She imagined them inflating like balloons, lifting her up into the leaves.

Her friends—Sophia, Grace, Averi—they all hated their older brothers. Brothers who teased and made fun, who scared them and hit them when their parents weren't looking, played innocent when their sisters cried. But her brother wasn't like that. She loved her brother; he helped her build the Lego Hogwarts Castle she got for Christmas, let her sleep in his bed when she was scared during storms. When her mom wasn't around (which wasn't often), he was the next best thing. Always there. Always knew what to say, what to do. Not like Daddy, who she also loved. But Daddy didn't *know* all the important things—like how she didn't like jelly, only peanut butter, how you weren't supposed to turn the lights all the way off at bedtime, just down really low on the dimmer, or that she wanted water only from the refrigerator, not from the faucet in the bathroom.

"What are we doing?" she asked her brother. She'd wanted to stay back with Mommy, but Daddy wouldn't let her. *Come on, kiddo. It's our time to be together.*

"Hiking," her brother said.

"Hiking to *where*?" she said, leaning on the word.

"Nowhere," he said. "We're just walking."

"I'm tired," she said. And she *was* tired suddenly—she wasn't just saying it so that they could go back to Mom. "My tummy hurts."

She *did* say that sometimes, because that was an automatic "let's go home" for her mom. Her dad didn't pay attention; he knew she sometimes was faking because she was bored or uncomfortable. *Just hang in there a little, okay?* he'd say.

"We'll go back in a minute," her brother said now. "Look at this."

It was a log that had fallen and was laying beside the path. "Remember that book: *Bug Hotel*—or something?" he said.

Oh yeah, that book about how when a log falls down, insects move in and find a home and help the log to decompose. Cool.

Her brother peeled back a wet brown layer of bark to reveal a congregation of tiny black beetles; she leaned in close to watch them move and shimmer, burrow into these little holes they'd made. She wasn't a girly girl. She didn't shriek about bugs the way her friends did. She reached her finger down, and one of them crawled onto her hand.

"He likes me," she said.

She turned her hand and let the tiny bug scuttle up her wrist and onto the cuff of her long-sleeve tee-shirt. Her favorite shirt, with the owl on it. She wore it all the time even though a hole had worn under the arm and the hem was coming down in the back.

Her brother was inspecting the log. There was already a deep, long hollow, and her brother was crouched down peering inside. While he was looking inside, she heard the birdcall she'd been hearing, this kind of sweet song, with lots of notes. She'd never heard one like it. Birds usually just sounded like they were cheeping to her, especially in the city. But this bird was saying something, something important.

Once when she'd been walking past the Alice in Wonderland statue in Central Park, she saw a man nearby with a monocular pointed up at a tall apartment building.

"What's he looking at?" she asked her daddy. The man had a table set up with brochures and photographs for sale. Her mommy would have said *I don't know* and that would have been the end of it, because they would have been running to this thing or that thing and there wouldn't have been time to stop. But Daddy didn't ever care as much about being on time, so they wandered over.

The man had white hair and a plaid cap and a very nice blue coat. He reminded her of her grandpa, how quiet and careful he was. He talked about the hawks and other wildlife that nested right in New York City.

"Natural beauty is everywhere," he said. "It finds a place for itself even right here. You just have to know where to look."

He let her daddy lift her up to the monocular, and the man adjusted the lens until it came into focus and she saw two fuzzy gray baby hawks in their nest, their beaks open, surrounding their mama, who was red with white feathers on her chest and who had alert, bright eyes. Penny watched, mesmerized, until her daddy said it was time to go. When she moved away from the monocular, she saw only the building again—except now with the small cluster of brown up high on a ledge. She never would have seen it. After that, she started noticing birds in the trees and always tried to listen to their songs. The squirrels that danced across branches in the park. A woodpecker one day. Her daddy even showed her an article about someone who'd woken up to find a wild turkey sitting on his balcony. What the old man with the monocular said, about knowing where to look, it stayed with her. He was right.

Before they'd left for the hike, Daddy had downloaded an app on his iPhone that would help them identify birdcalls. He also had the binoculars. She looked around at the leafy tops of the trees, shielding her eyes against the bright yellow light (was it *ever* this buttery yellow in the city?). She tried to catch a glimpse of the bird that was singing, but she couldn't. She glanced back down the path—she wanted to show her daddy the log, to use the binoculars. Where *was* he?

"Where's *Dad*?" she asked her brother, a little whiny.

A single echoing crack came in answer. Then a kind of cry, a fluttering of leaves. She turned to her brother, who she could tell had heard it, too, because he was looking down the path toward where they had left their dad. The light shined on his white blond hair and turned the lenses of his round glasses weirdly golden.

"What was that?" she asked. He shook his head to say he didn't know.

"Dad?" he called out. The birds had gone quiet. Louder: "*Dad?*"

When there was no answer, her brother said they should go back for him, so they did.

They walked back down the path, her brother taking the lead. She felt wobbly, a quiver in her stomach, tears threatening. She couldn't even say why she was scared. What had they heard after all? Maybe nothing. They turned the corner to see the path empty. The rocky dirt surface was edged by trees that sloped down toward the river valley. "It's not that steep," her father had said. "But you could still fall a good ways and hurt yourself. So be careful."

She was the first to hear the low moaning.

"Daddy!" she cried. "Daaaddd*dy*!"

"Kids!" his voice was low and far away. He said something else, but she couldn't hear what. They moved toward the sound, her brother edging toward the side of the path, looking down.

"Stay back," her brother said. She pressed herself up against the trunk of a tree, feeling the rough bark through her shirt. Her father was still calling to them. It sounded like he was saying *Get out of here! Run!* But that couldn't be right.

"I see him," her brother said. "He must have fallen. Dad, what happened?"

Then another one of those strange echoing cracks. Her brother froze stiff, then grabbed his leg and started screaming, fell to the ground. It was a terrible sound, high-pitched and filled with fear. It connected to something deep and primal within her, and sheer terror rocketed through her, a lightning bolt. She heard herself shrieking, too, a sound that came from her and didn't.

A black flower of blood bloomed on her brother's thigh. He'd gone a frightening white, couldn't stop screaming. It was a siren, loud and long, deafening. She wanted to cover her ears, to tell him to stop. Her father was yelling down below. Her name. Her brother's name. Then a command as clear as day: Run!

She went to the edge of the path and saw her father lying among the trees, sloping downwards, arm looped around a slender birch trunk as if he was holding on, leg bent strangely. And then she saw the other man. Dressed in jeans and a flannel work shirt, heavy boots. He wore a baseball cap, the brim shadowing his face. In his arms he had a gun, long and black.

She froze, watching him. Her brother's screaming had quieted; he was now whimpering behind her. Her father was yelling still. But she couldn't move; she was so afraid, so confused, that her body just couldn't move.

She heard something, a chiming. A little tinkle of bells. The phone. Her father's phone was ringing. She turned and saw it down the path, screen bright, vibrating on the dirt path. It broke the spell, and she ran for it. She was fast. She was the fastest girl in her third-grade class, always pulling effortlessly ahead of everyone else on the soccer field at relay races in PE. Coach said she was a rocket. But she wasn't fast enough today.

Another man, whom she hadn't seen, was coming up the path from the opposite direction. He got there first, crushing the phone beneath his hard black boot as she dove for it, skinning her knees, the dirt kicking up so that she could taste it in her mouth.

He looked down at her, his expression unreadable.

"Don't bother running," he said. He sounded almost sad for her. "He's got you now."

But she did run. Her daddy had always told her if a stranger tried to take her that she was supposed to run and scream at the top of her lungs and fight with everything she had. *Don't ever let them take you*, he warned. *No matter what.*

Why? she used to ask. The conversation frightened and excited her, like a scary movie. *What happens if they take me?*

Nothing good, said her father grimly. And the way he said it meant that the conversation was over.

She used to lie in bed at night sometimes, thinking of how she would get away from a bad guy that tried to take her away from her family. In those imaginings, she was always strong and brave, fiercely fighting and punching like the kids in *Antboy* and *Kick-Ass* (which she was way too young to watch but did with her brother on those nights when Mommy was working and Daddy was in charge).

It was nothing like this. She couldn't *breathe*; fear was a black hole sucking every part of her into its vortex. Her brother was now yelling, too, telling her to run. And she did. She got up from the ground and she ran past the strange-looking man, leaving her brother and her father behind. She was going for help. She had to be fast, faster than she'd ever been. Not just for herself, but for her daddy and her brother.

How far did she get? Not far when a great weight landed on her from behind, bringing her hard to the ground, knocking all the wind out of her. There was a foul smell and hot air in her ear.

"You come like a nice little girl, and I won't kill your father and your brother. I won't go back and kill your mother, too."

She couldn't even answer as the man yanked her to her feet and started dragging her back up the hill—past her brother who lay quietly crying on the ground.

"Let her go," her brother said faintly. "Please let her go."

They locked eyes; she'd never seen anyone look so afraid. It made her insides clench. She couldn't help it; she started to shriek and scream, pull back against the man. But he was impossibly strong; she was a rag doll, no muscle or bone. Her movements were as ineffective as the flap of butterfly wings.

When she looked back, she couldn't even see her daddy. And after a while, walking and walking with the man holding on to her arm, pulling her so roughly, talking so mean, it started to get dark. She had never been so far away from where she was supposed to be. Maybe it was a dream.

It couldn't be happening, could it? Could it?

PART ONE

NEW PENNY

Millions of spiritual creatures walk the earth
Unseen, both when we wake and when we sleep.

—John Milton,
Paradise Lost

A girl, spindle thin, rode too fast atop a motorcycle with an electric-purple gas tank and fenders, shiny chrome exhaust pipes. The engine roared, scaring the birds from their perches and causing the animals in the woods to skitter into their burrows. The road before her was a black ribbon dropped carelessly on green velvet, a twisting, turning skein between the trees that had not yet started to turn color. She took the bends tight and in control, feeling the confidence that only youth allows, still blissfully ignorant to the hard fact that consequences can be as unforgiving as asphalt on bare flesh.

The Hollows watched as she flew, the tall pine trees reaching up all around her, the last breath of summer exhaled and the first chill of autumn hovering, not yet fallen. The girl was of this place; she belonged here, more than she knew. But she was a fox in a trap, more likely to chew off her own leg than stay and wait for the hunter to come find her. She was unpredictable and wild, powerful, foolish, stubborn, like many children The Hollows had known.

She rode past the woods, past the high school and the small graveyard with the dilapidated caretaker's shack, past the small pasture. Then she turned onto Main Street, which would lead her into the heart of town. She slowed her speed. If she was seen driving too fast, then it would get back to her grandmother, who would then worry about her more than she already did, which by Finley Montgomery's estimation was far too much.

She wound through town slowly, looping once around the square, lifting a hand at the light to the man who waved from the crosswalk. Then she parked near The Fluffy Muffin, took off her helmet, revealing a shocking

11

head of hot pink and black hair. She hung the helmet on the handlebars, not worried about anybody taking it. That wouldn't happen here, not in The Hollows. Mrs. Kramer, owner of the bakery, smiled indulgently at the girl from the shop window. Then Finley disappeared inside the shop, where she would buy some fresh croissants for her grandmother, which she would try to get home before they got cold.

Across the street, Miss Lovely cleaned out the annuals from in front of her bed-and-breakfast establishment while her daughter Peggy balanced the books inside, worrying about the financial health of their business, which was poor. Expenses far outstripped income, and Peggy wasn't sure how to tell her mother, who never liked to talk about such things.

Around the square, shops were opening. Yogis lined up outside White Orchid, shouldering their mats in stylish bags and clutching water bottles as they stood, chatting. From the Java Stop the scent of roasted coffee beans drifted out, luring in passersby. Marion March, owner of Gentle as a Lamb, lay out on a wooden stand a beautifully crocheted blanket made from the lamb's wool she sold in her boutique of handmade clothes and linens. She'd thought by this point in her life that she'd have been a famous fashion designer living in Manhattan. But instead, she'd never left The Hollows. Marion was born and raised here, married her childhood sweetheart, and raised two girls, one of whom was currently studying at the Fashion Institute of Technology, with aspirations of her own to design (inspired by her mother). If Marion was disappointed at the way her life had turned out, no one knew it, especially not her girls, who thought she was the most wonderful mother on the face of the earth.

Around the corner and down the road, private detective Jones Cooper mowed the lawn in front of the house he shared with his wife, Maggie. His wife had been nagging him to hire the neighbor's son Greg to do the yard work. The boy was a boomerang, unable to find a job in banking after college and living in his parents' basement; he needed the work. But Jones Cooper needed the exercise. Of course, it was only a matter of time before he did what Maggie told him. He was a man who loved his wife and was smart enough to know that she was right about most things, even if he took his time getting around to admitting it.

There were 9,780 living souls populating The Hollows. There were good people and bad ones, people with secrets and dark appetites, happy people, and people buckling under the weight of grief and sorrow. There were people who were looking for things and loved ones they had lost, and people hiding. There were lost people, trying to find their way home. Each of them was connected to the others in ways that were obvious or as hidden as the abandoned mine tunnels beneath the ground. Each had his purpose and his place in The Hollows, whether he knew it or not. Every thing here had its time and its season.

After a few minutes, Finley came out of the bakery with a pink box that she carefully stowed in her backpack, mindful not to crush the contents. Then she climbed on her bike. She zipped out of town, returning home the way she came. Even though she had been born and had grown up someplace else, The Hollows had kept its tendrils reaching out to her, tugging at her, keeping her connected until very recently, when it was time for her to come home.

Finley had noticed that all the warmth had gone from the air and knew that it meant winter, her least favorite season, was approaching. She didn't know how fast it was coming or how hard it was going to be. She didn't know that something would be asked of her, something she didn't want to do but in which she had little choice. And she certainly had no inkling that she might not see another spring.

Even The Hollows couldn't tell the future.

ONE

Squeak-clink. Squeak-clink. Squeak-clink.

Oh my God. Finley Montgomery rolled over in bed and pulled the pillow over her head. *What the hell is that?*

Squeeeaaak. Clink.

It wasn't *loud* exactly. In fact, it was faint but unceasing and arrhythmic, like the dripping of a faucet in another room. It was its stuttering relentlessness that made it so annoying.

The unidentifiable noise had leaked into her dream, where Finley had been repeatedly turning a knob on a door that wouldn't budge. In her dream, her frustration grew as she tried in vain to enter the room, tugging and pulling, twisting the rusty knob. Finally, the sound had woken her, tickling at the edges of her awareness as she came to wakefulness, her irritation lingering.

Sitting up, she looked around the mess of her bedroom—open laptop on her desk, stacks of books, laundry in a basket to be put away, more clothes on the floor, boots in a tumble by the door. She was alone, the door closed. She knew that the sound was inside her, not outside.

Squeak-clink.

"Okay," she said, drawing in and releasing a breath.

Finley focused on the details of her room, listing off what she saw. *The gauzy curtains are billowing in the cool breeze. The wind chimes are tinkling outside. The golden sunlight of an autumn morning is dappling the hardwood floor.* She took another deep breath and released it. By staying in the present moment, she could—allegedly—control "the event." This is what her grandmother—who had a way of making it sound so easy, as if it were just a choice Finley could make—had told her. But it required an unimaginable amount of discipline, of psychic (for lack of a better word) effort.

Not that she was trying to *get rid* of the sound precisely, not for good. At this point, she understood that if she was hearing something—or seeing something, or whatever—there was a reason. It was just that she was trying to train herself to take in information in a time and place that was appropriate for it. She was trying to learn how to set boundaries so that "this thing" didn't destroy her life. *I let it take too much*, her grandmother confided. *You can do better than I did.*

"Not now," Finley said firmly. "Later."

The sound persisted, oblivious to Finley's desires.

Downstairs, Finley's grandmother Eloise was moving about the kitchen, making the music of morning—the opening of cabinets, setting of dishes, the gong of a pan on the stove. Then wafted in the scent of coffee, of bacon on the stove.

Squeak-clink.

It was fading as Finley climbed out of bed and stretched high, then bent over to touch her toes. Usually Finley took care of breakfast, thinking it was the least she could do, considering she was living with her grandmother rent free while she finished school. But on important days, Eloise made a point to get up early and cook—which was really just *so nice*. Finley marveled at how different were her mother and her grandmother.

Squeeak-clink. It was fainter still. But *what* was it? It wasn't a sound that was familiar to her. As soon as she put her attention on it, it grew louder again. She made her bed, still breathing deep. *I am in control of my awareness*, she told herself. *My awareness does not control me.*

As Finley turned toward the window, she saw the shadow, faint and flickering like a hologram, of a little boy in the corner of the room. He sat playing with a wooden train. She'd been seeing him for a couple of days. He wasn't any trouble, but she had no idea what he wanted from her yet. *Choo-choo*, he said quietly, moving the train across the floor. She watched him a moment, but when she took a step closer, he was gone, a trick of light.

The woman in the black dress, as usual, stood by the door to the hallway. Finley knew from her grandmother that the woman was Faith Good, a distant relative on the maternal side. Finley *did* know what Faith wanted. *She wants you to be careful*, Eloise had told her. Of course, that's what everyone wanted from Finley.

The sound wasn't coming from either of them, was it?

Finley stood another moment, thinking, listening, watching. She yanked her thumb away from her mouth as soon as she was aware that she was biting her nails again. Finally, she walked over the creaking wood floorboards, down the hall to the bathroom. She stripped off her pink tank top and gray sweatpants and stepped into the shower.

Letting the hot water wash over her, she scrubbed herself vigorously, sang loudly—Jeff Buckley's "Hallelujah." She was a bad singer, completely tone deaf. But she didn't care. All these actions kept her present in her body, in her life. And when she was done, the sound was gone. *It worked*, she thought gratefully as she grabbed the handle and turned off the water. Steam plumed around her, rising, dissipating. She was getting better at saying *when*—something her grandmother taught but had never herself learned to do. Later, after her exam, Finley thought, she'd deal with *them*.

Faith and the little boy were both gone when Finley returned to her room to dress quickly—pulling on soft jeans, a black tee-shirt, Doc Marten lace-up boots. She grabbed her motorcycle helmet off the dresser and her backpack off the floor and pounded down the creaky staircase, jumping the last few steps and listening to the walls rattle in response.

Finley, please! her mother would surely chide. But Eloise let Finley be. Finley and her mother were all hard angles, their edges always knocking up against each other, hurting. But Finley and her grandmother fit together like mated puzzle pieces.

She trailed past the familiar wall of family photographs: Finley and her brother Alfie on horseback—Alfie roaring with laughter as Finley tickled from behind; her mother Amanda's high school graduation day, a grainy, orange-hued shot in which eighteen-year-old mother looked pale and decidedly not joyful; Finley's grandfather Alfie and her aunt Emily bent over a book while a golden light shined on them through the window.

Finley always looked the longest at that one as she passed. Grandpa Alfie and Aunt Emily were both so present in Finley's life, though they had both died long ago—killed in a car accident that Eloise and Finley's mother, then a teenager, had survived but never really got over. Her grandmother never remarried. Her mother Amanda moved away from The Hollows as soon as she could and never came back to live.

Amanda talked about Grandpa Alfie as if he'd been the one who put the stars in the sky. She talked about Emily less, except to say that Finley was *just like her*—wild, fearless, creative, headstrong. Finley got the sense that it wasn't a bad thing necessarily, but it wasn't exactly a *good* thing either, since Amanda usually said it in anger or exasperation or just wonder.

Amanda hated that Finley was living in The Hollows, with Eloise—both things Amanda had fled. *It is driving her absolutely batshit crazy*, thought Finley with only a little bit of malicious glee. She dropped her stuff by the door, but not before kissing her fingers and putting them to a picture of her mother and father Philip on their wedding day. *Good morning, guys.*

In the kitchen, Eloise stood at the stove, a relic that had been there since Finley was small, and according to Amanda, longer than that. The knobs were worn smooth; the cooktop was so brown around the burners that had no hope of ever being white again. The back left burner no longer lit. Like everything else in the house, it was in need of replacement. But Eloise never replaced anything that wasn't beyond repair.

"Grandma, you need a new stove," said Finley for the hundredth time. She caught herself sniffing for gas like her mother always did.

"Why?" said her grandmother, turning off the burner. "It still

18

works. You don't just get rid of an old thing because you want something new."

"Yeah," said Finley, "ya *do*."

"Hmm," said Eloise. "Maybe *you* do."

Finley wrapped Eloise up in a hug from behind and squeezed gently. Her grandmother was small but powerful, giving off some kind of electricity even though she was skin and bones. Then Finley gave Eloise a big kiss on the cheek and released her.

"There's nothing wrong with new things," Finley said.

Eloise offered a patient smile as she brought the pan to the counter and slid scrambled eggs onto two plates. Finley's stomach rumbled.

"Did you hear it this morning?" Eloise asked.

Finley nodded quickly as she grabbed the orange juice from the fridge. "Squeak-clink?"

"I thought it was something in the basement," said Eloise. "But no."

"Can we talk about it later?" Finley asked.

She could already hear it starting up again. She poured orange juice into cloudy glasses. *I am in control of my awareness.*

"Sure," said Eloise. She knew the drill, changed the subject. "Are you ready for your exam?"

"As ready as I'll ever be."

Finley sat and Eloise put the plate of eggs, bacon, and fruit in front of her. She caught her grandmother's eyes lingering on her bare arms. Even though Eloise didn't say anything—and never had since the first day she discovered that Finley's arms were sleeves of tattoos—Finley wished she'd worn her hoodie.

When she first got to The Hollows a little more than a year ago, she'd sought to hide the richly colored dragons and fairies, butterflies, graveyards, mysterious-looking women in long gowns, dark shadowy figures of men and ghouls, a witch burning at the stake, a vicious dog on a chain. Each piece of art on her body meant something—was someone or something she'd seen in her visions or dreams. She'd started getting the tattoos when she was sixteen and hadn't been able to stop.

"Oh, Finley," Eloise had said that day. "Your beautiful skin."

19

"I'm sorry," she'd said. She wasn't sure what she was apologizing for—for the tattoos, for hiding them, for shocking her grandmother. "But this is me. This is who I am."

Eloise had rested a gentle hand up Finley's arm. Some of the art on Finley's body, which started at her wrists and snaked up her arms, over her shoulders and down her back, was still just a black outline at that point.

"It's a work in progress," said Finley.

"Meaning you're getting *more*?" asked Eloise. "When are you going to stop?"

Finley had lifted a defiant chin. "When the outside looks like how I feel on the inside."

Eloise had seemed to consider this. If anyone could understand how different was Finley's inner life from her outer life, surely it would be Eloise. Who knew better than a renowned psychic medium that the world of the spirit was altogether *other* from the world of the body?

"Okay, dear," Eloise had said. "I understand."

They hadn't discussed it much since then, and Finley didn't seek to hide her tattoos any longer. At home with her mother, she would never even dare wear a tee-shirt—because Amanda had no boundaries whatsoever. Or rather, Amanda didn't think that *Finley* deserved to have any. Amanda would stare and harp and moan about what Finley had done to her perfect skin, and how could she mutilate herself like that and what kind of life was she going to have and *oh my God, what about your wedding day*? Because *everything* was about Amanda and her anxieties, her need to have control, and her dashed expectations—even and maybe especially Finley's life.

Eloise sat with her own plate. "It's a beautiful day, isn't it?"

Even though the temperatures were still warmish, Finley could feel the icy lick of winter in the air. When the roads got bad, she'd have to put the bike in the garage and borrow her grandmother's Prius to get around.

"Yes," said Finley. "Gorgeous."

Finley's mood was growing sourer by the second. That was the thing she still needed to figure out. The boundary setting? The pushing off until such time as she could devote her attention to *their* needs? It was completely exhausting and tended to make her cranky. As if she had to build a wall of stone every day, only to have it knocked down again.

"You're going to do wonderfully," said Eloise. Her grandmother grabbed her arm and Finley felt the warmth of her. She was a giver, a recharger. "At everything."

Finley forced a smile, taking comfort in the fact that her grandmother was almost always right.

At the door, Finley pulled on her leather jacket and walked outside to her Harley-Davidson Sportster. The purple gas tank gleamed, filling Finley with a familiar tingle of excitement.

No one wanted her to ride a motorcycle—not Amanda, not Eloise, not the woman in the black dress. Not even Jones Cooper, her grandmother's occasional business partner, approved. *At your age, you think the world forgives mistakes*, he'd warned grimly. *It doesn't.*

Only her father Phil understood her need for speed and the silence she found there. He knew that the single place she was ever alone was on that bike. Eloise and Amanda hated him for helping her buy it; if anything ever happened to her while she was riding it, neither of them would ever forgive him. But he'd helped her anyway—not just because he was a jerk and liked annoying her mother (which he was and he did). But because he got it; he *got* Finley. Her father never claimed to understand the things she saw. But he knew all about the desire to run away.

She climbed on and with a kick of her foot and a squeeze of the clutch, she brought the motorcycle to life. Just the sound of it—that deep unmistakable rumble—gave her a measure of relief, like the first drag of a cigarette.

She waved to her grandmother and tried to measure her speed up the road. But once she turned the corner out of sight and the empty span stretched out before her, she opened it up. She couldn't help it. The bike wanted to go fast; it begged her to push faster, faster.

With the wind racing around her and the engine roaring beneath her, the sound of it living inside her body, she was only herself. All the shackles that held her, all the things that frightened and pained her, fell away. She could think; her own voice was clear and true. All the other sounds went quiet and she was free.

She found a safe spot for her bike in the parking lot of Sacred Heart College, bringing it to a stop as far from the psychology building as possible, in front of a tall, shading tree that was raining leaves in a shower of gold and red. Students and faculty usually parked their vehicles close to the low glass-and-concrete building, one of the newer structures at the college. But Finley tried to leave the roadster far from other cars when she could, afraid that it would get dinged or knocked over. The glittering purple of the gas tank and the fenders seemed to invite damage; she'd already been keyed. There was something about a motorcycle that drew attention, not all of it good. Except on the road, where other drivers often seemed not to see her at all.

Shouldering her backpack, she slipped her phone from her pocket and checked the time. Forty minutes until the exam, more than enough time to get an espresso from the commissary and go over her notes in the classroom.

"I'm ready," she whispered to herself. "I've got this."

As she drew nearer to the building, she saw two girls she recognized from her abnormal psychology class. They were walking arm-in-arm, laughing at something they were viewing on a smart phone. She lifted a hand in a timid wave, but they didn't see her, never glancing up from the screen. Lowering her arm awkwardly, she thought with a sting that she hadn't made any friends in The Hollows, and she probably never would, freak that she was. Meanwhile, her few friends in Seattle were drifting further and further away, and maybe they'd never been real friends in the first place. Maybe they'd just been people with whom it was easy to get into trouble. And once you weren't looking for trouble, suddenly you weren't fun anymore. Her sour mood deepened.

When the noise came back it was so loud that it actually startled her, stopping her in her tracks.

SQUEAK-CLINK.

Her heart fluttering, she glanced around at the idyllic college campus in autumn, a near-perfect catalog picture of trees and buildings and kids with bright futures carrying backpacks. Nothing dark or odd or out of place. *I control my awareness*, she said to herself pointlessly. *It does not control me.*

A swath of gray clouds washed the sun away, and the air grew cooler. Finley kept moving, passing a beat-up landscaping truck parked near the sidewalk. Beside it, an old man in a wide straw hat languidly trimmed stray branches with an enormous pair of clippers. She felt his eyes on her, but his face was in the shadow of his hat brim.

He wasn't the only one staring. A few feet away stood another man, this one young, tousled, leaned against the wall of the building, smoking a cigarette, pinching it between his thumb and forefinger. Baggy jeans, sweatshirt too big. Looked like he could use a shower. Had she seen him before?

"Nice ride," he said as she drew nearer.

He had sunken hazel eyes and the determined slouch of the very tall. He must have been over six feet. She *did* know him, actually. He always sat in the back row of the lecture hall. He had a look about him that she knew too well, heavy lidded and glassy—a stoner like the people she was trying to get away from in Seattle. She could even smell it on him a little, that sweet tang under the tobacco.

"Thanks," she said, glancing behind her. The roadster was out of sight, but he must have seen her ride in.

"Ready for the exam?" he asked.

The noise had quieted a bit, but she could still hear it. What did it mean? Was she supposed to know why the noise had come back?

She glanced around, but as per usual in The Hollows, there was nothing to see but trees and sky. Not that it was a bad thing, really, the nothingness. She needed a little less excitement in her life, didn't she? That's why she'd come here—to get quiet, to study, to learn more about her abilities from Eloise, to figure out what the hell she was going to do with her life. In the absolutely-zero-going-on department, The Hollows seemed happy to oblige.

"Maybe," she said. "You?"

"I might do okay," he said.

He offered a smile that managed to be sweet and a little mischievous all at once.

He stuck out a hand. "Jason," he said.

"Finley."

The sound was gone. She looked around and there was just the landscaper trimming, *snip, snip, snip*. Finley sensed that the gardener was still staring beneath the wide brim of that hat. She couldn't see his face really, but she could feel the heat of his gaze.

Dirty old man.

In another life, she'd have flipped him off. But she was trying to invite less trouble into her life. *Our choices, even the small ones, all have consequences*, her mother always said. Giving some old gardener the finger was probably a fine example of a bad choice.

She was about to go inside instead when she saw them in the distance by the tall oak tree. The Three Sisters—Abigail, Sarah, and Patience, daughters of Faith Good and Finley's distant relatives on the maternal side (obviously). They had been dancing in the periphery of Finley's life since she was a little girl, her constant companions, friends, troublemakers, confidantes, and whisperers of secret things. They'd been strangely quiet, in fact mostly absent, since Finley had arrived in The Hollows. Now, here they were. Patience sitting quietly, bent over a book, her dark hair pulled back into a tight bun, collar buttoned up to her chin; Abigail spinning around pointlessly, long skirts and wild auburn hair flouncing, like a child playing a game only she understood; Sarah, pale and blonde, watching her, laughing. As ever, Finley was as pleased to see them as she was wary. *What are you up to, girls?* And then they were gone.

"I was going to grab some coffee," she said after a moment of watching. "And go over my notes."

If he wondered what she was staring at, he didn't ask.

"Sounds like a plan," he said. He followed her inside to the small commissary adjacent to the psych building.

The coffee at the commissary wasn't too bad. She ordered a double shot and sat down at a table by the window, opened her notebook. Jason sat across from her, took out his laptop.

"You're old school, huh?"

"I guess so," she said.

She took notes in class, then copied them over when she got home. That's how her mom had taught her to study. Even though most people had their laptops or tablets in class, tapping all through the lecture, Finley still preferred the black-and-white mottled composition notebook. Things didn't seem real unless they were written in ink on paper. Words on a screen floated, seemed virtual and insubstantial. Ink sank in and stayed, rooted in the real world.

Finley hadn't exactly invited Jason to sit, and she was afraid that he was going to keep talking, but he didn't. In fact, there was something so easy about his energy that she forgot he was there as they read in silence and then walked together to class. He gave her a nod as if to say good luck, and they each went to the seats they had occupied all semester. Then she pushed him out of her head. No boys. She had enough trouble with Rainer, her ex-boyfriend from Seattle who had followed her—unbidden—to The Hollows and was now, annoyingly, tending bar at Jake's Pub, a cop hangout just off the town square.

Finley took her exam, losing time and herself as she focused on the pages in front of her. The *squeak-clink* had receded to just the faintest whisper on the edge of her consciousness, and for a time she forgot about it altogether.

TWO

Trees made Merri Gleason anxious now, especially when there were so many of them and nothing else. They stood sentry, an impenetrable green wall on either side of the road, ancient and knowing, looking down. How long had they stood there, she found herself wondering, watching in that impervious, detached way? What had they witnessed? If she was honest, she'd always been a bit suspicious of nature—unlike her husband. All the things he loved about it— the quiet, the solitude, the separation from the hectic busyness of modern life—made her nervous and edgy.

She glanced at her cell phone mounted on the dash. No signal. That made her nervous, too. The car *wouldn't* break down, but if it *did*, how long would it be before anyone drove past? How long would she sit on the shoulder of the road among the trees? Would she be forced to walk? She hadn't seen another vehicle in she didn't know how long. And P.S.—what was she *doing* here? Her errand, which seemed so right and true, so hopeful a few hours ago, now just felt a little crazy.

As if in answer to her anxious thoughts, a car rounded the bend behind her. She breathed through a welcome pulse of relief. But before long, the sleek black BMW with dark tinted windows flashed its blinker, then passed her and sped out of sight. She glanced at the speedometer. She *was* driving too slowly, not even forty miles an hour in a fifty-mile-an-hour zone. The truth was, she wasn't the best driver. A New Yorker born and raised—a *Manhattanite*—she'd rather *never* be behind the wheel of a car. She had her license but

27

hadn't driven regularly in years when her husband Wolf insisted that they needed to start getting out of the city more with the kids. Why they needed an eighty-three-thousand-dollar Range Rover was another matter. *Because we live in an urban jungle, baby*, he'd joked. More seriously: *And you need a lot of metal around you.*

She picked up speed, feeling more alone and vulnerable by the second. The trees were soldiers, surrounding her, menacing and grave. Give her the bustle and chaotic energy of an urban landscape any day. There was *life* in a city, the unmistakable throb of people doing, thinking, wanting, rushing.

Merri hadn't even *wanted* to rent the cabin last summer. If Wolf hadn't gone ahead and booked it without even asking her (*It's called a* surprise, *honey. Remember those?*), she'd have said no.

The idea of being unplugged, of long walks through the woods, of canoeing and picnics, of days where they could *just be together as a family*, cooking, reading, whatever it was that people did before they were slaves to schoolwork, and activities, and play dates, and endless birthday parties at Extreme Bounce? Before Netflix and iPads and smart phones and laptops? Well, when it came right down to it, it didn't exactly thrill her.

Because mainly what would wind up happening was that Wolf would go off and try to connect with his inner adventurer. *It's the only place where we're truly free*, Wolf would exclaim. To Merri, the kind of "freedom" Wolf was talking about just meant "without structure." And without structure, there was no control. No mother liked being out of control when her kids were part of the equation. But Wolf didn't get that, because he never factored in his kids when he was making plans.

And the kids wouldn't want to go with him on the excursions he planned because Wolf's idea of fun was not fun for anyone else. (And when the kids got tired, started complaining as they would invariably do, or Merri dared to utter even the slightest note that maybe they'd had enough, Wolf would get peevish and he and Merri would start fighting. And what was supposed to be fun would just wind up sucking hard, as Jackson might put it.)

So to avoid that inevitable scenario, Merri would just let Wolf go off and do whatever he wanted to do, while she, Abbey, and Jackson would stay behind and play Monopoly (or Sorry! or Old Maid)—until someone had a tantrum. Or maybe she'd read aloud from *The Giver*, which she wanted the kids to read (but neither of them really wanted to). Or they'd go for a short walk until Abbey fell and scraped her knee, or Jackson started complaining about bugs. Like Merri, neither Abbey nor Jackson shared Wolf's exact degree of enthusiasm for the out of doors.

So, Merri had been envisioning a weekend where she would end up entertaining Abbey (eight going on thirteen) and Jackson (thirteen going on eight) while her husband (forty-six going on eighteen) would disappear on hikes or whatever and take a bunch of selfies. He would then create a narrative of the trip, and in the *telling* of it later to friends, it would sound like the perfect family vacation. Because that's how it went with Wolf, no matter where they were. Though, of course, he would completely deny that. *What do you mean "create a narrative"? That's what happened! You were there!*

But those were the thoughts belonging to another version of Merri. The woman she was today as she drove up the winding rural road was so far away from that woman who worried about things like vacations, and not having time to work out, and whose turn was it to do the laundry. Those were luxury problems, the kind of problems people had when they had no real problems.

When she thought about the petty complaints that used to bring her and Wolf to screaming matches that sent the kids scuttling to their rooms—the ones that spanned days, had him sleeping on the couch—she was ashamed of herself. Literally *ashamed*. She would pay money to care about things like that again—his adrenaline addiction, how he spent too much time on the computer, how she *knew* he still jerked off to porn, how his "epic" nights with the boys left him reeking and completely useless the next day. But these days she only cared about one thing. Everything else in her life had turned to ash.

A big sign loomed to her right: Welcome to The Hollows. Population 9780. Established 1603. She breathed a sigh of relief, knowing that the town was just another fifteen minutes away. If the car broke down now, which it wouldn't, she could theoretically walk. (Though her ruined knee ached at just the thought.)

Silence. No radio, she couldn't stand the sound of chattering voices. Even NPR with its dulcet tones of liberal self-righteousness, or the classical music station on Sirius, things that once had been soothing, now grated on her nerves. Jackson and Wolf were back in Manhattan. Even *they* were moving on in the ways that they could: Wolf was working again; Jackson was back in school. But not Merri. No. She had stepped into quicksand and she was up to her chin, stuck and sinking fast.

If Wolf knew where she was, he'd have her committed—again. The first time, she barely remembered. She couldn't recall the exact events that had led to her hospitalization or the time she spent there—except for these kind of shadow memories—soft lighting and gentle voices, a kind of floating cloud feeling. She liked to think of it as a brownout. Just a momentary dimming of circuitry, her system overwhelmed by grief and rage and loss. Anyway, she couldn't go back to that place—literally or figuratively. Time was running out; she didn't know how she knew that, but she did. Her instincts were powerful and usually dead on, even when she ignored them, which she often (too often) did.

She followed the signs and pulled off the rural road and into the quaint and tony town square. She remembered being impressed by just how pretty and clean The Hollows was when they'd first arrived; she'd even briefly (like for five seconds) entertained that fantasy about moving from the city out to a place like this. *Wolf was right*, she'd thought. *This is going to be a nice getaway. And we are overdue for some time off.*

On their way to the cabin, they'd spent the first afternoon having lunch at the little diner. Then they'd wandered around and browsed in the cute boutiques—blankets and sweaters made from wool harvested from local sheep; simple, stylish clothing as nice and high quality as anything you'd find in the city; a glass and pottery shop—grabbing (really great!) lattes for her and Wolf and frozen hot chocolates for the kids at the Java Stop. She made a mental note to come in the morning to pick up pastries at The Fluffy Muffin.

"Where did you hear about this place?" Merri had asked.

"You know," he said, shaking his head. "I can't even remember. An article in the *Times* maybe? One of those 36 Hours pieces?"

"Such a weird name for a town, isn't it?"

"I like it," he said. "It's a little creepy-cool."

"Must be pretty in the fall," she'd mused.

Then they'd driven up to the place he'd rented on the lake. She had to admit when they got there that he'd been right; it was idyllic. She immediately felt lighter, more relaxed than she had been in a long while. A beautiful log cabin sat nestled among tall oak and pine trees. A wide blue lake glittered at the end of a long dock.

"Wow!" said Jackson, looking up from his iPad (for the first time in three years). As soon as the car came to a stop, Jackson burst out and made a beeline for the tire swing. Abbey hung back with Merri, always the cautious one, the careful one (at first). She clung to Merri's hips.

"I saw a wasp," she said.

"It's okay," said Merri, pulling her close. "It's pretty here. We're going to have fun."

Wolf spun around, arms open. "So? Did Daddy do good?"

That he was energized by natural places was one of the things she first loved about him. She used to say that Wolf, in the beginning, before the kids, brought her out of the controlled climates and sanitized and quiet environments she preferred and into the air. And he would say that she'd taught him it was okay to have his feet on the ground sometimes. He was the writer; she was the editor. He was the one repelling into the ravine; she was the one making sure the rope was secure. They were proud of how they'd balanced each other, yin and yang. She was disappointed at the cliché they became

31

later, how the things she'd loved at first grew to infuriate her. And visa versa. More than anything else, resentment was the death of love. It killed slowly.

"You did good, Daddy," Merri conceded. You did *well*, she said inside. If she'd corrected him out loud, the smile he wore would have faded. He hated when she did that, when she acted the "grammar Nazi." But language was a precision instrument. Used imprecisely it could level all kinds of damage.

"I know, I know," he said. His smile faded anyway. "I did *well*."

"I didn't say anything," she said too quickly.

But they were *at that point*, even then. The grooves of anger and resentment were dug so deep, words weren't even necessary to start an argument. Just a glance could do it. Even things unsaid were as loud as a shout.

"Jackson," she called. "Be careful."

The swing chain, rusty where it wrapped around the branch, was wearing a deep gash in the wood. It *looked* as though it could break apart at any moment.

"He's fine," said Wolf. Just the shade of annoyance, nothing more, but it evoked all the criticisms he leveled at her. She was too protective, hovering, coddling. *You're turning him into a pussy*, he'd spat at her during one argument. Which managed to be vulgar and misogynistic and unfair to both her and Jackson all at once. He'd apologized for saying it, but she hadn't forgotten it. Because, according to Wolf, she never forgot *anything*, and she *never* forgave.

The house was beautiful, too. A log cabin, with big plush furniture, a fireplace and chef's kitchen, a sleeping loft for the kids, a beautiful master bedroom for them, with a hot tub outside sliding doors, looking out onto a mountain vista beyond the lake. They swam all afternoon. Jackson and Wolf tried fishing but didn't catch anything. They'd bought groceries in town, grilled burgers that night.

After the kids fell into an exhausted sleep, Merri and Wolf made love in the big king bed. And it was still there, all the heat they'd had the first time. She loved the look of him, his lean body, his wild tangle of dark curls, the curve of the strong but not huge muscles on his arms. The caramel color of his skin, the stubble on his jaw. Her body *always* responded to his; he could *always* make her his. They'd made promises for this trip. They both had skins they wanted to shed and things they wanted to give up. They'd each made big mistakes, done damage to themselves, to each other, to their marriage. But the love was there, something deep and true between them. It was enough to get them through the mire of their problems. Merri believed that then.

She fell asleep that night thinking how funny it was that in a bad (was it bad?) marriage, vitriol and intimacy lay side by side like the stripes on a tiger. *As* the stripes on a tiger. Maybe, she thought, there was still hope for them. They'd come through their struggles, stronger and better than they were before. She'd actually thought that back then.

That night seemed like a lifetime ago, though it hadn't even been a year. The navigation computer told her to turn left now and she did so.

"Your destination is on the right in one-tenth of a mile."

She drifted down the pretty block until she saw the address on a mailbox up ahead. She slowed in front of a gorgeous Victorian house that sat beneath the shade of a big oak tree. Leaves drifted onto the hood of her car in the wind. The day was overcast, neither sunny nor especially gray. She crept closer, heart thumping. This was it; she knew this. It was her last chance. Far worse than that, it was Abbey's. Desperation clawed at her insides; she was bleeding from it.

It might be time to let go, her shrink had advised.

Let go? she'd asked. She must have stared, incredulous. *Let my daughter go?*

When we've reached the end of our resources, we have no choice, do we?

I haven't reached the end of my resources, she answered. *I'm still breathing.*

She never went back to see that doctor; he was her third. Wolf thought that they were all quacks, and he hadn't seen anyone. He was into dulling pain, not exploring it. He wasn't doing any better than she was. But he was, she could see, letting go.

"You have arrived at your destination," the navigation computer announced in its impassive way. It couldn't care less whether you'd arrived at an amusement park or a funeral home or the last stop on a futile search to find your missing child.

Merri hadn't made an appointment with the man she'd come to see, hadn't even called. She'd read about him and his partner on the internet, and the idea of them filled her with a swelling, irrational hope. She didn't want to be turned away on the phone. Wolf used to love that about her; that she never gave up. It was just one of the many things he disliked now. *Christ, Merri, it's over. She's gone.* Of course, he'd said that when he was drunk and ended up weeping into her lap for the next hour. He wanted to move away from pain. But that was not an option for Merri.

She'd die before she gave up on Abbey.

Merri climbed out of the car and stood in the cool fall air for a moment. Adrenaline pulsed through her, putting butterflies in her stomach, causing her hands to quake. Then she walked up the drive and onto a narrow, shrub-lined path that led off to the side yard, finally coming to a structure that looked like it adjoined to the main house. She read the plaque mounted on the wall: JONES COOPER PRIVATE INVESTIGATIONS.

Please God, she prayed. It was just something to say to herself. Merri believed in nothing except her own iron will. *Please*. She pushed through the gate.

THREE

By dinner the sound was driving Finley absolutely crazy. *Squeeaaak—clink. Squeeak—clink.* She'd successfully pushed it away all day, taken her exam, attended a class, and spent the rest of the afternoon studying in the library. She felt good about herself. Studious. Doing the right things. Jason, the guy she'd met before class, had left before she'd finished her test. Finley had halfway expected him to be waiting for her, and was relieved (and a little disappointed) to find he wasn't. He was the kind of guy you could get in trouble with; she could just tell. She could just see herself, back at his place—some seedy studio somewhere—smoking a joint. So, better not to even have the temptation.

On the ride home, she couldn't hear it at all. She drove around for a while, just for the pleasure of the silence inside her head. But that evening, when she was preparing dinner for herself and her grandmother, feeling the weight of mental exhaustion, the sound just grew louder.

At the table, she finally lost it, put down her fork with a clatter. "*What* is it?"

Finley didn't even know what to call it. An auditory vision? There had never been just a sound before.

"I don't know," said Eloise. "But it's *loud*. It must be important."

Her grandmother was frustratingly calm, her eyes tilted up to the air as if considering a puzzling but benign trivia question. The world-renowned psychic, responsible for the solving of countless cold cases and the rescue of abducted women and girls, guest on

Oprah, and Finley's personal mentor should have more to contribute, shouldn't she?

Of course, there was nothing about her gray-haired, bespectacled grandmother, who sat primly in a pressed denim dress and white cable cardigan, that communicated her sheer power and ability. And in truth, it was hard for Finley to think of her as anything but her kind and loving grandmother. Right now, though? She'd happily trade her adoring grandma for badass psychic medium Eloise Montgomery—*if* she would help make the goddamn *squeak-clink* go away.

"What am I supposed to do with this?" Finley asked.

"You have to listen, dear," Eloise said. She took a nibble of stir-fry. "Listen until you *hear*."

"I *am* listening," said Finley.

"Are you?" asked Eloise. "Or are you trying to make it go away?"

Finley blew out a breath and dropped her head into her hands. "I had other things to do today. I can't give my life over to this."

When Finley looked up, Eloise nodded in that way that she had, understanding and nonjudgmental, as if there was little she hadn't heard before.

"In my experience, these events are like children. You may be able to delay attending to them, but they won't grow any quieter from being ignored."

This was a point on which Agatha and Eloise differed. Agatha Cross was Eloise's mentor, the one who had advised Eloise on all things related to her abilities, helped her to navigate her new life after the accident that took her husband and daughter and left her with a gift she didn't understand. And Eloise often directed Finley to Agatha when she felt the other woman had more to offer her granddaughter. Agatha was more about tough love; *they* get dealt with on *your* schedule, *they* don't get to demand and dictate. (After all, Agatha said, *they* have all the time in the world.)

Eloise, on the other hand, felt that if someone needed her, it was her responsibility to give herself over, that there was no point in delaying it. *If you don't give, they take*. Who was right? Finley had *no* idea, though she was well accustomed to two authority figures having strong differences of opinion, thanks to her constantly arguing parents. The good news was that she got to choose a little from column A, a little from column B. No one was right all the time; sometimes you just had to trust yourself. Of course, that was the hard part.

The lights flickered a little. The wiring in the old house also needed addressing. But Eloise seemed content to let that go, too, as if it were too earthly a concern to trouble her. "I need your help," said Finley. "I don't understand this."

"You will," Eloise said. "And I'm here. You know that."

She sounded so tired. There were blue smudges of fatigue under her eyes. And was it Finley's imagination, or did Eloise look thinner?

"Are you okay?" Finley asked. Eloise hadn't touched her food, had just pushed it around.

"Don't worry about me," said Eloise, rising quickly with her plate. "I'm fine, dear. Let's worry about you and figuring out what they want."

"How do I do that?"

"How do you find the answer to any of the questions you have?" asked Eloise. She cleared her plate into the garbage.

"Internet search," said Finley.

"Okay then."

"That's it?" said Finley. "That's your advice?"

Eloise offered an easy shrug, a self-deprecating smile. "That's what *I* do when I'm lost these days."

"Ugh," Finley groaned, anything more articulate almost impossible. "I don't even know what to search for."

"It's mechanical," mused Eloise, now with ear tilted to the air as if that would help her hear the noise better. That was true; it *did* sound like the operation of some kind of mechanism.

"But it's not totally rhythmic like a machine," said Finley, glad to finally be talking about it.

"Hmm," said Eloise. "But there *is* a rhythm."

Finley's phone buzzed on the table. There was a text from Rainer. *I'm thinking about you, Fin. Dirty things. I get off work at 11.* A chaos of emojis followed—a bikini, a pair of lips, a purple devil. She bit back a smile, quashed the rise of giddiness and arousal that he never failed to ignite.

"I thought you weren't going to see him anymore," Eloise said lightly. She hadn't even looked at Finley's phone. It wasn't a psychic thing; it was a grandma thing.

Finley scrolled through a list of excuses: *He's new in town, doesn't know anyone yet; I feel bad that he followed me here; I'm trying to let him down easy.* But in the end, she didn't bother. She just didn't say anything. Besides, Finley wasn't *seeing him* exactly. It was complicated.

"So how was the exam?" asked Eloise, maybe sensing the need to change the subject. Finley had put too much soy sauce in the stir-fry, so neither of them had exactly eaten with gusto. They would dutifully put the leftovers in a glass storage container, which would surely sit in the fridge for a few days and then get tossed.

"I feel good about it," Finley lied.

She'd never been a great student in spite of best efforts and being reasonably intelligent. There was a lot of chatter going on in her head, a lot of distractions without. She was a notoriously bad judge of whether she'd done well or not. Finley and Eloise cleaned the dishes, listening to the sound, trying to figure out what it was.

"Some kind of pulley?" said Eloise.

"A gate opening or closing?" said Finley.

"A wheelbarrow?"

When Finley moved to scrub the pan, Eloise waved her away.

"Go figure it out," she said. "It won't stop until you do."

Finley let her take the pan but lingered. It wasn't like her grandmother to be so distant from the problem. Since she'd arrived in The Hollows, it was Eloise who had the visions or visits and Finley who supported, more like an assistant or apprentice. She had never felt like anything was her responsibility exactly. Why was this different?

"Grandma," said Finley.

Eloise turned from the sink and dried her hands.

"I'm lost on this one, kid," she said. She released a slow breath. "I think it might be up to you."

38

Finley's head was starting to ache. *This* was the kind of feeling, the kind of place where she got into trouble. Rather than deal, if she were in Seattle, she'd go out with her "friends," drink too much, get into some kind of mess. In The Hollows, she had nothing to do and no place to go. She had no choice but to pay attention to the problem.

Finley reluctantly climbed the stairs to her room, the *squeak-clink* coming from everywhere and nowhere. In her room, she tried to do other things—make her bed (which she hadn't made that morning, and she could just hear her mother nagging), put away her laundry. She took out a textbook to do her reading. But the sound wouldn't be silenced. Finally, she sat cross-legged on her bed and opened her laptop.

She placed her fingers on the keys as if it were a Ouija board and eventually tapped "squeak-clink" into the search engine bar—for lack of any better ideas. Sometimes it *could be* as easy as that, Eloise had told her. The amazing thing about the internet was that it was alive with all the ideas and conversations and questions in the universe. One would be hard-pressed to enter a thought, question, or word and not find a hundred people already discussing it. Jung's collective unconscious at your fingertips.

The first thing that came up was the call of the rose-breasted grosbeak, a North American bird—white, black, and red—with a melodious call of up to twenty notes similar but far more beautiful (according to some birdwatching blogger) than the call of a robin. When Finley listened to the call, it didn't sound anything like what she'd heard. She bookmarked the page anyway. The bird lived up north in the summer and migrated along the east coast to South America in the winter. It might be something, a piece that would fit into a larger whole. It was too soon to tell.

Next, she typed in: "things that squeak." An article from *Better Homes and Gardens* topped the list with a bunch of potentially squeaky things—the door, the floor, drawers, a bed frame, a mattress, a faucet. The faucet gave Finley pause, the image of the running water. She closed her eyes and saw a rusty stream of water pouring onto the ground. But was it connected to the sound?

Squeaking engine, definition of *squeak* (a short, high noise), bicycle noises, a common problem with the rear wheel of an Audi; the coins on the bus go *clink, clink, clink*—a children's rhyme; the sound one blogger said the rusty wheel on his old wagon made. Finley chased links and read chats and articles and blog posts until hours had passed and her back started to ache from hunching over her laptop.

Finally, she closed the lid on her computer, her brain fried. How did it get to be ten thirty? She noticed then, with a giddy sense of relief, that the squeaking was gone. She got up from the bed and stretched high, hearing her neck crack. Then she walked down the hall.

In the bathroom, she looked at herself in the mirror, ran fingers damp from the faucet through her spiky pink and black hair. She put the glasses she wore for reading on the white porcelain of the old sink, lined her eyes with black pencil, put on some lipstick.

Back in her room, she changed from her cotton bra to a lacier affair, something her mother sent with a designer label and a big price tag. (Amanda was the queen of mixed messages. Really—what kind of mother buys her single young daughter lingerie after a lifetime of hammering into her the consequences of casual sex?)

Finley pulled on a tight black tee-shirt—cotton, not too sexy. Sexy enough. Still in jeans and boots, her jacket over her shoulder, helmet under her arm, she walked quietly down the hall. The television was on in her grandmother's room, but Finley didn't knock. She didn't want *the look*, the *not-saying*. Downstairs, the little boy was playing with trains in the living room. Faith—in her old-timey black dress, with her salt-and-pepper hair pulled tight into a bun and her perpetual disapproving frown—stood predictably by the door, that look of warning on her face.

"Go away," Finley told her.

And Faith obeyed, but only to turn and clomp up and down the hallway, calling attention to herself. Finley really couldn't stand her. Even though the woman had suffered and was ostensibly (according to Eloise) well meaning, she *really* got under Finley's skin—for all sorts of reasons.

But then Finley was gone, straddling the bike, the engine beautifully loud in her head, traveling fast, too fast, up the long rural road into town.

Finley couldn't remember how old she was when she first started seeing The Three Sisters. Young—maybe even as young as five. Or maybe they had always been there. However old she'd been, Finley already understood that there were people around her that were not visible to others. And she already knew better than to say anything about them, because it scared her mother.

There was a certain frozen look Amanda would get on her face when Finley asked about the old woman at the table or the girl sleeping under her bed. There was a blanching of the skin, a dropping of the jaw, kind of like the look her mother got when their cat Azriel brought dead mice or birds into the kitchen and deposited them on the kitchen floor. A gift certainly, but not the type anyone would ever want.

There's no one there, Finley.

She's right there in the blue dress.

Stop it right now. This is not funny.

Confused, Finley would fall silent. Thinking about that now—how her mother knew what Finley was and what was happening to her—still made her angry. Finley had been so ashamed and afraid, confused, had held so much in, when all Amanda would have had to do was pick up the phone and call Eloise.

She never wanted this—for either of us, her grandmother explained. Eloise was always making excuses for Amanda.

You can't ignore a thing just because you don't want it, countered Finley.

Parents make mistakes, usually out of love.

Control is not love.

Oh, Finley. A sigh. *There's a lot you don't understand about motherhood.*

Finley knew right away that The Three Sisters were different from the other people she saw. Those who came before them were almost like images on a screen, projections with no awareness of Finley. They often repeated the same action—like the old woman knitting the same row on the same blanket over and over. Or the girl clutching her teddy bear and turning over onto her side in sleep— over and over. Finley had been too young to intuit that perhaps they wanted or needed something from her. Anyway, the others never stayed for very long.

The Three Sisters had movement, awareness of Finley and their surroundings. They were curious, talkative. Patience was the youngest, the sweet one—slender with dark hair and big doe eyes. Sarah was the middle girl; she was a follower. There was a pleasant plumpness to her, a twinkle to her eyes, roses in her cheeks. She didn't talk much. And then there was Abigail, the oldest. With her mane of auburn hair, that mischievous *knowing* to her gaze, she was the one who always got Finley in trouble.

But since Finley had come to The Hollows they hadn't been around as much—maybe because Finley was busy with school and helping Eloise with "the work" and the house. She was busy in ways she hadn't been before. *Engaged* was the word. Finley wouldn't say she was happy exactly, but she wasn't raging, miserable, or looking to act out the way she had been when she was back in Seattle. She understood herself better here; she was calmer.

The girls were attracted to negativity, to bad energy. Finley was doing her best these days to stay away from drama. And she was looking to stay out of the kind of trouble that brought The Three Sisters around. So maybe that was part of it.

Or maybe, as she had come to suspect when Eloise revealed that the Good sisters were her distant relatives, that they got what they wanted. Finley was in The Hollows, where they were from, and where she apparently belonged.

Finley brought the bike to a stop in front of the pub. Inside, the lights were already low and the open sign turned off. The street had a quiet, deserted feel. All the shops that surrounded the park in the town square (complete with precious gazebo) were shuttered. The

Hollows went to bed early and slept all night. The only twenty-four-hour diner was ten miles outside of town by the highway. You wanted pizza at two in the morning? Too bad. Pop's, the only pizzeria in town, closed at nine thirty.

She knocked on the red door and after a few moments, it opened. Rainer stood there smiling his crooked smile—oh, those icy blues and wild dark hair. Her heart fluttered a little at the sight of him; it always did. Stupid. Stupid. Because he towered over her, she had to gaze up at him—which always made her feel small (which, in turn, annoyed her a little). He was wide, too, powerful through the shoulders, with big arms sleeved with tattoos—a dragon, a geisha, a python, a panther, Dali's melting clock, Leonardo da Vinci's flying machine. Escher's *Relativity* traveled over his right shoulder blade, a raven perched on his right pectoral muscle. He was the only one she knew with more ink than she had.

"I didn't think you'd come," Rainer said, standing aside so that she could enter. "You didn't text me back."

Jake, who was at the till, gave her a friendly wave. He was at one with the wood floors, like a pillar holding the place up. A dartboard hung on a ruined wall, pocked with holes from failed throws. Rows of bottles stood behind the bar; pictures of cops all over the walls. Rainer pulled a cover over the pool table, while Jake gave the counter its final wipe-down for the evening. A scent of sawdust, smoke, and beer hung not unpleasantly in the air. Windowless, dark, Jake's wasn't a place Finley would come to hang out. It was mainly cops and construction workers who came here, as far as Finley could see. It had a decidedly *male* vibe. There was one other bar and restaurant in town, Tipsy's, where you could get a middling cocktail, a more upscale atmosphere, decent food. But that wasn't Finley's scene either. She didn't need to be hanging out in bars.

"How's your grandma?" Jake asked. She sat on a bar stool near him.

"Doing well," she said. "Planning a little trip to San Francisco."

He was a big man, with a mustache that dominated his face and glittering green eyes. Though he was smiling at her, he had a powerful aura of sadness. So much so that Finley got up almost as soon as she sat down and moved to the wall, pretending to look at all the photographs—Jake as a young cop in New York City, stiff portraits from decades ago, celebrations at the bar, memorials to fallen officers, a picture of the World Trade Center pre-9/11.

"To see Ray?" he asked.

Jake had some kind of history with her grandmother; Eloise had helped him with something once. Finley didn't know what it was and Eloise wouldn't say. Then again, Eloise had history with a lot of folks in The Hollows. Good or bad, Finley tried to stay out of it.

"Yeah," she said. She had to smile a little. Her grandma had a boyfriend, *and* she was going to visit him. *I might be out there awhile. That okay?* Finley didn't really want Eloise to leave, but who was she to stand in the way of love?

"Well, good for them," said Jake, maybe a little wistful. He was missing someone. Finley could feel that. Someone long gone.

Rainer shifted on his jacket and walked over to her.

"Feel like working?" she asked softly.

"Always," he said, dropping an arm around her. He turned to Jake. "Okay if I get out of here?"

"Yeah, we're done," said Jake. "Good work tonight, kid."

Rainer walked over to give Jake a high five, and then he and Finley were out on the street where a light drizzle had started to fall.

They walked a few doors down to the plain storefront that Rainer was renting. Called simply Hollows Ink, it was his tattoo shop. Not surprisingly, Finley was one of just a few clients—The Hollows wasn't exactly a tattoo kind of crowd. But an investor friend had fronted him some money, enough to buy top-of-the-line equipment and get a sign for the window, cover nearly a year of rent. Rainer figured he could make the shop work inside that amount of time. He had a blog with lots of followers, a Pinterest page where he posted his best work. A wealthy couple that had found him online had come in from the city recently, promising to send friends his way. In the meantime, he was working at Jake's to pay the bills. Rainer *looked* like a total slacker, but he could be industrious as hell when he wasn't high. And he didn't give up—on anything.

Inside, Finley shivered as she stripped off her shirt, her exposed skin tingling in the cold.

"Is the heat on?" she asked.

Rainer was watching her in the floor-to-ceiling mirror that dominated the far wall. When their eyes met, he smiled. Then he turned on the ultrasonic and its hum filled the shop.

"I'll turn it up," he said. He rubbed his hands together, his breath coming out in white puffs. "Trying to keep costs low so I'm turning it all the way off when I'm not here."

He walked over to the thermostat and a few seconds later warm air blew through the vents above Finley. She stayed where she could feel the heat, rubbing at her skin. She hated the cold; it hurt, made her feel vulnerable and lonely.

The walls were fresh-painted black, and Rainer had placed two tattoo chairs and a table, some armrests against the mirrored wall. An impressive rainbow of ink colors—blood red, fuchsia, electric lavender, cerulean, sunshine yellow—stood sentry on a floor-to-ceiling rack. Through the curtain that covered the door to the back room, she could see his mattress on the floor, the sheets a rumpled mess.

"It looks good in here," she said. He'd hung some pictures, too. Nicely framed images of some of his best work, much of it from Finley's body.

"I'm getting there," he said. His smile told her he was feeling good about things. "I have an appointment tomorrow, and another one the day after that."

"Who's coming in?" she said. Frankly, she was a tiny bit shocked that he was making this work, that he seemed sober enough even though he was tending bar, and that the shop didn't smell like weed.

"A kid from the college wants his girlfriend's name on his arm— big mistake. But I'm not going to tell him that."

Finley looked down at her nails. Was that a dig? Rainer had Finley's name tattooed on his arm—a design around his right wrist that looked like a tribal band. Maybe that's why he couldn't let go. Once it's written in ink on your skin, it's forever. You can laser it off—if you don't mind the scar.

"Oh!" he went on, as he readied the equipment on a tray. Like a doctor preparing for surgery, he washed his hands vigorously in the small sink, then dried them. "Guess who followed me on Twitter? Ari Ash. You know—from Miami Tats? His work *kills*."

"That's—*great*," she said. The night she'd told him she was leaving—him, Seattle, her family, everyone—he'd cried. They'd been alone in his parents' house, sitting at the dining room table, lights off, the dim light of dusk washing in through the windows. Things had not been good between them, and she really hadn't had any idea that it would come as a shock. But she couldn't forget the look on his face—the sad wiggle of his eyebrows, the drop of his lower lip. In her heart, she didn't really think he loved her, not the way she loved him. She was surprised to see that she'd been wrong.

"Please, Fin," he'd said. "Don't do this. I'm sorry. I'll do better."

He'd actually dropped to his knees from the chair where he'd been sitting.

"It's okay," she said, dropping down with him. "It's not forever. I just need to get away from things here—my parents, our friends, all the mess."

"Me?"

No, she thought, the "me" I am when I'm with you. With Rainer she was jealous, possessive. She drank too much, smoked too much pot. She was lazy, neglected her studies, fought all the time with her parents about him. When they were out with their friends, there were fights, high drama. The other stuff—Finley's visitors, her dreams—it was all reaching a crescendo. When Eloise told her about Sacred Heart College and suggested that she apply and come live here so that Eloise could help Finley understand what she was, she agreed.

"I love you, Finley," he'd said. "I'm sorry I'm such a screw-up. Please don't go."

He'd messed around on her as recently as the week before. Then he felt so guilty that he told her about it right away, like a little boy who wanted to be punished, then quickly forgiven. It wasn't the biggest deal in the world because they were "taking a break" and Rainer

46

was weak. Girls loved him, those big blue eyes and meaty biceps, all the tats. He was a hottie, and girls just *stared*. He was oblivious most of the time, wasn't one of those guys with a wandering eye, always looking at someone else. It's just that if the opportunity presented itself, and he was high enough, he didn't exactly put up a fight.

When he'd figured out that she was serious—in that she'd applied and been accepted at Sacred Heart, even had her plane ticket—he dropped his head to her shoulder and held on to her tight, crying. She'd cried, too, holding on just as tight. But she knew with a stone cold certainty that it was time to go. She didn't imagine that he had the gumption to pick up and follow her across the country. She'd been wrong about that, too.

Now, he moved in close, putting strong hands on her arms. Soap, wood, and something else, a scent that was uniquely him. The soft cotton of his tee-shirt, the warmth of his body, the strength of it, his pulse, his heartbeat—all of it was a drug, calming her, luring her. It's why she tried to move away from him. He was nearly impossible to resist.

"Rain," she said, trying unconvincingly to push him away. She pressed her forearms against his chest, but he held on.

"I think about you all day," he said. Finally, she let him wrap her up because she was cold and he was a furnace, giving off heat and light. "And all night."

"Don't," she said.

"Tell me you don't think about me." His voice was gravelly and male, a note that resonated in her body. Oh, she *did*. She thought about him all the time.

"Let's not do this, okay?" she said. "We had our talk about boundaries."

About respecting her decisions and what she needed to do for her life, about understanding that what she *needed* might be different from what she *wanted* but how that didn't give him the right to push her in the wrong direction. His lips found hers, and she let them linger for a second, *just* a second, before she moved away from him. He released her, pushing out a resigned sigh.

She hadn't wanted him to follow her here. In fact, she'd told him not to. But he couldn't be stopped. His idea to start a tattoo parlor in The Hollows seemed outlandish enough that she didn't think it would last, figured he'd be gone inside a month. But The Hollows must have wanted him here, because it looked like things were going okay. She knew better than anyone that The Hollows got its way. No matter what.

"Who are we working on today?" he asked.

Of course, she needed him—maybe that was why he was here. He was the only tattoo artist to ever work on her. And he had a way of knowing what she wanted, and how important it was. He understood her, everything about her. He believed and never judged. The images Finley held in her mind somehow communicated themselves to Rainer. It was beyond words; she and Rainer were connected.

She lay herself down on the table and turned on her side, her back to him. They were running out of room. Her arms and most of her back were heavily populated, a growing collage of the people she could see that others could not. The old woman, the girl under the bed, the man in the suit, the teenager with the gun. And more, so many more.

"There's a little boy," she said. "He's about four, with blond hair and a cherub's face. His eyes are wide and far apart; his lips are full and pouty. He looks like a troublemaker, but sweet."

"Kind of like me," Rainer said. He ran his hands along her back and over her hips. She watched him in the mirror she was facing. His head was bowed, so that those dark curls fell, hiding his face.

"Yes, like that," she said. "Sweet but always in trouble."

His hand rested on her bare waist. The heat hummed to life again and warm air blew through the ceiling vent.

"I'm trying to be a better man, Fin," he said. "You see that, right?"

She *did* see that, but it was more complicated than even he knew.

"You *are* good, Rain," she said, feeling guilty for no reason.

"Then what?" he said. "What do you need me to do?"

She didn't answer. It wasn't about him, or not just about him. It was about her, how he made her want to go to dark places. She'd come here to learn about herself, to absorb the things that Eloise could teach her about what she was and how to control it. She had so much to learn about herself. She couldn't do that if she was lost in Rainer and all the drama that always seemed to crop up around them, between them: the fight in the bar when Rainer thought she was flirting (she wasn't); the day she missed an exam because she was sleeping off a high in his bed; the girl in love with Rainer who tried to cause trouble by constantly calling and hanging up on Finley's cell phone; the argument he'd gotten in with her mother where he'd called her a controlling bully. (Not a deal breaker, but still.)

"He's wearing jeans and a striped tee-shirt," she said. "He loves trains."

He rubbed her shoulder, kneading it with two strong hands. "What about The Three Sisters?" he asked.

There was an uncompleted tattoo on her inner right arm, an image of Patience, Sarah, and Abigail. It was the black outline of their faces, hair wild, eyes bright, all leaning in together with no space between their bodies. Rainer had started it for her before Eloise even told her who they were.

A few months after he'd done the initial outline, her grand-mother showed her a drawing that was identical to the tattoo, some-thing Eloise had found in The Hollows Historical Society archives. Eloise told Finley their dark history then—that The Three Sisters were tried and burned at the stake as witches in the 1600s. They were only girls when they died—twelve, fourteen, and sixteen. Faith never got over it. Centuries later, poor Faith was still hovering, trying and failing to keep bad things from happening.

Rainer had started some shading on Abigail—her dress, her hair. But the other two were still just outlines, waiting. As Finley under-stood them better, they would get their colors, their details, their shading.

"Not tonight," Finley said.

If he was disappointed, he didn't show it. She knew he was dying to continue his work on The Three Sisters, Abigail especially. Instead, he took out a sketchbook and charcoal pencil. She waited, her eyes closing, the exhaustion of the day pulling at her. The sound had quieted, which must mean she was on the right track with her research. She found herself thinking of the rose-breasted grosbeak, its pretty black and white and red body, its sweet and joyful song. *Little Bird.* The phrase stuck in her head, repeated itself—a loving term of endearment, a nickname. Yes, that was it.

"How's this?" he asked. He walked around in front of her and held up the sketch. It was nearly perfect, almost exactly as she'd seen the little boy—from the glint in his eye to the train in his hand.

"His face could be a little chubbier," she said. "But yeah. You're amazing."

He gave her a deferential bow and then went over to the copier to make the stencil. She liked him best in the shop, where he was focused and knowing. He was less wild in here, less dangerous. She flashed on that moment in the bar when Rainer came out of nowhere to punch the guy she was talking to in the face. Blood gushed from his nose and he'd cried like a girl. That was the first time she glimpsed Rainer's dark side, the anger deep inside him. Once she'd seen it, she couldn't forget it. She couldn't even remember what the guy had said to her. He pressed charges, though, and Rainer went to court, paid a fine for drunk and disorderly.

"Hold still," he said now.

As he spoke, the hint of movement in the dark corner of the shop caught her eye. She wasn't surprised to see Abigail leaning against the wall. Rainer pulled his cart over, unwrapped a new needle, put on surgical gloves. He was a professional; he did things right even when it was just the two of them. He arranged the pile of gauze, which he'd use to mop away the blood and ink. Abigail walked over until she was standing behind Rainer, who held the tattoo gun.

"How about here?" he asked, laying a hand on her lower back, close to her hip.

"That's fine," she said. He pressed the paper there with a crinkle, then peeled it back. She knew it was just a starting point, all the magic would happen with his freehand work.

Rainer pressed his foot on the round pedal, making the machine hum with its electric sizzle. Finley breathed deep in anticipation of the needle, the heat, the pain. It was a hurt that brought with it a kind of relief. Eloise had expressed concern that Finley's "tattoo addiction" was a form of masochism. Maybe.

She released a low moan as the needle pierced her skin, close to the hipbone. The closer to the bone, the worse the pain. There was no denying that it hurt, but Finley could sink into the pain, embrace it. Fighting, bracing against it only made it worse.

Rainer had his head bent over, totally focused on the task before him. Abigail walked across the room and stood beside Rainer. To Finley, Abigail had real substance—the fall of her hair, the swoosh of her dress, the sound of her shoes on the floor. Finley watched Abigail watching Rainer. She looked at him with such naked longing that Finley finally averted her eyes.

FOUR

Merri let herself into the apartment. Wolf had insisted she take the key. *If it's Jackson's home, it's your home, too*, he'd said. He wasn't ready to end the marriage.

"We can't split up," he'd urged. "Not now, not like this. Think about Jackson, Merri. How much more can a kid take?"

She wasn't one of those people who subscribed to the idea that kids were better off in a miserable but intact marriage than they were in a broken one. Not anymore. In fact, if she'd left Wolf years ago when she first knew it was over, none of the horrible things that came later ever would have happened. Why do people cling to these old ideas about family and marriage? Why do they stagnate, forcing the universe to deliver ever more severe lessons? Fear. It was fear of change that had kept her marriage together. Now that the worst possible thing had happened, Merri found that she was free from fear. She was untethered from what people thought, her terror of failure, the desire for stability. Rather than the joyous release she had always imagined, instead she had a sense of being unmoored in her life. She was drifting, unable to settle, emotionally homeless.

She dropped her coat and bag by the door. The lights were low, the big (enormous, a truly ridiculous sixty-five inches; God, he was such a child) screen television tuned to a soccer game. Wolf was hunched over his keyboard, his eternal posture. The tall windows of the TriBeCa loft looked out onto a field of lights. There was money. His. Hers. Not a fortune, but enough. That had never been one of their problems. They had never struggled to make ends meet.

They'd always fucked like rock stars. No, it wasn't one of the big three—money, sex, infidelity (though he'd never been faithful)—that split them apart. What was it then—other than the enormous, unthinkable tragedy that ultimately blew them to smithereens? Nothing. Everything. She still wasn't sure. The worst part about it was that she'd never stopped loving him. Even after everything, the sight of him still thrilled her.

"Hey," she said, keeping her voice low so as not to wake Jackson.

He leapt up as if she'd Tasered him, then put a hand over his heart.

"Merri," he said. "Christ."

His relief, his happiness at seeing her was palpable. She glanced at the screen out of habit. She didn't see any images of enormous breasts, or girls kissing, or wild porn sex—just an open Word document. She knew he was on deadline.

Not that she cared about his deviant sexual appetites anymore.

Porn isn't so bad, he'd childishly insisted more than once. *Lots of guys look at porn. It doesn't mean anything.*

It means you're a man-baby. That's what it means. And no working mother wants a man-baby as a partner in her life, just FYI.

She sank into the plush couch they'd purchased together at Jensen-Lewis. She remembered paying for it and thinking that people who didn't love each other anymore had no business buying furniture together. Now she felt comforted by its butter-soft leather, by the solidity of the thing. It wasn't going anywhere. Everything had changed around it, but it was still there.

"Where have you been?" Wolf asked.

"I talked to Jackson before bed," she said, a little defensive. She was unhinged, obsessed, yes. But she was still there for Jackson; she hadn't abandoned him in her grief. In fact, he was the only thing keeping her from going over the edge completely.

"He said you FaceTimed from your car," said Wolf. "Helped with his essay."

"Yeah," she said.

"Where were you?" he asked again.

She wasn't sure how to approach the subject, how he was going to take it.

"I found some help," she said.

He walked over to the enormous kitchen island—open plan, great room, of course, fifteen-foot ceilings, miles of bookshelves, spare amounts of furniture and décor. Wolf took a box of peppermint tea from the cupboard and brewed her a cup with the instant boiling water from the Hot Shot.

"Have you eaten?"

"Yes, thanks," she lied. She couldn't remember the last time she'd eaten anything. A protein bar this morning? Or was that last night? She really did need to manage her blood sugar better. HALT, was it? Never let yourself get too hungry, too angry, too lonely, too tired? She'd gleaned that much from her brush with addiction therapy. It seemed like a good rule of thumb, in general, that one should manage the conditions of hunger, loneliness, anger, fatigue. If you could manage those things, you were in good shape. But she was way too far gone on all counts. She hardly even recognized her own reflection anymore. Who *was* that middle-aged, gray, drawn-looking woman in the mirror?

"What kind of help?" he asked, coming to sit across from her. Wolf kept his distance lately; he knew that she didn't want him to touch her. Even though she really did. She wanted him to wrap her up. She wanted to disappear into his arms the way she used to when she was younger. Then, back when she'd first loved him, he was the safest place she'd ever found in her life. Now, he was quicksand.

"What kind of help?" he repeated.

Still, she didn't answer him right away. She didn't want him to shit all over it, which he was almost guaranteed to do.

"A private detective—" she started carefully, only to be interrupted.

"Merri—" Exasperated, hand to forehead.

"This one's different."

"Different *how*?"

How much money had they spent in the year that Abbey went

missing? When the Amber Alert yielded nothing. When the news conferences and manhunts had ceased. When the volunteers had gone back to their families, and the fliers weathered away on the trees to which they'd been tacked. When calls stopped coming into the tip line—even the crackpots and voyeurs and sadists got bored eventually. When the police stopped looking them in the eyes. How much money had they spent trying to find someone, *anyone* who wouldn't give up on their child?

"He—uh—works with a psychic."

Stunned silence, jaw dropping—actually this was worse than raging, which she had expected. Wolf had a hell of a temper; he could really throw down. And she was ready to go to the mat with him. But his silence deflated her. She braced herself for the barrage of questions: What are you thinking? Are you high? How long before you accept that our daughter is gone? These stories you see on the newsmagazine shows, about the people held captive for months and years are statistical anomalies. She's gone. She was gone probably within hours of losing her.

Instead: "A psychic." The word was flat with fatigue, disbelief.

"That's kind of a weird word," Merri acknowledged, not liking the sound of it from his mouth. "They're partners—sort of. She's solved cases, a lot of them. You can search her: Eloise Montgomery. And the detective is Jones Cooper. He used to work for The Hollows PD, retired now."

Wolf was slowly shaking his head, mouth open, at a rare loss for words.

"I'm doing this," she said finally. "It's our last chance."

He put his face into his palms.

The thing was, she didn't blame Wolf for any of this. She blamed herself. She blamed herself for taking a nap (or trying to) while he took the kids hiking. She had just wanted a couple of hours of silence; that was it. He'd promised her that on this trip, she'd get a little bit of time to herself—to read, to watch television, to nap. She wasn't one of those women who took trips with "the girls," leaving husband and kids behind. She didn't take spa days. She didn't go out with her pals for drinks, unless it was work related. Merri was a mother and wife first. She worked. She worked out (obsessively, religiously)—or used to before her knee injury. That was it. She wasn't sure that it was the right way to be, or healthy at all. That's just how she was hardwired—for better or worse. Sometimes it took its toll; she got frayed, impatient with everyone. Her mother always said, *You have to find some time for yourself, sweetheart. Just for you.* But Merri didn't even know what that meant anymore.

The irony was that she hadn't even slept that afternoon, though the air was cool and sunlight danced hypnotically on the floor of the cabin. The windows were open, and everything smelled *fresh*—the flowers outside the window, wood still burning in the outdoor fireplace where they'd made s'mores after lunch.

But a niggle of guilt kept her from relaxing: she *should* have gone with them.

"Take the time," Wolf had insisted. "Just chill for a bit. We won't be long."

She wanted to hike; lunch feeling heavy in her belly. They *should* be together as a family. Did he bring enough water? Abbey got dehydrated so easily.

All Merri's lists of should haves and must do's were an endless parade. So, in the end she neither relaxed nor hiked. She wound up sitting down with a book; which was okay and a bit of a luxury in and of itself.

But part of her was keeping vigil, just waiting for them to come back. She could envision them coming through the door. One of them would almost certainly have skinned a knee or have incurred some other minor injury. There would have been some kind of drama; Wolf would be out of sorts that the outing had been nothing like he'd imagined it. Perhaps because he always treated the kids like they were twenty-year-olds who didn't need his assistance in any way—when they needed his assistance in almost *every* way. Jackson maybe less so. But Abbey was a little drama queen—no event could occur without some theater from their girl.

Merri read awhile, did some crunches. Then she walked over to the refrigerator, thinking she could whip up something great for dinner. But they needed another trip to the store. Maybe she'd take the car into town. She tried not to think about the bottle of little blue pills in her bag, the one she'd promised not to bring with her. She'd taken too many already, *couldn't* take more. She waited as the shadows started to grow long. The light had taken on a particular pretty golden quality when she started to worry a little.

"Fine," Wolf said now. "If you think it will help."

He stopped short of saying "help *you*." Wolf had given up on Abbey. No, that wasn't true and wasn't fair. He'd closed off the part of himself that was alternately raging and catatonic with grief. Part of him had died; she could see it in his eyes, which grew haunted in the evenings. The other part had slipped into survival mode. He'd slowed his life down to one day at a time—home and family. As far as she could see, he did nothing but work and take care of Jackson, try to take care of Merri.

He'd forced them all to move out of the Upper West Side building that had been their home for fifteen years and into this loft. *Too many memories, stagnation, clinging to a past that was gone, one way or another.* She'd raged at him. How could they leave their home, pack up her room? The only solid thing left in their lives. The callousness of it rocked her. What would Abbey think when she came back and found that they'd moved her things to another home, put her iPod Touch, her first teddy bear, her endless rows of books, her school uniforms, her dresses—into a room that she'd never seen.

"None of that matters," said Wolf. "Can't you see how worthless it all is? Without her *energy*, it's just junk. If—when—she comes home, no matter what, we'll all need a fresh start. Especially Abbey."

Wolf had been adamant; even Jackson seemed eager to move on. But their son had always been desperate to please his father. He'd do anything Wolf wanted; the man could do no wrong.

That's when she left—not left, exactly. She didn't have another place to live. She was homeless; when she didn't sleep here, she slept in her car somewhere up by the cabin. How could she have a home, a life, when her daughter was missing, when every moment she wasn't *in motion, doing something*, she was imagining every possible horror?

"I want to go up there for a couple of weeks," she said.

This was it; this was her life. Gone were the normal routines that once seemed as immutable as the rising and setting of the sun— make breakfast, take the kids to school, hit the gym, work till lunch, eat, get the kids, run around to various after school activities, work again after the kids went to sleep. How hectic it all seemed, such a grind sometimes—dishes, laundry, homework, clean your room, did you remember to do this or that or the other thing. The task list only grew, as soon as one thing was accomplished, three other things were added. Holidays and school events, birthday parties, and parent-teacher conferences. How beautiful and distant it all seemed now, like a village you saw from a cliff, far below and nestled in rolling green hills. She wanted to go back there, but it was too far.

"What about Jackson?" Wolf said.

She bit back the rise of sadness, helpless rage, that feeling of constantly being pulled apart. "I need to do this," she said. "For her."

He blew out a big breath, sad and hopeless, took off his reading glasses, and rubbed his eyes. His thick curls fell in a careless tousle. He hadn't shaved in a couple of days. She liked him best like this— rumpled, tired. This was the real Wolf. The one who didn't feel like he had to put on a show of himself—adventurer, travel writer, Ivy League–educated man of the world.

"And if nothing?" he asked. Just a whisper, like they were speaking to each other in church.

She'd anticipated that question, had thought about making grand promises, that she'd try to move forward, that she wouldn't spend so much time up there, that she'd start therapy again, doctor of his choice. But she didn't have the energy to make promises she didn't mean.

"I don't know," she said.

He came to sit beside her, and she didn't shift away from him, turned to face him instead. He put his arms around her and she held her body stiff, then let go, wrapped her arms around him, too. He buried his face in her hair; then he was shaking. It took her a second to realize he was crying. She held him tighter, feeling less alone in this thing. He was whispering; she couldn't understand what he was saying at first. *I'm sorry. I'm sorry. I'm sorry.* Over and over again like a prayer.

FIVE

Penny dreamed of a room with glow-in-the-dark stars on the ceiling and yellow sunlight washing in through big windows. A mobile of red painted wooden fish dangled at a tilt by the bookshelf; there was the smell of toast and coffee. Blankets soft as powder, smelling of fabric softener, tiny marshmallows bobbing in creamy hot chocolate, a chalkboard wall where she could draw whatever she wanted. The last thing she'd scribbled there was a frowny face with tired eyes: I don't want to go to school today! She could remember the smell of the chalk and how the pink dust got on her clothes.

But as soon as Penny woke in the musty, windowless space she occupied now, all of that disappeared like fairy powder—a sparkling, insubstantial thing that everyone knew didn't exist—like so many of the dreams that Penny had.

She was never sure what time it was now. Her room didn't have a clock or a television. She didn't have an iPod Touch. She'd had one once, though. She remembered it with its cover that looked like a penguin. She'd been angry because her brother accidentally smudged it with purple marker that wouldn't come out. The ink made a little smear by the eye. *It looks like he got in a fight with another penguin,* her brother said. *And lost.* (That, for some reason, had made her *really* mad.) But all that, too, was gone. It was better not to think about the things from before; otherwise that feeling came up. That sad, angry twist like a tornado inside her that made her do things that got her into trouble.

She sat up now in her hard cot that squeaked and wobbled beneath her. There was only one too-thin wool blanket that scratched, no sheets. The blanket was so dirty it made her skin itch and crawl, like something you'd see in a homeless person's cart. It had that dirty-body smell, the kind that got into your nose and stayed. Penny climbed out and straightened the blanket, put the flat, yellowed pillow right, so they wouldn't get mad at her. *Lazy, ungrateful, stupid thing.*

Then she walked over to the little mirror and combed her hair, pulled it into a ponytail at the base of her neck. *You're so pretty. Your hair looks like spun gold.* Her mommy used to tell her that. But her mommy was gone. Now, Penny's hair looked like straw; she had to pull her hardest just to get the cheap plastic comb through. Her mom used to spray something that smelled like apples, and the tangles would just fall away. But no one did anything like that for her anymore.

Slowly, she pulled on the jeans that were too big for her, and the boots that were too big for her, and the coat with the sleeves rolled up. Then, pushing out the narrow door into the cool air, she shuffled over toward the old red water pump. It was dark outside and the moon hung low and wide like a sad face looking down on her. She had to use both her hands and all her strength to get the pump to work. But after a few tries, the water started spilling and filling the bucket that Poppa had left there for her.

You never tasted better water out there, I'll bet. Right?

She'd agreed because she always agreed now. She used to argue with her daddy, and he'd roll his eyes and tell her to *lose the attitude* and *was she planning on becoming a lawyer when she grew up.* But her daddy was gone, too. And when she disagreed here, bad things happened. Really bad things.

She dragged the bucket over toward the barn where she could already hear the cow lowing. A little bird was singing a sweet song up in the trees, which meant that dawn wasn't far off. That was something she had learned here. Birds start singing before the sun comes up, just before there's even a lick of light in the sky. She'd read in a book once, *The Bumper Book of Nature*, that the quiet of dawn was the very best time to hear birdsong. She wanted to write to the author and tell him that really it was right *before* dawn. That's when the songs were the prettiest, as if the best singers got up before everyone else.

When Penny pulled open the big barn door, the squeaking hinges let out a sound that cut through the night and seemed to vibrate in the silence that followed. All the birds went quiet, listening. It couldn't be helped; it wasn't her fault that the hinge squealed like that. No matter how slowly or quietly she tried to open it, that's the sound it made.

Penny stopped and turned around to the big house, watching. Dreading the moment when the lights came on upstairs, she drew in one breath and released it. The windows stayed dark, the birds starting chirping again, and Penny went inside the barn. The chickens fussed cluck-cluck-clucking in their coop, and Cow called out for her.

She let the chickens out into their outdoor pen and spread their feed around as a milky light broke over the horizon. Out in back, she tipped the water bucket into the trough for the pigs. There were only three, but they were *huge*, brown and white, dirty, rutting. There was something mean about them, something ugly. They weren't cute and pink, like she used to imagine them. In school, she and her friends used to draw little pig snouts on the notes they wrote to each other and imagine that they wanted to have pigs for pets. But the truth was, none of them had ever even seen a real pig. Maybe there were other kinds of pigs. Pigs that didn't have beady, intelligent eyes. Or ones that didn't make horrible grunting noises, that weren't twice or maybe three times as large as a girl.

She was just glad she didn't have to feed them. Poppa did that. It was disgusting to watch them eat. She didn't like pigs anymore.

Stay away from the pigs, the other girl had told her. She'd been blonde like Penny, with sweet, smiling eyes.

Why? Penny wanted to know.

The other little girl, who was skinnier and dirtier than anyone Penny had ever seen, swallowed hard and looked like she didn't want to say. *They're mean.*

Cow was still calling, low and mournful, but more urgently. Penny pulled the stool over and put the other bucket under the big pink udder. Then Penny petted Cow on her big nose and gave her a kiss. She loved Cow, her muscular softness, her gentle presence. Penny wrapped her arms around the cow's big head—even though the cow was a little smelly—and gave her a hug.

Cow was the only nice thing. Her mom always asked when they were having a snack after school: *What was your favorite thing about today?* But Penny tried not to think too much about her mom, because it just made her sick inside, opened a big wide hole in her belly. Anyway, the answer every day now was Cow. If her mommy had asked, that's what Penny would have told her.

She sat and squeezed the udders in her hand, they were soft and warm and malleable as clay. She was getting good at it and soon the creamy liquid shot in sharp streams, hitting the side of the bucket with a *zing*.

The work was hard, and it used to be that she had to take a lot of breaks—her fingers and arms burning with effort. But she was getting stronger. The other girl had showed her how to do it, the same one who told her to stay away from the pigs. She'd never told Penny her name, even when she'd asked. *I don't have a name*, she'd said. *Everyone has a name*, Penny said. But the girl just shook her head and looked so sad that Penny dropped the subject.

"The trick is not to squeeze too hard. And don't yank," the girl said. "You have to hold the teat in your whole hand, thumb and forefinger closed around the top to keep the milk from going back up into the udder. Pull and let go. Pull and let go."

But the other girl was gone now. Bobo said that there had been more girls, too. But they made Momma angry. They thought too much of themselves, or they made too much noise, complained, weren't helpful. They were too pretty, made Momma jealous. *Not ugly like you.*

Penny slowed down toward the end, because she didn't want to bring the bucket up to the house. She rested her forehead against the velvety brown cow, enjoying every squeeze. But eventually the job was done. So she kissed Cow and lifted the heavy bucket by the handle and carried it to the door that stood open. Her stomach bottomed out when she saw the two upstairs lights on, glowing like two staring monster eyes. All around the clearing was a thick, dark stand of trees.

Those woods are haunted, Bobo had said. *Full of demons and ghosts.* She didn't believe him at first, but she knew now that it was true. In the night, when she lay sleepless, thinking of that faraway place, crying, she'd heard all kinds of things—screaming, weeping, angry voices yelling. Sometimes there was howling. Worse than all of that, on certain nights there seemed to be a strange whispering coming from the trees themselves. The sound was nowhere and everywhere. Even if she covered her ears, she could still hear it, the sound of a million voices talking ever so softly.

Still every night, she wondered if she shouldn't just take her chances in those woods. *Don't bother trying to run. He'll get you. And anyway you have nowhere to go.* Bobo was right; her family was gone, she had no idea where in the world she was. In the end, she just lay there praying. *We can talk to God*, her daddy had always told her. *He listens.*

She wasn't sure that was true. Because she had been talking every night, but the answers that came didn't seem like they were coming from God.

With the woods dark around the clearing, and the light breaking, the moon fading, Penny hauled the bucket toward the big house.

SIX

Squeak-clink. Squeak-clink. Squeeeaaak-clink.

"Oh. My. God," said Finley, pulling the pillow pointlessly over her head.

Squeak-clink. Squeak—clink.

When she finally yanked the pillow away, the light in her room was too bright, too golden. She'd overslept.

"Seriously?" she groaned to no one.

Her back ached like the worst sunburn or like someone had repeatedly punched her there. And she had a Rainer hangover—head pounding with regret, stomach queasy with self-recrimination. Even though nothing happened, she shouldn't have gone to see him. Wasn't it just really leading him on? Why was she so *weak* when it came to him? She reached for her phone and checked the time. If she hustled, she could go for a run, then make class. But she had *no* hustle that morning. None.

Instead, she got out of bed and went downstairs, still in her pajamas, still with the sound in her head. She smelled coffee. Caffeine and sugar, the answer to many of life's problems—that's what she needed.

"I'm still hearing it," she called out.

When she pushed into the kitchen, Eloise was sitting at the table with Jones Cooper.

"Oh, sorry," she said, pausing in the doorway for a second.

She thought about beating a hasty retreat to change. But then she just didn't and continued walking over to the coffee pot instead.

She figured that Jones Cooper, retired cop turned private investigator, had probably seen a few people in their pajamas before—which in her case consisted of a black, long-sleeve tee-shirt and a pair of gray sweatpants. And Finley wasn't exactly shy. Even though she didn't know Jones that well, there was something safe and familiar about him, like he *belonged* in the kitchen. He had big energy, took up a lot of space. He filled the chair he sat in and made the table look small. She felt like he could get away with wearing a cowboy hat and she wished he would.

"How was your night?" asked Eloise. She rose and came to give Finley a kiss, and to get the milk for her coffee.

"Okay," Finley said.

Her grandmother would never ask anything further like where had she gone and whom had she seen—not like Amanda, who would already have her cornered with a hundred questions. Eloise didn't have to; even if she didn't know precisely where Finley had gone, she knew the nature of the encounter—good or bad, healthy or unhealthy, safe or unsafe.

"Good morning, Mr. Cooper," said Finley, glancing over at him. She could tell it wasn't a social call. There was a seriousness to him, a gravity, as well as a manila folder in front of him.

"Good morning, Finley," he said. "And call me Jones."

Finley and Jones had shared a few moments early on when she'd first moved to The Hollows, one where he told her that she was driving her bike too fast, that the consequences for careless behavior were often unforgiving. Coming from anyone else, she'd have blown it off. But after his warning, she'd slowed down for the sake of her grandmother, if not for herself. At least in town, where everything she did was promptly reported back to Eloise.

As she poured her coffee and put slices of bread in the toaster, the sound ceased. It took her a second to realize that Jones Cooper was the reason it was gone. She also became aware that neither Eloise nor Jones had said a word since she entered, that Jones was looking at his cup, and Eloise was watching Finley.

"Squeak-clink?" she asked her grandmother.

"Maybe," said Eloise easily. "It's been quiet since he got here. For me anyway."

"What are you talking about?" asked Jones. The way he asked it suggested that he wasn't sure he wanted the answer.

"Jones has had a visit from a young mother looking for her missing daughter," Eloise said, ignoring his question. "You might remember; it was in the news last year. The family vacationing from the city?"

"I thought it was the father," said Finley. She came to sit at the table with them, her curiosity piqued. "That he'd disappeared with both kids. Custody thing."

"No," said Jones.

He opened the file, revealing a swath of papers that looked like printed articles from the web.

"You're thinking of another case about eighteen months prior to the Gleason girl abduction," he said. He leafed through the pages and pulled out an article. "The Fitzpatrick family moved here from Manhattan back in 2013, and within a year, they were going through an ugly divorce and custody battle. The husband came to take the kids—a girl Eliza, age nine, and a boy Joshua, age fourteen—for his scheduled visit and didn't bring them home. It was treated as a parental abduction. I did some research last night. The case is still open, no sign of the husband or the children—which I find odd. It's really hard for anyone to disappear these days, especially with two children."

Eloise made a confirming noise and looked down at the article.

"There was no criminal history, domestic violence," said Jones. "There were no allegations of abuse or neglect. Their passports weren't used, so they didn't flee overseas."

Finley looked at the poor-quality image of the children with their father, obviously on some kind of outdoorsy adventure, since they were all wearing backpacks and leaning on walking sticks. They looked beautiful and marked for some ill fate. But wasn't that always true of the photographs of the missing?

"There are similarities between the two cases," Jones went on when Finley and Eloise stayed quiet. "Namely that Betty Fitzpatrick, the mother, said that the children and their father were planning a hike. Which is the circumstance under which the Gleason girl was abducted.

Still nothing from Eloise.

"I'm not saying that the cases are connected necessarily," said Jones. "But I do know that The Hollows PD took another look at the Fitzpatrick case when Abbey Gleason disappeared."

Eloise leafed through the articles, pushing her glasses up on her nose. The expression on her face had gone from lovingly benign to tightly focused on the work in front of her. She was a stranger to Finley for a moment, someone distant and untouchable.

"The woman who came to see me last night, Merri Gleason," Jones went on. "Her daughter Abbey disappeared ten months ago when the family was up here vacationing at a lake house."

"I remember," said Eloise. Even her voice sounded different, grim and soft. "I kept waiting to get something. I never did."

Jones shifted back in his chair, and it groaned beneath his weight. He folded his big arms around his chest, kept his storm cloud eyes on Eloise. Were they blue or hazel or a kind of misty gray, those eyes that missed nothing, Finley wondered.

"There was a big police effort, of course," said Jones. He coughed to clear his throat. "Lots of media. Weeks passed, then months. Leads went cold. I was one of the volunteers who searched the woods where she went missing."

Finley remembered but only vaguely. She'd still been in Seattle living with her mother, hadn't she? She hadn't been thinking or paying much attention to anything but the drama in her own life. *It's not the Finley Show*, her mother used to chide. *It's not just about you.*

"The girl's brother and father were both shot; she was taken," said Jones. "Hours passed before the park ranger came out looking for them."

"Right," said Eloise. She took off her glasses and pushed the papers away. "There were two men. One man shot Wolf Gleason and

70

his son, then took the girl as they watched, helpless. But he couldn't see their faces, couldn't identify them afterwards."

Jones nodded, took a sip of coffee.

"And allegedly the other man stayed behind with a knife while the older man disappeared with Abbey Gleason."

"A nightmare," said Eloise.

"Must have been," said Jones. He said it oddly, not cold exactly, but with the acceptance of one too accustomed to the unfolding of nightmare scenarios.

Finley didn't have anything to add, just watched the interplay between them. It was easy, respectful. Eloise and Jones worked a number of cases together, always to good success, their talents balancing and complementing each other's. There was something powerful about their energy, as if there was no case they couldn't solve.

Finley was aware of something else then, an almost giddy sense of relief, the sense of a weight being lifted. She'd heard her grandmother describe this, the feeling that came when you were doing what needed to be done. But she wasn't doing anything. She was just sitting there.

"It's been nearly a year now," said Jones. "The Gleasons have hired other detectives before. And Mrs. Gleason? She's brittle with grief. There's a lot riding on this for her; she feels like it's her last chance to find her daughter."

Eloise nodded, whether in understanding or agreement Finley wasn't sure.

"She knows the realities of the situation," said Jones, looking down into his cup. "That a child not found in the first twenty-four hours is likely not to be found alive. But she hasn't given up. She says that she can feel her daughter's *life force*."

He leaned with a very slight skepticism on the last two words. Finley knew that when Eloise and Jones first met, he'd not been a believer, not at all. Because of their many unexplainable experiences together, he now had a grudging acceptance of Eloise's abilities. He trusted her, even if he didn't understand her, Eloise had explained. *It takes a big person to accept what they can't intellectualize.*

"Did you take her on?" Finley asked.

She didn't imagine he'd be here if he hadn't. But she had learned long ago not to seem like she knew things she couldn't know. It made people uncomfortable.

"I did," he said. "I didn't see how I could turn her down."

He was a thick man, solid on the earth, the kind of guy you'd call to fix your problems—get your kitten from a tree, watch your house while you're away, help you find a missing loved one. It seemed to Finley that there were far too few totally reliable people around. People who did what they said they were going to do. People who showed up at the appointed time. That was why she liked Jones Cooper—a lot. He was everything her father wasn't. Phil was flighty, unpredictable, prone to tantrums. Not that she had daddy issues.

Jones's brow was creased with concern as he lifted a big hand to rub at his crown.

"You're going to help?" Finley asked Eloise.

Finley knew that her grandmother was planning her trip to go see Ray, though an exact date had not been set. *Soon*, Eloise kept saying, as if she was waiting for something and didn't want to say what. Finley suspected that Eloise was worried about leaving her alone, especially since Rainer showed up a few months ago. Finley had offered assurances; she wanted her grandmother to experience a little freedom, a little happiness. No one deserved it more.

"This one's not mine," said Eloise. She held Finley in a kind but unwavering gaze. Finley's heart did a little dance. "It's yours, Finley."

Jones and Finley exchanged an awkward look. She saw a mi-cro-expression cross his face. *She's just a kid. I can't work with her.* All the walls came up inside her. *No way*, she thought. *I'm not doing what you do.* Then they both turned their eyes to Eloise, who leaned back in her chair, took a sip from her coffee.

"*Squeak-clink* is yours," said Eloise evenly, putting the putty-col-ored cup down on the table. "I'm just overhearing."

Finley choked back a flutter of panic, a deep sense of resistance. She hadn't done "The Work" yet, as Eloise liked to call it, not re-ally, and she wasn't sure she even wanted to. At the moment, Finley was thinking about psychology (maybe, probably)—which made her mom deliriously happy. It was a profession where Finley surmised her abilities might be helpful—though she couldn't say *how* exactly. It was just an instinct.

The truth was that Finley wasn't at all sure how she planned to use her "gifts." The way Eloise lived, a slave to it, constantly in service to . . . *them?* Finley wasn't certain that she wanted that for herself.

We are chosen, Eloise said ominously, more than once. *We don't choose*. Finley had rankled at the idea of having no choice. The idea of fate, of a predetermined course to one's life did not jell with her beliefs.

"How do you know *I'm* not the one overhearing it," Finley said. She didn't like the way she sounded, young and peevish.

"We both know it's you, dear," said Eloise, putting a gentle hand on Finley's. "I'm sorry. I'd take it from you if I could."

There was something strange about the way she said it, something unsettlingly final in her voice.

Finley glanced back and forth between Jones and Eloise. She expected Jones to speak up, to insist that it was Eloise he'd come for, not Finley. Instead, he cast his eyes down at the table. He grabbed onto the edge and gave it a little wobble. It was uneven. He looked underneath, presumably to determine the problem.

"You need to put something under there," he said to Eloise. "To stabilize it."

She raised her palms at him to indicate that he was free to do what needed doing but that if it were up to her it would wobble forever.

Jones got up and opened Eloise's junk drawer, came back with a folded-up piece of cardboard, and kneeled down on the ground with a groan.

"How do you know that *squeak-clink* has anything to do with *this?*" asked Finley weakly. She pointed toward the papers on the table.

Eloise smiled, that sad, gentle smile she had. "You tell me," she said. "Does it or doesn't it?"

"I don't know," Finley lied, looking down at her hand. She'd bitten her nails down short, and the black nail polish she wore was chipping. *Really, Finley. Get a manicure*, her mother's voice chided.

"Look," said Jones. He rose slowly, stiffly to his feet and then tested the table; it stayed solidly in place. "Seems like you two need to talk. And I have plenty of work to do on this one, lots of threads to pull, some gaps to squeeze into. Let's just leave it that when and if there's *something*, one of you will get in touch. No pressure."

Eloise got up to see him out, while Finley nodded mutely and stayed seated.

"Should I leave it?" he asked Eloise, casting an uncertain glance in Finley's direction.

"Why don't you?" said Eloise.

He took a little crocheted change purse from his pocket, each row of stitching a different color of the rainbow. There was an applique cat on the front, with the letter *A* on its belly. Finley found herself reaching for it—even though she didn't want to—and Jones handed it to her. She held it, staring. There was no denying that the sound was gone, that she felt that wave of relief Eloise had described. But Finley didn't like being told what to do. She was like her father that way. Once he was *expected* to do something, once something was *demanded* of him—he made excuses, weaseled out, or just disappeared altogether.

She gave Jones a lackluster wave good-bye. Listening to him and Eloise talk quietly as they walked down the hall, she dropped her head into her arms. It grew quiet. The front door shut, making the plates in the sideboard rattle like they did. When she lifted her head, the little boy was standing in front of her with his train. She could hear the sound again, but just faintly.

"Not right now," she said—to the boy, to the sound—rising and walking away. She passed Eloise in the hallway.

"Should we talk?" asked Eloise.

"No," said Finley, too sharply. She was instantly sorry. More softly: "Later, okay? I have class in an hour."

Her grandmother put a hand on Finley's shoulder, then tugged her in close. Finley dropped into her, holding on tight. Amanda was not an affectionate mother, not with Finley. She was far more loving with Alfie. And over the years, as Amanda seemed to want more physical contact with Finley, the girl wanted less from her mother. In fact, now, she just endured Amanda's embrace, almost shrank from it. But Finley had always been physically close to her grandmother—hugging, holding hands, sitting on her lap when Finley was smaller.

"I don't think I'm ready for this," Finley whispered.

Her grandmother released a breath. "I have bad news," she said. "We almost never feel ready for any of life's passages. And yet we often must move through them all the same."

"You make it sound like I don't have a choice," she said.

Eloise pulled back and put a palm on each of Finley's cheeks. "Life is an impossible twist of choice and circumstance, one rarely exists without the other."

"I don't know what that means."

She headed toward the stairs, wanting the conversation to be over, Eloise let her go, didn't try to hold her back.

"It means that we choose within the context of what happens to us," she went on, even though Finley was moving away. "We don't always choose who we are, or what we experience. We just choose what we do with it all."

It sounded like resignation to Finley, like admitting that she didn't have any true control over her life. She wasn't sure she could believe that.

Faith Good stood on the bottom step, staring at the front door. Finley slipped past her quickly because she didn't like to be close to Faith, her presence leaving a cold spot that leaked into Finley's bones and that she'd have a hard time shaking all day.

Halfway up the stairs, Finley turned back to Eloise. Her grandmother looked up at her, smiling a little. It was a look that made Finley feel stronger, better. It was a look that said: I know you'll do the right thing, even if you're not sure yourself.

"When are you leaving for San Francisco?" Finley asked, a tingle of worry tickling at the back of her mind.

"Not quite yet," said Eloise.

Finley tried not to show her relief. "You don't have to stay because of me," she said. "Really."

"Oh, I know," said Eloise easily. She waved a dismissive hand. "I just have a few loose ends I need to tie up."

Outside, they heard Jones Cooper pull from the drive, his tires crunching on the gravel. Finley continued up the stairs, clutching the little change purse in her hand.

In her room, instead of getting ready for class, Finley lay down on her bed, looking at the change purse. It was light and insubstantial in her grasp. Eloise might be shunted into a vision by an object; Agatha could absorb all kinds of energy, thoughts, and intuitions that way, too. But Finley had never had that experience. On the other hand, she'd never had an opportunity to try. Most of her childhood, she'd just worked to ignore the people she saw. And it was only recently that she understood that they wanted something from her.

Only The Three Sisters had ever encouraged, sometimes pushed, her to actually *do* something. The first time, it was Patience, who told her what her grandmother was. That was how Finley learned about Eloise—not from Amanda, not from Eloise herself, and not from accidentally seeing something on television.

Finley had been dreaming about Eloise, who in the dream was eating a pie with a fork, straight from the pan, digging into its middle, leaving a gaping hole that resembled nothing so much as gore spilling from a wound. She didn't seem to be enjoying the pie at all, her expression grim, her posture hunched.

"Grandma?" asked Finley uncertainly in her dream. "Is that *good*?"

Instead of answering, Eloise stood and knocked the pie to the floor. Then the old woman dropped to her knees, somehow managing to get the cherry filling on her clothes and in her hair as she struggled to clean it up.

"Grandma," Finley asked, alarmed. "What are you doing?"

"I'm trying to fix the mess I've made."

"Let me help you," said Finley. She attended a Montessori school, where Finley's teachers had taught her well how to clean up a mess, demanded that she was responsible for herself. So, she knew what to do. She looked around for a cloth, but there wasn't one.

"You can't help me, sweetie," Eloise said. "You're far too young."

"I'm not," said Finley, a little miffed. "I'm a big girl."

Finley woke from her dream to see Patience sitting by her bed. Abigail could never be trusted. Sarah seemed unknowable. But Patience almost—almost—seemed like a friend.

"Your grandmother is just like us," she said. "She sees what other people don't see. Knows what other people don't know."

"That's not true," Finley said. It couldn't be true, could it? Surely her mother would have told her.

"She has a lot to teach you later," Patience went on. "But tonight she fell and hit her head, and she's very alone."

Finley woke her mother that night and demanded that they call Eloise; she'd cried and raged until Amanda finally had no choice.

While Finley talked to Eloise on the phone, Amanda lay on the bed and openly wept. And that was the first time Finley ever felt free to talk about her dreams, the people who came to see her, the things she saw. Eloise listened, and understood, and didn't have a total freak-out like Amanda did when the topic came up. And it was such a relief to let it out, to not hide it.

"Try not to pay too much attention to the dreams just yet, okay," Eloise had said when Finley was done. She sounded sad, but strong and sure. "They're not bad or wrong. Just try to ignore them for now. You can't do anything for anyone until you're older."

Finley didn't talk about The Three Sisters that night. She wouldn't share that with Eloise until many years later.

"Why didn't you tell me about Grandma?" Finley asked her mother when the call was over.

"Because I didn't want this for you," Amanda said helplessly. "This is my worst nightmare."

Amanda was in despair, and watching her, Finley felt the first dark flower of rage bloom. She saw too young how powerless her mother was, how inadequate, how weak. Abigail, of course, couldn't have been more pleased with all the drama this event caused.

"She can't keep you from this," Abigail said from the corner of the room. "No one can."

The second time had been much worse. Finley had been seven years old. Her parents were in a screaming match upstairs, while Finley watched cartoons.

Finley barely heard them; this was happening all the time. Phil and Amanda were either screaming their heads off at each other or making big displays of love and affection, supposedly because her mother had read that it was okay to fight in front of your kids if you showed them when you made up, too. It just made them seem crazy to Finley, and their behavior was very confusing, so she tended to just block them out altogether when things got heated.

It was a particularly bad argument, because Finley had to turn up the television to hear her show better.

Irresponsible. Never here. We're drowning, Philip.

Overreacting. Controlling bitch. Get off my goddamn back.

It was Abigail she saw first—wild auburn hair, deep-set dark eyes, wide mouth. Then Patience, who stood quietly by the window, almost disappearing into the light. She looked outside at the milky, rainy sky that was the same color as her skin. Sarah sat on the hearth smiling, full of mischief. Abigail was the most powerful, and Patience was the sweetest. Sarah was the easiest to be around because she never asked anything of Finley.

They hate each other, Abigail said without saying.

"I know," said Finley. She did know that. Her parents might have loved each other once, but no more. It was clear; their terrible energy together was a noxious gas in the house making them all sick.

Make them shut up, said Abigail.

Finley looked at her, finally turning away from her cartoon— what had it been? The X-Men. Finley had always been obsessed with superheroes—cartoons, comics, and movies. She loved the idea of the ordinary person turned into something extraordinary by fateful accident or terrible design. Secret identities, crime fighting, supervillains all in the brightest colors and most outrageous costumes. Way cooler than anything her friends were into—My Little Pony, American Girl dolls—yuck.

Finley's eyes fell on her father's cigarette lighter, which he left around everywhere, even as he tried to pretend he'd quit smoking at Finley's behest. She wasn't fooled, of course, because he always smelled of cigarettes beneath an obnoxious layer of Stimorol gum and Acqua Di Gio.

The lighter rested on top of the pile of bills that had started the fight in the first place. His cell phone bill, his American Express, the Mercedes payment, whatever else. Abigail just looked at it, and Finley found herself looking at the lighter.

Abigail didn't make her do it. Finley *wanted* to do it. In fact, just minutes before she'd been looking at the offending paper, the pile of which her mother had been waving at her father in anger, and wished she could just set them on fire. Abigail just gave her permission to do what she already wanted to do.

Little Finley got up from the couch and picked up the papers. Then she took the lighter and after a few tries managed to get the small blue flame to flicker out. Then she held it to the curled corners of the bills.

First, they just turned a little brown, the metal flint of the lighter growing hot against her thumb. Then there was a twist of gray smoke. Soon a dancing orange flame began to eat away at the papers in her hand. She let the lighter drop and stared. It was mesmerizing, hypnotic to watch the flames grow, the papers disappear into ash. It wasn't until she felt the heat on her face that she snapped out of it, realizing what she'd done. She dropped the papers in fear, where they scattered on the coffee table, still burning, quickly setting the magazines beneath them on fire, too. She watched as the flames spread. The Three Sisters were gone.

Finley started to scream for her parents, and they came racing down the stairs just as the smoke detectors began to wail. Her father quickly put out the flames with a towel from the kitchen, while

Amanda shuttled Finley from the house, then held on to her tight, weeping in the front yard.

I'm sorry, she just kept whispering. *I'm sorry, Finley*.

Though Finley was frightened and sorry for what she had done, she also acknowledged that she had, in fact, shut them up. There wasn't another harsh word spoken between Phil and Amanda for the rest of the afternoon. They behaved like two chastened children, tiptoeing around each other, being extra gentle with Finley. She didn't even quite get why they were being so nice.

That night while Amanda lay next to Finley in bed, stories read, lights low, she asked: "Why, Finley? Why did you do that, honey? Didn't you know how dangerous it was? You could have been burned, or worse."

Finley told her mother about The Three Sisters. Amanda already knew what Finley was, of course.

"Don't worry, baby," her mother whispered that night in bed. She was quietly crying again, holding on to Finley. "We're going to get you the help that you need."

And Finley felt deeply relieved. But that was before she knew what her mother meant—which was that she'd spend the next year seeing a kid shrink.

Now, in her grandmother's house, Finley held on to the little change purse and closed her eyes to see what she could see.

SEVEN

Kristi was so easy. It was, by far, the thing Wolf Gleason had liked best about her. And he, even now, liked a good many things about her: those wide, always surprised blue eyes; her round, bouncy ass; her teardrop breasts. Not necessarily in that order. He'd never seen Kristi without her nails done—a perfect French manicure *and* pedicure. Not just a bikini wax, a Brazilian—now *that* took guts.

Her hair was a perfect white-blonde frame around her heart-shaped face. She wasn't beautiful precisely—her nose was just the tiniest bit crooked. Her face, in fact, was weak—one of those faces that is pretty only in youth, plump and dewy with health. Once time and gravity got to work, there was no strong scaffolding underneath to fight the sag, the inevitable lines and wrinkles. Her body was nice, soft—muscles not too ripped by countless desperate hours at the gym. But she wasn't *hot*—not like boyhood fantasy hot. Few women were, off the pages of a magazine; there were always physical flaws in real life. But Kristi was the kind of girl who knew how to take care of and maximize the gifts nature had bestowed on her, however fleeting they may be.

The other thing he'd liked about her (at first) was that she was perfectly sunny all the time. Merri (contrary to her name) could give Sartre a run for his money—hell is other people and all of that. But Kristi was always bright-eyed, continually looking for the silver lining, the best in people and situations. She relaxed Wolf. She rolled his joint for him and held it to his lips—literally and figuratively. She got on top and rode him until he quivered beneath her, spent and gorgeously exhausted. She giggled when she laughed, light and mellifluous. She liked Hello Kitty. She didn't mind that he was into porn. In fact, she watched it with him. To his delight, it turned her on.

"Be careful," his buddy Blake had warned. "Those are the girls who always turn."

Wolf figured Blake—always the straight arrow all through Regis, at Columbia, now partner at a big law firm, faithful husband, perfect dad to two girls—was maybe just a little jealous. Blake and his wife Claire had been together since high school (she was a Chapin girl whose daddy had founded Blake's firm), so he had to be at least a little curious, especially since Claire didn't exactly impress Wolf as the kind of girl that would get wild at all in the bedroom. (Of course, Blake would never talk about anything like that, got all prudish when the topic even came up.)

Though Wolf had to admit that Blake didn't exactly *seem* jealous. *Pitying* would be a better description of his attitude. Anyway, Blake had been right. Wolf should have listened. His lifelong friend was an uncanny judge of character.

Wolf glanced at the clock. It was 2:35 in the afternoon. He had to leave in exactly fifteen minutes to pick up Jackson from school. Last year, Jackson was raging that Merri wouldn't let him take the subway home. *Everybody takes the subway, Mom! You're turning me into a freak show!* Now, the poor kid wouldn't go anywhere without one of them. He was as fragile a person as Wolf had ever seen. And Wolf *would* be there on time to get his kid, who needed him. He wasn't going to let anyone else down. Ever.

"Look, Kris," he said, trying not to sneak another peek at the clock. "Can't we talk about this later?"

"Later when?"

She sat on the red felt bar stool, leaning on the quartz countertop. Her face was blotchy and red from crying. She held a tissue, regularly dabbing the corner of each eye in a practiced effort to keep her mascara and eyeliner from running. He moved toward the door, hoping she'd take the hint and follow.

"I have to get Jackson," he said. "This is not a good time to talk."

She subtly—*almost* imperceptibly—rolled her eyes. He was trying not to hate her.

"I need to know *when*, Wolf," she said. "It's been almost a year. I've been patient. Most women wouldn't have waited around this long."

There was a wide, unbridgeable gully between them. Why didn't she see it? Did he have to spell it out for her? Maybe he did. He had been sleeping with Kristi for a year and a half. It had started a few months before they lost Abbey and had, in spite of his desire to end it, dragged on after. And the longer he was with her, the less knowable she seemed. The less he *wanted* to know her. Beneath that well-coiffed, (once) sunshiny exterior—what was *really* there? What moved her? Inspired her? Frightened her? What did she love? Hate? How many times had he heard her say blandly, "Wow, that's awesome." Or, all pouty: "That's so *not*-awesome." Had she ever been truly *awed* by *anything*? He didn't know.

"Your marriage is over," she said. "It has been for a long time. You said so yourself. I know it's been hard."

She bowed her head here. Why did it seem like she was *trying* to look sad, understanding—like she was acting? "But we need to move forward."

That she could be sitting here, saying this to him, made him think of Blake.

"Man, that girl is—"

Wolf thought Blake was going to say "hot" or "sweet." Wolf had kind of sprung Kristi on Blake. Blake was his best friend, and Kristi at the time, in the beginning, was making him so happy; he needed to share it. So he had her pop in just quickly at the Upper East Side bar where Wolf was meeting Blake for a drink.

"Empty," Blake finished. "She's completely vacant. No offense, man—you know I love you. But when you have a woman like Merri, and two great kids, why would you do something like this to your family?"

That moment, after which Blake paid the bill and left, had put a real strain on their friendship.

(*Blakey and Claire canceled for the cabin*, Merri told him the next day, disappointed, mystified. They'd been vacationing together most summers for a decade. *Any idea why? She's been acting so weird. They'd tell us if they were having problems, wouldn't they?*) Wolf had been pissed, knowing that Blake had told Claire that Wolf was fucking around, breaking the sacred man code.

Now, Wolf inched toward the door. He didn't move fast anymore, which is one of the reasons he needed to leave soon. The city that he used to navigate with the arrogant ease of the young and healthy was now a painful obstacle course of stairs and uneven sidewalks, crushing crowds, and uncomfortable subway rides where suddenly younger people offered up their seats—seeing at first his crutch, then his obvious limp. Even the kindest touch could hurt when you were a raw and bleeding open wound, which he was.

He was healing, but not quickly. But he was glad for the almost constant pain. He deserved it. He deserved a lot worse. The bullet had just missed the major artery but broken the bone, lodging itself into his femur. (In dark moments, he'd wished it had killed him.) The doctor had opted to leave it in, rather than risk nerve injury. The bone would heal around it, apparently. Wolf imagined that he could feel the cold bit of metal inside the knitting flesh and bone, a hard, icy reminder to carry with him forever, to remind him how he had failed his beautiful Abbey. How he had failed them all. Ever since they'd been kids, Wolf had always wished he were more like Blake. Nothing like this could ever happen to his friend; Blake wouldn't allow it.

"You know, Wolf," Kristi said now. "I've been suffering, too."

He almost laughed. A young, pretty, childless woman of privilege did *not* know suffering.

"Did you just say that?" he asked. "Do you have *no idea* what we have been going through?"

Of course, she didn't. She was a spectator, had no skin in the game. He didn't want to blame her. Everything rested cleanly on his shoulders. But deep down inside where he might hold a little bit of love or affection for her, there was only a cold, angry feeling. If it hadn't been for you—

But that was the old Wolf. The Wolf who had not yet been harshly punished by the universe. The new chastened Wolf was trying to be there for his sundered, shattered family. He was trying to wade through the deepest, most unimaginable mire of horror, grief, and regret possible for a human to endure. And he only kept moving because of his beautiful, damaged boy who needed him to get whole again somehow. But Wolf was still fucking Kristi. How could he excuse this? He couldn't.

"I'm sorry," she said. This time she looked sincere. "I know how hard it is. I can see that."

He waited for it.

"But we had a plan. You made promises to me. Do you remember? I can't put *my* life on hold forever."

Here was what he should have said:

Kris, you're right. I can't string you along anymore. For a moment, a brief blistering moment, I thought that what we had was love. But I don't love you. I never did. It's only now, sifting through the debris of my life, the one I didn't appreciate, that I realize what I've lost. You should just find a nice guy your age (yeah, she was only twenty-five). Find a nice guy with a blog and a Facebook page, maybe even a fat publishing contract. Someone who is young enough to confuse lust with love, someone who is shallow enough to never notice that you have the emotional depth of a kiddie pool. I have been sleeping with you because you are simply the only easy pleasure I have had in my life for ages. Now that you are no longer easy? You are just not worth the effort.

Instead:

"Look, Kris, my mom and dad are coming to spend time with Jackson tonight. I'll come over, okay? We'll talk more."

She wiped her tears, that bright smile coming back a little.

"And we'll figure it out?" she said. "We'll make another plan?"

"Yeah," he lied. He lifted her bright red wool coat from the hook on the wall and handed it to her. "We will."

"You promise?" She stretched up to kiss him softly on the lips. He let her because honestly she was the only person who kissed him anymore—other than pecks on the cheek from his mom. Jackson endured Wolf's kisses to the forehead. Merri wouldn't come near him; she actually recoiled from physical contact with him. Who could blame her?

"I promise," he said.

As they exited the building, she had that little bounce in her step again. She had no idea that they were never going to see each other again. He had always been an excellent liar.

Uptown, Wolf got off the train a stop early to force himself to walk the extra distance even though his leg screamed in protest, and his physical therapist told him that he might be overdoing it.

"For injuries," the physical therapist said, "rest is as important as the right exercises."

Their family therapist had said something similar. That they should be finding ways to relax and even have fun together again, just the three of them. That it wasn't disloyal to Abbey to find joy again. Which was complete and utter bullshit.

He ignored all the Abbeys he saw. The Abbey in the purple jacket and pink cheetah print helmet riding a Razor scooter beside her mom. The Abbey as she might look twenty years from now— wheat-colored hair pulled back, wearing jeans and a stylish black poncho, holding hands with her hipster boyfriend, whom Wolf was sure to despise. The Abbey as she had been, a little pink peanut in a stupid-expensive stroller (It's a pram! A car seat! A high chair! A booster!) with Mom jogging behind trying desperately to lose weight she didn't need to lose.

All the Abbeys that were and would never be because of his careless, shitty brand of fatherhood. The smart phone dad—always taking pictures and posting beautiful filtered shots on Facebook and Instagram for others to admire, forgetting almost entirely to look with his own eyes.

He saw Jackson standing outside the school, resting against the gray brick wall and staring at his iPhone. It was the perfect fall afternoon—cool but not cold, leaves shedding, street full of kids and parents heading home from school, not yet crushed with commuters rushing to and fro.

His kid looked like a scarecrow, balancing on one thin leg, blond hair spiky all over, so fragile as if he could blow away or burst into flames. All of this was hardest on the kid. Wolf thought for a moment that Jackson had ditched the crutch he was still using. As Wolf drew closer, he saw it leaning against the wall next to Jackson.

"Hey, buddy," he called. "What are you doing out here?"

Maybe it was progress. Usually Jackson wouldn't step outside without one of them. Though what help the kid thought his useless father would be, Wolf couldn't imagine.

"I don't know," said Jackson as his dad approached.

Wolf bent down with effort and took Jackson's book bag. In doing so, he caught a glimpse of Jackson's phone. The *New York Times* app was open to a breaking story about a school shooting in Texas.

"Jacko," said Wolf. "Come on. You're not supposed—"

"I know."

"The doctor said—"

"I know." He almost yelled—the sweetest, most gentle kid that ever was. An angel baby, Merri had called him. Sleeping through the night by two weeks old, rarely a peep out of him. Softer: "I can't help it, Dad. I just can't."

Wolf ran a hand along the back of Jackson's silky, beautifully shaped head, fighting back a powerful rush of sadness and pain. Was there no end to it?

"I get it," he said. "I get it. Let's go get a smoothie at Papaya King."

A longish walk that would do them both good. He hoped.

EIGHT

Something was different. Something had shifted. The air had a peculiar scent; the gray of the sky was darker punching against the bright white of the high clouds. Something. *What was it?* Eloise watched Finley go—the girl's thin form crouched over the roaring machine, speeding away. That girl thought she owned the world; maybe she did. She didn't believe that she could make a mistake, get hurt. Eloise envied her arrogance a little, even as she cautioned against it. As Finley turned the corner out of sight, Eloise smiled, in spite of herself.

It had been on the tip of her tongue, the thing Eloise wanted to say. "Finley," she almost said. "Can you be late today? We should have a talk." But she'd never found the courage to push the words out. What point was there, really? What good would it do?

Back inside the house, the old clock ticked, the floorboards creaked, the pictures of her family stared at her from the wall. All these things seemed real and solid, permanent. Of course, it wasn't so. Everything tended toward breaking down, entropy. Time and gravity were immutable forces that pulled the world apart. If not for constant vigilance, the fabric on the sofas would mold and rot, the roof would start to sink, shingles and shutters would fall. The house would be a ruin one day. And that was right, as it should be. Nothing is forever.

Eloise took her bag from the hall table and headed out the door.

In the car, she drove down the road. So many years later, she never failed to remember the day Emily and Alfie died whenever she passed the place where the tractor-trailer drifted into their lane, forcing them all into a head-on collision. After which: Alfie and

Emily were gone; Eloise and Amanda were left to go on; and Eloise began to hear the dead—their voices, their stories. It had been a day like any other day, not the shade of any warning, not a tingle, not a sense of anything to come. Lives lost, lives altered from one moment to the next. Other people would have moved, left this place, at least not forced themselves to drive the same road every day. But Eloise was not other people. She didn't want to forget, to move on. You didn't have to do those things to let go.

She drove through town, past the Java Stop and Miss Lovely's Bed & Breakfast. At the light, Jake, proprietor of Jake's Pub, waved to her as he crossed in front of her car. She lowered her window to hear what he was saying.

"I can feel winter coming," he said again.

"Me, too," she said, smiling. "Have a good one."

He smiled in that way they sometimes do afterwards, after they'd laid their problems at your feet, and she'd helped the best she could. Sometimes it was enough and they were grateful; sometimes not, and they were disappointed. But it was always awkward when there was nothing left to do but accept. Jake had asked her for answers about a woman he'd lost long ago. He'd given her a necklace, and Eloise had a dream. It was never easy to watch a big, strong man break down and cry, even though she should be used to it by now. Every time they saw each other now, Eloise and Jake, they each remembered that moment, when he cried and she held him.

She passed the yoga studio where some lithe women lingered chatting outside the door after class. Then past the hardware store and the community garden that a group of mothers had started in an empty lot owned by the city. Finally, she took the road out of town, toward Agatha's.

It was a short drive. Agatha was outside what was now formally called The Hollows, but she was still part of the place. The old-timers knew that The Hollows was bigger than the modern town boundaries dictated. The Hollows went on and on, up into the hills. Just because some civil engineers decided to demarcate a proper line between towns didn't make it so.

She drove along the quiet road, between the towering pines until she came to Agatha's drive, and then she turned. She moved through the gate that stood open, took the long driveway up. When she arrived, she sat and watched the house for a minute. She had a feeling that her old friend would be out back. Why had she come? She couldn't even say.

She didn't bother walking up to the door but made her way around the side of the house. She had been right; Agatha was sitting out in the gazebo past the pool that used to gleam with bright blue water but was covered now. The house had gotten too big for her, a rambling old thing. But she stayed on. *I can't leave here any more than you can*, she'd said once. And Eloise had bristled at this. *I can leave here whenever I want*, she'd thought then. But Agatha had been right about that, as she had been about so much.

"You're here about Finley," said Agatha as Eloise approached. "Among other things."

"You must be psychic," said Eloise. Agatha gave a little chortle at that.

She was smaller than she used to be, frailer. When Eloise had first known her, nearly thirty years ago now, Agatha's power used to radiate off of her in waves. She was a big woman, always clad in tunics and scarves and flowy pants. Just her presence brought comfort; it energized. That was at the height of it, when the waiting list for her speak-to-the-dead business was three years long, when she traveled on her private jet to help law enforcement agencies, make talk show appearances, help families find their lost. The years had slowed her down. Toward the end, she saw fewer people, was able to do less, see less.

Eloise sat opposite Agatha, whose long white hair was tied back in a bun. She was dressed in white, a flowing tunic and linen pants. She fingered a strand of big black beads around her neck. From where Eloise sat, the beads looked like skulls, faces pulled taut in anger and sadness, fear, misery.

"We're getting old," said Agatha.

"Yes," said Eloise.

The Whispers were usually quiet here, but today they were loud. Most people would hear the sound as just the wind in the leaves. But it was so much more, a million voices telling their stories, the full rainbow of human experience—birth and death, joy and grief, fear and love. Eloise had been listening for a long time now. Too long.

"It's her time," said Agatha. "She'll take the seat of her power. Whether she wants to or not."

Eloise felt a pang of grief. She didn't want this for Finley, any more than she had wanted it for herself. Under that, there was a selfish current of relief.

"And me?"

Agatha looked at Eloise with eyes that were blue and knowing, her gaze expansive and forgiving.

"Ray wants me to come to San Francisco," Eloise said. Even as the words were out of her mouth, she finally knew that she wouldn't be going to him. She'd been putting him off since Finley came, thinking that it was Finley who needed her. But it wasn't as simple as that. Finley thought she needed Eloise, but she didn't, not really. She was just leaning on her, finding a balance she already had.

Poor Ray, he'd been waiting so long. There hadn't been enough of her for him in the end. She'd never stopped loving Alfie, and there were so many people who had needed her help. There wasn't anything but a sliver of her left over for Ray.

"But I won't be going, will I?"

Agatha lifted a hand to Eloise, who took it.

Once long ago, Agatha had turned up on Eloise's doorstep. She'd seen Eloise on the evening news, shortly after Alfie's and Emily's passings, and knew immediately that Eloise needed a visit. Eloise had been in the throes of despair, grieving, trying to understand what was happening to her. And Agatha, a seasoned medium with years of experience under her belt, had guided her with a firm and loving hand into the next phase of her life. If it hadn't been for her friend, Eloise might have been consumed by misery. Still, Eloise always thought of herself as a bad student. So many things Agatha had tried to teach, Eloise never learned. Finley was already better at those things—setting boundaries, saying when. Agatha was a vastly superior teacher for Finley than Eloise because she had, like Finley, grown into her abilities at a young age. They hadn't been thrust upon her in midlife, in the wake of tragedy.

"You are a part of this place, Eloise," said Agatha. "Like the tree in your yard, rooted deep into the earth, your branches reaching up to the stars."

The Whispers reached a crescendo, then fell off, growing softer. They demanded that she listen. And Eloise *had* been listening. She'd done little else, her life devoted to answering the call. She didn't have any regrets. Sorrows, but not regrets. She closed her eyes and let the cool wind caress her. When she opened them again, Agatha was gone. Eloise was alone in the gazebo.

She sat there for she didn't know how long, listening. And then finally, perhaps for the first time, she took the advice she'd just given to Finley that morning. She *heard*.

As Finley climbed off her bike, her cell phone chimed.

howz it goin freakshow?
Her brother Alfie.
id try to explain, but ur such a muggle u wont get it, she typed back.
hangin with dead people cuz u can't make frenz who breathe
at least my friends dont drag their knuckles on the ground
    and beat their chests
oo oo ah ah—seriously
its ok the hollows is a little lame. hows mom?
misses u. seems sad. seeing dad again.
Ugh. wus up w/u?
Ssdd
come on
all good—school, soccer, board—livin the dream
nothing weird?
i wish.
no you don't
tell rainer I said hey

Finley's brother Alfie was three years younger than she was and her opposite in every way. His hair was as sunshiny blond as hers was midnight black. He was big—tall with broad shoulders—where she was tiny. And he was totally normal, not a hint of any ability. He wasn't even especially intuitive. He was the good boy—never in trouble, never causing their parents any grief—did well in school, total jock, competitive skateboarder. Alfie Max Montgomery was their mother's favorite child. But Finley didn't blame her for this. Alfie was Finley's favorite, too. He was a soft place in a family full of hard angles. He was even nice enough to go by Alfie when he really wanted to be called Max—a way better name for a skater punk.

Finley always thought *her* name was a living symbol of how badly her parents got along, even in the early days. Her given name was Emily Finley Montgomery; her mother had insisted on naming her after Finley's deceased Aunt Emily. Phil was totally against it, something about the cyclical nature of existence and *One Hundred Years of Solitude*—bad juju. There was a big fight, which ended in the compromise that they'd give their baby both names and let her choose when she was old enough. Finley was three when she made her choice. She didn't want to be named after a dead person.

Same deal with Alfie; Amanda wanted to name her son after her father; Phil wanted Max—because it was a cool name. Both children bore Amanda's last name; she'd kept her last name in the marriage and felt her children should have it, too. Another thing that drove Phil crazy.

"After I carried them in my body for nine months, delivered them naturally, and breast-fed for a year—why in the world would they get *your* last name? Because of some anachronistic idea of paternal lineage? Grow up, Philip."

Control, control, control. That was Amanda's thing.

If she misses me, Finley thought (with a little twinge of guilt), *it's only that I've escaped her grasp.* Of course, that wasn't quite true or entirely fair, but Finley didn't want to think about her mother right now.

She stuffed her phone in her jacket pocket and walked up the drive to Cooper's office as a golden patina of early afternoon light broke through gunmetal clouds. The house had a bright red door with a gold knocker, an autumn wreath. On the stoop sat a chaos of brightly colored ceramic pots.

She walked past the home, following a discreet sign tucked in the shrubbery that read: JONES COOPER PRIVATE INVESTIGATION. A small structure, which looked to be adjacent to the larger house, had two doors—glossy black with brushed nickel handles. The one on the left read MAGGIE COOPER, FAMILY AND ADOLESCENT THERAPIST.

Finley had been to enough therapy that she suppressed a shudder. Endless hours on couches, Dad stone-faced, Mom crying, therapists who thought they were dealing with a standard-issue troubled child, not even realizing how far out of their depth they really were. That feeling of being totally misunderstood by every adult around her had stayed with her.

She knocked on the other door, and after a few seconds Jones Cooper opened it for her and she stepped inside. There was a small foyer, with desk and chair that looked as if they had never been used—a spot for a secretary or an assistant. She followed Jones through another door, into a room that was nearly blinding in its blandness. White walls, beige carpet, desk, computer, phone, and couch—that was all, a totally utilitarian space.

"Ever think about decorating?" she asked. He motioned toward the couch and she sat.

She thought she saw the shade of a smile, but it was quickly gone, as if it hadn't been there at all. He pointed to a picture of his wife and son that sat on his desk in a simple wood frame. "I've got that."

"It's all just kind of, I don't know, *beige*."

"It works," he said, with a shrug. "I haven't had any complaints until now."

She nodded, looking at the carpet, which was not beige but dove gray, out the window, everywhere but at him.

"I guess you're not here to talk about my decorating skills," he said. "Or lack thereof."

What *was* she doing here?

"I'm not like my grandmother," said Finley abruptly. She realized that she was wringing her hands and tried to stop, tucking them beneath her.

"Okay," he said.

He leaned back in the chair behind his desk, put his hands behind his head, fanning his arms out like the wings of a cobra. He had her in that stare. Not unkind, but seeing everything. *Note to self: Don't bother bullshitting Jones Cooper.*

"But I want to help you, I think," she said without meaning to. She hadn't even *meant* to come here. "Can I try?"

He tilted his head slightly to the right. Had she expected him to seem happier about it? Like relieved or something?

"Yes," he said slowly. "But remember we're dealing with a family here, people experiencing the worst possible case scenario. We can't afford any false leads—or false hope. This is not a game."

She hadn't really thought about that part of things. It—this thing, whatever it was—had always been about *her* and whoever was hanging around. She'd never had to consider the component of the living looking for answers. It added a layer of pressure she hadn't considered. Maybe this wasn't such a good idea. She thought about just getting up and walking out. Instead, she stayed seated.

"So how do you work with my grandmother?"

Jones leaned forward on his desk and rubbed at the bridge of his nose. She'd Googled him once and read a slew of articles about him, seen photos from when he was young—a jock, hometown heartthrob, lacrosse star turned local cop, until a scandal from his past caused him to retire. He'd kept secrets that came back at him—those consequences he was so worried about. In the old pictures, he'd been handsome, beautiful even. She could still see it in him, though he had deep wrinkles around his eyes, a fuller face.

"It's been different every time," he said. "The first time she came to me. A couple of times I went to her. But I do the real legwork, as if I'm working alone. If she comes up with something, we talk. There's a lot of talking."

Finley kind of liked that Jones Cooper was a reluctant believer, though she couldn't say why.

"But *you* deal with the client, right?" asked Finley.

"Right," he said. "And I was very clear with Mrs. Gleason that there were no guarantees. I told her that Eloise can't always help. But, of course, in a case like this, expectations and desperation levels are high."

"Yeah."

Finley felt the weight of it all. According to Eloise, Finley was some kind of natural. But she didn't disappear into visions like Eloise did, or actually communicate with the dead like Agatha Cross. Although she sort of did both of those things. But there wasn't a whole lot of cohesion to what she experienced. Like in this case, she had the *squeak-clink*, the Little Bird, and the change purse in her pocket that gave her nothing.

Still, she had come here to see Jones not entirely of her own free will. She had been on her way to class when she stopped by his home instead.

"You're growing into your abilities," Eloise had said. "Be patient. Be mindful."

These were two items that were not exactly high on Finley's list of personal strengths. Anyway, what if Agatha and Eloise were wrong? What if her abilities never truly blossomed? What if she had to live this half life, the dead all around her, no way to ever know what they wanted? The thought of it filled her with a shuddering dread.

"So where were you going?" she asked. She felt her phone buzz in her pocket, but she resisted the urge to take it out and look at it. Too millennial in front of Jones; he was sure to disapprove.

"How did you know I was going somewhere?" Jones asked.

"You're wearing your jacket," she said. "I can hear your keys in your pocket. You're holding your hat."

Jones Cooper smiled, a rare thing. "I like observant better than psychic."

"Maybe I'm both." She knew it sounded like the statement of confidence. But really she just wasn't sure.

He stood. "Don't you have class?"

"I missed it already," she said, rising as well. "Take me with you." She could feel reluctance in his silence.

"You're heading somewhere relating to the case, right?"

He looked longingly at the door, obviously preferring to go alone. Why he agreed to take her along, she wasn't sure. But he gave her a nod and held the door for her. She followed him down the path and climbed into the passenger seat of his maroon SUV without another word between them.

"About a year ago, the family rented this cabin," said Jones. They had been driving for a while down a long rural road, studded with mailboxes but no homes visible from the street.

"Destination is in point five miles on your right," said the navigation computer.

He turned off the road and they drove another few minutes up a dark, rocky drive before they reached the clearing, a pretty log cabin coming into view.

"This is a rental property," said Jones. "But since the Gleason girl went missing, the owner hasn't had many takers. It was a crime scene for a while, after which there was a bit of stigma attached to the place. Then the season ended."

He brought the vehicle to a stop, and they climbed out. Was there a new chill in the air, a sudden drop in temperature? Finley zipped up her leather jacket, digging her hands deep into her pockets. She hated the cold and was already grieving warm air and long days and the sound of crickets.

"I read the police report," Jones went on. "I still have connections at The Hollows PD. No physical evidence was recovered here."

She looked at the swing hanging from the tree; it swayed listlessly in the breeze. A short red plank attached to a blue-and-white rope.

What do you think? Did Daddy do good? She heard and she didn't hear it. It was a whisper in the leaves, an echo.

"What are we looking for?" asked Finley.

"We'll know it if we see it."

They broke apart, Jones to the left, Finley to the right. She walked around the narrow side yard and into the back, where a sturdy wooden playhouse dwelled in the shade of trees. Adjacent was a slide, and a ladder leading up to a roofed surface. It reminded her that she and Alfie had always wanted a tree house. Their dad always promised to build one, but he never did.

On a wide deck there was a picnic table, frayed lounge chairs, a covered barbeque. A path led down to the lake that glittered gold and copper in the afternoon sun. She walked toward the water, then out to the edge of the dock. All around, as far as she could see were trees and mountains off in the distance. These lake properties backed up against The Hollows Wood, a state park that sat on over a thousand acres.

Then she heard something, faint and sweet.

At first she thought it was the *squeak-clink* but quickly realized that it was the call of a bird. Lilting, twisting notes lifting joyfully into the air. She remembered the birdsong she'd heard online just the night before and looked around for it, the little fluff of white, black, and red, the rose-breasted grosbeak. But she didn't see anything. It was too late in the season, wasn't it?

Finley moved in the direction of the sound, away from the house, along the perimeter of the lake until she came to a trailhead. Wildflowers were still blooming around the wooden post that marked the opening with a sign that included a map. The trail, about two miles long, looped back to the entrance, an easy hike. There was a list of birds and plants one might see, a warning to bring water and a cell phone.

There he was, perched on top of the sign, a little black, red, and white ball of bird, puffed up proudly, with an ash-colored beak. As Finley approached, he flew off with an alarmed *squeak*, alighting in a branch above her. He looked down accusingly. *Don't go far, Little Bird. Stay where Daddy can see you.* It was an echo on the air, something uttered long ago.

Finley stared at the bird, wondering. If she'd come here yesterday, before hearing the *squeak-clink*, which caused her to research the sound and finally discover the call of this bird, would his song have caught her attention? She asked herself her favorite question: What would Carl Jung say? He'd say that when there was a series of acausal events—the *squeak-clink*, the appearance now of the bird she'd read about online—that there must be a cause, even if that cause wasn't explainable by science. Jung never discounted the rarity, the anomalous occurrence; he embraced it, explored it. He knew that science didn't have all the answers to the true nature of the universe.

"They took this trail," said Jones coming up behind her. She didn't startle; she'd heard him approach.

She was still waiting to feel something, to have some kind of experience. But there was nothing, just the slightest buzz of unease, a tickle really at the back of her consciousness. This wasn't going to work; she should have known. Nothing ever worked the way it was supposed to; she was going to let everyone down, just like she always did.

"Merri Gleason watched them walk off together," he said. He turned and pointed back at the bay window that had taken on the gold of the sun.

She listened as he recounted what she'd already read online. A young man had stopped Wolf Gleason about a mile down the trail, pretending to be lost. While they spoke, someone hiding in the trees shot Gleason in the leg. He fell off the path, down the slope. The children had gone up ahead but came running back at the sound of gunfire. Gleason's son was shot; the girl was taken. It was four hours and near dusk already before the ranger came looking for them.

"Local and state police were out here three days looking. Dogs. Choppers," said Jones. He walked as he talked, looking everywhere—down on the ground, up into the sky, farther up the path. "The whole thing. Ten miles north through the trees. I was one of the volunteers."

He shook his head, looking back at her. She dug her hands deeper into her pocket, feeling useless, searching for warmth.

"There must have been a vehicle waiting," he said. "They could have been long gone by the time anyone started looking."

He took out his flashlight, and they stepped onto the trail, started walking. They walked for a while, Finley clutching the girl's change purse in her hand. Jones moved up ahead of her just a bit, now shining his flashlight about, though he really didn't need it, the sky still held a little light. What was he looking for? She was about to ask.

It happened just like that, as if she had stepped through a doorway. Suddenly the sun was brighter, and she was moving fast, breathless. Up ahead, a man old, skeletal but strong, his face a jagged mountain, yanked a screaming girl by the arm up the path. He was dragging her as she kicked and fought like a wild animal.

"I *swear* to you," he said through gritted teeth, yanking her hard. "I'll kill you, you little brat."

He had a rifle strapped around his back. "Then I'll go back and kill your family."

The girl quieted for a moment, whimpering. But then she dropped her weight to the ground. She was tiny, with a wild mass of blonde hair.

"Daaaaaddddddyyyyyy," she shrieked, desperate, panicked. The sound cut through Finley, sharp, serrated. "Daaaaddddddyyyyy."

The old man delivered a hard blow to her face, and the girl opened her mouth wide in a silent wail of pain and misery.

Finley was there, but she wasn't there. She moved to stop the man, but she had no body, no will. She was just an observer. The helplessness of it was excruciating. *She's a child. Let her go!* The words were loud, but she had no voice to speak them.

"Go back and finish it," the man growled at someone Finley couldn't see. He expertly removed a hunting knife from a sheath at his waist and handed it over, never losing his grip on the child who thrashed and shrieked.

"I don't want to, Poppa." It was a young voice, but thick and slow. "*Do it.*"

Finley felt a churn of petulant anger, a sullen resistance, but also the cold finger of fear poking into her belly. Then she was moving back down the path away from the man and the girl. A disembodiment, a floating.

Up ahead, a boy, towheaded and slender, lay on the path, his expression blank and glassy, a great stain of blood on the thigh of his khaki pants, his shattered glasses next to him on the path.

"No," he whispered. "Bring her back. Mommy."

She wanted to go to him, to comfort him somehow. He was so young and so frightened, in pain. She ached with it. *Do something for him!*

"Leave him alone," called a distant voice. At the edge of the path, she looked down at the man twisted, down on the slope off the path, his face obscured by the trees. He tried to claw his way back. Moving so slowly, grunting with effort.

"Where's my daughter?" he managed. "Where is she?"

There was a blade in a young man's hand. Was Finley *in* him? *Beside* him? Finley didn't know. She could see his dirty, calloused fingers wrapped around the black handle, as if they were her own. Not a man's hand, a boy's thick, soft fingers. Oh, God, thought Finley. I don't want to watch this. I don't want to *be in* this.

You can look away, Eloise had said of her own visions. *But if you do, you risk missing what you're there to see and you'll have to go back again and again until you figure out what you missed.*

But whoever Finley was in (or near, or above, or *what?*) just sat down on the edge of the path, watching. He lay the knife down beside him. The little boy on the path closed his eyes after a time; he stopped whispering. The man on the hill stopped struggling, lay still. *Do something!*

But there was nothing she could do.

What do you see? Finley tried to quiet the roil of panic and anger, and be present. *What do you see?* The black-handled hunting knife. It's late afternoon, the sun golden and low in the sky. She could still hear the girl screaming distantly, which meant that she and the old man were on foot. The man on the slope didn't look like the pictures she'd seen of Wolf Gleason, but it was hard to tell.

Then Finley heard it, the sweet song of the rose-breasted grosbeak. It was quiet except for that, and the wind in the leaves.

His thoughts and feelings were hers. He liked to be alone in the woods, liked nothing better. He didn't want to hunt like Poppa. He didn't like to watch the light drain from things that never hurt anyone, that flicker of pain and terrible fear just before the end, the convulsion of life leaving. Where did they go? He had so many questions and never any answers. The world was such a confusing place and there was so much pain.

He sat there for a long time, his thoughts dull and heavy, then chaotic. The man and the boy had both lost consciousness. Maybe they were dead. He was supposed to kill them and then hide their bodies. He knew a place where they wouldn't be found. But he didn't, couldn't. Not again. He wouldn't tell Poppa. Finley stayed with him.

When the sun got very low, he got up and followed Poppa and the girl.

And then Finley was back on the trail, finding herself on the ground. It was nearly dark, and Jones sat beside her as if he were waiting for a bus, untroubled. He was still shining his flashlight up into the sky. Why did he keep doing that? What did he think he was going to see up there?

"I thought you said you weren't like your grandmother," he said as she started to stir.

"What happened?" she asked. God, her *head*. It was *pounding*. Is this what it felt like? Is this what happened to her grandmother every time?

"You went boneless, kid," Jones said. "You just—went down."

There was a rock digging into her back. Jones had rolled up his own jacket and put it under her head. She struggled to sit. He took a mini-bottle of water out of his pocket. Had he had it all along? A big Boy Scout, always prepared. She cracked it open and drank a few sips.

"So what did you see?" he asked. She told him everything.

"The man and the girl went up that way," she said, pointing north. "There was no vehicle. They were on foot."

Jones stayed quiet, frowning.

"Someone else—a boy, I think—was supposed to come back and

kill the brother and the father," she said. "But he didn't do it. They weren't supposed to survive."

Jones seemed to take that in, offered a slight nod. "I wondered about that. Why they had been left alive. Why didn't he kill them?"

"He didn't want to," Finley said. "He said—he thought? Felt?—that he didn't 'want to hunt like Poppa.'"

The experience was already slipping a little, like a dream. Had she *inhabited* him? She wouldn't have been able to explain it to anyone except someone else like her. And even then, there were no words to explain it. Either you understood or you didn't.

"They couldn't have gone on foot," said Jones, with a shake of his head. "The search team went as far north as they could go into the woods. There was nothing up there."

"They did," said Finley. She was certain, though she couldn't say why. Jones looked in that direction, as if he was considering.

"There's something wrong with the kid," said Finley. "He's impaired—or something."

Jones didn't say anything, but he was watching her now, waiting for her to say more.

"What did they look like?"

It was fading fast. "I didn't see the young man," said Finley. "I was in him, seeing through his eyes."

She described the old man, tall and thin but with a wiry strength. His face wasn't clear, covered with white hair. He wore a hat that obscured part of his face.

"And what about the father and the little boy?" he asked when she was done. "The Gleasons?"

"I don't know," she said. "The faces were . . . fuzzy or something, hard to take in."

Finley struggled for their features, something she could hold on to, but she couldn't bring them to the surface of her consciousness. She just kept hearing the little girl, seeing her struggle to get free.

"She fought," said Finley. "That's why the man didn't come back and kill the others himself. She fought him every step of the way."

NINE

A man came in the morning. A stranger. At first, Penny wasn't even sure what she was hearing, a loud crunching, the hum of something. Then she realized it was a car on the long drive. Penny felt a deep startle, a jolt of fear, as she stood at the pump. Then she ran to her hidden room next to the barn, as she'd been taught to do, and closed the door, watching through the gap.

The car pulled up slowly and came to a stop. A man sat at the wheel, staring down at something, then looked up and around him. She gasped as he got out of the car. It *wasn't* her daddy, but he looked kind of like her daddy did—tall and strong, with clean clothes and shiny hair. He wasn't dirty and wrinkled with a big gap in his teeth, and dirt under his nails, like Poppa.

He was more like the people she used to see in the world before. He had nice shoes and strong shoulders, shoulders you could ride on. And arms that hugged and never hurt. She *knew* she wasn't ever supposed to show herself, to talk to anyone. If she did, Poppa said he would leave this place and find her mommy and daddy and kill them both. She knew he could do it. She'd seen him do things that she tried to forget as soon as she saw.

Even so, there was a voice in her head.

Show yourself to him, the voice said. Her feet moved, leaned toward the door.

Poppa came out on the porch, his filthy overalls hanging, his baseball cap askew. He had a face full of white stubble and cheekbones that jutted like cliffs and eyes that sunk like dark canyons into his head, and she knew he smelled rank when you got up close—sweat and cigarettes.

"Hey, there," the clean man said. He lifted a hand, gave a nervous smile. "Sorry to trouble you. But I'm lost."

"Where you headed?" asked Poppa. He could be so nice to people, even to Penny. He gave her Baby, the rag doll with the missing button eye that she slept with every night. Sometimes he rested his big hand on top of her head, like her daddy used to. They fed her, gave her clothes. They weren't always bad.

"I'm looking for a town called The Hollows," the clean man said.

"Yeah," said Poppa with a squint and an understanding bob of his head. He stayed rooted on the porch. "You took a wrong turn back at the river. You need to shoot left instead of right, then it's about twenty miles north."

"The creek?" said the man squinting. "At the bottom of the hill?"

She moved quickly. There was a door in her room that led to the barn, one that couldn't be seen from the outside. It was where they hid her when she first came here and the people were searching. She could hear them, but she stayed quiet, Poppa's threats that he'd kill her, kill them, kill her family keeping her bound and gagged. Now, she pushed out that door. Bobo had showed her how. She walked softly, stood at the tall doors that led outside. *Hurry. Now.*

"You don't have one of those computers?" Poppa said. His voice had taken on a darker tone. "With the directions?"

The clean man had a beautiful black car, a BMW, which she knew because her mommy always sighed when she saw one. *My dream car*, she'd say.

The man laughed a little, held up the device in his hand. "My phone died. We're lost without technology these days, aren't we? Literally."

Poppa didn't say anything. He didn't like computers. It was the first thing he did; smash her iPod Touch.

"Well," said the man, turning back toward the car. "Thanks—and sorry again to trouble you."

Penny pushed the door and it emitted that long creak, just as she knew it would. She moved into the light even though she didn't want to. The man saw her, his polite smile fading a little, brow wrinkling.

"Hey there," he said. "Hey, little one."

She didn't say anything, just stared at him. She didn't have a voice anymore, could hardly get any words out, as if they'd all dried up, blown away like leaves. He took a step toward her, the sun dappling golden through the trees. If only she could say: *Help me! Take me home!* She took a step closer, the words were right there.

But then a cartoon spray of red blew out of the clean man's right ear. And his face went from worried to peaceful and blank as if he'd fallen asleep while standing before her. Then he slowly dropped to his knees. He wobbled there a moment, rocking, and fell to his side in a soft heap of himself. Penny's throat closed up as she turned toward the porch and saw Poppa standing there with his hunting rifle, still aimed. Penny couldn't breathe, a strange rasping sound in her throat.

"Look what you did," said Poppa. He lowered the gun and glared at her accusingly, as if she held the gun in her hand. "Look."

Penny found sound—a deep wail, a thunderous scream from the ground beneath her that traveled up her legs and into her gullet. It exploded from her, scaring the birds from the trees, making the animals in the barn restless and afraid. She screamed and screamed and couldn't stop, even when Poppa took the belt to her right there on the ground in front of the barn. The lashes were sharp and hot against her back and her thighs, a nasty, searing pain that only made her scream louder until everything went a blessed black.

Later when she came to, in the same place on the ground, Bobo was standing over her. The clean man and the beautiful car were gone, except for a long red stain on the ground where the clean man had fallen that was as big as Penny and still wet. She felt nothing, just an icy numbness.

"Come on," Bobo said. "Get up."

He had a chipped tooth and a slow way of talking. She struggled to stand and stumbled after him. Inside, he stripped off her shirt and ran it under the water from the faucet. He used it to dab away at her back, which burned like fire. But she didn't scream or cry out from the pain. She used up most all the sound she had left. All that remained was a weak whimper.

Then he took off his sweatshirt and put it on her. It was way too big. He helped her into her cot and covered her with the blanket.

"Try to be good now," he said. "They're getting tired of you."

They sky was growing dark outside and the air cool. Then he stood over her, watching; she tried to ignore him. She was always tense around Bobo; she never knew when he was going to be nice or be mean. Sometimes he was both. But tonight he just let her be, stood there a while like he was trying to think of something else to say.

"That's going to be trouble—what happened today."

Then he walked off. She didn't sleep, just lay there thinking, listening as the whispering in the trees grew louder. They were trying to tell her something, but she didn't know what. Finally, she got up from her bed and walked toward the window. She stood listening, the black space between the trees like a doorway she might walk through.

TEN

Merri and Wolf were not B and B people. Well, *Wolf* wasn't. Mr. Adventure. He'd rather sleep in a tent in the woods, go to the bathroom in a chemical toilet, than socialize at breakfast with other travelers over fluffy flapjacks and fresh coffee. Merri always thought there was something nice about the whole enterprise, though. The quaint rooms in beautiful homes, a couple cooking in the kitchen, serving guests, telling stories, giving advice. There was a connectedness, a sincere friendliness to it that Merri found comforting. Kindness, courtesy, true warmth—it was disappearing all around, wasn't it? Especially in the city. In elevators, on the trains, on the street, people didn't even lift their eyes from the screens in front of them anymore. The world had become such a crowded, frenetic, and terribly lonely place.

She could have chosen the Hampton Suites off the highway that led up to The Hollows. It would have afforded her a certain amount of distance, some anonymity. Instead she chose Miss Lovely's Bed & Breakfast, a charming little guesthouse off the main square. She pulled into the small, gravelly parking lot as she'd been instructed over the phone, shouldered her small tote, and walked toward the entrance.

"How long are you going to stay up there?" Jackson had wanted to know at breakfast that morning.

"I don't know," she'd answered. "Until . . ."

What could she say? Until she found Abbey. Or something that told her that she'd never find Abbey. "I'll come home on Thursday nights to spend the weekends with you."

He nodded, pushed his glasses up his nose. "Maybe we could come up on the weekends and help."

Jackson, unlike Wolf, wanted Merri to go to The Hollows. He'd go with her if they'd let him. As much as he wanted Merri to stay, he wanted someone to be up there looking. *Families don't give up on each other*, he'd said when they first came back to the city. *We can't just leave her.* His words, the shattering of his voice, had stayed with her.

"We'll see," she'd said this morning, ruffling his bangs.

They wanted him to go back to life. Maybe it was unfair, unrealistic to expect him to do that. But it was even less fair to allow him to think that there was anything he could do for Abbey.

"Dad said you loaded the *New York Times* app onto your phone," Merri said after she forced down a few bites of granola.

Jackson didn't look up from his bowl, clinking his spoon against the edge.

"We talked about this with the doctor," she said.

He nodded. "Bad things happen in the world every day," he said in bored monotone, the tired repetition of a phrase he'd been forced to memorize but didn't believe. "Good things happen every day, too. There are no patterns."

Since the day in the woods when a strange man shot him and his father, then took his sister, Jackson had been obsessed with the news. They'd catch him on his computer with ten windows open, shuffling back and forth between CNN, the *New York Times*, the *Washington Post*, the *Hollows Gazette*, BBC. Murders, abductions, terrorist attacks, mall and school shootings. He had developed the idea that by monitoring world events, he could make sure that their family didn't fall victim to any more tragedies.

"The worst thing can happen to any of us any day," their family therapist had told Jackson. "We can't control how events unfold, even through constant vigilance. Watching and waiting will only serve to rob us of the joy of the normal, good days."

But Jackson had an idea in his head that he couldn't get out. He claimed that he *knew* something bad was going to happen that day in the woods. He knew because when the news had been on in the morning, there had been a story about two missing children who had never been found. And he'd had a *feeling*.

"It makes me feel better," he'd said, rinsing his bowl in the sink and putting it in the dishwasher. "To know what's happening."

"I don't think it makes you feel better," said Merri.

In fact, it kept him up at night. It fed his idea that the world was a terrible and unsafe place, which was why he wouldn't leave the house without one of them, couldn't be alone in the apartment. It was lucky that Wolf's parents were so present in their lives; other-wise things would be really hard. Harder.

"It does," he said, solemn, certain.

She didn't know what to say. She didn't want to argue right be-fore she was going to leave. So she decided to drop it, walked around to the other side of the island to rinse her own bowl and put it in the dishwasher.

"Mom," he said, careful, tentative. "I saw something online last night."

This was the other thing. He thought that by scanning all the various local and international news sites that he might find some-thing that would lead them to Abbey. It was compulsive behavior, not pathological exactly. He didn't have OCD, per se, according to their doctor. More like a mild case of PTSD. But both Merri and Wolf were against medication for him if they could help it. Nobody knew better than she did what a rabbit hole *that* was.

"Jackson."

"Just listen," he said. He had that kind of nervous energy that he got these days. He grabbed onto the hand she was reaching toward him. "Somebody else went missing up there."

She shouldn't ask, shouldn't encourage him. But if another child had gone missing . . . "Who?"

"A real estate developer," he said. He already had his phone out of his pocket, was holding it up to Merri. "He's been missing a couple of days."

She looked at the article, squinting and holding it away from her because she wasn't wearing her glasses. A man in his late forties had left his office in Manhattan for a meeting in The Hollows for which he never turned up. There was a photo—smiling, clean cut, bespectacled.

She handed the phone back to her son. "It doesn't mean anything, sweetie."

They stood eye-to-eye, which was the weirdest thing. Jackson, her baby, would probably be taller than she was in a few months.

"It gave me a feeling," he said. "It made me think about Abbey."

"Sweetie."

"She's alive, Mom." He took his glasses off and a big tear fell down his cheek. She reached up to wipe it away, feeling a dump of anxiety.

"If she is," said Merri. "I'll find her. I swear it, Jackson. I *swear*."

It was irresponsible to make promises like that. She couldn't help it; she wanted it so badly to be true. She took him into her arms and let him cling, trying not to cling back.

Now, Merri walked up the porch steps at the B and B and into the foyer, where a pretty young woman sat at a desk. Strawberry blond hair pulled back into a high ponytail, freckles, a youthful sweetness—just the kind of girl Wolf would like. He liked them young and bubbly, the opposite of his uptight middle-aged wife. She pushed in a door and a little bell rang.

"Miss Lovely?" Merri asked.

The girl smiled warm and bright, getting up from her seat and walking over with outstretched hand. "I'm her daughter Peggy. Mrs. Gleason?"

"Yes," said Merri. "Call me Merri."

Her hand was warm, her energy so welcoming. No, she was too smart, too genuine for Wolf. She wouldn't fit the bill as a fling. He liked his side dishes (as Merri came to think of them) a little empty, that way he could fill them up with himself.

"My mom's in the kitchen," said Peggy. "She wanted you to have something fresh for afternoon tea."

Merri could smell something baking, the scent of cinnamon wafting on the air. There was a vibe to the place, the girl, the aromas that relaxed Merri in a way that she hadn't experienced in a long time. The place wrapped itself around her like a blanket.

"Your room is ready and waiting for you."

Peggy walked around the desk and took Merri's bag from her. Merri let her take it, because it just seemed rude not to, and followed her up the stairs.

The room was lovely (no pun intended), a plush four-poster bed with a cozy sitting area around a small fireplace. A writing desk by the window, on which sat fresh flowers—bright pink Gerber daisies—in a vase. The bathroom had a claw-foot tub and black-and-white tile floor.

"If there's anything we can do for you, Merri," said Peggy, looking suddenly solemn as she put Merri's tote on the luggage rack, "please don't hesitate. We want to help any way that we can."

When Merri made her reservation, she hadn't told anyone why she was coming and why she'd need a room indefinitely. But she had informed Detective Chuck Ferrigno of The Hollows PD that she'd hired Jones Cooper, and he promised to cooperate fully (apparently they knew each other well). She should have known that word would travel fast in a place like this. She remembered how the town had rallied around her family, how the volunteers had helped search, feed them, manned the hotline, organized vigils.

Merri barely remembered those early days—caring for Jackson and Wolf in the hospital and searching for Abbey. Every nightmare she had was unfurling around her in a blood-soaked blur—her daughter *missing*, her son and husband *shot*. The whole world was a stuttering horror reel. But as shattered as she had been, she remembered the feeling that arms were around her, holding her up. Strangers comforted her, ran errands, brought food and flowers. The owner of the cabin let them stay free of charge, as long as they needed. If the rest of the world had grown disconnected and lonely, people happier in front of a screen than with each other, the opposite seemed true in The Hollows.

"There's a safety net here that can only be seen when tears are shed," someone had said to her in those early days. *Even for outsiders?* Merri had wondered aloud. *If you're in The Hollows, you belong here,* the person had replied. She couldn't even remember now who it had been.

"Thank you," Merri said now.

"I hope you don't mind my saying that we're all still praying for your daughter, that she'll come home safe to you."

Merri nodded, wanted to thank her again, but she lost her voice to a sudden rush of tears.

Come home safe to you. It was such a benign phrase, implying that all could so easily be well again. Merri was holding on to that. Only Wolf had dared to ask who Abbey would be if she came home. If all this time she'd been missing, alive somewhere, what horrors had she endured? How would it have changed her? Would she ever be well and whole again? Merri became obsessed with the women in the news, the ones who had been abducted and held for years, watching their interviews, reading their ghostwritten stories. The girl who had been taken from her home and held in the woods, walking through the town where her parents lived with her captors, never calling out for help. They all had the appearance of wellness in varying degrees. But what cracks, what fissures lay beneath the media-ready surface? Who will Abbey be if she comes home to us? It didn't matter. Whoever she was, Merri would hold her until she was well again. They would all be changed, irrevocably. But they would be together.

The girl—what was her name?—hovered by the door, looking at Merri uncertainly. How long had Merri sat there, lost in her thoughts?

"Thank you," Merri said, trying to recover herself.

Peggy—that was it—smiled sadly, seeming to understand, and turned to leave the room.

"Of course," she said. "Again. Anything you need."

People—Wolf, her doctor, even her mother—were starting to treat Merri like a crazy person, someone too delusional to move forward from tragedy, grasping at the very slim hope that Abbey was still alive. It was such a relief to not be treated that way. In The Hollows, it seemed like people were hoping along with her. No one here seemed to think she should have moved on by now.

They're just being polite, Merri, Wolf would surely say. *No one says what they're really thinking.*

Maybe so. But the world could do with a few more kind, polite people—even if it was fake.

Her phone pinged, and she drew it out of her pocket to see a text from Wolf.

Arrived safely?

He knew she had. They each had a Find My Friends app on their phone, so he could have easily seen that she was in The Hollows. Although service up here *was* spotty.

Yes.

She slid her wedding ring up and down her finger. She didn't wear it all the time anymore, had grown quite careless with it, leaving it on the edge of the sink, the kitchen counter, the dresser in the bedroom. Wolf was forever returning it to her, looking injured. As if he had any right to look injured about anything.

What now?

That was Wolf. What now? What's next? What should we do? A man in perpetual motion, always on to the next thing.

I don't know. I see Jones Cooper in an hour.
Sure you don't want me to come up?

She *did* want Wolf to come up. She wanted the man she had first loved. The Wolf who was strong but kind, funny but sensible. The world traveler—his work as a travel writer had taken him to places of which she'd never even heard. She'd found that so exotic. She loved how he could just pack a bag and go anywhere without a hint of stress. He was so calm in every circumstance, always seemed in control. To Merri who was scattered, a worrier, the one who got lost and showed up late, he was a steady hand to hold on to. She followed him places that she never would have dared to go on her own, homebody that she was—trekking on the Inca Trail, scuba diving in Belize, an eco lodge in the Amazon. When she was with Wolf, at first at least, she was less afraid of the world. Of course, that was before the children came. And before he had all that trouble with work. Before she discovered that in their fifteen years together, he had never been faithful to her for more than a year at a time.

No, I'm okay, she typed. I'll keep you posted.

I love you.

She didn't doubt his love for her, odd as that was to say of a faithless husband. But she didn't say it back anymore, though she did still love him. More than she wanted to.

She flipped open her laptop and logged on to the free wireless offered by the guesthouse. On the ride up, she hadn't been able to stop thinking about what Jackson told her, about the missing man. It was nothing, of course. Jackson was a worrier, a ruminator like Merri. Still.

She found a small item in the *Times*. Real estate developer missing. Gerald Healy, forty-four, left his Manhattan office for a meeting with a construction company in The Hollows. He never arrived. His car hadn't been found, cell phone signal lost. Family—wife and two small children—were pleading for any information. There was a picture of a handsome man with dark hair and glasses, wearing a bright smile and a green-and-white checked shirt. She felt a rush of impotent urgency.

The wallpaper on her laptop screen was an image of Abbey. She was the wild child, the kook. When you first got to know her, you might think she was cautious, even fearful. But in her heart, she was an adventurer like her father, a warrior. After she'd hung back a bit and assessed the situation, she dove right in. The image was a shot from above with Abbey looking up at the camera, her mouth wide open in laughter, her purple skirt twirling. She was unabashed joy, raw energy in that captured moment. How could she not be here with them—all that wild love, all the crazy little kid energy? How could her Abbey, those other two children, this man, just disappear and not be found? It just didn't seem right. Was the world that big, that dark, like a maw that could swallow you whole?

She scrolled through the few articles, which were all similarly lacking information. It was less of a news story when adult men went missing, probably more likely that he'd just abandoned his family than come to any harm. But he didn't look like the type to run off. He had a goofy smile, was cute in a geeky sort of way. In fact, he reminded Merri of their friend Blake. Blake, who was the consummate good father, a loving and faithful husband, always honest and upright. In all their years of knowing him, Merri had never seen his eyes stray in the direction of a pretty waitress when Claire was around. It wasn't even that he was *not staring*; it was that he did not notice. Not in the way that Wolf noticed every tight piece of ass within a certain radius, the way he was always browsing.

It was actually Blake whom Merri had met first on the night she met Wolf. She'd been getting her MFA at Columbia. Blake was studying law. And Wolf was at the journalism school. She was at some sports bar that she'd gone to with a guy she thought she liked. But he'd quickly revealed himself to be an arrogant asshole—like most male MFA students who invariably thought that they were going to be the next F. Scott Fitzgerald.

"No offense, but your date is a jerk."

Her date—*What had his name been? So long ago*—had left her at the bar to go to the bathroom, and Blake had slipped in beside her.

"I couldn't help but overhear," Blake said apologetically. "His voice was *booming*."

"Really?" she said. "Because I stopped listening an hour ago."

Blake asked her what she was drinking and ordered her another vodka soda. Then they just started talking, and he felt strangely familiar, one of those people who feel like an old friend before you've even exchanged names.

"Don't look now," Blake had said. He nodded in the direction behind her with a mischievous grin. "But I think your friend has found a more enthusiastic audience."

She glanced over and saw Bruce (yes, that was his name) leaning into a woman from their short-fiction class. The woman was as talentless and dull as he was; they were a perfect couple.

"Good for him," she said.

"You can't keep the pretty ones all to yourself, Blakey." Wolf had joined them.

Just the sight of him, even that very first moment, lit her up inside. Those silky curls, those glittering eyes, those muscled forearms. Something else, too, of course. What had it been in him that made her choose Wolf over Blake? Was it something good? Or was it something bad?

Whatever it was, Blake, however sweet and good looking, immediately receded from her view. And it was Wolf she wound up going home with that night. Blake and Claire had broken up, just briefly. (He was single for the first time since high school the night they met.) The following week, however, Blake and Claire got back together. And they were married before Blake had graduated law school. Merri and Wolf were married two years later. But there had been one night when she could have chosen between them. She'd spent a lot of time over the years thinking about how things would be different if she'd kept talking with the man she'd *liked*, instead of sleeping with the man she *wanted*.

But then there would be no Jackson, no Abbey. And that had always given her comfort because her children were the center of her universe, the right things that made every other mistake and mishap okay. Until. Until their failings as people and parents were harshly punished with the loss of Abbey.

It was that thinking, that mental maze that had led Merri to her nervous breakdown in the months after Abbey's disappearance. This idea that if she could atone for all the mistakes she made, maybe she could stop the fall of dominos or even reverse it. It was easy to see from which parent Jackson had inherited his obsessive thinking.

Her phone pulsed on the table, startling her.

Mom! Aced my math test. 99!
Good job, Jacko!!

She scrolled over to see him on the little map on Find My Friends. There he was, at school where he belonged.

Are you okay up there? She could see his worried frown.
Don't worry about your Mom, kiddo. Let me worry about you.
Okay. Love you.

She glanced back over at her computer screen. The missing man stared out at her. Merri's psychiatrist told her that the most stressful condition for the human mind is simply not knowing. Even if the worst thing happens, the mind recovers eventually, returns to its natural baseline of happiness. But the wondering, the crushing weight of disappointments, the violent swing between poles of hope and despair. It's almost more than a person can endure.

She was attuned now to the wobble, that edgy feeling that meant she was losing her grip. She forced herself to close the computer and lie down on the bed, breathe deep. *Let go. Let God.* It was such a simple phrase that did bring comfort if you let it. But not as much comfort as those smooth, fat white pills, which she still thought about every day.

ELEVEN

This Penny was different from the other ones. It took him a while to figure out what it was. He'd seen it the very first day when Poppa had noticed her in town. Poppa hadn't *said* anything. He had just stopped his work and went very still, and Bobo followed his gaze to the family moving up the street. They drifted right past without even seeing Poppa and Bobo.

The pretty woman, with her raspberry-colored tee-shirt and faded blue jeans, holding the hand of a boy with white blond hair. The man had strolled up ahead, was looking in the window of a shop and pointing at something. The girl trailed behind, licking ice cream from a cone. She gazed up at the trees, spun around—daydreaming, in her own world. Then it was like she sensed him looking at her. She turned slowly, and she *saw* him. Looked right at him, not through him or over him or around him, like most people. She smiled, white teeth a little crooked. Then she ran ahead, back to her family, taking her daddy by the hand. She didn't look back at him again, though Bobo kept watching her.

Poppa gathered up his things, even though they weren't near done. He threw everything carelessly into the back of the pickup. Then they were driving slowly down the street, following a distance behind the family. Poppa smiled, waving to folks as they called out to him—the old lady from Orchard Street, the owner of the hardware store, Mr. Jenkins. Everybody knew everybody in The Hollows.

The family walked a while, and finally all piled into one of those big, expensive cars. It was shiny and blood red. They were like a television family, too perfect. They weren't real. Especially the girl with her round cheeks and pretty mouth, golden hair. She was like a doll.

"You know how much one of those things cost?" asked Poppa. Bobo didn't answer.

"You could feed a village in Africa for a year," he went on.

Poppa couldn't care less about villages in Africa. He just hated rich people, people who thought they were smart because they had money and lived in the city. People who came in from outside and bought land that they had no business buying and built big new houses that didn't belong in The Hollows.

He followed them out of town. Poppa wasn't worried about being noticed. Normal people didn't think about being followed. And Poppa's truck made him invisible; no one ever noticed them. The family drove slowly, then sped up, then slowed down again like they were looking for something. Finally they turned onto a drive that led to one of those new big houses.

Poppa kept driving, silent, his jaw working. He wore a faded blue baseball cap over his tangle of white and gray hair, which he pulled back into a ponytail when he was working. With his free hand, he twisted at the bottom of the full beard that was the shape and color of a gnarled old tree branch. Bobo knew just what he was thinking. Bobo was thinking about her, too. That little doll of a girl, that crooked smile that was pretty anyway. She wasn't the first little girl Poppa had noticed.

They went back to work after that, worked until the sun started to get low in the sky. Doing what needed doing, then collecting cash at the end of each job.

Poppa liked to think of them as living "off the grid." *We don't exist*, he always said. They lived in a house that Poppa's poppa had built with "his own two hands" on property that had been in his family since The Hollows was settled. They didn't have a phone, or a computer, or a television. There was a generator and a fuel tank on the property, so there were no dealings with the electric company. In the winter, when the snows came, the roads became impassable except for Poppa's snowmobile. He could get into town if he needed to; but mainly they didn't need to. They worked hard all spring and summer, and in fall stocked the food cellar. And Poppa liked to hunt.

Up way back in the woods, there were other people like them. Folks who lived off the land. They lived in houses that didn't have a street address; they hunted, fished, and gardened for their food. They schooled their children, not just with books, but by teaching them how to survive like the men and women who first settled The Hollows. They buried their own dead. The townies called them hill people. But Poppa said that the people in the hills, they were "true descendants of our founding fathers." The Hollows belonged to them.

New Penny cried at first, but not like the others. The others whimpered quietly, went limp with fear, obeyed right away, got used up and discarded. But New Penny, she screamed, she raged and fought. There was a something deep inside her that couldn't be touched. Even when she had decided to be good, there was a wild sparkle in her eyes. Bobo liked her better than the others, even though she made more trouble. A lot more trouble.

But Momma and Poppa were getting tired of her now. She had been there longer than anyone. There had been another, too. But she was gone.

Poppa was angry about the man with the Bimmer, as Poppa called it. Poppa was skinny, so skinny that you could see the shelf of his collarbone and the dip behind it. His knees were rocks in a sock, elbows hard as hammers. But he was strong. He didn't need any help lifting the stranger into the trunk of his car. There was a neat black suitcase in there, which Poppa took. He searched the stranger's body, lifted his wallet from his pocket.

"There's nearly five hundred dollars in here," Poppa said, pocketing the cash. Bobo wondered if that would make him less angry at New Penny. But it didn't seem to. In fact, it just seemed to make him more agitated.

"Real estate man," he said. Though how Poppa knew that, Bobo couldn't be sure. Maybe because all the new rich people up here were either buying, selling, or tearing down what was already here and building something new. "Developer."

Up here that was the dirtiest word. Developers came up all the time, finding their way where locals from town wouldn't even dare to go. These strangers offered big money for land, never understanding that the folks who lived here were *part* of the land. They could no more sell it than they could sell the skin off their bodies.

Poppa took the developer's watch, too, a big glittery thing. And his belt and shoes. Those shoes that city people wore to the country, leather with big treads and fancy laces. Nice looking but not waterproof, not really.

Then they drove out to The Chapel (as the local kids called it) a run-down old barn out in the middle of The Hollows Wood. There were several long, wide trails behind the house on their property (one of several) that led straight to it. And Poppa did a good job of keeping the paths wide and passable for the truck and the snowmobile. So even a fancy car like the Bimmer could make it at least to the clearing. And since the ground was still dry because there hadn't been as much rain this year, Poppa was able to drive it right inside the old barn.

It didn't seem like the best hiding spot, because local kids came up here all the time. Bobo snuck out on full-moon nights and watched them smoking and kissing and more inside. Even though the place was so tilted and sagging that it looked like it could come down at any second, they came up here with six-packs of beer and cartons of cigarettes, sleeping bags. They made fires in the field, played music sometimes, and danced. There was a place in the back where Bobo could sit and watch them through a triangle opening in the wood. Whispered words, exposed skin, sometimes laughter, sometimes raised voices and tears. Bobo wanted to be one of them.

But there was no one up there now. Big fingers of sunlight streamed in through the gaping holes in the roof. That's why Bobo thought of it as The Chapel, because it looked like church somehow. Like God was reaching down to touch it.

Poppa drove the car back as far as they could go into the shadows. Then he got out and started pacing, which he did when he was thinking about what to do. Finally, he started taking things from all around—broken-up crates, pieces of wood that lay around. There was an old tarp by the door, a balled-up blanket in the corner.

They worked for a while to hide the car behind a pile of debris. From the door, where the car was parked toward the back, you couldn't see it. And the kids didn't do much exploring. When they came up here, they weren't interested in the barn or the woods around it. They were mostly just interested in each other's bodies, seemed like. The car might not be discovered for a good long while. And once the snow started falling, no one would come up here again until spring. It was supposed to be a long, cold winter, according to Poppa. And the way the air felt, it wouldn't be long before it fell over The Hollows.

The walk back to the house was long, but Bobo didn't mind. He wondered if Poppa noticed that they were leaving tracks in the field and on the trail. Tracks that would lead back to the house, if anyone was looking. Of course, he did; Poppa had taught Bobo all about tracking, about looking for the print on the soft ground, or the succession of broken branches, the nibbled berry or the scat in the leaves. Every creature left his mark, if you knew how to look. If you were quiet and patient, you could almost always find him. Poppa wasn't being careful, because he knew that most people weren't quiet or patient and certainly didn't know how to look at the woods to see what had journeyed down the trail before them. That must be why.

When they got back to the house, New Penny was still on the ground where she'd been lying unconscious since Poppa took the belt to her. Poppa told Bobo to get her cleaned up. In the chair on the porch, Momma rocked wearing that blank look she often wore, as if she were looking at something no one else could see. Maybe she was watching. Maybe not. She could stay that way for a long time. Bobo carried New Penny to her cot, head lolling, blond hair wild and dirty. Then he got the chain and locked her up again.

New Penny was whispering something that Bobo couldn't hear at first. When Poppa left, Bobo stood listening.

IhateyouIhateyouIhateyouIhateyouIhateyou

That was the thing about New Penny that was different from the others. She wasn't just afraid. She was full of fire. That's why he liked her better than the others. She was angry, just like him.

TWELVE

Finley rode her motorcycle to Agatha's big old house, not knowing where else to go. Eloise had been clear that Finley must find her way, that she was more or less on her own with the *squeak-clink*. But Finley felt lost. So she wound her way out of town to see Agatha. The vision was receding to the point of being inaccessible, like a dream that had just slipped away, and the few remaining pieces seemed disjointed and nonsensical.

She looped the town center and then took the small highway away from The Hollows. The farther she got, the better she felt, as if her lungs could take in more air, her shoulders straighten.

The negative energy of The Hollows could not be denied. It was no secret to Finley, who felt it constantly. The Hollows boasted an anomalous number of missing persons, of miscarriages, of accidents and unexplained events. Throughout its history, there had been brutal murders, witch burnings, and horrible mining accidents. *There's a powerful energy here*, Eloise had said more than once. *It's not always positive, it's not always negative, but it always demands something of people like us.* Though to look at its bustling, precious town center, you'd think it was the prettiest, most idyllic place on earth. People moved their families here to get away from the crime and chaos of the big city, vacationed here for its natural beauty and places like the Old Mill and the apple orchards and the famous pumpkin patch in autumn. The Hollows didn't mind visitors; it put on its Sunday best for those folks.

"It's a hell mouth," Amanda was famous for saying. But Finley's mother was the ultimate drama queen. It wasn't enough just to say that she didn't like The Hollows, that the town where she grew up was full of bad memories. She had to *hate* it, to disavow it completely. But Amanda was like that about everything—restaurants, fashion trends, Finley's friends. It wasn't enough to just say that something was not for her; she had to declare it unfit for others as well.

As soon as she was able, Amanda had gotten as far away from The Hollows as she could without leaving the country, as far away from Eloise and her abilities as national boundaries would allow. Finley's childhood visits to the place were brief and tense. Any mention Finley made of liking it there or of missing Eloise was met with a very particular kind of ashen-faced silence from Amanda.

When Finley decided to come to The Hollows to be with Eloise, to understand herself better, Amanda took it as a personal affront. "You're doing this just to hurt me," her mother had said, holding back tears. Finley denied it. But in moments in which she was being honest with herself, she had to admit that it was a little bit true. Her move to The Hollows was proof positive that Amanda couldn't control Finley, as hard as she tried. The Hollows, the motorcycle, Rainer, the people who weren't there. There was nothing Amanda could do about any of it.

Now, as Finley sat in front of Agatha's house for a moment, head aching, hands shaking, she wondered if her mother had been right after all to try to keep her away. And if she'd been right about that, what else might she be right about? Finley tried to keep from going down the rabbit hole into a universe where Amanda might actually know what she was talking about.

Finley climbed off her bike and jogged up the porch steps, knocked on the big white door.

She'd gone home first, to Eloise. But Eloise was not there, which was surprising because Eloise seemed always to be at home lately. Finley had walked through the house and in the kitchen checked the calendar. There was a single entry for the day. Eloise had scribbled: Dr. A. Finley made a mental note to ask about it.

After another knock, she pushed through the open door. Agatha's house was as big and white, as still and curated as a museum. The triple-height foyer, with its gigantic entry table and towering vase of flowers, made Finley feel tiny as she walked down the long hallway that led to Agatha's big sitting room.

Agatha got up from her seat by the fire and met Finley with a warm embrace in the center of an enormous oriental carpet. Finley's nerves immediately calmed as they sat on the plush white sofa.

Over in front of a row of windows that looked out onto a pool surrounded by a beautiful garden of trees and flowers was a long glass table. Agatha used it as a desk, and there were two large silver computers sitting there, as well as a laptop. Finley knew Agatha monitored the world news obsessively, always in tune with what was going on—she was a wellspring of facts and knowledge. *Education only makes us better at what we do. The more we know, the more we can understand. The more we can understand, the more we can help* them *and each other.*

"Tell me," Agatha said. They sat on the couch facing each other, Finley kicked off her boots and pulled her feet up beneath her to sit cross-legged.

Finley told her about *squeak-clink*, the little bird, the boy with the train, the reappearance of Abigail. She recounted her visit with Jones and what happened at the lake house. When she was done, they sat a moment, looking into the fire.

"You're shaken by your experiences," Agatha said finally.

"I thought you said there was time," said Finley. "That I could set boundaries and choose how I use my gifts."

Agatha nodded slowly, her face serene. She was ageless—might be sixty years old, though Finley and Eloise surmised she was in her nineties. She wore her white hair long, adorned herself with bangles and big necklaces and wide rings studded with gems. Finley thought of her as a big woman, always draped in tunics in long skirts, but lately she seemed thinner, more frail. Today, Agatha wore a pendant with a sky-blue gem, and Finley found she couldn't take her eyes from its glittering depth, its layers of color.

"I told you that you could *learn* to set boundaries and choose how to use your gifts," said Agatha. "I didn't say it would be easy."

"I've never had a vision like the one I had today," said Finley. "Where I've been taken out of myself."

"Like your grandmother," said Agatha. "That's hard. What I do is not exactly like what you and your grandmother do; you're far more tapped in to frequencies than I am."

Finley had suspected that she would be more like Agatha than Eloise. That she would connect the living with the dead, that she might use that in work as a psychologist or therapist to counsel the living. She had imagined herself possibly as a grief therapist, when she imagined herself as anything at all. Which was rarely. She hadn't really projected herself into the future.

The truth was she didn't know what she wanted at all, except that she wanted to be the exact opposite of her parents, especially her mother. And she really didn't want to be like Eloise, either, though she loved her grandmother, maybe more than anyone on earth other than her brother Alfie. But anyone could see that Eloise had let her abilities drain her. Finley wasn't prepared to live like that.

"What is this place?" Finley asked. She grabbed a cushion and hugged it to her middle. The trees outside were wild in the strong wind.

"The Hollows?" said Agatha. She looked around the room, offered a shrug. "I don't know. If I had to hazard a guess, I'd say it was an energy vortex."

"What does that mean?"

"There are certain places on earth that are spiritual centers, where the energy has particular characteristics," said Agatha. "Like Red Rocks in Arizona is supposed to be a place of healing energy. I have lived here all my life, and my ancestors before me, and I still don't quite know what The Hollows is and what it wants. I know I am less powerful when I'm not close to it. I don't have all the answers."

Agatha was the most powerful person Finley had ever met. *She just likes to downplay it*, Eloise had told her. *It might be a way she has of protecting herself.* Though Agatha claimed not to have dreams and visions at all, she always seemed to know everything that was going on before you said a word.

"I tried to put it aside and go to class," said Finley. "Instead, I wound up at Jones Cooper's place, and the next thing I knew we were heading to the lake house. And then I was *there*—seeing everything. I felt hijacked. I *couldn't* have avoided it."

Agatha reached out and Finley took her hand.

"I wasn't with *her*," said Finley.

"Who were you with?" asked Agatha.

"I don't know," said Finley. "A boy, I think. Someone *with* the abductor."

This had happened to Eloise, as well. She had inhabited rapists, pedophiles, kidnappers, murderers. Her grandmother didn't like to talk about those experiences, except to say that you could learn to turn away, to "draw back."

"You have to honor that," said Agatha. "And try not to judge. You were where you were supposed to be. And maybe the girl can't help you."

"Maybe she's already gone," said Finley. The thought had come to her on the ride over, and it made her sick, physically nauseous. When she thought about herself doing "the work," she only ever imagined herself helping people, saving people, finding the lost.

"Not everybody can be saved or is even meant to be saved," Agatha said, giving Finley's hand a squeeze. "You know that, don't you?"

"Then *what* am I supposed to do?"

"What do you think?" asked Agatha. "No. What do you *feel*?"

"I don't know," said Finley. "I truly don't."

"Be patient," said Agatha. "Follow your instincts. That's all you can do."

Finley got up quickly and paced the room, from the window to the door. Agatha was unperturbed, looking at her a moment, then back to the flames. She was a rock, and Finley was the wave, crashing against her.

"Is *this* what I do?" asked Finley, coming to stand in front of Agatha.

"I think it's too soon to tell," said the old woman. "But I'll tell you one thing and you might not like it. The Hollows doesn't like a void."

Finley shook her head, then wrapped her arms tight around her middle. She was freezing suddenly. Agatha always kept the house so cold.

"What does that mean?" Finley asked.

"It means that Eloise wants to leave," said Agatha. "And if she does, there will be a space to fill."

We are chosen, Eloise had warned. *We don't choose.*

"And if I don't want to *fill it*?"

Agatha gave her a wide, beautiful smile. But she offered only a shrug and a light shake of the head. "Too soon to tell."

"What if I *can't* help?" Finley said. "I mean, I didn't get anything out of that vision. I don't know any more than I did before. Well, not much."

"Are you quite sure about that?"

Finley had to admit that she wasn't totally sure about anything really.

She sat on the hearth and buried her eyes in her hands. The tattoo on her back burned; it was really uncomfortable, beyond normal levels. Maybe it was getting infected. That happened sometimes. In the dark of her palms, she saw the girl being dragged up the path.

"I was certain that they went north, deeper into the woods," Finley said. "But Jones Cooper says that the whole area was searched, and nothing was found."

"They're wrong so often," Agatha said indulgently, as if she were talking about children at play. "That's why they need us. Don't let anyone talk you out of what you have seen. Don't let other people make you doubt yourself, even those who are good and well meaning. They simply don't see what we see."

Finley blew out a breath.

"So what do I do?" Finley said.

"Sleep on it," said Agatha. "You'll know what to do when it's time."

"That's it?" said Finley.

Agatha chuckled a little. "Did you think I was going to hand you a rule book? The good news and the bad news is that no one knows better than you how to find your way with your abilities."

She'd said this before, and it never failed to remind her of Glinda, the Good Witch and Dorothy. You always had the power, or whatever it was Glinda had said. Finley was always so annoyed by that. If Glinda could have spared Dorothy from the beginning, why didn't she? All she had to do was tell her that those slippers were magic and that she could go home. But she didn't. *Nobody can give you the power over your destiny*, her mom had tried to explain. *You have to claim it, sometimes through trial. Otherwise you never know it's yours.*

To Finley, it just sounded like a crock, something grown-ups said to cover up their own failings.

"You're more powerful than you know," said Agatha.

Finley looked over at Agatha, who was pouring them each some tea from a set Finley hadn't even noticed, looking peaceful and unconcerned. She was embarrassed by how much faith Agatha and Eloise had in her. They thought she was some kind of prodigy, and they were clearly wrong. As Finley rose to help Agatha (the teapot was shaking in the old woman's hand), she wondered which of the three of them was going to be the most disappointed when they figured out that Finley's abilities were middling at best.

THIRTEEN

Penny had promised herself that tonight was going to be the night. But now that it was time, the woods were whispering, solemn with warning. *Don't go. Not yet.* She heard it and she didn't hear it.

After the house went dark, she'd lain in bed, wide awake, vibrating. Waiting for the right time. She couldn't stay here. Whatever was out there, even if the woods were alive with ghosts and monsters, witches and ghouls, screaming and wailing and chasing—it couldn't be worse. Could it?

Don't go. Not yet.

Her daddy had told her that if she ever got lost in the woods, to find a river and follow it downstream. At least she thought that was what he said. He was always talking about things like that: what to do if.

If we get separated on the subway, get off at the next stop and find the token booth clerk. Ask her to call the police.

If there's a fire, get out of the house. Don't stop to get any of your toys.

Never talk to strangers. If someone ever tries to take you, fight with everything you have. Scream as loud as you can. (He'd never told her what to do if the man was too strong and there was no one to hear her screaming.)

She knew there was a river; she'd seen one on the way when Poppa first brought her here. She told herself that she'd find her way back to it by going downhill, and then she'd follow it like her daddy said. But now that she was really about to do it, she couldn't remember how far it was, or exactly how to get there, or what she might encounter on her way. She was shaking, from cold, from fear.

Outside the moon was full again, just a sliver less than full, and high like a platter. She could see it through a wide gap in the planks that comprised the walls of her room.

"When the moon hits your eye like a big pizza pie," her daddy used to sing. "That's *amore*!"

He'd sing it loud and goofy, dance her around. Mommy used to roll her eyes, but in that funny, happy way she did when Daddy was being silly. When Mommy was *really* mad at him, her face went very still, and she got very quiet. Penny pushed the thought of them away. She didn't like to think about her mom and dad, and how angry they must be with her. She hadn't *listened*; she'd broken the rules. They didn't love her anymore because she'd been bad. That's what Momma had told her. Even though it didn't seem right, she thought it must be true because no one ever came to get her.

Don't go. Not yet.

The whispering was loud tonight. When she first heard it, she thought it was just the wind in the leaves. But night after night as she listened, she realized that it was voices, a million voices saying she didn't know what. She listened now, with the moon shining through that gap, falling on the dirty floor. Her blanket was itchy. Her back screamed from the lashes of the belt she'd received from Poppa. She'd stopped crying, though.

The day after the clean man came, Momma and Poppa took the truck into town. Momma was wearing her uniform, the yellow-and-white dress and shoes that looked like sneakers but weren't. She went into town dressed like that a few days a week.

Or had it been longer ago that they'd left? Two days? Three? Penny was wobbly with hunger; she was being punished and hadn't been fed. Still, as soon as she was sure they were gone, she managed to get down on the floor and work on the circle. It was screwed hard into the ground, but she kept trying to unscrew it. She imagined that it was loosening a little. The shackle on her ankle was so tight that it rubbed the skin raw until it was bleeding. She'd tried to slide her foot out, but she couldn't.

A little while after she heard them pull down the drive, Bobo came into her barn room. She hadn't heard him and didn't see him until he cleared his throat, startling her.

"That won't come loose."

"It might." *If you want something bad enough and you work hard enough at it, you can usually get it.* That's what her daddy had always told her.

Bobo didn't hurt her like Poppa did; he didn't do the same kind of horrible, not understandable things. But he *did* hurt her. Once he slapped her so hard across the face that she saw stars. Once he took Baby, who was her only thing, the one thing she held and told her secret thoughts, the one thing she cuddled at night. He ripped Baby's arm off, held her over Poppa's fire pit. But when she'd cried, Bobo gave Baby and her arm back. He even returned the next day and sewed Baby's arm back on.

She didn't understand Bobo, who was tall like a man but spoke like a boy, who was pale, with straw hair and misty blue, blue eyes that sometimes looked sweet and sad, but more often just empty, blank like Baby's button eyes.

He walked up closer, held up a shiny silver key. Then he leaned down and unlocked her ankle.

She sat, rubbing her ankle, which was black under the broken skin. Her foot was swollen, an odd grayish blue color and painful to the touch.

"Come on," he said, stepping to the door. She got up and limped after him.

Bobo walked up the porch of the big house and in through the front door. It was the first time she'd been unchained since the clean man came, and she thought hard about running. There was a moment when Bobo was in the house, and she was still outside about to step in.

Is it time now? she asked the voice.

But there was no answer.

From where she stood, she could see the rocky road down which the truck had driven. She saw the tracks etched there in the soft dirt. How far could she get before he caught her? Could she hide herself in the woods and then sneak away?

But then she thought about how big Bobo was and how fast, and she imagined Poppa's weight on top of her pressing all the breath out of her body, and the belt on her flesh. And she was so hungry and thirsty. Maybe Bobo was going to give her something to eat. And she didn't have any shoes. Poppa took the boots he'd given her. And her ankle hurt so bad. So she followed Bobo inside.

Bobo was smiling at her, a strange, not nice smile from the top of the stairs.

She was surprised to see what a pretty house it was and how clean. She thought it would be like a horror movie house with cobwebs and locked doors, creaking floorboards. She thought it would be filled with dark corners and mysterious passageways leading to ugly hidden rooms. But it was bright, free from dust with old but nice furniture—dark woods, flower prints, sparkly lampshades.

There was a ticking grandfather clock in the living room. Sunlight washed in through a stained-glass window beside it, casting a confetti spray of rainbows on the wood floor. There were pictures of a happy young couple on a rickety old piano. Two china dogs sat pretty on the fireplace hearth.

On the candy-striped walls, there were portraits of children—a boy playing baseball, riding a tricycle, opening Christmas presents. There was a pretty girl on horseback, a chubby blond toddler on the beach, a young woman with a baby wrapped in pink. Family pictures, like the million pictures her parents had—except the photos at home were on phones, computers, digital picture frames. Different people, different places, but the same *energy* (her mommy's favorite word)— happy, beautiful, look at us and all the little pictures of our life.

Penny followed Bobo to the upstairs landing and down a wide, carpeted hall, where he pushed open a door. Warm sunlight washed bright and yellow, spilling onto the rug. Penny blinked against the brightness as she walked inside.

It was a princess room, pink and lace with a four-poster bed and plush carpet. Tiny roses on white wallpaper. Shelves of dolls and teddy bears, rows of 4H trophies for riding horses and raising chickens—and not the small plastic ones that everyone gets. Tall, glittering towers with horse and rider on top, emblazed with First Place. Little golden horses jumped or stood regal beside the little gold rider. Ribbons in blue and green, red and white. Looking closely she saw that they were from long ago—1979, 1981. A million years ago. The room *did* look old-fashioned—no posters of rock stars, no computer, no iPad. Just a desk with shelves of books above—books about horses: *Black Beauty*, *The Black Stallion*, *National Velvet*. And lots more—who knew there were so many.

She sat on the bed, bouncing a little. It was so soft; she wanted to climb beneath the covers and sleep and sleep. On the bedside table was a picture, the young woman from the portraits downstairs. Familiar.

"Is that Momma?" she asked.

Bobo nodded, still wearing that same smile. What did he want? Why had he brought her here? The girl in the picture pressed her cheek against Momma's. They smiled bright and happy, but didn't it look a little strange, a little tense—like all the pictures of Mommy when she and Daddy went white water rafting (*before we had kids*) in New Mexico and she was actually terrified the whole time.

"She looks like you," said Bobo. "But prettier."

Penny knew she was pretty. His words didn't bother her. "Who is she?" she asked.

"She's the one they loved best," he said. And his smile was gone, replaced with a kind of still anger that caused Penny to avert her eyes. He hadn't meant to, but Bobo had given her something. Now she knew how to hurt *him*.

Afterwards, he made her a peanut butter sandwich, then another. He let her drink two glasses of milk. Then he brought her back to her room and locked her up again. The sun sank down, and Poppa and Momma still didn't come back. She lay still, thinking. Thinking about the clean man, and what Poppa had told him. Thinking about the princess bedroom and all the pictures. Thinking about the other girl who had been here and wondering where she'd gone. Thinking about the pair of riding boots she saw in the closet full of pretty clothes.

Her mother always said that when you were sad or worried or angry, that you had to do something. Anything. Go for a walk. Make cookies. Draw a picture. Clean your room. Never just lie there and feel sad or mad, because those feelings become like weights, holding you down, and they only get heavier, and you only get less likely to move them. As the sky went dark and the stars started to shine, Penny decided that she was going to do something.

FOURTEEN

The Egg and Yolk was the newest restaurant in The Hollows. An overpriced, fifties-style diner—complete with red leather and chrome counter stools, a jukebox, and *Leave It to Beaver*, *Father Knows Best*, *The Andy Griffith Show*, and other classic American television shows playing in a continuous loop on wall-mounted, flat-screen televisions.

Merri knew that it was a place frequented mainly by tourists and people passing through town to see the fall foliage, or packed with weekenders for the Sunday brunch. She'd chosen it as the place to meet Jones Cooper because she thought it would be empty at three o'clock on a Thursday afternoon and so it was. The locals stayed away because it was too flashy, too expensive—too *new*.

She walked in and took a seat in a booth toward the back, following the directive of the sign, which encouraged her to: Sit Wherever You Like!

Even so, she felt the eyes of the cook behind the counter and the older waitress over by the cash register. People in The Hollows knew her because of Abbey. Folks were always kind to her, but after a while their kind and pitying glances were heavy and brought Merri down. But it was more than pity, too. There was a current of fear, of distrust. As if the horror that had befallen her family might in some way be contagious. Merri could just *imagine* other mothers wanting to hug their children away when she was around. She didn't blame them. She would have felt the same way once upon a time.

She stayed bent over her phone, scrolling through news. In true

Jackson fashion, she'd set up an alert for stories relating to that missing man. A shadow caused her to look up, and the waitress was standing over her with an ice water and a menu.

"Thank you," said Merri.

The woman placed the red plastic tumbler on the table with a ringed, elegant hand. Merri glanced up and saw her own reflection in the woman's glasses, then the cool, ice-blue eyes behind that. Her smile was warm, attentive.

"Mrs. Gleason?" she said, laying the menu down.

Merri nodded. *Shit*.

"I was one of the volunteers that helped search for your girl," she said. "I want you to know that we're all still hoping you'll find her."

"Thank you," Merri said. Her face felt like ice, like it might crack into a million pieces.

People didn't even know how cruel kindness could be, how much it hurt.

"I pray for your family every night," she said. She smoothed out the front of her yellow-and-white uniform, something odd, uncomfortable about the gesture.

Yes, from the safety of your home, where your life is perfectly intact, you pray for us. Why did that always sound so condescending? She'd asked Wolf once. So goddamn superior. Because you're a hard, cold bitch, Merri Gleason, Wolf would joke. Or half-joke.

"That's very kind," said Merri, even though she wanted to gather up her things and run. There was absolutely nowhere to hide from people, though that's one thing she *had* learned. You couldn't get away from good-intentioned folks who hurt you without even knowing.

Jones Cooper came through the door then with a jingle of the bell. The woman looked at him and back at Merri with an understanding nod.

"I'll get another water and a menu."

He slid into the booth across from her. She liked his face, strong brow, high cheekbones. Those eyes—what would she call them? Penetrating. The bad guys must squirm before him. Even she felt a little uneasy, wondering what he could see when he looked at her: Someone unstable? Someone desperate? Was she unstable and desperate? Would any other type of person have hired a psychic to find her daughter?

"How are you holding up?" he asked.

"Okay," she said.

"You're at Miss Lovely's?"

When she confirmed, he nodded his approval. "That's a good place for you."

He didn't go on, but Merri thought she knew what he meant. Better than a rental or one of the impersonal places she might have picked outside of town. At Miss Lovely's she felt safe and cared for, a rare experience.

The waitress came back with the water and menus. Cooper ordered coffee and a patty melt. Merri ordered a pot of tea and chicken noodle soup.

"I have a couple of things I want to get straight before we continue," Cooper said when the waitress had gone.

"Okay," she said.

"After Abbey disappeared, suspicion turned to your husband for a time."

She bowed her head, took a breath. She tasted the familiar flavor of shame and anger in her mouth. She had to force herself to say the words she'd repeated too many times to too many hired detectives.

"At the time of the abduction, Wolf—my husband—was having an affair," she said. Merri never got used to the word *girlfriend*. It sounded so sweet and innocent, when in this case, it was anything but. "The police discovered that pretty quickly, and a lot of time was spent on Wolf and his *mistress*." Another strange word, somehow antiquated, with an almost permissive quality.

"They didn't have anything to do with this," she concluded.

The police didn't believe Wolf that he couldn't identify the men on that trail. That he'd never seen the perpetrators, had his glasses knocked off in the fall, as had Jackson. That all he saw were some vague and fuzzy dark forms through the trees, listened to Jackson get shot, the kids screaming. But he was in shock, terrified for the kids and himself, not thinking about identifying anyone. He'd been plagued by nightmares since. Merri told Jones all of that.

Jones nodded gravely. "I'm sorry to have to bring this up, Mrs. Gleason. But are you absolutely certain he had nothing to do with it?"

It was a question she almost couldn't bear to answer again.

"What motivation would they have to hurt or abduct Abbey?" asked Merri, trying and failing to keep the annoyance from her voice. "Their thing—it was tawdry, insubstantial."

She hated the way she sounded, like a jaded New Yorker.

"He was careless, stupid," she continued. "But he loves his children. He's—broken by this. Just as I am."

She looked away, swallowed back the tightness at the base of her throat.

"What do you know about the girlfriend?" asked Jones.

Merri lifted her palms. "Just a girl, some publicist, twenty-five. A total slut, sure." She didn't like that word; it was misogynistic wasn't it? Wasn't *Wolf* a slut, someone careless about sex and who they hurt with it? Though why should she be concerned about referring to her husband's mistress that way? "But not someone who would steal a child. Anyway, they were both cleared of any foul play."

There was that tone again, cold, disinterested in her husband's infidelity. Boys will be boys.

Cooper nodded slowly but held her eyes. He saw it all, she thought, every shade and layer of her. He'd already decided that the affair had nothing to do with Abbey; he was just doing his due diligence.

"I understand," he said. "I'm sorry to have to dwell on uncomfortable topics."

"Topics?"

He cleared his throat. "There were questions about the prescription drugs you were taking at the time."

Where do you get your pills? Do you have a dealer? Do you owe anyone money? Would they have come after you? Hurt your family? God, she could still taste the humiliation, the rage, the sick dread. It was a toxin. She might carry it in her body forever, like grief. Maybe it would kill her, show up as cancer or as some mysterious blood disease a couple years from now. When it manifested itself in her body, she would know precisely when she caught the germ.

A tragic event like this put your whole life under scrutiny. If Wolf had been having some petty affair, if she'd been taking too many Vicodin and Abbey *hadn't* disappeared, none of it would mean very much. They'd still be shitty parents, but their flaws and mistakes wouldn't be on display for everyone to see and judge. When you'd failed to safeguard the life of your child, people wanted answers, reasons why such a thing could never happen to them. Nothing like a good public flogging to make everyone feel better about themselves.

"A couple of years ago I had knee surgery and was prescribed some pretty powerful pain relievers to which I became addicted. I was in the throes of that problem when we lost Abbey, and that came to light as well. I had a nervous breakdown about three months after she went missing, and I was hospitalized."

"Where were you getting your pills?"

Merri shrugged. "I did a little doctor hopping," she said. "I got some online."

"You didn't have a dealer?"

Merri drew in a sharp breath. Could you call a colleague whose family lived in Canada and who on his regular trip up north picked up various prescriptions for friends a dealer? Ambien for his friend that didn't have insurance? Tylenol 3? Vicodin? That friendship was over; she'd had no choice but to give his name. He didn't get in any real trouble, but his drug-trafficking days, however benign, were over.

She explained this to Cooper.

"I understand," said Jones again. Something about the way he said it was comforting, not judgmental, and put her at ease.

"Although it might not make me mother of the year," she said. "I was fully functional, and my problems had nothing to do with Abbey going missing."

Was that really true? She still didn't know.

"Except that I should have been with them and I wasn't always myself," she added.

He reached out a hand and put it on her arm. Usually, she drew away from people, hated their touch. Especially since Abbey, and since she'd been off the pills. She felt like there was an electric current constantly running through her. But she was okay with him.

"I know you didn't have anything to do with what happened to your daughter," he said.

She looked down so that he couldn't see how close she was to tears. It was embarrassing to be crying all the time in front of people. She had never gotten used to it, how raw she was, how near she always was to breaking apart.

"Please don't waste any more time on those things," she said. "I didn't hire you to get stuck in old grooves in the road. I need a fresh approach."

She was trying hard not to sound edgy, but she was practically vibrating with urgency. There was a clock in her head; she could hear it ticking. Every second Abbey was farther away.

"I had to hear about those things from you," he said. "I wouldn't be doing my job if I didn't ask."

He explained to her how he was going over the files, and how he had gone to the lake house, and to the trail. And Merri was sure that was the right way to do things. But it was just more of the same.

"What about Miss Montgomery?" she asked. "Will she be able to help?"

He'd been clear with Merri that there were no guarantees, and she got that. There had been a number of private detectives before Cooper, and she knew how it went with them. With the presentation of that first big retainer check, every single one of them believed that he'd be the one to bring Abbey home. But then when the weeks wore on, the calls would be less frequent; then Merri's calls would go unreturned. Inevitably there would be a conversation about how all the leads were cold, the police had done a decent job, nothing had been missed. Nothing missed—except her daughter.

Now she was that mother who, in her desperation, had turned to a psychic. A terribly sad cliché, something people had laughed about (mirthlessly) in one of the groups she'd visited for families of missing children. *They're waiting like vultures for us, these charlatans*, one father had said bitterly. *How do they live with themselves, taking our money when we've lost everything else?*

But Merri had an aunt who'd had prophetic dreams, the stuff of family legend. And there had been a few strange things about Abbey, too. She had a dream that her hamster Daisy was going to die, and the next day he (there had been some gender confusion) did. Sometimes when Abbey had tantrums, the lights in their apartment would flicker. And she hadn't wanted to go to the lake house. She'd had nightmares about it for weeks leading up to the trip. But, of course, they'd dismissed it.

There's a monster in the woods.

No such things as monsters, kiddo. You know that.

"I went to see Eloise," said Jones in response to her question. "Her granddaughter thinks she might be able to help. Eloise isn't getting anything yet."

"Is her granddaughter a psychic?" asked Merri.

"So I'm told."

"You're not a believer?" she asked. She had to say the guy wasn't into selling himself, which was a bit of a change.

The waitress brought their food but seemed to linger nearby, needlessly wiping down clean tables and fussing with condiment trays that acted as centerpieces. Was she listening to their conversation? Would what Merri said become fodder for the gossip mill around town? Jones went quiet, took a bite of his sandwich. She sensed that he, too, was waiting for the waitress to leave the proximity. Finally, she did.

"I've been around long enough to know there's more to this life than we can see or understand. Let's say I have a healthy respect for Eloise, as well as a healthy skepticism."

Merri nodded. That put them on the same wavelength.

"And her granddaughter?"

"Eloise seems to think she's something special. I trust Eloise. And Finley seems like a good kid."

"Kid?"

"She's twenty-one."

"Wow."

"I know," said Jones, rubbing his eyes. "I don't even remember twenty-one."

Merri smiled a little.

"This is not a bait and switch if that's what you're thinking," said Jones. "It's not an exact *thing*, whatever it is we do. But I will say Eloise has had some big successes. Finley is untried, but she's the one who's picking up the signals—or whatever it is. So, up to you if you want me to continue."

He was giving her an out. Maybe she should take it.

"We didn't discuss your fee," said Merri.

"There's no fee unless we find your daughter," he said. "Then we can discuss what you think is fair. We don't do this for the money."

Merri, who was not surprised very often, found herself taken aback. "Then *why* do you do this?"

He looked up at her, as if considering the answer.

"It's just what we do."

He'd polished off his patty melt, and he was working on his fries. She'd barely touched her soup, which had grown cold while they talked. She thought about what that meant, taking money out of the equation for now, how it shifted the balance of power. She could hardly insist that he take money from her. She turned it over a moment, stirring at the greasy liquid in her bowl.

"So with that said, is there anything surrounding Abbey's disappearance, before or after that you *didn't* tell the police?"

Merri felt a rise of indignation, of defensiveness. There had been so many accusations, suspicious stares, brows wrinkled in a kind of curious pity. Like: *I feel bad for you, but surely this is your fault somehow.* Cooper lifted a palm, as if he could see the protest in her. And maybe he could; her shoulders had hiked up around her ears.

"What I mean is, is there anything that you dismissed as inconsequential, silly even? Ideas, feelings, suspicions. Given the nature of this investigation, is there *anything*?"

The waitress was behind the counter; there was no one else in the restaurant. Outside, the sky had gone a threatening white gray. Instead of censoring herself, she told him about Jackson's premonition instigated by the news story he'd overheard regarding the two missing children, about Abbey's dreams. She told him also about Jackson's fixation on the missing man. He took a small notebook out of his pocket and started scribbling. No judgment. When she was done:

"Does that help?"

He shook his head and offered a slight shrug. "I don't know. I'm not the psychic."

Here he smiled a little, which made his face surprisingly warm and boyish. When she'd researched him, she'd learned that he was a former school sports star turned cop. There'd been some kind of problem that caused him to retire early—she wasn't sure what. He was a big man, with graying brown hair, a ruddy complexion, and blue (or were they gray?) eyes, still handsome, virile. He was the kind of man that made women silly with the desire to please. And very married. Anyone could see that. It was one of the things that had always upset her about Wolf, even before she knew what it was. He never took himself off the market. He was always looking. Jones Cooper was taken—not that she was interested in him or anyone. Just an observation.

"I had already planned to go see Betty Fitzpatrick, mother of the other missing children," he said. "And that news story about the developer caught my attention this morning."

He was still writing.

"It's not so different, what they do and what I do," he said when he was done. She knew he was talking about Eloise and her granddaughter. "A lot of it has to do with instinct. Going where other people didn't think or didn't bother to go."

She took a sip of her tea, which had gone cold like her soup.

"Oh," she said, remembering. She dug into her bag and took

out Abbey's binky. It was so tattered and worn, so threadbare that it almost looked like a rag. Once pink with hopping bunnies, it had gone gray. It had been a gift from Merri's mother, and it had been in Abbey's crib since before she was even born. It became her most beloved binky; she never slept without it. Merri had slept with it every night since her girl went missing. "I brought this for Eloise— or I guess Finley. Please don't lose it."

It was a silly thing to say. A man like Jones Cooper never lost anything.

"The change purse I gave you," she said. "It didn't mean anything to her, just a trinket I bought her when we got to town. But this—"

She found she couldn't go on.

"I'd like to make promises," he said. His voice was soothing, even though his words weren't. "But we both know I can't do that."

"I know," she said.

This was rock bottom. That same man in the support group that she and Wolf had dutifully attended had said one evening: *When you engage the psychic, you have allowed despair to separate you from reality*.

She wondered if he was right. She really didn't care. Honestly, whether it was self-delusion or not, there was a sparkle of hope that had been all but lost before she came to see Jones Cooper. And that was something, wasn't it? Reality, especially Merri's, was highly overrated.

"Will I get to meet her?" Merri asked. "Finley, I mean?"

Did she sound desperate? She probably did. She didn't care about that either. That was the other thing she'd learned, that it didn't matter a damn what people thought of you. The world was a hard, unyielding place no matter whether people thought you were a saint or a sinner.

He drained his water glass. "Do you want to?" he asked with a frown, as if he hadn't been asked the question before.

"If you think it would help," she said. "*Would* it help?"

"I'll ask her how she wants to proceed," he said. "I'll say that Eloise didn't often meet with clients."

"Why not?" asked Merri.

"It just isn't how she works," he said. "It isn't always about the person looking. That's not always how she connects to the case. Maybe for Finley it's different. Like I say, she's untried."

He was very matter-of-fact about the whole thing.

"And it's hard for Eloise, I guess," he went on. "She can't always help, and it's very disappointing for folks, difficult to accept. Some people become hostile; she's had a lot of threats."

She nodded her understanding; she could see it, remembering how bitter the man was in her grief-counseling group. How would she feel if this investigation led her back to the place where she was when she drove up here—sick with desperation, lost, afraid that the day Abbey was taken was the last of any livable life? Would she be angry, hostile? Would she level threats? No. Most likely, she would just turn to ash, blow away on the wind, unable to keep herself together even for her remaining child who needed her so badly.

FIFTEEN

When Finley got home, her grandmother's car was still gone. Something about the absence of the car in the drive unsettled her. She didn't dwell on it long, however, because there was another car there instead. Rainer was asleep in his old Mustang, parked in the driveway. She pulled her bike up alongside him. He was so sound asleep, head leaning back, mouth agog, that he didn't even wake up. And her engine was *loud*. She'd always envied him his deep and untroubled, dreamless slumber.

His car was old, not as in vintage, but *old* as in a hunk of junk. The fact the he'd driven it from Seattle defied the laws of physics. The whole vehicle actually rattled when he got up over fifty-five miles an hour, reeked inside of pot smoke. With its black-tinted windows and primer-only paint job, it looked like something out of a postapocalyptic science fiction movie. Finley had a weird affection for that car, though. It was uniquely Rainer, and they'd had a lot of good times driving around in it—and parking it.

How could you go out with a guy who drives a piece of garbage like that? her father had wanted to know. *A man's car says everything about him.*

Her father had a brand-new black Range Rover and a Porsche 911 Targa 4 in electric blue, both cars that made people stare with unmasked envy. What did he think that said about him? she wondered. That he was an elitist jerk? A ridiculous middle-aged show-off? If so, then he was dead on.

I really don't think that's true, Dad.

153

It is. Trust me. A man who drives a piece of crap like that will never amount to anything.

It's what he can afford.

Exactly.

He's eighteen, she'd countered, which he had been at the time of the argument. The fact that he was still driving the thing was a testament to his endurance, his ability to make anything work. *I don't think that logic applies to teenagers.*

You're eighteen. You're driving an Acura.

That you bought for me. If it were up to me to buy a car, I'd be taking the bus.

Well, her father said. He never lost an argument; or rather never let you think that *you* had won. *It's different for a girl.* Add sexist to his many annoying characteristics. But still, her dad always made her laugh.

She knocked on the window, and Rainer stirred awake, not one to startle. He climbed out and stretched with the relaxed ease of someone who was deeply comfortable in his own skin. He had ink on his hands, a purple stain on his jeans. He was wearing the same charcoal-gray tee-shirt he'd been wearing last night, hadn't shaved. It was possible that he was a little high, his eyes slightly glassy. He smoked a lot of dope, nothing worse. But it was a problem for her. "Sober most of the time" was a top item on the boyfriend checklist.

"You skipped class," he said, lifting his arms to the sky in an elaborate reach, exposing his toned belly. A little flutter of desire made Finley blush and turn away.

"What are you doing here?" she asked. It came out a little sharp, but Rainer was tone deaf.

"I wanted to see you," he said. "Check your tat. Take you out for ice cream or something."

She walked toward the front door, and he followed her onto the porch. Finley gazed up the road, wondered about her grandmother again and when she'd be home. Eloise didn't exactly *love* Rainer any more than Finley's parents did, although she said she didn't think he was a bad guy. Just a little lost—*rudderless* was the word Eloise had used. It was true, to some extent. His mom was kind of a hard case, not exactly warm and fuzzy. His dad was a flake, a drummer for a Seattle band, and a lot more interested in the club scene than he was in Rainer. Eloise had never said that Rainer wasn't welcome, but Finley had the sense that he wasn't. She felt like she was sneaking around, having him here. Then she got mad about feeling that way. She wasn't a child, was she?

"So where were you?" he asked.

The warmth inside the house made her realize how cold the air had turned outside. The sky seemed moody and threatening. It was too early for snow, wasn't it? The trees weren't even bare. She shivered a little as Rainer shut the door behind him.

"I thought we weren't going to do this," she said. There was a simmer of anger that she wasn't sure was about him.

"I'm not hassling you," he said, stripping off his leather jacket and exposing those thick arms sleeved in tattoos. "I was just wondering."

Tracking her, being possessive, grilling her on where she'd been and what she'd been doing. Trying to catch her in lies she hadn't told. Then being cagey about his own activities. Screwing around with any hot girl that showed up at the tattoo parlor where he'd been interning in Seattle. Just thinking about how things were with him made her throat go tight with anxiety. He brought out the worst in Finley. Maybe they brought out the worst in each other.

When your relationship to a man makes you act like someone you don't want to be, you had better do some soul searching, Amanda had warned.

"Let me see your back," he said. He followed her into the kitchen. Finley turned around and leaned on the counter. She held up her tee-shirt, felt him peel away the bandage.

"Did you do Neosporin this morning?" he asked.

And *yet* he was loving, caring, talented, and good. He was a great listener, always willing to help with anything. Need to move your stuff, a ride to the airport, a place to crash—call Rainer. He was hardworking; when he had his mind on something, no one could stop him. Why were people so complicated?

155

"Yes," she said. His hands were strong, but his touch always gentle.

"Looks okay," he said. He pressed the bandage back and pulled her tee-shirt down. "Does it still ache?"

She took the ground coffee from the fridge and filled the pot with water, wondering about that for a second. Then, "How did you know it was aching?"

He smiled and gave a confused shake of his head.

"You texted me this morning," he said. "That's why I went to school. I didn't see your bike, so I came here."

He looked at his watch, an old analog Timex that belonged to his dad.

"I have to go soon anyway," he said when she didn't answer. "My shift starts in an hour."

Finley still didn't say anything, puzzling. She didn't remember texting him. She wouldn't have. Would she? He snaked an arm around her waist, careful to avoid the new tattoo. She felt his heat, then his lips on hers just gently, chastely. Then she was hugging him, not wanting to let go. Ever. Then she was pushing him away again. Poor Rainer.

No, she thought. *I definitely didn't text him.*

She took the phone from her pocket, scrolled through her texts. There it was.

Tat is aching. Can you come take a look at it? It really hurts. ☹

A pouty, childish text fishing for attention from someone she had been trying to push away. *Abigail*, she thought.

Rainer took the phone from her hand and put it on the table. Then he put his arms around her again. She tried to push back, but he held on, burying his face in her neck, kissing her there, sending tingles all over her body.

"Rainer," she said. "Let go."

He must have heard the anger in her voice because he released her right away and stepped back looking—what? Sad, confused, a little embarrassed. She knew that look; she'd seen it many times.

"I'm sorry," he said. "After last night, and since you texted this morning, I just thought—I'm sorry. Boundaries, right?"

He blew out a breath, crossed his arms in front of his body.

"*I'm* sorry," she said. "We shouldn't have. Last night. It was my fault."

It *was* her fault; *she* went to him. And she knew that Abigail couldn't make her do anything that she didn't on some level want herself—even if she didn't remember doing some of those things. *A haunting is a relationship*, Eloise had told her. *You play your part in it.*

Finley left the kitchen, and he followed her into the living room, where she sat on the couch. She stared at a picture resting on the end table of her mom, Alfie, and her taken a million years ago when she and her brother were small. She realized with surprise that she missed them a lot, even her mother, who was not just anxious, controlling, and overbearing. She was also loving and generous and good. Complicated. Everything was so complicated. She wanted things she knew were bad for her. She pushed people away, then pulled them close, then pushed them away again. She wanted to explore her gifts, see what she was capable of, and yet she was afraid to know. What was wrong with her? *You're just a kid*, her dad had said. *You're not supposed to have all the answers. You're allowed to change your mind.* But she wasn't a kid, was she? Time to grow up.

"Seriously, Finley. What's up?" Rainer said. He stood in the doorway, looking helpless.

"I'm—" she started. "I don't know."

"Talk it out," he said.

She told him about how the day had progressed, Jones Cooper, the events at the lake house. He sat on the couch beside her and just listened, keeping his hands to himself like a good friend. He was the only one outside her family that knew about her—the only one she had ever trusted enough to tell. Rainer himself was what Eloise referred to as an "Empath," someone sensitive, in tune with the frequencies that Agatha, Eloise, Finley, and others (so *many* others) received with such clarity. They weren't exactly gifted. They didn't do "the work" but tended to be in law enforcement, medicine, psychology—anything where intuition and instinct played a role. And there were lots of them, even in tattoo shops in Seattle that let underage kids get ink.

"That's pretty intense," he said. He looked at her with worry. "Is this what it's going to be?"

"Maybe," she admitted.

Faith Good walked into the room and pointed at Rainer, her face clenched into a tight, angry frown. Of all the people who didn't like Rainer, Faith liked him least of all. She started stomping around. The little boy with the train was over by the hearth. *Choo-Choo! Choo-Choo!* Then the *squeak-clink* started up again. *God! Seriously?*

"What's wrong?" asked Rainer.

He looked around the room to see what she was seeing. But of course he couldn't. The show was for her alone. She could barely hear him.

"Nothing," said Finley over the din. "Nothing. Look, I have to go."

"Okay," he said, drawing out the word.

She moved back toward the door, and he grabbed his jacket, followed her out. She climbed on the bike, while he stood by, still looking helpless.

"What can I do?" he said. "How can I help?"

"I'll call you," she said, gunning the engine.

She left him standing there, looking after her, as she took off down the road as fast as she could go, the engine wailing. She couldn't go fast enough, drive far enough. She wasn't going to be able to drown them out, to outrun them.

We don't choose, Eloise had warned. *We are chosen.*

She wound up at school. Maybe she could catch her professor, an older, somewhat joyless guy whom she had yet to see smile. Her other professors didn't seem much older than Finley; there was a casual air to them—jeans, call me Sam, a kind of easy aura to the lectures, lots of "like" and "um" in their speech. But Dr. Burwell was the real deal—balding, sweater vest, leather briefcase. He always had an outline for each class—a pile of them printed and stapled, sitting in a neat stack on the corner of his desk for the taking. He did not post his outlines or assignments online.

He was packing up his things when she knocked on his door.

"Miss Montgomery," he said. "Better late than never."

She wouldn't have thought he'd notice who was in class and who wasn't. He seemed pretty wrapped up in his lectures on Jungian concepts. He nodded toward the papers on his desk, and she stepped inside and took one.

"I'm sorry," she said. "I had to work." It wasn't exactly a lie.

He nodded easily, then started rifling through his briefcase. When he found what he was looking for, he looked up and handed her the essay she'd submitted last week about the Jungian concept of synchronicity. A patient of Jung's had reached an impasse in therapy, her rational mind not allowing her to accept some of the ideas of her unconscious. One night she dreamt of a golden scarab. The next day in therapy, she and her doctor heard an insect knocking at the window only to find that it was the golden scarab from her dream, a very rare occurrence for that place and climate. This experience led Jung to explore other strange coincidences that allowed his patients to receive information in "extra-sensorial ways." Many of Jung's theories delved into the paranormal, due to what he referred to as "uncanny happenings" in his early childhood. He even had a psychic medium in his family, had conducted séances, and had called for a serious scientific study of spiritualistic phenomena. Finley found this particularly fascinating.

"I enjoyed this," he said. "Very insightful."

She saw the letter A scrawled on the title page and felt a little rush of joy.

"I liked your thoughts on how the normal and the paranormal dwell side by side," said Dr. Burwell. "How the things we think of as extraordinary or impossible may really just be unexplored aspects of the normal human psyche."

She felt her cheeks flush; Finley was unaccustomed to praise like this.

"It sounded like you were writing from a personal interest," he said, pulling on his coat. "Have you had unexplained experiences?"

"Some," she said with a nod. He looked at her as if expecting her to go on. When she didn't, he said, "Well, good work, Miss Montgomery. Try to make it to class next time. We'll be talking about some of Jung's theories on the supernatural. I'd love you to share some of your points with the class."

She smiled. "I'll be there."

Outside, she took a breath. When winter fell in The Hollows, a low cloud cover seemed to block out the sky. She remembered last year feeling so closed in, so heavy with it. Having to garage her bike for three months and hitch rides from her grandmother had been a serious hindrance to her independence. She couldn't afford her own car, her savings account was dwindling fast. She needed to get a job, a real one with a paycheck. Something that didn't involve passing out in the woods and seeing dead people or working with desperate living people who needed help that she couldn't give.

She felt eyes on her and turned to see Jason sitting over by a tall oak tree in the middle of the lawn in front of the building. He waved and she waved back, then he beckoned her over. She walked across the lawn and took a seat beside him.

"You missed class," he said, looking up from an iPad. She saw the text they were reading for Dr. Burwell: *Man and His Symbols*.

"I had to work," she said. Again, not a lie exactly.

"Oh, yeah?" he said. "Where?"

"I, uh," she said. "I just started working with a detective in town. Part-time."

He raised his eyebrows, as if it were a different answer than he expected. "Doing what?"

The guy had a lot of questions. "I'm kind of an assistant."

"Like it?"

She shrugged, glancing over at him. He seemed pale and tired, hungover maybe. "Too soon to tell."

He turned off his iPad and stowed it in a battered old camouflage backpack. It looked military issue, with a big "US" embroidered on the flap.

He nodded sagely, then glanced down at the paper she held in her hand. "You got an A," he said. "Good for you. 'Jung and Psychic Phenomena.' You believe in that stuff?"

She thought about how to answer. "Don't you?"

"My mom had dreams, feelings, you know—*vibes*." He wiggled his fingers a little to demonstrate. "She was right a lot of the time."

Sadness etched its place into his brow and around his eyes. She wanted to ask him about his mother, whom he spoke about in the past tense. But something stopped her.

"Jung believed to some extent that psychic phenomena was an unexplored area of the human psyche," she said instead. "That just because a thing was rare, or unprovable in the context of the scientific method, didn't mean it wasn't real."

When Finley had first read this, it resonated with her as completely true. Because while she understood that other people might find her "ability" to be extraordinary, to her it was completely normal, nothing more exceptional than a musical or artistic talent, or a gift for numbers.

He leaned back against the tree. "Is that what you believe?"

"Yes," she said. "It is."

"Have you had experiences?" Wow. Jason was a very curious guy.

"I have," she said.

"I'd like to hear about them sometime."

Oh, Finley thought. *He's just trying to pick me up. Smooth. And I thought he really wanted to talk about Jung.*

She stood, dusted the grass from her jeans. She liked his energy. He was easy and nice to be around. Cute, too, in a pale, overtired kind of way. Nice hands. But she had Rainer to deal with, and school, and now whatever she was doing with Jones Cooper.

"Sure," she said. "Maybe sometime."

"Oooh," he winced. "Strike one. He hangs his head in defeat."

She smiled, not just a polite one. He was funny, and the smile swelled from a place inside her. Maybe they could be friends.

"Seriously, though," he said. But his smile wasn't that serious, it was full of mischief. "I was thinking I could use a private detective."

"Oh?" she said. "You have a mystery that needs to be solved?"

She waited for the punch line, but instead his expression darkened just a little. "Maybe," he said. "Too soon to tell."

"I'll be in class on Thursday," she said. "You can let me know then."

"Cool," he said.

She gave him a little wave and started toward her bike. She had the strange feeling that she should go back, that she should find out why he needed a PI. But the *squeak-clink* was starting up again, and the air was growing colder. And when she turned back to look at him, he'd shouldered his backpack and was walking off in the opposite direction. She let him go.

SIXTEEN

The sun was a white-yellow ball, fingers of its light spearing through the dark gray clouds. It was sinking low in the sky and soon it would be dark. It always amazed Penny how fast it dropped at the end of the day. If you watched, you could see it as it dipped below the tops of the trees. Once when she was another girl on vacation in Florida, she watched as it sank below the horizon, painting the sky purple, orange, and pink, the water growing dark, the air growing cooler. The sun was there one minute, then gone the next, like a Popsicle melted on concrete.

The golden light had washed all their faces and made her mommy look so young, and her eyes were smiley. She remembered that trip because her parents didn't fight. They were relaxed, building sand castles with her and her brother, sleeping late. They hugged and kissed a lot, which they didn't always do. She could feel how happy they were. It wasn't just that they were "trying not to fight." The energy was not tense or eggshell fragile. It wasn't that they "had nothing left to say." When that was the case, the air felt heavy and suffocating. Penny remembered how light and free everything felt on that sunset beach.

When the door opened to her barn room, softly, carefully, it wasn't Bobo or Poppa. It was Momma. Penny nearly let go of a scream, but instead she sat up quietly and pushed herself as far back on her cot as she could with her leg chained. Which wasn't that far. Momma stood for a moment, her spindly dark form just a shadow in the doorway. Then she stepped inside.

"No," said Penny. But the word just stuck in her throat and sounded more like a cough.

Momma knelt down beside Penny. When the old woman looked up, the fading yellow sunlight lit up the details of her face—deep lines, and strong ridges for cheekbones and sunken holes for eyes, which were a strange gray-green.

"Don't be afraid," said Momma.

"I don't want to," said Penny.

"Hush, now," said Momma. "You've always been such a hardheaded little thing ever since you were a baby."

She unlocked the chain on Penny's ankle, and it felt so good to be free from it as it fell to the floor with a clatter.

"That's better," said Momma.

She stood and held out her hand. Penny moved back, all the way into the corner.

Bobo could be mean. And Poppa filled her with dread and disgust. But she didn't fear either of them as much as she did Momma—though Momma had never laid a hand on her.

"Please," said Penny.

"She's waiting," said Momma. "Come now."

If she didn't go, Poppa would come and carry her. If he had to do that, any number of bad things might happen afterwards. So Penny slowly, reluctantly got up. She let Momma take her hand, and they walked outside into the semidark and growing cold. Penny still didn't have any shoes, and her clothes were threadbare. Her ankle was more swollen, more painful than it had ever been. It was an ugly black and blue and didn't even look like her other leg. Still, she kept up with Momma as she walked past the house, and out through the gate, Penny shivering.

On the dirt road, Momma let Penny's hand drop and Penny followed obediently behind her. *Now?* she wondered. *Should I try to run now?* But how fast could she go with her leg like that? Then, she heard a sound behind them and turned to see that Bobo was following. He stayed back, hiding behind the trees, then running to catch up.

Not yet.

After a while, they turned off the road and onto a path Momma had worn into the brush. Penny's feet were so calloused and her calves so scarred that she barely even felt the hard ground or the branches whipping around her ankles. But every step sent a rocket of pain up her leg. There was no choice but to ignore it, keep moving.

The trees whispered singsong. Penny started to cry a little; she couldn't help it. The place where she was going, all that trapped sadness and despair, all that loneliness and helplessness, it leaked into her bones like a chill in the air. Would she ever be warm again, safe and loved? Weak, puppyish whimpers escaped her though she tried to swallow them back.

"Hush, now, little Dreamer," said Momma. "We're almost there."

But it wasn't true. This walk was endless; maybe it was miles and miles. She had no sense of time or distance; she never had. *How long until the cookies are done, Mommy?* Penny used to ask. *About the time it would take you to watch an episode of Scooby-Doo*, her mommy would say. That made a kind of sense. But here, the hours, the days, the minutes, the miles had no beginning and no end.

Bobo trailed behind, a white spot in the dark. His pale hand was a starfish on the bark of a tree; his face a moon around the bend. He wasn't supposed to come, and he knew it, but Penny was no tattletale.

The moon was climbing high by the time they got where they were going, Penny growing sick from pain and fatigue.

The little church had been recently restored. It stood as white and stoic as the moon among the trees, with its black shutters and bright red door. It was a new thing in a place that was very, very old. The stones, which used to tilt at the heads of graves long overgrown and forgotten, had been righted. Where the names and dates of the departed had been worn away by time and weather, little plaques had been placed beside, naming the dead. Penny didn't know how she knew this, but she did.

She could see them, all the little girls who had been buried here.

Some of them played together, some of them sat and cried. Some of them were babies, and some were teenagers. One of them was on fire, and one of them was always wet, hair in filthy ringlets, skin blue.

Lately, there were three new ones, older, who lingered on the edge of it all, watching, sometimes laughing cruelly. One of those older girls never took her eyes off Penny.

"Where is she?" asked Momma. Her eyes darted around desperately. Penny knew that Momma couldn't see what she could see. No one ever could.

"Over there," said Penny.

Real Penny sat by the old oak tree. She was slouched and pale, her hands resting palms up on the ground, her head tilted to the side like a doll's. She didn't belong here anymore, but she stayed because of Momma, who couldn't let her go. Penny knew this like she knew all the things she shouldn't know. Things no one had ever told her or helped her to understand.

Momma knelt beside the tree and stared. "How is she?"

"She's happy," Penny lied. "She misses you, but she's happy."

The first time Momma brought Penny here, Penny was so stiff with fear that she could barely talk. Even when she was another girl, with another name, she'd had strange dreams and seen people who weren't there. But nothing ever like this place.

"Tell her to let me go," Real Penny had begged her the first time. "Please tell her I can't stay here anymore. She won't let me leave."

But when Penny told her that, Momma had fallen to the ground weeping, and when she recovered herself, she took a hold of Penny and brought her face in very close, so close that Penny could see the deep lines, the clumps of mascara on her lashes.

"You're a liar," she said. Her breath was hot and rancid. "A sick little liar."

And in the blankness of the old woman's face, she saw such fear and sadness, that Penny just lied from that day forward. She made up stories about Real Penny, how she loved to garden, and rode horses every day, how she ate all the ice cream and pizza she wanted. How she had friends and was with her grandma. And Penny knew these were the things Momma wanted to hear, even though she didn't know how she knew them. And as long as she told Momma things that made her smile, Penny knew she'd be okay.

"She went riding today," said Penny. "A big black horse with white socks."

It was a picture she'd seen in Real Penny's room. The picture was so old and yellowed, Penny figured it was safe to assume the horse was dead, too.

"Racer?" said Momma, with a pleased smile.

"That's right," said Penny, even though she had no idea.

That's why they brought you here, Bobo had told her. *Because you're a Dreamer. Poppa can tell a Dreamer from a mile away. There's a light that comes off, a golden shine. He collects Dreamers, for Momma, for himself.*

Real Penny tilted her head back and her eyes were two black holes, empty, bottomless things. "Tell her to let me go."

Penny closed her eyes, but she could still see two white spots looming like after you've looked at light that's too bright.

"Tell her!" the girl shrieked, and her voice was like the sound of the wind wailing. Her mouth opened into a maw, and inside Penny could see the girl strong and alive, atop a great black stallion. Then Penny saw her kissing a boy with long black hair, watched as they got into his car. Then there was nothing.

"She says she loves you," New Penny lied. "So much."

Momma put her head to the ground and cried.

When Momma lets her go, said the voice, *you can go home, too.*

SEVENTEEN

"Is this the right place?" asked Finley. The house in front of her was isolated at the end of a long wooded drive. With the flower-beds bare and the house in need of a coat of paint, the whole place had the aura of desertion, though a light burned in the downstairs bay window. A sadness hung around it like a fog, and Finley wrapped her arms around her center unconsciously.

"Yes," said Jones, who was annoyed with her. He was about to open the car door, but he stopped and held her in that steely blue-gray gaze of his. "I can't have you making a spectacle of yourself in there."

Finley forced herself not to look away from him. He was used to making people squirm, and she wasn't going to give him the satisfaction. Instead, she lifted her palms.

"What do you want me to do?" she asked. He came to her, after all. You can't invite this kind of thing into your world and then hope to control it. Didn't he know that?

"I wanted you to stay back at your grandmother's."

"I can't do that," said Finley.

She turned her gaze forward at the house, now. She knew she sounded as stubborn and intractable as Eloise could be. "I *have* to be here."

"Your grandmother never comes along on interviews."

"I told you," she said. "I'm not like my grandmother."

I'm not like anyone, she wanted to say but didn't. *Not my mother, not my grandmother. I am myself. Whatever that means.*

169

Jones heaved the sigh of a man who was used to giving in to the will of women. A long- suffering release of the syllable "ha."

"Well," he said. "Let's get to it then."

He hefted himself out of the car and shut the door—slamming it a little harder than was necessary? She sat for a moment, looking at the gloaming and the towering trees, watching Jones as he approached the house.

When she'd returned home after her flight from Rainer (and everyone and everything else), Eloise was back, and Cooper's SUV was in the drive, as well. She'd considered fleeing again—but she didn't have anyplace else to go. So she'd gone inside to find them at the kitchen table. Jones had filled her in on his conversation with Merri Gleason and he told her that Abbey had experienced prophetic dreams, and had nightmares about coming to The Hollows.

"Is she a Listener?" Finley asked Eloise, surprised. Eloise had her own language for their thing. Finley and Eloise were Listeners, people who heard (and saw, and experienced) what other people couldn't. Someone like Jones was a Sensitive—whether he knew it or not—someone with sharp instincts with the ability to see right through the layers of a person straight into their truth. In fact, Eloise and Agatha thought that everyone was on a kind of spectrum of psychic ability, from absolute Dead Head (Agatha's word), to Listener or Feeler or Dreamer, depending on the particular ability. It was far from an exact classification system, more like a slang between them.

Thinking about this made her think of Rainer. And thinking of him made her tattoo ache, which in turn got her thinking about Abigail. *What are you up to, girlfriend?* Finley wondered. But Abigail was nowhere to be seen.

"I don't know if she's a Listener," her grandmother said. She rubbed at her head with thumb and forefinger. "I'm not getting anything on this at all. It's yours, dear. I'm sorry."

Jones had handed Finley Abbey's binky, a pink and gray puff as soft as powder. She held it to her face, but it was as devoid of energy as any of the old rags Eloise kept under the sink. She stuck it inside her jacket pocket anyway, found herself worrying it between her fingers.

"If she was a *listener*," said Jones, "wouldn't she just be able to reach out to you or something?"

"At her age? *Probably* not," said Eloise. "Anyway, it doesn't work that way. We don't communicate telepathically. Whoever *we* are. If there's a pattern to all of this, if there are rules and ways, I never learned them."

They talked briefly about the missing developer and Jackson Gleason's premonition based on the news story he'd overheard.

"Are there other psychics in the Gleason family?" asked Finley.

"An aunt," said Jones. "Deceased."

"Do they have any connection to The Hollows, other than the fact that they were vacationing here?" Finley asked. A picture was forming for her, something nebulous, unclear. The Hollows had tendrils; it reached out for its children in strange ways.

"I don't know," he said, scribbling in his notebook.

"Why did they pick this place?" asked Finley. "To vacation, I mean. What drew them here? It's not exactly a tourist hot spot."

Jones shrugged, wrote a little more. "I'll ask."

He looked up at her, tucking his notebook away into his pocket. There was something like approval on his face. "Those are good questions."

She didn't want to be pleased with his praise, but she was. He rose and pulled on his jacket.

"Where are you going?" asked Finley, feeling a flutter of urgency.

"Betty Fitzpatrick—the woman with the missing children Eliza and Joshua," he said. Finley remembered their image in the newspaper articles Jones brought with him that first morning. "She agreed to see me."

It was late, after eight thirty. "It's a weird time to interview someone."

"She says she doesn't sleep anymore," he said. "Nighttime is the hardest time to be alone with your thoughts."

"I want to come," said Finley, not even meaning to. It wasn't even true, was it, that she wanted to go? She rose feeling her grand-mother's eyes on her, curious. "I think I'm supposed to go. The sound is gone."

"That's not a good idea," said Jones. He looked to Eloise for help.

"You came to us," said Eloise. "Finley has to do things her way."

"Still," said Jones. "We talked about this."

"What if we learn something because I'm there that we wouldn't if not?" asked Finley. She had a low-grade buzz of unease, a sense of urgency. If he didn't let her go, she was going to follow him.

Jones pressed his mouth into a tight line but raised his eyebrows in reluctant agreement.

"Get some rest," he said to Eloise as he pushed through the kitchen door and headed down the hallway. Eloise gave him a quick, dismissive nod, and Finley saw how pale she was, that there was a dullness around her eyes. Some worry butterflies fluttered from her belly into her chest.

"Grandma," she said. "Did you go to the doctor today?"

A look of surprise flashed across Eloise's face but quickly passed. "Just routine," said Eloise briskly. "Off you go."

"Don't make me late, kid," called Jones from the hallway.

"Kid?" whispered Finley. "Really?"

She and Eloise laughed a little. With a last look at her grand-mother, Finley followed Jones out of the kitchen.

"Not too late to wait in the car," said Jones now at the porch steps. He had this energy about him that he knew best and was waiting for her to come to her senses. It was pretty annoying.

"I won't embarrass you, if that's what you're worried about," she said.

"And if you pass out like you did earlier?"

But he was already ringing the bell, so she didn't have a chance to answer. Anyway, she didn't *have* an answer. Finley experienced a raw moment of self-doubt. What *was* she doing exactly? Why was she acting like a private detective, as if she *wanted* to be doing this?

She lingered, allowed herself to be aware that there was none of the usual restlessness she felt—in class, when she was studying, when she was trying to quiet the voices, keep her visitors at bay. Jones inspected a loose dowel on the porch railing as they waited. She half expected him to pull out some kind of tool and try to fix it. That's what he wanted, to fix every broken thing. He caught her staring at him, and she looked away, sat on a porch swing that hung to the right of the door. It squeaked as she swung it gently.

"Got an oil can in your pocket?" she asked Jones when he glanced over at her.

He gave her a flat expression. "I have one in my car."

"Of course you do."

All the running away and acting out she did when she was trying to deny what she was, maybe all of it was just a reaction to *that feeling*, the one that was suddenly gone because she was here with Jones. Eloise was so big on advising her to follow her instincts. But Finley had never been quite sure what that meant. How did you *know* when you were following your instincts, versus your fears or your desires? Were they ever the same? Was the choice that scared you silly sometimes the right one? Did the thing you wanted more than anything sometimes lead you down the wrong path? Her grandmother always seemed to think that Finley would know when she was doing "what was right." Finley understood, maybe for the first time, what that felt like tonight.

Jones rang the bell a second time. She rose and came to stand beside him again. Jones looked at his watch and seemed about to ring again when the door opened and a small woman stood behind the screen. She was younger than Finley expected. The pictures she'd seen of Betty Fitzpatrick had been grainy and taken on the worst days of her life. Finley just hadn't expected someone so dewy and fresh, looking like she'd just finished a workout.

"Betty?" said Jones. The woman nodded.

"I just got in from my run," she said apologetically, pushing a damp fringe of hair away from her eyes. She opened the door, and they walked into a pretty foyer, fresh flowers on the console table by the door. Jones introduced them, and she shook Finley's hand with a cool but strong grip.

"Eliza loves tulips," she said, following Finley's eyes. Eliza, her missing daughter.

Finley nodded and looked into a living room where a fire blazed and a wall-mounted flat screen was on mute, tuned to CNN. The picture of the missing developer was there; the news story was heating up. Cell phone signal dead. No calls out in several days. No credit card usage. No big withdrawals of cash or debt or anything untoward. Car still missing.

"Can I get you anything?" Betty asked.

They both declined and took seats on the couch, with her sitting across in a big wingback chair. On the mantel, piano, and every surface were pictures of a white-blonde, freckled girl and a towheaded boy who was unmistakably her older brother.

Though lovely, there was an emptiness to the space, to the woman. Something gone that had left a dark, cold hollow. Finley felt Betty's sadness, her anguish leaking into her own heart. It hurt.

"My husband came to take the kids for the day," she began when Jones prompted her. "They were just going to town to get ice cream, then for a hike. Everything was normal."

"But you were in a custody battle at the time?" asked Jones.

"Well," said Betty. "The media made it sound worse than it was. He wanted the kids every other week with him in Manhattan. And I thought that was destabilizing for them, so we were working on it. Would he move here? Would we move back to the city? It wasn't fun, but it wasn't necessarily acrimonious. Our marriage had ceased to be a good and healthy thing, but we didn't hate each other. He wouldn't have done this. He wasn't a controller or an abuser. He wouldn't have taken them, or hurt them."

Finley watched the woman. She seemed to deflate under the weight of the conversation. Much of the flush was gone from her cheeks. Finley could see her running, pushing her body to the edge of its endurance just for the fatigue that would follow. She didn't run for her health; she ran to quiet the grief.

"It's such a cliché," she said. "The police assumed from the beginning that it was him, and I'm not sure that they ever looked for any other possibility."

Jones made a noncommittal but affirming noise, and Betty turned subtly toward him.

"When the other girl—Abbey Gleason—went missing, they started to wonder if they missed something. But then they picked that family apart, too."

Again, Jones gave a sympathetic nod. He wouldn't trash the police work that was done, even if he didn't agree with the way the investigation had been conducted. That wasn't his way. Jones Cooper kept his opinions to himself.

"They reopened the investigation at that time," Betty said. Finley noticed then a kind of flat, glassy quality to the woman's eyes. She was on meds of some kind, understandably.

"You moved here about a year before their disappearance?" Jones asked. "Is that right?"

She nodded. "You know, the city is so expensive, we could give the kids a better life—all that."

"What drew you to The Hollows?" Finley asked. They had that in common, the Gleasons and the Fitzpatricks—they were outsiders, come to The Hollows from elsewhere.

"My family is from here," she said. "My maternal grandmother Hester Briar was born here. I never knew her, but I remembered visiting the town when I was a kid. When Jed and I were looking for a place to live, we came here and fell in love with it. I felt like I instantly belonged. Jed—not so much. I think it was one of the things that pushed us over the brink to divorce."

There was a kind of ripple in Finley's perception. And then the little girl appeared at her mother's feet, brushing the hair of a Barbie doll. The boy was over by the television, holding a video game controller in his hand, tapping it violently and jerking his body side-to-side like he was driving a racecar. Then they were gone.

Finley looked at the Xbox, cords wrapped and stowed on a tidy shelf next to a stack of game sleeves. There were books in a basket under the coffee table, and a small wicker toy box in the corner. It was a room waiting for children.

"Do you mind an odd question?" asked Finley. She felt the heat of Jones's eyes on her. But Betty smiled sadly and shook her head, as if there was no question that hadn't already been asked of her.

"Did either of your children ever experience prophetic dreams? Or maybe play with imaginary friends? See people who weren't there?"

Betty leaned back in her chair and looked up at the ceiling as if trying to retrieve the answer.

"Well, Eliza has a wild imagination," she said. "She's always making up stories, creating cartoon characters. I wouldn't say she had prophetic dreams. But now that you mention it, there *was* an imaginary friend for a while after we moved here. We didn't think much of it. Just her way of adjusting to a new life, missing her old friends and teachers."

Betty's eyes drifted over to one of the pictures of the kids on the mantle.

"Joshua, on the other hand, is all about math and science," she said. "Not even much of a reader. He has an engineer's mind, just like his dad. No imaginary friends for him."

A tear escaped Betty's eye, and she excused herself and got up, left the room. Finley and Jones sat awkwardly, waiting. Finley watched as the little boy returned, playing with his Xbox. He seemed familiar, not just from the photos she'd seen. Something about his energy was known to her. She watched as he rocked back and forth, his face grim with intent, his hands working at the game control.

"What are you looking at?" Jones asked.

"Nothing," Finley lied.

Finally Betty returned, looking utterly composed and dry-eyed.

"Did they hire you to find Abbey?" Betty asked when she sat again. Her hands twisted in her lap, like she was working in lotion.

"We're looking for Abbey," Jones said. "Yes."

"Then you're looking for Eliza, Josh, and Jed, too," she said. Even through Betty's flat affect, Finley could see that she was still daring to hope that her family might come home to her.

"It's not out of the realm of possibility that the two cases are connected," said Jones with a careful nod.

"Did Abbey have dreams?" Betty asked.

"Her mother says that she did," answered Jones.

Finley wondered how much he could tell or should tell about another client. She guessed he did what he had to do to make people comfortable, to get them talking without breaking important confidences. It must be a delicate balance.

"Why does it matter?" Betty asked. "I mean, why did you ask me about that?"

"Maybe it doesn't," said Jones, casting a glance at Finley. "We're just looking for connections, no matter how remote."

But Betty had her eyes on Finley. "I know you," she said quietly. "I know your grandmother."

Finley didn't say anything.

"Are you a psychic?" Betty asked.

"I don't know what I am," Finley answered honestly.

Betty seemed to accept this with a nod, but her gaze kept returning to Finley. Betty went on to answer more questions from Jones about whether there had been any sign or word from her husband, or people close to him. There hadn't been. Since the day eighteen months ago that they disappeared, there had been no cell phone or credit card activity, no word to friends or even his parents. The vehicle he'd been driving that day had never been located.

"Jed *wouldn't* do this," she said again. "He just was not that kind of man, not controlling or vengeful. He knew it would kill me to be away from my children. He didn't love me anymore, but he didn't *hate* me."

Jones took notes while Betty spoke, and Finley watched the children playing on the floor. They were in a loop, a repeat of the same actions over and over. A show for Finley; she watched, wondering what it meant. Yes! Joshua said for the tenth time. That's when she got it.

"Did your son ever play with trains?" asked Finley.

Betty stared at her, giving a slow blink. "My son is *obsessed* with trains. His father gave him a wooden train when he was two, and I swear that was all it took. It was nothing but trains for years."

She rose and motioned for them to follow. They climbed a narrow staircase and into a room at the end of the hall. The space was dominated by a huge train track, a total environment with bridges and tunnels, a little town, a wooded area. The shelves on the wall were lined with engines in all sizes and colors. It was an extraordinary collection, which obviously took years and a great deal of parental indulgence to build.

"Lately, he's more into his Xbox than his train collection," she said. "But I guess that's what happens."

The bed was made and the room smelled freshly cleaned, waiting for its occupant to come home. Finley expected to see the little boy, but he wasn't there. Strange.

"Can I see Eliza's room?" asked Finley. And Betty led them to another room down the hall.

Pink, dolls, more stuffed animals and books than the shelves could hold. There were glow-in-the-dark stars on the ceiling, an iPod Touch on the white bedside table, lamps shaped like flowers affixed to the wall. On the headboard a row of little birds had been painted and beneath them painted in a blue cursive: Little Bird.

"Little bird," Finley said.

"That's what her father calls her," said Betty. "Well, that's what we all call her. But it was my husband's name for her when she was a baby because she used to make this little chirping noise that he thought sounded like a tiny birdcall."

Finley waited for the flash of insight, the crashing into another space and time, a vision—anything. But there was nothing, just the flat, dead physical world.

Downstairs, Jones asked more questions about the days before the disappearance, where they were in town, where they ate. Other questions, too, about who worked at the house, local friends. Was there anything that made her uncomfortable, worried, seemed strange? It seemed dull, even pointless, to Finley but she got it. It was exactly like what she did on the computer, just searching for anything that offered the jolt of a connection being made. That's all it was, detective work—asking, listening, looking, making connections, or discovering that there were no connections to be made.

The boy with the train. Little bird. What did it mean? She still didn't know. Just pieces of a puzzle that she was unable to solve. Again, the rise of self-doubt, a restless kind of panic. She felt the urge to flee the house that had grown overwarm, the conversation that had grown dull and heavy, hopeless. But she didn't run. She forced herself to sit and listen.

"See, I told you I wouldn't embarrass you," she said in the car.

"You did okay, actually," Jones said. He cast her a grudging look. "But I'm used to working alone."

He turned the ignition, and the car hummed to life, cool air breathing out of the vents, causing Finley to sit stiff with cold until it gradually warmed. She told him about the *squeak-clink*, about the rose-breasted grosbeak, about the boy with the train.

He kept his hands at ten and two on the wheel, his eyes on the road ahead, a muscle working in his jaw.

"So what does that mean?" he asked. "Who did you see in the woods?"

"I don't know," she said. The faces were fuzzy and indistinct, like on television when identities were being protected. She tried to explain it to him, but she could tell it wasn't making a lot of sense.

"And 'Little Bird,'" she told him. "That was the phrase I heard in my head when I found the rose-breasted grosbeak online."

"Eliza's nickname," he said. "So that's who you saw?"

"I'm just not sure."

They drove, the road winding, rising, and falling, the trees thick and silent around them. *The woods are lovely, dark and deep*, she thought. *But I have promises to keep. And miles to go before I sleep.* Robert Frost. Miles to go.

"I went to see Agatha," she said. "She says that I need to follow my instincts."

"Agatha?"

"Agatha Cross? My grandmother's mentor?"

He flashed her a strange look, which she didn't understand. She guessed if he was still skeptical about Eloise, then someone like Agatha must seem like a circus freak to him. She waited for him to make some kind of crack.

"And what are your instincts telling you?" he asked instead.

"That you're wrong about the way they went," she said. "That they went north, deeper into the woods. That there was no vehicle."

"The area was thoroughly searched," he said, shaking his head stubbornly. "I was there myself. If they were on foot like you say, they couldn't have gotten far enough to hide by the time search teams descended."

"Unless they hid somewhere."

Someplace dark and quiet, she thought. Deep beneath the ground, a hole, tunnel. Finley could see it, her consciousness wobbling. The girl could hear the sound of the people searching, yelling, moving clumsily through the trees. The dogs were barking, and voices calling. And she couldn't yell, could barely breathe with his weight atop her, hand clamped over her mouth.

Help me. Help me. I'm here. The words pulsed through Finley, she found herself taking a labored breath as if there were a weight on top of her, too.

She expected Jones to argue that there was no place for them to hide, but she turned to him, he had the energy of consideration. He rubbed at his forehead as if an unwelcome thought had occurred.

"What are you thinking?" she asked.

"I'm thinking about the mines," he said.

North of The Hollows proper, up in the woods the land was laced throughout with abandoned iron mine tunnels. They were largely undocumented, few maps existing, but an acknowledged hazard locally. Every summer, some kid fell through the ground or got lost after having snuck in one of the openings. There had been several fatalities over the years, broken limbs, frantic days of searching. Many of the openings were marked, and vulnerable areas, where the infrastructures beneath the ground were giving way, were cordoned off when discovered. There were rumors among the local kids about people living down there. And a couple of years back, a fugitive had successfully hidden there for weeks.

"Where's the nearest opening to the trail?" asked Finley. She buried her frozen fingers deep under her thighs. This was it. Winter was coming. She was going to be too cold for months. A darkness crept into her spirit.

"I don't know," he said. "But if there was a mine opening up there, I bet it was searched. It's no secret. People have hid out down there before."

"Let's go there now," she said, leaning forward. She had her phone out, was Googling "iron mines in The Hollows New York." There were several news stories about injured and missing kids, the hazards of abandoned mines around the tristate area, historic tours, how they were a spelunker's (dangerous, deadly) paradise.

He held up a palm.

"If we head up to the mines, we need a team and the right equipment. We need to let someone know where we're going. Let me talk to Chuck Ferrigno first, and we'll go from there. Maybe he can spare someone. There's no point in going off half-cocked. You just make a mess of things."

She'd heard this advice before, many times. It's what grown-ups always said, not that she *wasn't* a grown-up. But Jones Cooper was way more of a grown-up than Finley could hope to be. She exhaled sharply with frustration.

"But what if there's something there? Something that was missed."

"Then it will be there in the morning when we come with enough people and the right equipment."

"What if it's too late then?" she asked. A niggling urgency pushed her forward in her seat.

"This is a cold case, kid," he said.

"Meaning what? That it doesn't matter? That there's no ticking clock? What if there is, though? Merri Gleason said that she felt Abbey's life force, that time was running out."

Jones gripped the wheel and looked ahead.

"The feelings of a distraught mother who's lost a child are not a reliable guide for an investigation."

"But what if they're the most reliable source of all? Maybe she's tuned in to her child, in to some kind of energy the rest of us aren't."

He tapped his thumbs on the wheel, beating out an impatient staccato. "Tomorrow morning first thing," he said. "In the light with the right equipment and an extra man. It won't be too late."

A wind picked up outside and bent the trees, sending a spray of leaves onto the hood of the car.

They're so often wrong, Agatha said. *That's why they need us.*

There was something about him, though. He was sure of himself, so knowing. And she was so inexperienced, so *not* sure of herself. And even if he was old school, she knew he was right. It was dangerous, and Abbey had been missing ten months, the other children longer than that. There was almost no chance of evidence still being there, and what difference would it make now? She sank back, disappointed, the energy leaving her.

"First thing in the morning," Finley said. "Fine."

You don't need him. He'll only hold you back.

In the rearview mirror, she caught the flash of red hair, the pale fire of skin. Abigail.

You're not a baby. You don't need him to take you to the mines.

Finley knew better than to answer her. But she wondered if Abigail was right.

Back at the house, Eloise was waiting. She had tea steeping, as if she'd known Finley was on her way home. At the kitchen table, sipping the hot, sweet drink, Finley recounted the evening for Eloise, who listened carefully, nodding, making soft affirming noises in all the right places. Her grandmother was one of the few people who actually listened when Finley spoke. Her mother was always talking over her, then barking "Let me finish, Finley!" when Finley tried to get a word in. Her father always seemed to be just waiting for her to stop talking so that he could tell her how it *really* was.

"If you hadn't been with him," Eloise asked when Finley was done, "what would you have done next?"

Finley had to think about it a moment. "I probably would have gone back up to the trail and tried to find an entrance to those mines."

Eloise rocked a little. She looked tiny, dwarfed in her big, soft gray robe that was nearly the same color as her salt-and-pepper hair.

"So, you would have gone up there alone, in the dark, with no supplies and no idea where you were going or what precisely you were looking for?"

"I'd figure it out," said Finley.

Eloise sipped her tea. "Or you might have gotten yourself hurt, or into a situation from which you couldn't extract yourself. And then you'd be no good to anyone."

Ugh, so *frustrating*. Everyone was so methodical, so cautious. Sometimes you just had to go out there and do what needed to be done. There was value to a seat-of-your-pants methodology, wasn't there?

"So what?" said Finley, that sizzle of frustration making her angry. "You just sit and do nothing while time runs out. What about following your instincts? Isn't that what we're supposed to do?"

Eloise wrapped her arms around her body as if warding off a chill, but she held Finley's eyes.

"There's a difference between following your instincts and being reckless, my dear. Only age teaches you that."

"Then what's the point of this?" said Finley. She leaned forward. "What's the point of *knowing* when you can't *do* anything?"

"Just because it's ill advised to go off unprepared," said her grandmother, "doesn't mean you *do nothing*. What's the next best thing?"

Finley leaned back in her chair, then got up and paced the room, from the door to the range and then back again.

"Maps," she said. "I'll find maps of the area, and research the mines."

Eloise gave her an approving smile. "That's my girl."

Finley gave Eloise a big kiss on the cheek, then bounded up the stairs to her laptop. Sitting on her bed, she entered "Maps iron mines Hollows New York" into the search bar and waited for the information to load. They were all there: Faith, the boy with the trains, the *squeak-clink*. But Finley barely noticed them.

EIGHTEEN

Wolf sent Kristi a text, turned off the phone he used exclusively for some of his less above-board activities. Then, on the corner, he tossed it into the trash. He didn't feel *that* bad about breaking up with Kristi via text. People of her generation were all about texting, which was just one example of their soullessness.

> I'm sorry, Kristi. I can't see you tonight. In fact, we should take a break from seeing each other at all. My family needs me and I can't let them down. Please forgive me. I do love you. It's just not time for us right now.

It was final without being hopeless. Romantic without leading her on, implying that in another time and place, they might be together. And anyway maybe it was even true.

Wolf ducked into The Parlor on West Eighty-Sixth Street, a kind of divey, not too crowded sports bar that he and Blake had been drinking at since college. He spotted his friend over by the bar, as usual with his face buried in the newspaper, glasses drifting down his nose. His blond hair was graying, his sleeves rolled up, and his jacket and briefcase rested on the stool beside him. Blake had been a middle-aged man since he was sixteen. Still, two girls at a high-top were looking over at him, whispering with curious smiles. But Blakey, as ever, was oblivious. He only had eyes for his wife, Claire.

*   *   *

Claire, who was *not hot* to begin with, had put on twenty since the kids and never bothered to take it off. Claire, who was a stay-at-home mom in spite of having a law degree, a searing, rip-you-to-shreds intelligence, and a knowledge of world events that shamed even Wolf, now seemed to care only about the kids—bedtime routines and the dangers of overscheduling and too much soy, or whatever was the hot parenting topic of the moment. Claire didn't even always take care of her roots. And still Blake looked at her like she was a Suicide Girls pinup. Wolf didn't get it.

"Hey, man," said Wolf, sliding in beside him.

College football roared on the television above them. Wolf was so out of it that he didn't even know who was playing. People cheering on the screen, happy faces, girls in hats and scarves. Who were those people with no fucking problems? Wolf hated them all in some nebulous, disinterested way.

"Hey, buddy," said Blake with a worried frown, his default expression for Wolf these days. "How's everything?"

"You know," said Wolf. He didn't even bother trying to put on an act for his old friend. He put on one for everyone else, not just because it made him feel better but because it made everyone else feel better, too. People didn't want to look into the face of grief; it was too terrifying.

"Yeah," Blake said, patting Wolf hard on the shoulder. "I know."

Blake folded up his paper and took off his glasses, put them in the pocket of his handmade Italian shirt. "How's Merri holding up?"

Wolf told him about the psychic Merri had hired, how she'd gone up to The Hollows for a while. The bartender brought Wolf a Corona with lime, gave him a nod.

"Is she—?"

"Losing it again?" said Wolf. He shook his head. "She seems okay."

When Merri went off the deep end a few months after Abbey disappeared, the psychotic break had hit like the strike of a baseball bat. One minute she was okay, on the phone with the detective who had been working Abbey's case. Wolf wasn't sure what the man had said, but whatever it was, it was too much for Merri. She just snapped. She put the phone down.

"What?" he asked her. They were back in the apartment, picking up some things to take back to The Hollows. Jackson, thankfully, was recovering at Wolf's parents' place in the West Village.

Merri had put her head in her arms, and when she lifted her face to him, she looked as glazed and blissful as a Hari Krishna.

"Merri?" For a second, his own heart had lifted. Had they found her? Was this nightmare over?

"Do you see them?" she'd asked. Her smile wide and beautiful; she looked so much like she had when they'd first met.

"Who?" he asked.

"The angels," she said. "They're all around us."

"Merri," he said, his heart dropping, growing cold.

"They're everywhere," she said, looking above him, starting to cry. "They're taking care of Abbey."

He'd called Merri's therapist and rushed her to the office, Merri dazed and pliant. She was committed at NYU Hospital within a few hours, and she'd stayed there for more than a week before snapping out of it as quickly as she'd succumbed.

"Her psyche, overwhelmed by the events of the last few months, did what it needed to do to survive," her doctor explained. "It gave her a little vacation."

As frightening as the episode had been, Wolf envied her.

"Shouldn't you be up there with her?" Blake asked now.

"She doesn't *want* me, man," he said. Wolf put his forehead in his palm. "Who can blame her?"

"Maybe she doesn't *know* she wants you," said Blake. "Maybe you need to be there for her so that she can remember what it's like *not* to be alone. Look, bad shit has happened, the worst things possible. But I think you two can find your way back to each other."

Blake was a hopeless romantic, a depraved optimist. There was no problem, in his view, that could not be solved by love.

"What about Jackson?" Wolf asked. "The kid's a wreck. I can't leave him. And I can't take him back up there."

"We'll take him," said Blake. "The girls love him. We'll make it fun for him, like a sleepover."

Wolf nodded, as if considering. Even Blake, who was so close to them, so well meaning, just didn't get it. There were no "fun sleepovers" in Jackson's immediate future. He'd been shot by a man who'd abducted his sister, almost bled to death while he thought he was watching his father bleed to death. He was shattered, glued back together, and barely holding on to the pieces of himself. It was true of all of them. Other people, even close friends and family, their lives were moving forward, as they should. But Wolf, Merri, and Jackson were still back in those woods while Abbey was being dragged away. That sick feeling of helpless rage was an echo in his psyche. How could he ever forget those moments, watching her while nothing in his mind or spirit could make his body do what it needed to do? He still regularly dreamed about it, woke up in a sweat, searching for their faces. But he'd never seen them, the men who took Abbey. Without his glasses or contacts, they were just dark, nebulous forms. He looked down at his hand. The beer bottle was empty. He lifted it to the bartender for another.

"I'll think about it," said Wolf. "Thanks."

"You know we'll do anything," said Blake. Wolf knew that his old friend was one of the few people in the world who said it and meant it. But there was literally nothing anyone could do for them. Except . . .

"I wanted to ask you something," said Wolf. He took the article he'd printed from the web and unfolded it, smoothed it out on the bar in front of them. "Hear anything about this?"

Blake put his glasses back on. "Yeah," he said. "I heard about this guy on the news and then there was some chatter about it at the office."

Blake was a criminal defense attorney, had lots of connections with other lawyers, cops, and detectives. He had been a huge help in dealing with the police, especially when they were tearing Wolf and Merri apart.

"What kind of chatter?" Wolf asked.

"Well, foul play is definitely suspected. The guy was like Mr. Nice, happily married, very successful, into his job, no debt, no affairs, not even a parking ticket. Not the kind of guy who typically takes off on his family. There's no signal from his phone, which means it was probably destroyed. No credit card activity."

Blake looked down at the article again. "The Hollows," he said. "Where Abbey—I'm sorry, man. I didn't make the connection."

Wolf nodded quickly. "Jackson's *obsessed*."

"The news thing?"

"Yeah," he said. "But it's more intense than it's been. He thinks the story has something to do with Abbey."

"Why does he think that?" asked Blake.

"I don't know," said Wolf. He took a sip of his next beer, which was ice cold and tasted good. Usually, he tried not to drink when he wanted it as bad as he did right now. Because when he felt this bad, it all went down too easy; he drank too much, did stupid things, was useless the next day. It was the only thing that smoothed out the jagged edges of his inner life. But he couldn't afford that kind of carelessness anymore. "I don't think *he* even knows."

Blake tapped a finger on the bar, thinking.

"I heard today that the guy had some kind of new technology in his car. If it's tampered with, reported stolen, or damaged, it apparently sends off some kind of beacon to the leasing company. They can control the car remotely, render it inoperable, find out exactly where it is in the event that it needs to be repossessed."

Wolf felt an unreasonable flutter of hope, in spite of himself. This was a symptom of Jackson's PTSD, and it was contagious in a way because the shattered, hopeless mind reaches for any kind of hope, no matter how dim. Ostensibly, Wolf was only asking because it helped calm Jackson down. Once he realized that there was no connection between whatever news story and the fractured lives of the Gleason family, Jackson moved on. Of course, Wolf didn't actually believe that this story had anything to do with Abbey. But still, wasn't there just the faintest glimmer of *maybe*? "So—"

"There are channels that need navigating, some initial resistance to the warrant that was needed because there's no real evidence of foul play," he said. "It's taking some time. They were talking about it today, privacy and legality issues."

Wolf thought about the man's family. How infuriating it must be to have a technology that could help you find your missing loved one and then not be able to use it. The delays for reasons of legality seemed inhumane to the point of being Kafkaesque when you were frantic with fear and everyone else was following rules. How many hours did the police spend grilling Wolf and Merri while Abbey's abductor was getting farther and farther away?

Wolf ordered another beer, and a shot of tequila. Blake looked at him but didn't say anything. Blake and Claire were real friends, and even if they didn't, couldn't, understand, they'd been there every step of the way. Blake had been in The Hollows hours after Abbey disappeared, advising them, supporting them.

"Will you keep your ears open about it, let me know if you hear anything so I can tell Jackson?"

Jackson's doctor had advised them not to dismiss the kid's fears, but to help him work through things. Help him to see that there were no patterns, no way to predict the future to prevent bad things from happening. Wolf wasn't sure what good it did for him to know that, that no one had any control over anything, that life could spiral out of your control in a moment.

"Sure," said Blake. "Want me to make some calls?"

"That would be great," he said.

"I'm interested anyway," said Blake.

The place was filling up, and the voices around them getting a little louder. They both zoned out on the game. During a commercial break, Wolf watched a preview of the weather. The first winter storm was on its way, and it wasn't even Halloween. Snowfall in the city was going to be light, but it looked like they were going to get dumped on farther up north. The sight of that gray graphic over the upstate region gripped him with sorrow. Another winter coming without Abbey, and Merri getting farther away every second.

"You should go up there, man," said Blake again, reading his thoughts. "At least bring her back before that storm hits."

"Maybe you're right," said Wolf.

A girl sat at one of the high-tops, surrounded by a crowd of co-workers, her blazer off, her sheer blouse revealing a cream-colored camisole. Her blonde hair was silky and a little wild around her face like a mane. She was smiling at Wolf, sweet and shy. She laughed at something, turned back to the young man beside her.

In another life, Wolf would have lingered after Blake went home. He'd have found a way to strike up a conversation with the pretty girl. If she'd been a certain type, he'd have wound up back at her place. But he liked to think that he was a different man now, someone who'd learned from his mistakes, made better choices.

So when Blake picked up the tab and gathered up his things to go home, Wolf left with him.

Back at the apartment, Wolf's parents had gone to sleep in the master bedroom, and his mother had made up the bed for him on the couch. He looked in on Jackson, who was sweaty and fitful in sleep, his leg kicked out from beneath the covers, still wearing his glasses, his night light on. The scar on his thigh was a large but tidy keloid mark that looked like a star. A book on quantum physics lay spine up on the floor. Wolf touched his son's head, took off his glasses, and turned out the light.

On the couch, he dialed Merri and was surprised when she answered.

"There's a storm coming," he said. "I think you should come home."

"I can't," she said. He could tell she'd been crying.

"Then we're going to come up," he said.

"Don't," she said. "It's not healthy for him."

"Then I'll leave him with my parents," he said. "Just for a couple of days."

She didn't say anything, her breath filling the space between them.

"I'm sorry," he said. "Merri, I'm truly sorry. I've been a shit husband and a worse father." How many times had he said it? Were there ever more pointless, impotent words in the English language than "I'm sorry." The words uttered when all was lost, when nothing could alter outcomes.

"Let me try to do better," he said. "Please."

There was only silence on the other end. He thought that maybe she had hung up, as she sometimes did, without a word. Even when she wasn't angry, she would every once in a while just absently end a call, her mind on to the next thing.

They were so different, always had been. He was a writer. She was an editor. He created; she corrected. *There's a right way and a wrong way to do things, Wolf. Most grown-ups know that.* Was it Ray Bradbury who said, Stay drunk on writing so that reality doesn't destroy you? On the page, you could write the world. Off the page, the world would crush you, if you let it, with its harsh consequences and brutal outcomes, with all its banalities and dull day-to-day slog.

"Merri?"

"Okay," she said. "Try to do better."

And then she hung up.

NINETEEN

It was Abigail who wanted the rings. Patience said not to. And, of course, Sarah said nothing because she never had an opinion of her own. She swayed between the two of them, following whoever was stronger, not unlike Finley.

Finley had noticed the rings a few times, when she'd been up at the chalkboard, working through equations with Mrs. Frazier. Finley knew all about diamonds from her mother, who never tired of leafing through Tiffany catalogs, showing Finley the jewelry she liked, teaching her about cut, color, and clarity. And Amanda had plenty of gems of her own, a drawer full of glittering stones—some costume, some costly. Finley had grown to associate jewelry with apologies. When Phil screwed up, a little blue box appeared shortly after.

Mrs. Frazier's engagement ring had a cushion-cut stone, more than a carat, but not quite two, with a neat row of smaller stones, alternating diamonds and blue sapphires around the band. It glittered and drew attention to itself, and Mrs. Frazier always had her nails done. And such pretty, soft hands. The wedding band was a simple matching ring of small diamonds.

Finley could tell how proud her teacher was of those rings. Leading up to her wedding, there had been a stack of wedding magazines in her drawer, along with a binder of all her plans. She was all business in the classroom; but Finley could see how happy she was, how excited. She'd slide the magazines out as soon as the classroom was empty; Finley would see them when she stayed after class for one thing or another. One afternoon, Mrs. Frazier had showed Finley a picture of her dress, her ring and manicured nails glittering as she pointed to the picture. So pretty. Finley wondered what it would be like to be so happy, to be in love. Had her mother been so in love with her father once upon a time? Amanda said, yes, she'd never loved anyone like she'd loved Phil. And she probably never would again and maybe that was a good thing.

Mrs. Frazier took her rings off sometimes, put them in a little ring dish on her desk.

Take them, whispered Abigail one day. Finley had been taking a make-up test, and Mrs. Frazier got up to go to the bathroom, an act of tremendous trust.

Finley knew better.

"No," she whispered. "Go away."

But wasn't there, deep beneath what Finley knew was good and right, a throb of desire? Was it hers? Was it Abigail's? The room was cold, smelled of chalk dust and mold, the fluorescents flickering their sickly blue-white light. Finley really *liked* Mrs. Frazier, formerly Miss Grant. Finley would *never* steal from her, or anyone. But those rings were so pretty. And what would it be like to have something like that?

He'll buy her another one. No one would ever suspect you.

Sarah stood by the chalkboard looking uncertain, glancing at the door. Her dress was long and sky blue, in tatters around the hem. The girls all smelled faintly of smoke. Patience was by the window, staring at Finley with dark eyes. Her dress was black, buttoned high up the throat, her hair tightly pulled back. She looked the most like Faith, though Finley didn't know that at the time. She never met Faith until she moved to The Hollows. There was anger etched deep around Faith's eyes and into her brow, even around the corners of her mouth. It was righteous, the anger of a person who had been done wrong. Abigail, Faith's most unruly daughter was angry, too. But she wanted to do harm. She wanted to hurt because she had been hurt. She didn't give a damn about justice. Finley knew all of this without exactly having words for any of it.

Follow her lead and you'll know nothing but heartache. Trust me, said Patience.

Shut up, said Abigail venomously.

"Go away," said Finley. "I have to finish the test."

She ignored them and went back to work, using all her mental resources to block them out. When she was done, she put her head down on her desk. She was so tired when the girls were around; they exhausted her.

She must have drifted off, and Mrs. Frazier was leaning over her, her walnut hair falling in a pretty sheet, her cornflower eyes thickly lashed and worried. "Finley. Finley? Are you all right, sweetie?"

Finley roused herself as if from the deepest slumber, disoriented, a little confused, and with the sense that something was terribly wrong.

"You must still be a little under the weather," Mrs. Frazier said, putting a hand to Finley's forehead. Finley had been sick with the flu for a week, that was why she had to make up the test. She didn't feel totally better. "I'll wait with you out front until your mother comes."

Somehow—and Finley honestly and truly did *not* know how— those pretty, glittering rings wound up in her pocket. She must have gotten up from her seat, walked over, and put the rings in her pocket. But she had no memory of doing it. Had she discovered them herself, she'd have tried to find a way to return them without getting caught. Instead, they dropped out of her jeans when her mom was cleaning up her room that evening.

The shit storm that followed was epic. The suspension from school and grounding were bad enough. The disappointment of her parents and a beloved teacher was worse still. More than that, from that day forward Finley felt like she was a "bad kid." Like there was something wrong with her that could not be fixed. She was a thief, a liar. Maybe that's what attracted her to Rainer and his friends; they were bad, too. Her kid shrink believed Finley when she said she didn't remember doing it. And he had suggested that it was some kind of fugue state, a dissociation, which in turn was a suggestion that Finley was seriously mentally ill. Which was scary enough that Finley tried to tell her mother the truth.

Naturally, her mother wouldn't even hear her about The Three Sisters.

"Stop it, Finley," she said. "Just stop it. You have to start taking responsibility for your own actions. I'm not buying this whole I-see-dead-people routine. It's pure bullshit."

What made it worse was that she knew her mother *did* believe her but just couldn't accept that something she had tried so hard to control was beyond her abilities to manage.

"I want to go live with Mimi," Finley had said miserably, using the name she'd used as a little girl for Eloise, during one of the million arguments that followed. "At least she understands."

Finley still felt a pang when she thought about the look on her mother's face—rigid with pain and anger, her eyes glittering with tears.

"Over my dead body," Amanda had said softly, then left the room.

It was midnight when Finley knocked on Rainer's door, fully aware of herself. He came to her sleep-tousled and let her inside. She shivered in the transition from cold to warm. She wasn't dressed warmly enough for her bike, and she felt so stiff and cold that she could shatter like an icicle.

"You're freezing," he said. He shut the door and wrapped her up tight in his big arms. Despite all the drama that had characterized their relationship in the beginning, his friendship was the safest place in her life. He was wide open and always there for her. She'd pushed him away hard, but he'd followed after her just the same.

He let her go for a minute, then moved over to the thermostat and turned up the heat. When he returned, he proceeded to vigorously rub at her arms until she laughed.

"You okay?" he asked.

"I think so," she said. "Yeah, I'm okay. I just had a weird night."

She shouldn't be here; she knew that. It was a mistake. Still, she found herself pouring out all the events of the day since she left him. She told him about her internet search and everything she'd found out about the mines. There was a lot of information—old drawings, unofficial maps, photographs posted by cavers and spelunkers, old news articles about kids falling in and getting hurt, town meeting minutes about making them safer. They sat cross-legged on his mattress, for lack of any other furniture, as she showed him everything and told him about the things that had happened. She held back the part about Abigail, about not remembering sending him the text. That was a little too weird, even for Rainer.

"So," he said. He held the maps she'd printed. "Are you working with him now? Are you a private detective?"

"I don't know what I am," she said for the second time that night. "But it feels right, what I did tonight."

"So then it must be right."

"Yeah?" she said. "Is that how it works? If it feels right, it's right?" Rainer shrugged. "How else?"

She looked at his face, so earnest and innocent in his way. Rainer followed his heart, no matter where it led—even to The Hollows. He didn't know another way to be. Maybe it was the right way to be, even when it hurt.

"I'll go up there with you tomorrow," he said. "If you want."

"You will?"

He gave a little laugh. "Don't you know I'll go with you anywhere, Fin?"

She did know that. He had the most faithful heart of anyone she'd ever known. Something in her that she hardened against him softened once more. She laced her fingers through his and felt his energy warm and good.

"You want to work?" he asked. He put the pages down beside the bed. They were photographs of historic documents, hard to decipher, but Finley had a mental model of the area now, some idea how close to the path an entrance might be. But a lot could have changed since those maps were drawn. Nature was in constant motion, always changing and renewing as much as it appeared to stay the same.

"No," she said. "Not really."

She wrapped her arms around his neck and pulled him to her. He pressed his mouth to hers. He tasted of peppermint; the stubble on his jaw was pleasantly rough on her skin. She disappeared into the sweet softness of his lips, the strength, the heat of him. She gave in. It felt good not to fight, not to always keep trying to do what was right, as opposed to what she wanted. Which seemed always to be two very different things.

"Fin," Rainer whispered, throaty and soft. "I thought you didn't want this anymore."

She didn't answer him, just peeled his shirt off as he unbuttoned hers. She let him lift her, wrapping her legs around him. His living space was spare and dingy with a small refrigerator and a hot plate on a countertop, a light bulb hanging from a wire in the ceiling. It was cold, a draft of icy air coming in from the back door that led to the alley behind the shop. There was no place she'd rather be.

"I love you," he breathed in her ear.

She let him slide off her jeans, and she ran her hands along his arms, over the dragon and the phoenix in flames, over the bouquet of black roses, and the burning man. She ran her hands through his hair, down the strong muscles of his back, shivering as he buried his face in the curve of her neck.

She didn't answer him. But she did love him. She loved his hot temper and his desire to possess her. She loved his talent and his kindness, his boyish sweetness. She loved the way she felt when they were together, desired, safe. She even loved all the wild emotions he invoked in her. All the other things, all the reasons why not, had receded from her memory. Or maybe they were the reasons why. Because the things that hurt were very often the things that made you feel most alive, like the ink on her skin, the storm of her emotions.

Even as she disappeared into Rainer, Finley was aware of Abigail who watched from the corner of the room, her face impassive and cool. What was Rainer to Abigail? Just another shiny thing she wanted, that she was using Finley to have. Or was it that she was trying to lead Finley to self-destruct? As often as she'd seen Abigail, as connected as they were, Finley still wasn't sure what she wanted, if she was good at heart or bad to the bone. Maybe like Finley, she was a little of both.

Finley pulled Rainer close, then pushed him down so that she could climb on top of him. He unlatched her lacy bra and tossed it, gave her that wild little boy smile that always thrilled her, lit her up inside. Then there was a flicker of worry across his face. He took her hand and kissed her fingers.

"Are you sure, Fin?" he said. "Don't play me, okay. I've got too much skin in this game."

He was so alive, such warm flesh, and so much light in his eyes.

"I'm sure," she said. When she put her hand to his face, she saw the shadow of Abigail's hand. In the mirror across the shop, Finley saw Abigail, hair flowing around her like flames, astride Rainer where Finley should be.

Finley felt a lash of anger, and she let it expel Abigail, push her back and away.

No, said Finley. *He's mine.*

Abigail retreated to the corner, watching. When Finley looked back at Rainer, he was staring at Finley, seeing *her*, not Abigail.

"It's you," he said. "It's always only been you."

She only has as much power as you give her, Agatha had told Finley. *You are flesh and bone. You make the rules.*

Up until that moment, Finley hadn't believed her.

i had a dream. hello. Fin?? heeeellllllloooo???
u know what time it iz luzr?
didja get dat? I had a DREAM.
really.
yeeaahh. im like u now.
ok. biting.
im gonna be the worldz most famous snowboarder. BAzillions
    in sponsorships. girlz toss their bras at me when I win the
    olympic gold yo.

way better than my dreams. wenz ur first snowboarding lesson?
Aw wrz the love? U know I kill on the boardz.

It was three in the morning, Finley tangled up in Rainer who
slept like the dead. The phone gave off its unnaturally bright glow,
lighting the room.

Ur not at gmas. Ooo ur at Rainers. Telling mom.
How wud u know?
Find my frenz.

Ugh, the Find My Friends app. She'd let her stupid brother follow
her and now all he had to do was look at his screen to find her on a
map. She clicked, scrolled over, and turned it off, making her status
unavailable.

I just shut it off.
ha ha too late.
donchu dare tell mom.
i won't. just like I won't tell you that dadz been here all week.
when are they going to grow up?
looks like never. they seem . . . happy.
good for them.
don't be a hater.
go to sleep luzer and dream of all your groupies cuz that's
closest ur gonna get to any real action.
Sooooo mean to your lil bro.
Love you.
Me too.

Finley put the phone down, staring at the ceiling. A big crack
in the plaster looked like a wave, water stains like faraway birds.
Rainer sighed in sleep, pulled her closer. She hadn't been sleeping
when Alfie texted, just lying there, at first looking at the maps in

the glow of her phone, then thinking about her visit with Betty Fitzpatrick, listening to the *squeak-clink* that was ever present now, but the volume on low. Abbey's dreams, Eliza's imaginary friend, Jackson's predictions, Joshua's trains. The little bird. A million little pieces floated in the ether above her, not coalescing, never taking any kind of shape.

Rainer stirred and pulled her closer.

"Go to sleep, Fin," he said.

She felt herself drift off in the warmth of his embrace.

But then the air grew cold and Finley was out in the night, a light snow falling all around her. She was running, running, running— sick with exertion and fear. Her heart couldn't work any harder, and bile rose in her throat, a burning acid. The trees were soldiers, towering above her, looking down in apathy. They'd seen so much, too much. They couldn't help and wouldn't even if they were able. Because the world turns, impassive, even as we all run wild, ripping the place and each other to pieces. We will destroy ourselves, and it will still turn at the same pace, and the seasons will come and go, not missing us at all.

Then Finley was kneeling on the ground, her chest aching. An anger welled in her, something so powerful and ancient that it barely fit in her tiny body. She looked down to see the bloody pulp of a woman's ruined face. It was a hideous mash, the skull had taken on an unnatural shape, like a deflating balloon. And in her hand she felt the greasy heft of a flashlight that was covered with blood.

She heard what she thought was the high call of a hawk and then realized it was her own primal keening.

TWENTY

Momma cried the whole way home; she always did. They walked the long miles back with her sobbing. She seemed to drag herself, moved so slowly. Even so, Penny was trailing behind, her bad foot aching, and she was so, so tired. If she lay down on the ground, she knew she'd fall asleep. And maybe the snow would cover her like a blanket and she would sleep and dream of home.

She'd always had dreams. Dreams so vivid and real that it was impossible to tell whether she was awake or asleep. Some dreams were fuzzy and strange, and she knew it wasn't real. But some of them, like the dreams she had about Zoe, where it was bright as daylight and there was scent and sound, were as real as anything that happened during the day. And she would ask herself, Is this real? She didn't know the answer.

Zoe was the little girl who used to sleep under her bed. Penny told her mommy about Zoe, even though she knew her mommy couldn't see Zoe. She overheard her parents talking about her imaginary friend. Mommy was a little worried, and Daddy thought it was normal. *I like Zoe better than any of her other bratty little friends*, Daddy said, which made Mommy laugh a little. Penny liked her better, too.

Penny had never had a friend as fun and funny, as easy as Zoe, who always just wanted to do what Penny wanted to do and never argued. Play dates with her other friends often ended in tears or hurt feelings or the idea that there wouldn't be another play date—and everyone usually acted as though it was her fault. But Zoe was always content to just be with Penny, and there was something nice about that.

One day, in one of Penny's dreams, she and Zoe were playing in the playground in Washington Square Park where Penny always used to go with her daddy. And while they were on the swings, Zoe said that it was time for her to go home. Not home, not back to her family—it was time for her to *go on*.

"To the next place," said Zoe.

"Where's that?" Penny asked, even though she already knew, sort of.

"Before and after," said Zoe. "The place we are before we're here and the place we go after."

"Are you scared?" asked Penny. Penny was scared just thinking about it. Where *had* she come from, and where *did* people go when they died? All the other questions had answers. Not that one. Not her parents. Not even on Google. *Nobody knows the answer to that*, her daddy said. *Some people think they know. But they don't. It's one of life's grand mysteries.*

So everybody dies and no one knows what happens then? Penny had asked her father, disbelieving. It didn't seem right that there wouldn't be an answer to a question everybody had.

Her father took a moment to answer. *I guess that's right. But you don't have to worry about that for a long, long time. Let's get some gelato.*

"No," said Zoe, in answer to her question. "I'm not scared." She swung high and fast, the sky a dazzling blue and white above her, her red sneakers reaching for it. "Not anymore."

When Penny woke up and looked under her bed for Zoe, her friend was gone. And Penny knew that Zoe wouldn't be back. She wasn't sad, even though she knew she'd miss Zoe. And she wasn't scared anymore either.

The air had grown colder, and Penny's ankle had stopped aching in a way. It was more like a strange tingling, growing numb. She dropped back a bit, and Momma didn't seem to notice, so Penny dropped back a little farther. She looked around for Bobo, but he was gone. She hadn't seen him since the graveyard. Maybe he had gone back to the house. He didn't like the graveyard; she knew that. He didn't like it when Momma went to see Real Penny. The moon was hidden by clouds and the woods around her were just shadows, those black doorways that could be the way home, or the way to something even worse. She could hear the frantic and chaotic whispering of voices.

She dropped back a little more and watched as Momma turned the bend, lost in her own grief, certain that Penny was right behind her. It took a second for Penny to realize that she was alone. Momma was far ahead, and Bobo was nowhere to be seen. The voice was quiet. It had told her that she couldn't leave until she convinced Momma to let Real Penny go. It was the same voice that told her to show herself, and then the clean man got shot. Her mommy told her that she didn't have to listen to anyone except her family and her teachers, and the parents of her friends. The voice wasn't any of those.

Maybe it was one of those other voices—like those of people who told you to keep secrets from your mommy, or who told you they had candy or lost a puppy and could you help, or who wanted you to try something that was very bad for you but would make you feel good at first. Maybe the voice was one of those. How were you supposed to know the difference? *If there's a little noise inside you that tells you something is wrong or bad or that your mommy wouldn't like it, listen. That's called your instinct. Always follow your instincts.* There were too many voices. It was so much easier when your mommy or daddy just told you what to do.

Those tall, dark doorways, they called to her. What could the shadows hold that was worse than being chained in a room, alone, afraid, hurt? Were any monsters that lived in the woods worse than Poppa? The people she saw in the graveyard, they never hurt her. Zoe had not been afraid when it was her time to leave. And Real Penny wanted so badly to cross over that she begged her Momma to let go.

Penny moved slowly at first away from the footpath, waiting for Momma to come back. Then she moved a little faster, her heart a bird in the fragile cage of her chest. She had nothing—no water or food or even shoes. She didn't have a coat. *The most important step in survival happens long before you leave the comfort of your home*, her daddy had told her. *It's all in the preparations you make for your journey*.

Then she was in the trees. Then she was running, even though she was in pain. Something about the excitement of being away made everything hurt less, even the cold.

She had only made it a little way before she heard Momma screaming, her voice cutting through the night like the cry of a bird. Penny ran faster, rocks cutting at the bottoms of her feet and branches whipping at her face. But Penny didn't stop.

She remembered, her *body* remembered, that she was the fastest girl in her PE class. That all the other kids, even the boys, dropped behind her when she ran, huffing and puffing. She dug deep the way her coach had told her, even though she was weaker than she had ever been, not wearing the bright orange sneakers that her brother said looked like flames when she ran.

All around her the trees were monsters, reaching high up into the sky. The ground was damp, full of debris—rocks and sticks cutting at the soles of her feet.

Penny! Penny! Momma was calling a frantic, desperate wail. The ground was a downward slope beneath her, and she let gravity pull her, making her faster, even as she knocked into trees, sliver branches slicing at her face. Twice she almost tripped and fell to the ground.

Breathe! Her coach would yell, *let your breath carry you*.

Penny liked him. He talked to her like an athlete, someone who knew her body could do amazing things, if only she could just tap into the strength inside. If only she believed that she was made of wind and air and sky, that she could fly, that she was lighter, brighter, faster than everyone else unlucky enough to be made from bone and muscle and thick heavy blood inside their veins.

The whispers were all around her, laughing, crying, jeering, cheering, a million voices, all saying something different. Penny ran even though it seemed like Momma was getting closer. She could hear the old woman rushing through the branches, hear her screaming.

Penny! Penny! It was so desperate, so very sad.

But the girl kept running because that wasn't her name. It never had been. And now that she was free, she allowed the sound of her own name back into her head. Her name wasn't Penny.

And so she ran. And she would have run faster, gone downhill because that was the way to go, according to what her daddy had told her.

But then, ahead, she saw a bouncing light, small and round moving through the trees. What was it? Who was it? It was moving toward her, getting bigger. Momma was screeching and running behind her and the whispering in the trees was so loud and discordant, it filled her head.

She turned away from the light and slowed down, looking for a place to hide. She found the carved out hollow of a tree and tucked herself inside, deep into the wet, smelly wood. She was shivering—fear, exertion, cold. Footsteps, shuffling steps through the leaves. The beam of a flashlight glanced the tree in front of her; she squeezed herself far back into the hollow. Something with a lot of legs skittered across her bare foot, and she stifled a startled scream.

"New Penny." Just a whisper. "I'll help you get away from here. Where are you?"

Bobo. She stayed hidden. He couldn't be trusted, not really.

"I can hear your teeth chattering."

She clamped a hand over her mouth and realized that they had been chattering like a cartoon cold person's teeth. She never thought that really happened. Her whole body was quaking, an involuntary palsy of cold and fear. She held her breath, waiting, willing her body to be quiet, to not betray her with whimpers and sharply exhaled breaths. Then Bobo's face appeared in the opening of the tree, he shined his light onto her, and she covered her eyes against the beam.

"Come on," he said. "I know the way."

He put the flashlight on the ground and shifted off his jacket and held it out to her. It was denim with a fluffy lining, probably still warm from his body. And she was so cold. She reached for it, and as she did, he grabbed her arm, yanking her out onto the ground.

"Momma!" he yelled, his face lit with malicious glee. "Momma, she's here!"

"*Shut up*, Bobo," she said. She ran at him and started hitting hard, beating her fists at his chest and trying to cover his stupid mouth. But he just smiled, leaning back, and swatted her blows away as if he were swiping at gnats. Her little fists didn't hurt him.

"Momma!" he bayed again, the word filling the night.

She tried to run, but he grabbed her and threw her to the ground hard and then climbed on top of her, his weight on her chest so heavy that she could hardly breathe.

"Why are you helping her?" Penny hissed. "She doesn't *love* you."

Bobo's face was blank. "Yes, she does."

But she heard all the notes of uncertainty and despair. She knew things about Bobo, things he didn't tell, things she wasn't even sure he knew about himself. That's what it was like for her. She could look at a person and see what that person wanted her to see. But she could also see what squirmed beneath the surface, raw and pink. Like when her mommy sounded angry and was using her stern voice, but she was really just tired. Or when Sophia at school acted like she knew better than anyone, but was really just afraid that no one liked her and had to prove she was smart so that no one would make fun of her. Or how her brother pretended not to like sports but was really just ashamed of being a little clumsy, so he stuck with the things he *knew* he was good at, even though he secretly wanted to play soccer. All the layers were exposed to her, always had been.

"No," she said. Cruelty was the only weapon she had now; she had no choice but to wield it. "She *doesn't*. If she *did*, she wouldn't spend all her time in the graveyard trying to talk to your dead sister."

"Shut your *stupid face*," he said, his eyebrows wiggling with sadness. "I'll let them put you with the other Pennys, the *bad* Pennys."

She saw a hole, then, a deep pit with no bottom. It was in a cave, with a high rocky ceiling. There was an old light burning. Where was it? It was a dream and a memory, but neither of those things. Then it was gone, and she was back in the woods with Bobo. A space opened inside her. A cold, deep abyss of fear emptied her out until she was one with the night and the cold. She went quiet, all her power, all her speed, all her strength leaving her. That was why, she knew with a clarity she didn't quite understand. That *hole* was why they had all been brought here. Not for Momma. Not for Real Penny. The girls that had come before her, they would never go home, and neither would she. They would all disappear into the maw where the voice lived, and they would be there forever.

But this is your home. It always has been.

"Don't," she whispered. And Bobo looked down at her, seeing her, she thought, for the first time. Not New Penny. "Please. I don't belong here."

"Where? *Where?*" Momma yelled. "I can't see you."

He waved the flashlight in the air, and she heard Momma moving toward them, clumsy, stumbling through the trees and debris.

"She's here!" he yelled. "She tried to get away, but I caught her."

A lash of anger and some of her power came back. She couldn't beg him. He wasn't going to help her. He was like a beaten dog, slinking after his master. Never to be trusted.

"Penny was the smart one, the beautiful one," she said. "She rode horses and did well in school. When she died, Momma died, too. There was no love for you. She never loved you because you're ugly and stupid. Who could *ever* love you?"

Bobo didn't say anything. He just looked so sad that she almost took it back.

"Let me go," she said. "Bobo isn't even your name, is it? It's what Penny called you. What's your real name?"

"Arthur," said Bobo softly. She picked up on the note of pride, used it.

"That's a nice name," she said, thinking quickly. "It's a king's name. King Arthur and the Knights of the Round Table. Do you know that story?"

He shook his head. Of course, he didn't. But he was listening. "Arthur was a king and he lived in a huge castle with a beautiful wife. And everyone loved him."

"And he was strong and brave?"

"Definitely," she said. "Just like you."

He smiled a little at that, climbed off of her. He was a little boy in a big boy's body. Just like her little cousin Jared, who was a wild toddler prone to tantrums. She could always talk him out of it, just by listening and figuring out what he wanted. He had a hard time making himself understood, and then he'd just go crazy because none of the adults around knew what he wanted. Somehow she always knew.

"Let me go," she said. "Come with me. We can both leave here. You won't have to work all day and hunt for Poppa. I know you don't like to kill the animals. I'll take care of you."

Momma came through the trees, looking haggard and terrified. She washed over with relief when she saw them. But then anger set her features into a tight fist. Her long gray hair was pulled back into a tight ponytail, and she wore a barn jacket that was frayed and dirty, jeans that were too big, and thick boots. Her face was a landscape of lines and grooves. A hideous storybook witch, a crone.

"Bring her back," Momma said, in that stony voice she had. "You're a bad girl, Penny. You scared your momma."

Bobo stood and yanked her to her feet, his grip an icy garrote.

Something big welled up from inside her, a sob of rage. "My name is *not Penny*," she shrieked. All the fear and rage that she'd kept buried exploded. "Penny *is dead*."

Bobo stared, wide-eyed with surprise.

"Penny can't find peace until you let her go," she yelled. Her voice was so loud, and all the other sounds around them, even that strange whispering went quiet. "She's trapped here even though she doesn't want to be because you *won't let her pass*."

People always thought that the dead haunted the living, but she knew now that sometimes it was the other way around.

Momma stood, white and stiff, her hands clenched into hard fists. Bobo still held Abbey tight, though she struggled now, trying to get free as Momma moved closer.

Momma drew her hand back and slapped Penny hard across the face, then drew back her hands to her mouth. Penny saw stars, felt the hot sting on her face, the ache in her jaw.

"I'm sorry, Penny," said Momma. "I'm so sorry."

Sheer hatred pumped through her. She spoke slowly but loudly, some blood spilling from her mouth warm and salty. "I'm. Not. Penny. And I want to go home."

Momma stared at her and long moments passed. Still the air around them was blissfully silent, until she started struggling against Bobo's strong hug.

"Put her with the others," Momma said to Bobo.

"Momma," said Bobo, pleading.

But Momma started to walk away. "I won't do it, Momma," said Bobo. "I don't want to."

Momma stopped in her tracks and turned around, her face ugly with anger.

"She doesn't love you," the girl said, rage pulsing. It was so big, so monstrous, like it couldn't fit in her body. She didn't even recognize the sound of her own voice. "She never did. She only loves Penny. You don't have to do what she tells you."

Momma moved in close to them, and Bobo shifted away, still holding on tight to her. She tried to drop her weight so that she could slip out of his arms, but still he held her, his grip strong as chains.

Then Momma had sandpaper hands on her wrists and started pulling. "Give her to me," she said, yanking her away from Bobo.

She dropped to her knees, and Momma, with her tireless, sinewy strength dragged her across the ground while Penny screamed and fought, using every ounce of power she had in her. *Digdeepdigdeep.*

It happened so swiftly, the shift of shadows. Penny wasn't even sure what she was seeing at first. Momma seemed to freeze, stunned. Her arm dropped like a doll's arm, falling limply to her side. Bobo held the flashlight aloft, the lens turned red with blood. He brought it down again, hitting Momma with a revolting crack across the head. Her head snapped to the right with the blow. It was almost comical, like cartoon violence. Then the old woman dropped to the ground, slumping into a stiff-legged seat. Bobo moved in fast knocking her flat. Then he sat astride her, hitting and hitting again.

An inhuman sound escaped him, a horrible wail of rage and misery.

Moooommmaaa!

The girl—not Penny—lay still, staring, her heart hammering. Then she got up and ran. She didn't even notice that it had started to snow.

TWENTY-ONE

Rainer could tell, just by the way she got out of bed, that Finley wasn't quite awake. Awake, she moved quickly, walked so fast that he almost couldn't keep up with her, all her movements purposeful and swift. But when she was like this, she moved slowly and deliberately. She sat up, her white skin glowing.

"Fin?" he said.

She stood naked, the perfect curves of her body painted from the light washing in through the curtain from out in the shop. In the darkness, he couldn't see the art on her skin, just her dark silhouette. She dressed, and he watched as he quietly pulled on his own clothes.

"I'm coming with you," he told her.

"Okay," she said easily.

That was the other thing. When she was like this, she never argued. If she'd been awake, she would have told him that it was time for her to go. And if he tried to stop her or go with her, she'd get mad. Tell him that he was trying to control her, not respecting her boundaries, being a Neanderthal. He didn't get it. Did girls want you to take care of them and protect them, or not? *Girls want what they want in the moment,* his dad always said. *The next moment they want something else. You just have to give it to them and not ask too many questions. That's the trick to getting along with the ladies.* So far, Rainer hadn't seen anything that proved his father wrong. *"All right, baby, whatever you say." That phrase right there is the key to my successful marriage.* Rainer's parents, unlike the parents of most of his friends, had been happily married for thirty years. So there must be something to that.

Rainer had first seen Finley in high school detention, though he'd heard about her before that. Freaky Finley they called her. Or Finley Firestarter. He wasn't sure why she had those names. But there *was* something different about her, those dark, bottomless eyes, that cool half-smile she wore, like she was in on a joke that no one else was getting. Rainer didn't believe in love at first sight—until he saw Finley.

Her hair was longer then, an impossibly thick jet-black mop around her shoulders. She didn't have any ink, just a row of piercings in her right ear. It wasn't anything physical: not her snowy skin, or the perfect curve of her ass, or the beautiful swell of her breasts. Something about her called away a piece of him, and it floated through the air and she breathed it in, and it was forever lost to her. Loving her was like trying to get that piece of himself back, a deliciously pleasant, totally lost cause.

"Miss Montgomery," said Mrs. Patchett that day. The gym teacher was affectionately known among the badly behaved of Roosevelt High School as Miz Hatchet. "What are we in for today?"

"Tardiness," said Finley quietly. A couple of the girls in the front row laughed. Even among the misfits, she was a misfit.

"Take a seat," said Miz Hatchet. "No phones, music, video or e-books. Homework only. Or quiet reflection on what brought you here in the first place. In your case, tardiness. You might do some thinking about what your being late means to others."

Rainer watched Finley walk up the aisle, a big pack over her shoulder, a notebook clutched to her chest, willing her to sit where he could watch her. She picked the seat over by the window, took out her notebook and textbook and proceeded to do what looked like algebra homework. The rest of the losers just sat, staring outside or discreetly texting each other. Miz Hatchet pretended not to notice, staring at her own phone.

School motto: *What I am to be, I am now becoming.* Rainer wasn't sure what that meant. It sounded more like a threat than a promise. He was in detention for smoking out behind the gym when he should have been in class—but every week it was something else.

Last week it was for arguing with a teacher. The week before he'd smashed a locker, pissed about something. A typical (for him) bad temper moment, where everything just crowded in on him and he needed to bust out of it all. What had he been mad about? A test he'd failed even though he'd studied hard? A comment that annoyed him? Someone knocking into him in the hallway? He honestly didn't even remember.

He was failing or barely passing every class, except for art. The only thing he cared about was ink, helping his dad with his gigs at night (unloading and setting up equipment, then taking it down again and partying in the meantime), getting laid by the band groupies (who would have thought a middle-aged Aerosmith cover band would have young, hot groupies?), scoring the occasional joint. He wasn't sure whether a high school diploma was going to be of much use to someone like him. He already made more with his dad than most people made working some shit nine-to-five job, and his apprenticeship at the tattoo shop was nearly done. And then he could make some real money, once he had his own clients. Would it matter that he was getting a D in algebra?

He'd thought about just getting his GED. But his dad wanted him to stay in school, said dropping out was the biggest mistake he ever made. So Rainer agreed to try to graduate. *Don't just graduate, son. Learn something.*

Rainer couldn't keep his eyes off of her that first day. He wondered how it was that he'd never seen her before—but of course they were in different classes, and he cut as much as he came to school. He had his sketchbook out and abandoned his drawing to try to get her profile—fine, high cheekbones, a cute little upturn to her nose. Big doe eyes, moppy black hair. She was like an anime princess. He found himself thinking impure thoughts. Then she turned and looked at him, right through him, as though she knew everything in his head. She smiled, a very bad girl, but still kind of a sweet little smile.

He looked away, but her spell was cast. That was four years ago. She was in him, under his skin—even when she tried to leave him, he couldn't let her go. Even though he figured that she was probably better off without him, he still followed her.

That's not love, she told him. *That's control. Different things, Rain. Really different.*

Now, she was moving toward the door, taking her jacket off the hook. Where was she going tonight? He'd followed her all sorts of places when she was like this.

"I'll drive," he told her.

"Okay," she said.

Outside, a light snow had started to fall. It was too early for that, wasn't it? He'd seen the news, a big storm coming. But he thought it was the usual hype. And truly it didn't look like much.

"Where are we going?" he asked. The engine rumbled to life. He was always a little amazed when it did.

"To the lake house," she said. Her voice was dreamy, her eyes blank. She wasn't sleepwalking, not quite.

"Where's that?" he asked gently.

"Drive out of town," she said. "North toward the mountains."

He did what she said, turned when she told him to turn, and finally they came upon a sign that said CLARABEL'S LAKE HOUSE.

"Turn here," she said.

He took the long drive and wound up before a dark house. No lights on inside or out. She climbed out of the car and moved purposefully around back. He followed, shivering in his tee-shirt and light jacket. She moved past the dock and up a small path until they were at a trailhead.

"He took her up this way."

Rainer knew that this had something to do with the case she was working on with Jones Cooper, the maps she'd shown him that night, the mines he hadn't wanted her to visit. Eloise and Cooper might have talked sense into Finley's *brain*. But whoever was she when she was like this? That chick didn't listen to *anyone*.

"Are you sure?" he asked.

She started walking.

"Finley," he said. It was so dark, unnaturally quiet for a city boy.

216

It made him laugh that people were always so afraid of big cities. These quiet rural places where no one was around to hear you scream? These were the places that gave Rainer the creeps. Anyone, anything could be lurking in those woods. "Let's get someone. This isn't safe."

He didn't really expect her to listen. She was already moving fast. He lingered, took his phone from his pocket. The signal was weak. They didn't have any food or water. They weren't dressed warmly enough, and the snow was still falling, heavier now.

"Do you hear it?" she asked from up ahead.

"No," he said.

He never heard what Finley heard or saw what she saw. Only when he drew for her body did he get pictures sometimes, things he saw as vividly as if he were watching it on a screen. People like The Three Sisters or the boy with the train. But he suspected that it had to do with her and not with him, some kind of vibe she was shooting off. He wasn't like her. If there was something more to the world than what he could see with his eyes, he'd never experienced it. Dreams that came true; people that weren't there; sounds that no one could hear? No. He'd dropped acid a couple of times, but even those hallucinations were tame and meaningless.

"Fin," he said. He'd lost sight of her, so he jogged a little until he came around the bend and saw her slight shadow up ahead.

Then he *did* hear something, some kind of distant wailing. All the hair came up on the back of his neck, his arms. Was it an animal? A person? Shit.

"Finley," he yelled. He had to run now to catch up with her. When he did, he grabbed hold of her arm. She stopped and turned to him, but her eyes were blank.

"Let's go back," he said. "We'll go get that guy Cooper. Or the cops."

He heard it again, the distant wailing.

"You go," she said and tugged her arm back, kept walking.

Rainer stood. He should go back; he knew that. He should get Eloise or Cooper, or even the police. Or he should pick Finley up and carry her back. She was no match for him physically; he could easily pick her up and throw her over his shoulder and carry her back to the car, even kicking and screaming. But he didn't do any of those things. He did what he always did when Finley took off. Into the dark, with the snowfall growing heavier, he followed. He couldn't be sure, but he thought he heard the faint sound of laughter.

PART TWO

ANGELS IN
THE SNOW

You cannot hide in snow
No matter where you go
You leave a trail behind
That anyone can find.

—Anonymous

Your vision will become clear only when you can look
into your own heart. Who looks outside, dreams; Who
looks inside, awakes.

—Carl Jung

*S*now falls on The Hollows, a silent silver glitter through the starless night, resting on trees, coating roofs, dusting the ground. The wind whispers through the branches and the temperature drops. Where water was, ice forms. Winter has arrived, bringing death with it. Everything green and bright will fade to brown, then rot to black, then return to the earth as all things must.

The Hollows sleeps; houses are dark and shops are closed. Most people are tucked into bed, dreaming. But out deep in the woods, a girl, small and barefoot runs through the trees. No one can hear her, and no one knows where she is. Except the boy who follows her, wailing for his lost mother who lies still and lifeless far behind them both.

Another girl with hot-pink hair and pictures on her skin kneels over the dead woman, getting blood on her hands, her clothes. A young man stands beside her, watching, saying that they have to go, that they need help and can't go on alone. It's too cold; they're lost, and the phone isn't working. They have to go back the way they came and find help.

Wake up, Finley, he says, pulling at her. But she can't hear him.

Off in the trees, he hears something, the sound of a little girl crying. He follows the sound.

Who's there? he calls. "Hello?"

The darkness swallows him. And the girl with the pictures on her skin doesn't notice, because she is there and not there.

A truck drives up the rural road from town. The man who drives it is as much a part of this place as anyone. His bones are as old as the trees, grown from this place, roots dug deep. He has lived here all his life, like his *father before him, and his father's father and so on. He will never leave, and when he dies, his body will become one with the ground. He will be part of The Hollows forever. He will be a blade of grass, a knot in the trunk of an old oak, the blossom on a flower. What he is in life matters little to The Hollows, which never judges its children.*

Outside of town, Eloise Montgomery stirs in her sleep, troubled. Maybe it's the wind moaning through the eaves, or The Whispers in the trees telling her that something is not right. In her yard, the oldest oak in The Hollows grows. Its branches reach high up into the sky, its roots dig deep, deep into the earth, burrowing, fingers taking hold. The leaves that were fresh and bright green in the summer have turned from gold to brown and fallen from the branches. What hasn't been raked away returns to the ground. Even as the death of winter comes to The Hollows, already it is that much closer to the rebirth of spring.

She wakes up with a start and sits up in bed, listening. She walks from her bedroom and moves down the hall. Standing at the doorway to her granddaughter's bedroom, she heaves a long worried sigh when she finds it empty. She hesitates, then goes back to her own room and starts to dress, pulling on warm clothes and heavy boots. Downstairs, she dons a coat and scarf. She stands a moment in the hallway, as if considering her actions. From the table by the window, she picks up a photograph and looks at it for a long time. Then she puts it down and walks out the door, careful on the slick porch, taking mincing steps up the snowy walk to her waiting car. She climbs inside and starts the engine, even though she doesn't like driving in bad weather. She doesn't see well in the dark anymore, and the going will be slow.

Off the main square, Jones Cooper gets out of bed and gets dressed, quietly so as not to awaken his wife. Sleep, which never comes easily to him, has eluded him altogether. He walks quietly down the stairs to the kitchen, where his files are spread out on the long table. The biggest part of him doesn't believe in psychics or visions, or anything beyond what he can see or touch. He is a man whose feet rest solidly on the earth. He knows, however, that there are no secrets in The Hollows. And if you just look hard enough at the facts, you will find the trail of evidence that leads you to the truth, no matter how ugly.

TWENTY-TWO

Run, Abbey! Run! The day was clarion blue and cool, the trees in Van Cortlandt Park a fire show of color. Abbey's track team was racing against Riverdale Country Day School. And they were all there together—Wolf, Merri, and Jackson—to cheer their girl on. It was one of those rare moments when everything was right. Where how they looked from the outside—happy, successful, intact—was how they felt on the inside. The air was clean, the wild chorus of voices cheering and shouting, lifting up high.

And the girls! So young and leggy! With focus and determination beyond their years, huddled together, whispering seriously to each other, sizing up the competition. Most of them didn't know how beautiful they were, certainly not Abbey, who wouldn't even comb her own hair if Merri didn't daily chase her down with the brush.

What amazed Merri about her children, both of them but maybe especially Abbey, was how self-possessed they were. Abbey and Jackson were both strong-minded, full of their own ideas and not afraid to put voice or action to those ideas. Where Jackson had said definitely no to sports, opting instead for Young Scientists' Club and Chinese, Abbey wanted to run; she came to Merri and told her so. Prior to that it had always been Merri suggesting—piano, ballet, horseback riding? All of which Abbey had gamely tried, quickly losing interest.

"I want to join the track team," she told Merri after school one day. "Coach says I'm fast."

"Oh," Merri had said, surprised. Competitive sports? Really? She'd dodged the soccer bullet with Jackson, who would rather take out an eye than participate in sports. He was a creature of the mind. Abbey was more physical.

Wolf wanted to know: "Does that mean we're going to be standing around on fields every Saturday? Driving all over the state if she's any good?"

"I suppose," said Merri, equally unenthusiastic about the prospect.

"All right then," he assented.

Whatever their differences in parenting styles, they were both on the same page when it came to supporting the kids. They were not into *pushing* extracurricular activities. (They were not *those* parents. They had no illusions, weren't thinking that their kids were going to win sports scholarships like *everyone* seemed to think no matter how middling the talents of their offspring.) But they were always present for what Abbey and Jackson wanted to do. That was their job, they figured, more than anything else, just to be there. A job at which they'd ultimately failed.

And so they found themselves at Abbey's first meet. Merri watched with fascination as her beautiful, lithe, and yes, *super*-fast daughter left everyone in the dust that her neon pink sneakers kicked up.

"Oh, shit," said Wolf, watching as Abbey sped by, jaw dropping. "She's amazing."

"Wow," said Jackson, looking up from the book he was reading. "She's *really* fast."

And Merri watched with the terrible mingle of pride and love and fear and sadness that was motherhood. As that girl raced past them, her family cheering from the sidelines Abbey was just Abbey. Not their daughter, their baby, not Jackson's little sister, not *just* those things. She was all herself. Merri remembered Abbey's plump little fingers, how they would grab for Merri's face and hair, how hot they always were. Now those long, thin fingers interlaced with Merri's. But one day, Abbey wouldn't need or want to hold hands anymore. And still Merri cheered like crazy, because Abbey *was* awesome.

That day was perfect, blue and crisp. They were so happy. *Maybe we've turned a corner*, Merri thought. She was in denial about the pills still that day, not even acknowledging that she was still taking them even though her knee no longer really hurt. It wasn't even a thought in her head. Things had been better with Wolf, or so she believed. And the kids were happy and healthy.

Run, Abbey! Go, Abbey!

Merri woke with a start, the happiness of her dream memory lingering. She grasped at it, but it faded away, blue draining to black. Joy replaced with a heart-pumping unease, those words hanging on the edge of her consciousness. *Run, Abbey!*

She reached over for the phone to check the time and saw that Wolf had texted her. She must have been so soundly asleep that she hadn't heard.

I'm coming up. Don't bother saying no.

She felt a mingling of relief and annoyance. They were joined together, wrapped around each other whether they always liked it or not. There was too much history, the children, shared investments, joint property. The very idea of legal divorce was as enervating as it was heartbreaking. It was one thing to drift like she was doing, neither here nor there. It was another thing altogether to bring the axe down on everything they shared, splitting it cleanly in half. Of course, nothing like that was ever clean.

It was midnight.

She picked up the phone and dialed. He answered after one ring, as if he had been waiting for her to call.

"Hey," he said. Merri could hear Claire's voice in the background. He answered her gently. "It's Merri."

Is she all right? "Are you okay?" he asked, echoing his wife's question.

"Yes," she said. "I don't know."

"She's okay," he said.

Merri listened to the covers rustling, heard their bedroom door close. She could envision their apartment as clearly as she could bring to mind her own. She could see the runner on the hardwood floor, the night light glow from the chaos of the girls' room. He probably walked into the gourmet kitchen, the white door swinging.

"What's happened?" he asked.

"Nothing," she said. The sound of his voice calmed her. "No news. I'm sorry. I was just dreaming of Abbey."

He breathed on the line, and she could see him. He'd be hunched over the phone, leaning against the counter, his brow wrinkled with worry. He'd be wearing a tee-shirt, some kind of flannel pajama bottom. Not like Wolf, who always insisted on sleeping naked. *It's the only time I'm ever free*, he'd say. *What if someone breaks in? What if there's a fire?* Merri wanted to know. That he could allow himself to be so vulnerable always annoyed her.

Blake had never touched her except as a friend—a warm embrace, a kiss on the cheek. The night they met didn't hover between them, not really. There was no wondering: *what if?* It simply didn't matter. The currents of their lives had swept them along parallel paths, close but never to touch. Neither of them could ever be unfaithful, even if they wanted to—which they didn't. Now there was friendship, deep and abiding. Somehow that was more solid than anything else in her life.

"I saw Wolf tonight," said Blake. "He's a wreck."

"He's coming up here," she said.

"Good," he said. He had a kind of relief in his voice, a tone he got when Wolf managed to do the right thing. "He should. You shouldn't be up there alone."

The wind was wailing outside, and Merri pushed back the covers to walk over the creaky floor to the window.

"It's snowing," she said, peering through the curtain. The streetlamp across the road gave off a weak amber light, the flakes glittering as they fell. The sight of it filled her with dread. *Abbey*. The second winter.

"He asked me about that missing real estate developer," said Blake. This surprised Merri. It wasn't like him to indulge Jackson that way.

"Jackson told me about it, too," Merri said.

"Well, apparently the guy had some kind of chip in his car put there by the leasing company. It's a new technology, allows them to locate and even disable the vehicle in the event that someone doesn't make their payment."

She didn't quite know why, but she felt a little lift, a rush of hope. It was ridiculous to think this had anything to do with Abbey.

"When I got home, I made some calls," he said. "I was debating whether to call Wolf or not. It's probably nothing."

"What is?"

"The leasing company released the GPS coordinates, and local police are mobilizing, probably as we speak if they're not up there already."

"Where?"

"About twenty miles north of The Hollows."

"Do you have the coordinates?"

"Merri," he said. "This probably has nothing to do with Abbey."

"I know that," she said. And she *did* know that. But then why was her whole body tingling? And why had she hired a psychic? And why had Abbey been dreaming about a monster in the woods? And why did Jackson know that something bad was going to happen that day? And why was he obsessed about the missing developer?

She thought about those pills all the time. She was thinking about them even now as she pulled on her jeans and her boots, her long-sleeve tee-shirt, and fleece, putting the phone on speaker and setting it down on the desk. Those pills that dulled her fears and her anxieties, that numbed her anger at Wolf and at herself, that quieted all the million shitty things she had to say about herself. Those pills, and the white sheet it draped over her ragged thoughts. If she had them, if she popped two in her mouth right now, in an hour she'd be sleeping or at least lying down, knowing that there was nothing she could do for Abbey, wherever she was. But she didn't have those pills. All she had was this vibrating feeling that wouldn't be quieted.

"What are they, Blake?"

"If I tell you, do you promise not to do anything reckless?"

She thought about it. They were too close, their friendship too strong for her to lie. "No," she said.

He told her anyway.

The first time Wolf did it, it was a big nothing. Honestly, it was little more than an embellishment. Everybody did that; it was part of being a storyteller, wasn't it? Your interviewee was somewhat *less* articulate than you might have hoped. You rearrange sentences so that they come closer to what the moron actually meant, so that the words on the page have more impact. It wasn't lying, not really.

It was a piece about New Orleans after Katrina, how the city was struggling back to its feet. The article he wrote wasn't even for a major publication, just an online travel blog called The Road Less Traveled. Wolf liked writing for them because they were light editors. They basically proofed his pieces and posted them. They paid peanuts, but the trips were always covered—air and ground transportation, and decent lodging—and they weren't looking for the kind of fluff that trade magazines wanted. Sure, those trade assignments were plum, all expenses paid trips to spas and resorts, guided excursions, luxury treatments. It was unspoken, but it was expected that the articles written after such star treatment be complimentary. Otherwise, you no longer got invited on press trips. But there wasn't much negative to say about five-star luxury, was there? The scallops were a little chewy? The massage therapist didn't use enough oil?

What Wolf liked about the smaller publication was that they let you do your own thing. The Road Less Traveled let him wander and *find* the article he wanted to write about a certain place. They sent him down to Jazz Fest a few years after Katrina. Attendance was back up, and though the city was still struggling, the music scene was making a healthy recovery. He talked to artists, music lovers, and bar owners, everyone echoing the same sentiment, that New Orleans was coming back, and that the music scene was alive and kicking. It's just that no one really said that *exactly*. So he just fudged something an old trombone player said. Most of the people who Wolf talked to had been drinking; hell, he'd been drinking. So what if the old guy didn't say exactly what Wolf wrote?

The only person who picked up on it was Merri.

"He really said this?" she asked when she was editing the piece. She read all his work, and he didn't feel good about anything until she liked it.

"Who said what?" he asked, even though he knew exactly what she was talking about. Merri had an eagle eye. She missed nothing.

"This quote: 'It's been hard, no one's denying that. But New Orleans is back, better than before. You can't crush the soul of a place like this.' "

"Why?" asked Wolf.

"It's just such a perfect quote, such a great way to end a story."

"Sometimes you just get lucky."

The guy *had* said *something* like that. But it had been somewhat less eloquent. What did it matter if you made people sound better than they actually did? No one ever complained about that.

Then, over the years, it just started to become a habit. You kind of knew what people were going to say, didn't you? After you'd been to enough places and talked to enough people and seen enough things, you had an idea of what you were going to find before you ever got where you were going. Nearly twenty years as a travel writer, and real surprises came few and far between. Except he *was* surprised when he finally got caught.

After he texted Merri, Wolf woke up his mother and told her that he had to go help his wife. She agreed completely and even seemed relieved to hear it.

Then Wolf pushed into Jackson's room and found him awake. As ever, the kid's room was weirdly neat. Jackson kept all his books organized by size on the shelves. He'd laid out his own clothes for the next day. Wolf didn't even bother asking whether or not he did his homework. He was a perfect student.

"You're going up there?" said Jackson when Wolf sat on his bed.

"I have to, buddy," he said. "Your mom shouldn't have to go through this alone."

"Can I come?"

"Maybe on the weekend, okay?" said Wolf. "But what I need you to do is to stay with your grandparents and go to school. We can talk every afternoon and you can call when you need me."

Jackson was such a trouper. Wolf remembered being his age; he'd never been half as smart or kind or mature as his son. He still wasn't.

"Do you think you can find her?" asked Jackson. He sat up and put on his glasses. He was a towheaded Harry Potter, his face a beautiful, delicate mask of hope and still, even after everything, innocence. He still believed in happy endings.

But the answer was no. Wolf felt with his whole heart that Abbey was gone; he didn't feel her, not the way Merri claimed to. He knew what the odds were of finding Abbey alive. The truth was, he wasn't going to The Hollows for Abbey. He was going because he needed to be there when Merri realized, too, that their daughter was dead. That someone had taken her because Wolf had failed as her father, her protector, and she wasn't coming back. He had given up on happy surprises long ago.

"I don't know, kiddo," he said. "We're going to try."

"Did you ask Uncle Blake about the missing man?"

"I did," said Wolf. "He's looking into it."

Jackson released a breath and looked up at his father. "Okay."

"Grandma will take you to school in the morning," said Wolf. "And she'll pick you up, too. I'll call you in the afternoon."

"You're going now?" Jackson glanced at his clock. It was nearly midnight.

"I don't want your mom to be alone up there."

Jackson nodded, seeming more relieved than anxious or upset as Wolf expected—which Wolf took as a positive sign that he'd made a good choice. He tried not to think about the fact that both his mother and his son had the same reaction, as if everyone was silently hoping that he'd do the right thing for once.

He threw a few things in a bag and was on his way out the front door by twelve thirty. He was surprised, though he really shouldn't have been, to see Kristi standing outside the building.

"What are you doing here?" he asked.

He knew he sounded cold, but he didn't have time for this, for her. Her face was blotchy from crying, her mascara running. It didn't soften him.

"What?" he went on when she didn't say anything. "Were you going to ring the bell—with my parents and my son up there?"

Something in her face shifted from hurt and vulnerable to angry.

"This is what you think of me," she said lifting up her phone, presumably to show him the text he'd sent. The street was quiet the way TriBeCa was at night. It was more of a residential neighborhood, and lights were dark, streets felt empty. It didn't throb and pulse like the rest of the city. Her voice echoed in the emptiness. "You think you can just send me a text and that's it. I just disappear like I never existed."

He couldn't stand the sight of her. For the first time, he saw her for what she was, the bleach-blonde embodiment of all of Wolf's failures and mistakes. His throat was thick; he had no words.

"Why are you looking at me like that?" she asked. "Like I'm something you can't scrape off of your shoe?"

They'd met at a press party. She was the publicist for a luxury hotel group and was hosting an event at their new Manhattan property on the stunning rooftop bar.

She'd been wearing a shift with sequins glittering on the front. He saw her when he first walked in; she'd greeted him at the door, looked at him with big eyes.

"You're Wolf Gleason," she said. "I love your work!"

She was just—shiny. Dress, nails, lips, eyes. Everything sparkled. Merri didn't exactly sparkle anymore, certainly not for Wolf. Lately, it seemed like his wife only noticed him when she was mad about something he'd neglected to do. Mostly they just fought and shuttled the kids back and forth to school, and worked, and stood around on fields or sat in small chairs at parent-teacher conferences. In fact, there was very little *sparkle* in midlife, it seemed to Wolf. That was maybe, more than anything, what had attracted him to Kristi—that she wasn't *everything else*. Of course, nothing sparkles forever.

"Why did you tell me about that place?" he asked now. He'd been wondering about it for a long time, could never bring himself to ask. He didn't even want to remember that it had been Kristi who first told him about The Hollows.

She blinked, confused. "What *place*?"

"The Hollows."

She blew out a breath of disdain, rubbed a hand to her forehead. "*Not* so that you would take your *family* up there on a *fucking vacation*."

Her voice had come up an octave, and a woman walking down the sidewalk on the street turned and stared, then kept moving.

"Then why?"

She shook her head, gave him the look that women always seemed to give him sooner or later—angry, disappointed, tired.

"You don't even remember, do you?" she said. Not really a question. "Because that's where I'm *from*. I was trying to tell you about myself. But you never heard that, because you never gave a shit who I was, or am, or what I wanted."

Had she told him that? She was right: he didn't remember. He never listened when she talked, kind of like the kids who tended to prattle on about nothing, some video game or drama with friends. *They know when you're not listening*, Merri had chided a million times. *We all do*.

Somehow, the name of that town had rattled around in his head until he Googled it when Merri said she wanted to spend a week "upstate." They were considering buying a country house—or he was. Thinking it might be fun to check it out for a week, he searched around and found a *New York Times* piece "36 Hours in The Hollows" Pick apples at the Old Cider Mill; wander miles of gentle nature trails; breakfast at The Egg and Yolk; take an iron mine tour with a local guide and learn some history, yadda yadda.

Wolf went to VRBO and impulsively rented Clarabel's Lake House. It all happened inside an hour, none of the usual back and forth between him and Merri—should we, shouldn't we, can we get away, aren't we spending too much money? In fact, he didn't even ask until after he'd booked it. She was happy enough about it, though. He remembered feeling like it was meant to be, the perfect getaway. And did they ever need it.

Merri had been trying to wean herself off the pain pills she'd been prescribed for her knee surgery a year ago and was *still* taking. They figured she had the mettle to cut back until she could go cold turkey; and she claimed that she'd been doing that, cutting back. She'd planned to stop taking them altogether when they were away. (He had no idea that she'd brought a bottle with her, just in case. On the day Abbey disappeared, she'd taken three Vicodin before noon.)

Wolf himself was still reeling from having his piece pulled from *Outside* magazine. The editor was a good friend of his, so things had been handled delicately. *Some of your quotes can't be verified; sources can't be reached. Why don't you get me those contacts, and maybe we can reschedule the piece?*

They needed a rest. The Hollows seemed like the perfect place to go to get some distance, some perspective. They'd come back refreshed, renewed—Merri would be well, he'd break up with Kristi, talk his way out of the *Outside* magazine thing. Everything was going to be fine. That's how he felt as they loaded up the Range Rover and headed upstate.

But he hadn't even been up there a full afternoon before the place—the kids and all their incessant whining and complaining and Merri's aura of enduring yet another thing that Wolf wanted to do and she didn't—started closing in around him. He was suffocating before they even got to the lake house. The town—with all its precious (overpriced: *Christ*, it wasn't SoHo!) shops and mediocre coffeehouse, and allegedly farm-fresh ice cream parlor—fell short of his expectations. He thought it would be somehow *more*. In fact, what was suffocating was that he thought all of it—his life, his marriage, his kids, *vacations*—should somehow be more. He had these grand visions of what things *should be* and it was never that.

Life is not a travel magazine article, Wolf. One of Merri's endless "grow-up" speeches. *No matter where you go—no matter how the water sparkles, or how they serve champagne in flutes at sunset—you still have to haul yourself there, deal with all the moments in between, pay for it in the end. That's real life—all the time between those beautifully filtered images you post on Facebook.*

He'd texted Kristi while Merri was getting the kids some ice cream or something.

I'm dying up here without you.

Usually she texted him back instantaneously, as if she were always just waiting for him to reach out to her. This time she made him twist. She didn't respond for more than an hour. Finally:

who told u to go? ☹
I'm sorry. I miss you.

Kristi had, just a few days earlier, delivered an ultimatum (which was one of the real reasons he was trying to get away from her): tell Merri, or she was going to break it off. End his marriage? Destroy his kids' lives? For a girl like Kristi? Not going to happen.

So he'd started distancing himself. Before her there had been flings, one-night stands, nothing lasting, nothing emotional. He'd expected her, like the others, to recede from the stage at his cue. But Kristi wasn't having it. Lately, she'd been texting and calling, once even dared to ring the landline.

Someone named Kristi Blaire? Merri had called that night, reading from the caller ID but not answering. *She's one of your press contacts, right?* Merri was the least jealous, least suspicious woman he'd ever met. It was one of the reasons he'd married her. Anyway, the night of that call was when he decided they needed to get away. But up in The Hollows, fully immersed in "family time," he found that he *missed* Kristi.

With the kids finally zoning out in front of the television and Merri taking a shower, Wolf called her from the porch.

"I don't want to be without you," he'd whispered, listening to the water run in the bathroom.

He'd meant it in that moment. But what was it that he thought he couldn't live without? It wasn't about her, not at all. It was about how she made him feel about himself. She wanted him, needed him, admired him. She asked his advice, lapped up his compliments like cream from a bowl. She soothed him when he was angry. There was an expression Merri wore, a kind of tired scowl of disapproval that he'd never seen her direct at anyone else but him. When Kristi looked at him, it was the shiny look of love.

"Maybe this would be a good weekend to tell her," said Kristi. "I could come up tomorrow. After the kids are asleep."

It wouldn't come as any surprise, would it? Merri must know the marriage was over. With the kids asleep in the loft, there would be little opportunity for drama. He'd leave with Kristi, and Merri could bring the kids home the next day. The details would be worked out later. Looking back now, he saw how insane it was, how depraved and utterly narcissistic. But that evening, he was an animal in a trap. Chewing off his arm seemed like a viable alternative. That was the problem, he reasoned. He was a wolf, a ranger, being asked to live the life of a Labradoodle. Domesticity was against his nature. Kristi, unlike Merri and the kids, wanted him to be himself.

They made a plan. He'd tell her after the kids went to sleep the next night. Kristi would drive up to get him, and they'd go back to her place.

"I love you, Wolf," she said through tears. "I'm going to make you so happy."

"I love you, too," he said. But the words felt big and fake in his mouth. He hung up, and Merri was behind him.

"Who was that?" she asked.

"My mom," he said easily, turning around to meet her embrace.

"The kids are asleep," she said. "Crashed out in front of the television."

He smiled. "That's an argument for letting them have televisions in their bedrooms at home."

She laughed. The nighttime routine of stories and putting the kids to bed had been the same since Jackson was born, hours of reading, and cajoling, and can I have some water, I need to use the bathroom, promises, threats, and finally silence.

"This was right," she said. The moon was high and the night was clear, the sky riven with so many stars. "It's beautiful here and so peaceful. This is just what we needed. Thank you for planning it."

And just like that, he was back in her thrall. Maybe it was their shared laughter, or her relaxed look of happiness, or just the reality of the call he made and how it would shatter all the years they had together. Whatever it was, he felt that unmistakable tug he always felt to her, even when he didn't notice it. Merri was a force, a planet with her own gravitational pull. He was her moon and had been since the night he met her. No one and nothing had ever thrilled him, excited him, challenged him, forced him to be a better man than Merri had.

When they were sure the kids were well and truly asleep, they made love that night, and it was everything it had ever been and more. The porn he had with Kristi was theater. He knew she faked it 75 percent of the time. Merri was incapable of faking anything; she was the real deal. They shed it all that night—all the domestic cobwebs, all the million tiny arguments over nothing, all the boredom and the drudgery of running a life. Flesh on flesh, heart to heart. It was still there, that electricity of the first time, grounded in a life built together. How could he have imagined giving that up?

"We can do better than we've been doing," Merri said that night as she drifted off. "I can do better for us."

"Me, too," he whispered. And he meant it. "God. Me, too."

He called Kristi as soon as he was out with the kids on the hike. "It's not going to work," he said. "Not here."

The silence on the other end of the phone was leaden with her anger and disappointment. Jackson and Abbey were lingering; he waved them up ahead. They both gave him a look, suspiciously confused. They knew he was doing something wrong, but they couldn't fathom what. What had he been thinking? How could he ever dream of leaving them? It was a midlife crisis, wasn't it? A sad cliché? That's what he'd become, the man who couldn't manage the mundane day-to-day of his life. Cage dive to see the great whites on the Barrier Reef in Australia, trek to see the mountain gorillas in Rwanda, zip line in Costa Rica—all totally doable. Fill out Valentine's Day cards with his daughter, work with Jackson on his fractions for the millionth time, run out to the store at 9:00 p.m. because there's no milk for the morning—utterly terrifying. Terrifying to think that really Merri was right: those things were the stuff of real life. Little more.

"Then we're done," she said. Her voice was liquid nitrogen.

"Kris," he said. "What do you want me to do?"

"I want you to do what you said you were going to do."

"It doesn't have to be over," he said. "I just need more time."

"Don't." And she hung up. That's when the first shot rang out. The next one took him down.

It was hard not to see it as retribution, a harsh correction for all his many failures. If he'd never met Kristi, he wouldn't have brought his family to The Hollows. If he hadn't been on the phone, his kids so far from him; if he hadn't introduced Blake to Kristi, Blake would never have told Claire, they wouldn't have canceled. If he'd never booked that cabin without asking Merri. The parade of "what ifs" and "if onlys" was endless. If any of those things had been different, the most horrible thing would never have happened. Or at least it might not have. He'd let too much space come between them. He'd let them out of his sight. That day and long before that. It was his fault.

The distant wail of a siren brought him back to the dim TriBeCa street.

"I'm a person, Wolf," Kristi said now. "You get that, right? I don't just exist for your pleasure and amusement, to be shoved aside when you've used me up."

It was hard not to hate her. But at least he was smart enough to know that, really, he just hated himself.

"I'm sorry," he said. Those two useless words again.

"Everyone told me, you know?" she said. She laughed a little. "That you were using me, that you would never leave your wife, especially not now. I really didn't believe them. I really thought that you just needed time."

She looked up at the sky. "What a cliché, right?" she said when he didn't answer. She lowered her eyes and smiled at him sadly.

He saw her then, maybe for the first time: a young woman who was not blank, not vacant, but naïve maybe even a little foolish. If she had seemed empty to him, probably it was because all he saw in her was his own reflection. Poor Kristi was just in love with the wrong guy, trying to make something that started off cheap and tawdry into something real. Confusing him with the man she thought he was, she'd believed his promises, mistaken lust for love. She was just a little girl looking for the happily ever after, the redemptive narrative. She wanted to be able to say, "We had a rough beginning, but we came through tough times to find happiness." But there was no redemption here.

"I'm sorry," he said again. "I've made mistakes. A lot of them. What can I say? I have to be here for my family now. I have to try to fix what I've broken."

A siren wailed up the avenue. They both turned to look, then back at each other. He could tell that she almost understood, that she was glimpsing the truth about him, about life in general. That no matter how hard you tried, sometimes things were just as they were, not how you wanted them to be.

She lifted her palms, a helpless tear drifting down her cheek. "But what about me?"

"I never wanted to hurt you." Wow. Did he really just say that? The only thing more pointless than "I'm sorry." As if what we want or intend matters more than what we actually do. The truth was he never gave a moment's thought to Kristi or what would happen to her in all this mess.

He watched her for a moment; her eyes were glistening and she bit her lower lip. Was there going to be high drama? Would she slap him? Try to seduce him? Would she weep and wail as he tried to get away from her? Would he let her lure him back to her apartment, abandon his plans to go up to The Hollows?

But no.

"I hope you find your daughter," said Kristi. She shook her head. "I really do. I can't tell you how sorry I am that I ever told you about that place."

"It's not your fault," he said. "This is all on me."

She gave him a little smirk. "I know that," she said.

She bowed her head, shoving her hands into her pockets. Then she just walked away, her heels clicking on the sidewalk, echoing off the buildings around them. She turned a corner and was gone. He felt nothing, except a vague regret for everything that had passed between them. It certainly hadn't been worth it, for either of them. But that was another truth of life that Wolf had only recently learned. Very often, there was no redemptive narrative. The consequences for some mistakes would not be undone. He headed toward the garage.

TWENTY-THREE

The problem with going *fast*, was that you couldn't go *far*, too. Her heart throbbed, and her ankle hurt so much that she cried while she ran, seeing white stars of pain every time her foot connected with the earth. Finally, she slowed to a limp, breathless, having lost her bearings completely. She stopped and looked around the dark woods. No light from the moon. *Don't panic*, that's what her daddy would have told her. *Find shelter. That's the first thing you have to do if you get lost in the woods.*

Exposure was the greatest threat to survival, her father had told her. She kind of didn't get it. She thought it would be food or water that was the most important thing. Then, she'd never been too cold for too long. Her skin never ached from the frigid air. She was separated from snow and rain by boots and coats, mittens and scarves. It never touched her, not like this.

The snow was falling in big thick flakes. And she remembered how it looked when it fell out her window. How it would seem to melt into the black river of the street and never accumulate. But here, a white blanket was forming. The snow was clinging to leaves, forming little piles on branches.

"What do I do now?" she asked the voice.

But there was no answer. The voice was probably mad at her because she had disobeyed. Now, she was on her own. She tried to rid herself of the image of Bobo hitting Momma over and over again with that flashlight, but she couldn't. Had *she* made him do that? Was it her fault? She thought that she should be sorry, that somehow it was she who drove him to do it. But she wasn't sorry. If she'd been strong enough, she'd have done it herself.

Once, when she was in first grade, her gym teacher—a big goofy guy who thought nicknames were funny—called her something she didn't like. He called her Lazy Daisy because she made a face one day when she didn't want to do a hundred sit-ups—like, *who did*? He had other nicknames for kids too, like Big Red for Ben who had red hair, and The Rock for Brock who was kind of a big kid. He wasn't mean exactly, but he was a teaser.

He teases because he likes you, Daddy said.

Grown men should know better than to give children nicknames, her mother said. *If you don't like it, sweetie, you're entitled to politely say so.*

So one day, she said nicely, very nicely, "Mr. Turner, can you please stop calling me that?"

"*Aw*, Lazy Daisy doesn't like her nickname," he said, not nicely.

Then he just started saying it more. She got angrier and angrier until one day, on the field when he said it again, she picked up a rock and threw it at him. It was just a small rock, a pebble really. It didn't hurt, but she could tell by the way his face flushed that he was mad. She got sent to the principal's office and her parents were called. She remembered that stubborn *not sorry* feeling she had, even though she was forced to apologize. Mr. T stopped using nicknames after that.

She kept walking, but it was getting harder and harder. Impossibly, she was starting to get sleepy, too. The snow on the ground looked like the fluffiest white blanket, as though she could lie down on it and rest. It tugged at her, even though she knew how the freeze of it would cut like knives on her skin. She felt the pull; it was hard to resist.

No, no, said the voice. *Don't do that. Keep walking*.

She heard a snap and a crackle and turned around to see that white light bouncing in the distance behind her. Bobo. He was not her friend; she knew that. She kept moving, aware suddenly of a sound that was growing louder. He was crying, moaning. She'd seen that in him, that tangle of love and hatred he had for Momma.

She didn't understand it, but she'd used it to hurt him. And more than that. Somehow, she didn't know how, she'd made him hit Momma with the flashlight. She wondered if he knew it. Would he do that to her, too, if he caught her? Would he use that flashlight on her?

The pulse of fear woke her up a little, caused her to pick up her pace. Drawing on a well of energy she didn't even know was there, she was about to run again. Then she saw something up ahead that stopped her dead: the eyes of the big house, glowing orange. All this time she thought she was heading *away*, instead she was just heading back in the direction from which she'd come.

She would have cried out in anger and frustration, but she stayed quiet, choking on it, swallowed the big sobs that came up, and moved behind a big oak tree. Wrapping her arms around herself, she tried to calm down, take deep breaths. The sound of Bobo's moaning was getting louder, growing closer. What would he do to her?

Then a thought came: those boots in Real Penny's closet. There was a warm jacket, too. In the kitchen she could get some food and water. She'd have supplies and a better chance of surviving in the cold. She had her bearings now, knew the way to town because of what Poppa had told the clean man. Maybe it was a blessing *in the skies*, like her mom always said, even though Penny had no idea what that meant. When something was good that seemed bad? But what did that have to do with the sky?

Poppa hadn't been home all day and sometimes he didn't come back from town until the next day. Where he went or what he did, she had no idea and didn't want to know. The house might be empty. She waited for the voice to tell her what to do, but the voice was quiet again. It was kind of like when her mommy was helping with homework. *Is this the right answer?* she would ask. *What do you think?* her mom would answer. But she could always tell whether the answer was right or not, just by the expression on her mommy's face—a tiny, slightly worried frown or a hidden smile in her eyes. But the voice was just coldly silent. She hated the voice.

Bobo's wailing cut through the night like an alarm, startling her into action. If Poppa was home, he'd surely come out in answer to Bobo's call—probably with his gun.

She moved through the trees fast and quiet—her pain and fatigue forgotten for the moment. She paused at the clearing for the house and saw that Poppa's truck wasn't there. She waited, scanning the area, looking in the windows of the house, checking the shadows by the barn. It was quiet, just the lamp over the barn shining, casting a weak white circle of light, and the glowing orange eyes of the house.

She took a deep breath and then she sprinted to the house, limped up the creaky porch steps, turned the rattling old metal knob, and pushed inside. She shut the door hard and leaned against the wall, panting.

"Poppa!" she called. "Momma needs your help! Hurry!"

If he was there, he would race out to help Momma, wouldn't he? Then Penny would have the time she needed to get supplies and go. She listened. Was he there and not answering? If he caught her in Real Penny's room, what would he do to her?

But there was only silence; she waited, listening to her own breath, then started slowly up the stairs. The warm air in the house was a blessed relief but it made her skin tingle, and that heavy, tired feeling had come back. The snow tapped against the glass as she inched up one creaking step at a time.

On the landing, the hall loomed long. She wanted to be quiet, but instead she ran the distance to Penny's room and burst inside, carelessly letting the door hit the wall. She moved immediately to the closet and removed the shining black boots, as well as the jacket. She didn't know where Poppa was or when he'd be back. She didn't know how long it would take Bobo to reach the house or what he might do when he got here. He was crazy; she'd seen it in his eyes, a kind of wild, horselike fear and a terrible rage.

She found a pair of socks in the drawer and slid them on. They were so warm, but it hurt, too. It hurt to go from cold to warm, a kind of throbbing pain. Then she pulled on the boots. Even though they were too big, her ankle screaming in protest at the pressure. Abbey wobbled with the pain, struggling to keep going.

A flash of light against the wall, a thud from outside brought her to the window, hiding behind the curtain.

She saw Poppa climbing from the truck, the snow falling heavily around him. He wasn't alone. They were there, too, the other girls—though she knew Poppa couldn't see them anymore. The girl who taught her how to milk the cow was standing by the barn. The other girl, the one who'd come after her and had only been here a short while, stood by the trees. And someone else lay on the ground, wearing a white dress, arms and legs spread wide, as if she were making an angel in the snow. She wanted to help them all, but she knew it was too late.

She ran noisily in the too-big boots, down the hallway. She had to get downstairs and toward the back of the house before Poppa came in. But she only made it to the landing in time to see the door open, then close. She was trapped upstairs, no way out. He moved into the house.

"Momma," he called. He stood in the foyer a minute, listening. Then he moved toward the stairs.

TWENTY-FOUR

Finley and Eloise lounged on soft chairs, the sound of the ocean loud around them. The water was jewel green, white capped, lapping against sand as white as sugar. Finley wore a black bikini; Eloise was conservative as ever in a chambray skirt and cream sweater set.

"You asked me what it is," Eloise said.

"You didn't answer," said Finley.

Finley's legs were covered with tattoos—a girl dancing, a gun, a glade of towering trees morphing into The Three Sisters—none of which she remembered getting. She ran her hands along her skin, which was greasy and smelled of coconuts. She only remembered lounging on a beach in a bikini a couple of times—once in Florida, once in Hawaii, both trips that were characterized by her parents bickering and arguing from dawn till dusk. But today there was only silence, except for the white gulls and the sound of the surf.

"There is no answer," said Eloise. She sipped from a straw punched into a hollowed-out pineapple. Finley had one, too. The drink inside was like nectar, sweet and refreshing, the most delicious thing she'd ever tasted. It made her relaxed and lightheaded.

"It's something different to everyone," Eloise went on. "Like life. You take from it what you bring to it."

"But it's not like other places," said Finley.

"No," said Eloise. She, too, looked peaceful.

"It wants something," said Finley.

"We all want something," said Eloise.

Finley was annoyed. Why must Eloise always be so vague? Maybe she didn't have the answers, after all. When she looked over again, it was Abigail. The girl, with her wild auburn hair, wore that eternal blue dress, tattered and worn. She tilted her face toward the sun with a smile.

"Too many bad things have happened here," said Abigail. The voice that came from her mouth was Eloise's. "It might have started with just one thing, one tragedy or injustice."

Finley closed her eyes. When she opened them, there was a little girl in an owl tee-shirt, the knees of her jeans ripped and bloodied. The voice was still Eloise's.

"That anger was a seed that grew. The energy expanded and spread itself, like violence runs in families. Now a blockage has been created, and nothing can pass through as it must. It's like a clogged drain. And the muck gathers, collects, rots, and festers."

Finley listened, though Eloise's voice was barely audible now over the sound of a strange whispering. And more so, Finley didn't want to hear what the old woman had to say. She was tired of all the darkness. Why couldn't she just stay here on the beach, with the sun on her skin? She looked down and it was all gone, all the ink on her arms, on her legs. Her skin was clean, clear of any marking. She felt such a tremendous sense of release, but loss, too.

"Someone at peace has to show them the way out," said the little girl with the very old voice. "Once the negativity has been released, it won't attract more."

"I don't know what that means," said Finley.

She turned back to Eloise, but the woman was gone, her seat empty, her drink tipped, leaving a dark stain on the sand.

Finley had blood on her hands, and a long dark streak marred each leg of her jeans as if she'd tried to wipe it off there. Far from being warm, basking on some unnamed beach, her body felt rigid with cold, shivering from her core. *Where was she?* Awareness came in pieces. She was alone in Rainer's car, engine running, sitting in the driver's seat. The car didn't have heat, and her breath plumed out in great clouds. She gripped the steering wheel hard, as if she were bracing herself for a crash.

She was parked on a tree-lined street—Jones Cooper's street. A light came on in an upstairs window. Shit. Her heart thumped; there was a big blank space where her memory should be. Panic beat its wings in her chest. What was the last thing she remembered? Think. THINK. A text from Alfie. Abigail in the mirror. Rainer's hands on her body. The old maps of the iron mines.

Rainer. Where was he?

She felt around for her cell phone, finally fishing it out of her jacket pocket. It was a block of ice, and her hands were so chilled that she couldn't get the touch screen to work. She blew on her fingers, rubbed them together, and then tried to call. It rang and rang. Then he finally picked up.

"Rainer?" she said. "Where are you?"

But there was only static over the distant sound of his voice.

"Down here—" That was all that she could make out, or something like it.

"I can't hear you," she said.

Then the line—infuriatingly—went dead. She tried again, then again. But the call wouldn't go through. Why were they not together? Why did she have his car? Had she taken it? Was he back at the tattoo shop and cell phone reception was just bad because of the weather?

The snow fell in big fat flakes, powdering lawns and the trees. The world was a hush, a breath held, her own coming out deep and ragged.

How could she have driven to the Coopers' and not remembered it? It was troubling. She rubbed her eyes hard, willing the last few hours back. Ironically, they'd just been discussing this in abnormal psychology class, about cognition in fugue states. Though the subject is functioning—even as in Finley's case, driving—information that is assimilated during that period is generally not accessible once the state has passed. Finley couldn't think of what she'd experienced now, or the first time with Jones, as anything but a fugue. A separate part of herself was conscious. Last time, she'd remembered. Why not this time? She might never get the last few hours back. Why was there *so much* blood? A sweet, gamey smell sat thick on the air, sickening and yet oddly familiar.

The porch light came on, and the front door to the house opened. Jones stepped out onto the porch wearing jeans and a Georgetown sweatshirt under a barn jacket. He looked up at the falling snow, nonchalant, as if everyone popped out onto his stoop at three in the morning to check the weather, then he dropped a steely gaze across at the car.

Finley remembered the dark-tinted windows, the general condition of the vehicle. She opened the door and stepped out, waving her hand.

"It's me," she called. Her voice bounced down the street, sounding high and weak to her ears like the voice of a child. "Finley."

He closed his eyes and bowed his head, then looked up with a deep frown. He moved down the path and up the drive.

When he reached her, "What the hell are you doing out here, kid? Whose car is that?"

"I—" she started. "I don't know what I'm doing here. It's Rainer's car."

"You almost got yourself shot."

She wrapped her arms around herself, still disoriented and confused. "Why would you come to the door with a gun?" she asked. She looked for it, and saw the hard edge of it pressed against his sweatshirt.

His assessing gaze made her feel stupid—really stupid.

"Strange, beat-up old car, dark-tinted windows pulls in front of your house in the middle of the night? Cops never stop being cops, I guess," he said. He peered inside the car, then back at her.

"What's all over you? Is that blood?"

She tried to keep herself from shivering, but she couldn't.

"He killed someone," she said. It came back in a rush then—the raised arm, the heavy flashlight, the revolting sound of metal on flesh and bone. But why was the blood on her? Had she been there, too?

"Who did?" he asked, alarmed. His hand on her shoulder now was warm and steadying, a bolster. In that moment, something about him reminded her of Eloise. He was someone who fixed, who helped.

"The boy who was in the woods, the one I saw," she said. "He killed someone tonight."

"You witnessed this?" A simple question without a simple answer. She shook her head. "No," she said. Then, "I don't know."

"Whose blood is that?" Jones said. "Are you hurt?"

"I don't know." She could hear the screaming. *Momma! Momma!* "No, I'm not hurt."

"That's a lot of blood," he said, lifting her hands and looking at her palms. "Where were you just now?"

There was a flash. She fought for it. Where? Where?

"On the trail," she said quickly. Yes, yes, that was it. "The trail you and I visited."

"And on the trail you witnessed a murder?"

"No, not exactly," she said. "I don't know."

He watched her a moment, shaking his head as if she were an equation he couldn't solve.

"What were you doing up there, alone in the middle of the night?"

"After I left you, I researched the iron mines," she said. She patted at her jacket and found the folded pages there. Fugue or not, at least she'd had the presence of mind to bring the maps. She handed them to him. "I found these."

He took them from her and squinted at them. "These are too old to be useful," he said. "Trust me. I grew up in this place and I was a cop here for a good long time. I've pulled kids out of those mines. There's no accurate map in existence."

"There was a man," said Finley. "A guy named Michael Holt who dedicated himself to mapping out the mines. It wasn't that long ago."

251

"The guy you're talking about was a nutcase," said Jones.

"And his father before him," she said. "He was a professor, wrote a couple of books."

"Another crazy person," said Jones. "He was a hoarder."

Stubborn, Finley thought, holding on to fixed ideas that he didn't want changed. Or was it that he didn't want to think that they'd missed something when they were all looking for a missing girl? That they'd all been up there searching and she'd been there, just out of sight.

"Didn't Michael Holt hide in the mines for a while?" Finley asked.

"He did," Jones admitted.

"So it's possible then that whoever took Abbey did the same," said Finley.

Jones blew out that sigh again. "Even if he had, it was ten months ago."

"But it would mean that maybe they didn't have to go far," said Finley. "That there was no car waiting. That *maybe* Abbey is still right here, in The Hollows."

He looked at the maps, then up at the sky.

"All right," he said after a moment. "Let's head out there and see what you saw or didn't see. We'll take my vehicle because, I'll tell you what, it doesn't look like you should be driving. I'll call Chuck."

Finley guessed he was talking about Chuck Ferrigno, the only detective at The Hollows PD. There had been others, according to Eloise, but budget cuts had reduced the department to the bare bones, which is why Jones Cooper consulted regularly.

A pretty woman appeared in the doorway as Jones and Finley were headed over toward the SUV. He walked to her and they exchanged a few quiet words, a quick embrace, and she went back into the house, casting a motherly, concerned glance in Finley's direction. Maggie Cooper offered Finley a wave, then disappeared back inside. She came back a minute later with a blanket and some towels, and handed them to Jones. After giving him a quick kiss on the cheek, she closed the door.

In the car, Finley used the towels and some antibacterial ointment Jones had in the center console to wipe some of the blood off her hands. Then she wrapped herself in the blanket, still shivering, foggy headed, afraid.

"There was a girl there, too," Finley said, as he pulled out of the driveway. Finley could see her, slight and dirty, standing among the trees. Her face was a strange blur, in focus but not. A pulse of frustration moved through Finley. *What was happening to her?*

"Are you sure?" he asked.

Finley nodded. She wasn't crazy; she knew that much. Whatever she saw was real; she just couldn't get the pieces to coalesce, couldn't understand where she'd been when she saw what she saw.

"Who was she?" he asked.

"I don't know," she said. How many times had she said that? She thought that she must sound like an idiot. She bet Eloise was never so uncertain. "Her face is unclear. They were deep in the woods."

"How did you get up there?" he asked. "Did you walk from the path?"

She wasn't going to say "I don't know" again.

"Is there another way up into the woods?" she asked instead. "Is there a road that goes up to wherever someone who veered off that trail might go?"

Jones seemed to consider her question. "There's a rural road that leads to private drives connected to old properties—all of which were thoroughly searched when Abbey disappeared."

She'd never been up that way on her bike. "Who lives up there?"

Jones shrugged. "Back when I was a kid, we called them hill people. I suppose that wouldn't be considered politically correct these days."

"Hill people?" asked Finley. The phrase sounded strange, made up.

"Yeah, you know, folks who live off the grid. They have generators, hunt for their food, come into town to do odd jobs, get supplies. But mostly they stay up past The Hollows Woods."

Finley tried to process this. It was totally new information to her, something her grandmother had never mentioned, something she'd never read online. "You mean like a *Deliverance* kind of thing?"

"Well," said Jones. "That's a little oversimplified. They're just people living the way folks used to live. They've rejected the modern world. Some might argue that they have good reason. Not everybody wants wireless internet, a smart phone, and a latte or whatever from Starbucks."

"So they just live up there and never come down? The kids don't go to school? What if someone gets sick, or dies? What if a crime is committed?"

Jones shook his head. "The kids get homeschooled, some of them. We've had a few people come down for medical care—but you know they don't have money, insurance. Most of the babies aren't born in hospitals. They bury their own dead up there."

"Is that legal?"

"It's legal to live the way you want to live," said Jones. He had pulled out his phone and was dialing. "Within reason, anyway. This is America."

"That's not true," said Finley. "You can't just *not* have a Social Security number, not pay taxes, bury your own dead. Can you? Don't the police ever go up there?"

Jones pushed out a little laugh. "Not unless they absolutely have to. These folks don't like visitors. Locals know to stay away."

Locals know to stay away. Something about this cleared the fog from Finley's head.

"So when you say these properties were thoroughly searched . . ." said Finley, letting the sentence trail.

Jones dialed the cell phone in his hand and put the phone on speaker. The tinny ringing ended when a deep, resonant voice answered. "Ferrigno."

Jones identified himself and ran down the situation—Finley Montgomery, blood on her hands, someone hurt, heading up north on the rural road.

"Actually, I'm heading up there, too," said Chuck. They could hear rustling, a car door slamming, an engine coming to life.

"Why's that?" asked Jones, casting a glance at Finley.

"We got a lead on that missing real estate developer. The beacon on his car is sending out a GPS location, and the warrant finally came through allowing the NYPD to get the information. I was just going to call you, actually."

"Where is it?"

"Out in the middle of nowhere, where a BMW has no business being," he said. "From the signal, it *looks* like the middle of the woods. We're heading up to search. Got some guys coming in from the next county, too."

Finley watched Jones, who wore a deep frown. Without thinking, Finley reached for the glove compartment, where (of course) there was a notepad and pen.

"What are the coordinates?" asked Jones.

Finley jotted down the numbers. Outside the snow was collecting in the gaskets of the windows, on the shoulder, and in the trees. But the road ahead of them was still black, slick, and wet.

"Satellite image shows a clearing in that location," said Ferrigno. "Course this weather is not our friend at the moment. We have to try to get up there before it gets any worse."

"Could be The Chapel," said Jones.

"That's what I was thinking," said Ferrigno. Finley saw a muscle working in Jones's jaw.

"Coming up?" asked Ferrigno.

"We have to check on the other incident first," said Jones. "Someone might be hurt up there."

"Need some backup?" Ferrigno asked. "I can spare a guy if you think there's an emergency."

"I'll call you if I need someone," said Jones. "Hey, just one other thing. When Abbey Gleason went missing? How thorough was the search on the properties of the folks living up there?"

"Pretty thorough," he said. "The few families that are still there cooperated fully. But there aren't that many people anymore— maybe five or six total. There are a few shacks, one or two houses. The landscaping guy has a pretty nice place up there, Abel Crawley?

Makes you think, you know, that there's something to shedding the modern world. He's got a generator, chickens, pigs and a cow, a deep water well. Works all spring, summer, and fall, off all winter."

Squeak-clink. Squeak-clink. Squeak-clink.

The water pump for the well; Finley could see it. Things that squeak. She saw the red metal pump resting on a wooden platform. There was a girl, using all the strength to pump it, the barn off in the distance. *Squeak* as the handle went up, *clink* as it came back down.

They pulled off the paved road and onto a smaller dirt one. Jones shifted the SUV into four-wheel drive. Finley looked out into the darkness, the same questions scrolling through her mind. What had happened to Rainer? Why did she have his car? Whose blood was all over her?

Finley's whole body pulsed with tension and fear now, her mind a whirl of images and disconnected thoughts. Then, out in the night, she saw a bobbing white light. It went dark for a moment, and she sat forward looking. Then it came on again.

"Stop the car," she said.

Jones put on the brakes and the vehicle skidded to a stop.

"Do you see that?"

"I don't see anything," said Jones. "It's pitch-black out there."

She saw it clearly, and then she was outside, running toward it with Jones calling after her.

TWENTY-FIVE

She crouched low, making herself very small in the tiny space she found between the wall and the shelves. She could be quiet; she was a good hider. She listened as Poppa clomped up the hallway, big boots on hard wood, then climbed back down the stairs. She waited; she didn't hear an outside door open and close, but still it grew very quiet as if he had left. She waited a long time, crouched inside the linen closet.

It was moldy, the dust tickling her nose, a sneeze threatening. She buried her face in her jacket, plugging her nose. *If you hold your sneeze in*, her brother had warned, *you'll explode your eyeballs*. For the longest time, she'd believed him.

She waited and waited, until finally she got up painfully from her crouch and quietly moved toward the door. The hallway was empty, the stairs waiting to lead her down and out the door.

She didn't know where Poppa was, or Bobo. But she knew she had to go. She didn't have to listen to the voice. She only had to listen to her mommy, and she was sure that her mommy would tell her to get out of that house and run the way Poppa had told the clean man to go.

The door squeaked a little, but not too loudly. She crept down the hall, trying to be quiet in those boots. At the top of the stairs, she paused, listening. If she tried to tiptoe down the stairs, they'd creak. If he heard her, he'd trap her upstairs. She had to run and burst through the door, and then head straight for the gate and then keep running. She took a deep breath and got ready.

"What are you doing in here, girl?"

An electric shock of fear spun her around to see Poppa standing behind her.

"You think you're the only one who can creep?" he asked, his smile mean.

She had no words. She stared at his sunken blue eyes, his white hair wild. His hands she knew were rough and hard. He was so skinny that his face looked like a skeleton and she could see all his bones. Behind the fear, another feeling vibrated. Hatred. She hated him. She wished he were dead, that he'd rot and the bugs would eat his flesh. She lifted her chin at him.

"I'm leaving," she said.

She stepped down a single step and he reached for her arm, but she slunk away, down one more step. He inched slowly toward her, as if she were a bird he was afraid to startle.

He laughed a little. "Who said so?"

"Momma said I could leave."

He frowned, his jaw working. He was missing a tooth on the side of his mouth, and it made his smile ghoulish. She'd never seen an adult with a missing tooth. Plenty of kids had big gaps in their smiles and that was normal. One of the doormen in her old building had a gold tooth. And she always stared at it when he smiled at her. *Good Morning, Little Rose!* he'd say when he saw her before school. Her name wasn't Rose, but he made her wish it were.

"No, she didn't," he said.

"She said I couldn't help her anymore," she said. "She needs a new Penny."

She moved down a few more steps, and he came slowly after her. His smile broadened. She could smell his scent, like grass and wood.

"Was Penny your daughter?" One more step.

"Shut up, girl," he said. "Mind your business." It sounded like "yer."

"Did you hurt her?" she asked. "Like you hurt me."

It wasn't right what he had done, what he was still doing. Real Penny wanted him punished. The voices in the trees wanted that, too. He was a pain giver, someone who hurt and wasn't sorry.

One more step down, the wood creaked loud and long. She was standing on her bad ankle, and the pain was so bad she was seeing those white stars again. The door stood open, a cold draft snaking up the stairs. She wobbled a little, knocking one of the picture frames from the wall. It fell and shattered on the stairs, littering the floor with broken glass.

"Did you touch her?" she said. "She told me you did. You weren't a good daddy."

His smile didn't waver.

"She started a fire because she wanted to kill herself and you, and Momma for letting you hurt her. You're a bad man," she said. She took one more step down. "That's how she died."

Bobo's wailing voice carried in from outside, sounding like the call of a dying animal. Just as Poppa lunged for her, she ran down the stairs. The old man lost his balance and came tumbling after her, crashing down with a series of grunts and then a hard landing. The walls rattled.

She burst through the door onto the porch. Bobo was moving up the road she needed to be on, staggering, his flashlight shining. As Poppa came roaring out the door, she ran back toward the barn, the opposite of the way she needed to go. She knew that there was a path that led back into the woods. She headed for that, her mind going blank with panic.

She ran and ran until she had to stop, a big stitch in her side, breathless, her leg screaming with pain. Sobbing, exhausted, she kept moving forward. Everything had gone quiet. No one was chasing her; the lights from the house behind her were no longer visible.

There was no way to know how long she walked, or why Poppa and Bobo didn't come after her. Maybe Bobo told Poppa that Momma was hurt; maybe they went back to help her. She'd almost forgotten that it was snowing. It accumulated on the path, not much, just a dusting. She looked up and watched as all the zillion little crystal flakes fell. The next thing she knew she was on her knees, overcome. She bent down and started to cry.

One of the girls she'd known here had been the fastest girl in her school. But she wasn't that girl. She was lost and afraid and she wanted to go home. She let herself rest on the cold, hard ground. Real Penny and Zoe weren't afraid, she reminded herself. They wanted to go wherever it was they were going, to whatever was waiting *after*. Wherever it was, it had to be better than here. She heard the sound of her very own name whispered in the leaves around her. *You are home*, the voices said.

She let herself fall to her side. Even though it was cold, it felt good to rest. She was about to let her eyes close when she heard voices. Not the voices in the trees, or calls on the wind. But real voices. Men. Deep and rumbling. A conversation, people talking to each other.

"Up here, to the right." It was real and solid.

"There's *no way* to get a car up here." Another voice, breathless with effort.

She looked up and saw off toward the end of the path, a strange flashing red-and-white light. She almost got up and ran in the other direction, then she realized what it was. The police. Using all her strength to pull herself to her feet, she started to run, opened her mouth to scream for help when she felt strong arms on her, a hard hand over her mouth. A white-hot flash of pain took her words away. Then, there was nothing.

TWENTY-SIX

The bouncing light was gone, and Finley was alone in the dark, debris thick and slick beneath her feet, trees reaching, tilting into the sky. She kept moving, oddly sure footed. A calm, a new and yet familiar feeling, rose up from her center, giving off a kind of inner heat that kept the cold at bay. She'd heard Eloise describe this, a knowing beyond knowledge. It was a kind of engine that powered you through, even when you weren't sure exactly what you were doing. Something glowed up ahead, diffuse and large. She moved toward that as quickly as she could, without quite knowing why.

Jones Cooper was behind her; she could hear him moving heavily through the trees, grunting like an old bear. She saw his flashlight and called out to him occasionally so that he would know where she was, though she assumed he was following her tracks. There was enough light to see forms and the way through the trees. The snow was accumulating, growing thick on the branches, powdery slick beneath her feet.

She knew the way as if she'd been here before many, many times—even though she had no conscious memory of when that might have been. Once, after she first moved to The Hollows, she found herself in a small graveyard deep in the woods. She had no idea how she'd gotten there, apparently waking in the night and riding her bike to the edge of the woods, then walking through the trees. Eloise had followed her and brought her back to herself.

Finley knew that Abigail had wanted her to see that place, the place where she, Sarah, and Patience wanted to be buried. But their

261

ashes had been fed to dogs after they were burned as witches. There was nothing to bury. They were so tired, Abigail had told her, and they wanted to rest. *How do I help you rest?* Finley wanted to know. But no answer came then and it still hadn't. But she kept finding herself back here in The Hollows Woods. What would Jung say? How would he explain what was happening to Finley?

She came upon the body first, nearly tripped over it. It was deflated, snow settling in the valleys of her eyes, in the folds of her clothing. Finley should have recoiled in horror, that would have been a natural reaction for someone who'd never seen a dead body before. But there was something so unreal about it, so curious, that instead Finley kneeled beside the woman with the ruined face.

Finley had *been here* when the woman died, when she'd been beaten to death with a flashlight. Not *there*, not in the flesh. But she had borne witness from some vantage point. Finley could hear the wailing she'd heard in her dreams, and the cracking soft thud of metal meeting flesh and bone. Was it this woman's blood on Finley? She swayed between her dream memory and the present moment. The cold, the sound of Jones coming through the trees, the wind, that was now. She held on to it.

Jones came up behind her, his breathing labored with effort, and he shined his light on the corpse.

He came to his knees beside Finley and pointlessly put a hand to the woman's throat. If there was ever a person more obviously dead, Finley didn't want to see it.

"Who is she?" he asked.

"He calls her Momma."

"Who does?" he asked.

"The boy from the trail," she said. A name swam in her consciousness: Arthur.

"He killed her?" Jones already had his phone out.

Finley shook her head, not certain now. "I don't know," she said. "Maybe."

She could see the flashlight coming up and down and hear him wailing. But it wasn't a boy's arm that she saw. It was a girl's hand, small and pale but powerfully strong. She couldn't explain what she was seeing. Was it memory or vision or some hybrid of both?

"We have a body up here," said Jones into the phone. "I'll send you a pin of my location. You'll see my vehicle where we came in through the trees. It's possible we have a lead on Abbey Gleason."

He released a breath, listening to whoever was on the line. Then, "Don't ask."

His flashlight beam fell on the white trunk of a birch that was red with a dripping, bloody handprint. Finley could see the broken branches, a smear of blood on the next tree. She got up and started to move, Jones's voice growing fainter as she drew away.

"Jesus, kid, where are you going?" he called after her.

But she didn't stop to wait for him, kept moving toward that light.

"Head for the light," she called back.

"*What* light?" he called. "Wait for backup."

But he was already far behind her, and she kept moving. She heard the call of the rose-breasted grosbeak, even though she knew that they had long ago flown south to warmer climates. The only other sound was the crunching of her movements, the wind.

When finally she came to the narrow road that ended in a low gate, she saw the tiny bird. He was black and white, with flashes of red, fat and happily singing his pretty song. *Little bird*. As she watched him, the white became snow, and the black faded into the darkness, and the red became the bloody handprint on the gate. His song faded into the wind.

Finley saw the source of the light she'd been following: a lamp burning over the doors of a barn, the ground around it a field of white. The door to the main house stood open. A red water pump sat on a raised platform, a bucket beside it. *Squeak-clink*. And she heard the worried lowing of a cow. This was it, the place she was supposed to find. She knew it. She'd never been more sure of anything in her life.

"Abbey!" she called. "Abbey Gleason!"

The wind picked up and blew a drift in the accumulated snow, sprayed glitter into the air, but that was the only answer.

"Abbey!"

Finley felt the cold for the first time as it seeped in through her thin jacket. Her shoes were soaked, the blood on her jeans cold to the touch.

She was about to call out again when a girl slipped from between the barn doors, which stood ajar. Finley took an eager step closer, her heart filling with relief, when another girl, this one with dark hair, emerged from the trees. Finley stepped through the gate, only to see another terribly thin child laying on the ground making snow angels.

Finley's heart dropped, and she stood rooted watching them as they watched her. Waves of emotion pulsed through her—fear, anger, sadness. She gripped the icy gate to support herself, and the cold was razor sharp on her skin.

When the girl from the barn drew closer, Finley recognized her. Finley moved to go get her, to scoop her up in her arms and carry her away. But something stopped her. She stayed rooted as the girl moved closer, walking through the snow but leaving no trail behind her.

"She's gone," the girl said. "You're too late."

"No," said Finley.

"You're too late for all of us," she said.

Finley bowed her head against a powerful rush of shame and anger. The blow of failure was so brutal that it nearly doubled her over. It filled her throat and took her breath. If she'd followed her instincts, she'd have come up here sooner. She *knew* that time was running out. Instead, she listened to everyone else. And now it was too late. How did Eloise stand it? The failures. No wonder she always looked so haunted, so sad. Instead of sadness, Finley felt the heat of anger. This was so wrong, so unfair.

When Finley looked up again, fists clenched, all the girls were gone. Jones came up behind her, panting with effort.

"Is this the place?" he asked.

"She's not here," said Finley. She bit back her tears of rage. "She's gone."

"You don't know that," he said. He put a strong hand on her arm. But she did know it. The whole place vibrated with negativity. Terrible things had happened here, just a few miles away from people who could have helped. It was infuriating, like trying to keep sand from slipping through your fingers.

Jones pocketed the flashlight he was holding, drew the gun he had in a leather holster at his waist. Finley looked at it and realized that she'd never seen a gun up close. It was flat and black and full of menace, gripped in his hand that was red and raw.

"Stay here," he said. He gave her his signature frown—something between concern and disapproval. "Meaning, don't go running off by yourself. You're flesh and bone, you know. You're not invincible."

She was shivering now and hung back at the gate, trying to collect herself, while Jones knocked loudly on the door.

"Investigator Jones Cooper," he said. "Your door is open and I'm coming inside."

When he disappeared, she marveled at his nerve. Could he do that? Just walk into someone's house? Then she thought about following him inside. But unarmed she was just a liability, wasn't she? There were other sounds now, sirens and the approach of vehicles, though still distant. The police were coming. Too late.

Finley walked across the clearing to the barn and pushed open the big door, its hinges emitting a long squeal into the night. She saw the cow she'd heard, some chickens in a coop. The relative warmth of the indoors was a relief, even though she could still see her breath in silvery clouds. Her sinuses tingled with the smell of hay and the scent of animals in an enclosed space.

The little bird perched on an overturned bucket, singing its pretty song. She moved closer to it. It sat, puffed up and pretty, black eyes shining like jewels. When she reached for it, it disappeared. She moved to where he'd been, looking hard at the area around her. What had he wanted her to see? And then she saw a seam in what from a distance had looked like the wall of the barn. It ran from the ceiling to the ground. She looped her finger into a knot in the wood and pulled. It was a door and it opened out toward her, revealing a hidden room.

A tiny cot, a chain with a cuff attached to a ring in the floor, a battered baby doll, a broken mirror on a beam over a small, cracked sink. Finley pushed away the ugliness of it, the horror that radiated from the floors, the wall. She bit back another choke of tears, that terrible anger that burnt like acid in her throat. This is where they hid her. When the police came looking, she was in here. How many others? *Where* were they now?

Over in the corner, a small girl wearing a pair of jeans and an owl tee-shirt, her hair white blonde, her skin moonstone, stood.

"He took us because we're like you," she said to Finley, as if she had been waiting. "He calls us Dreamers. We see the other things, the people who aren't there."

"Who took you?" Finley asked. "Who calls you that?"

"The old man," she said. "You've seen him. He knows you."

Finley took a step closer. For a moment Finley flashed on the girl's face as it had been, bright with innocence, the glitter of mischief, a big toothy smile that could light the world. This girl was solemn and grim, her eyes just shining black holes containing all the knowledge of the world. Not a ghost, just a form of energy that Finley could recognize and understand. She couldn't stop shivering.

"You can still save her," the girl said.

"How?" asked Finley, moving a careful step closer. A rush of hope. "How can I save her?"

A shot rang out, shattering the quiet of the place. She felt the sound rattle her bones, spinning toward it. When Finley turned back, the girl was gone.

TWENTY-SEVEN

Wherever he was, it was so dark that he was essentially blind. He couldn't even see his hand in front of his face. And he had some vague awareness that he was hurt in a significant way; his leg felt odd, as if it didn't quite fit on his body the way it was supposed to. There was pain, but it was oddly distant like a siren just out of earshot. Where was he? How had he gotten here?

He had a foggy recollection of Finley kneeling over a woman who was obviously dead, her face smashed. And Rainer had been trying to pull her away. Clearly, they were out of their depth, and the snow was getting heavier. They were both getting frostbite; Finley's mouth was literally blue. It was time to take charge of the situation, he remembered, thinking, and if Finley thought he was being controlling and overbearing, well, that was too bad.

"Finley," he said. "She's dead."

Finley hadn't said a word, just kneeled there, rocking in a weird way. She'd gotten blood all over herself, and it was seriously freaking Rainer out. He was about to lift her to her feet and carry her out of there, when he saw something in the bushes, a dark form that slipped in and out of the trees and then was gone.

"Who's out there?" he called. He didn't like that his voice sounded high pitched and scared.

Man, he really hated the fucking woods. There was a primordial wildness that unsettled him. It was like you could die out here and your body would just become one with all the other organic debris. Animals and insects would come and feed on your flesh; your body would decompose in its own acids, and the earth would rise up to swallow it. No grave, no headstone. There was nothing clean or sanitized or palatable about it. There was not some part of you that stayed forever, body preserved in a coffin, ashes in an urn on someone's mantel. You'd be gone as if you never were, just absorbed like a rotten log. Only your bones would bear witness to the form you'd held.

"But that's what it is," Finley had said, though Rainer hadn't said a word. She'd done that before when she was like this. "That's as it should be. We are one with the earth."

"Sure," he said. "But not today. We are *out of here*, Finley."

He saw the shadow again, and then there was the laughter he'd heard before. Or was it just the strange way the wind sounded, caught in the hollows of the trees, whistling?

"I have to help her," said Finley.

He leaned in as close as he could stand to the bloody mess on the ground. Dead. Definitely dead, skull smashed in, face just a mass of ruined flesh.

"She's dead," he said. "The only way we can help is to get the police."

Finley was light, and he hoisted her easily.

"Put me down," she protested weakly. Rainer headed back the way they came, with Finley pounding on his back. That's when he saw her.

"What the fuck?"

He put Finley down, and she immediately ran back to the dead woman's body.

That girl in the shadows; he'd know her anywhere. It wasn't just the moonlight of her skin or the ice of her eyes. It wasn't just the twisted spools of her fire-kissed hair, or the delicate lines of her neck. It was her scent—something grassy and clean; it was her essence. He'd come to know her as he etched her picture into the delicate flesh of Finley's body. Abigail, the oldest of The Three Sisters.

There was a deep intimacy to ink work, especially when he worked with Fin. He *saw* what she wanted him to see. And when he put the needle to her skin and inked those images onto her flesh, he was closer to her than he was at any other time. She trusted him, opened herself to him. She let him mark her body with total faith in their connection. Even when their other connections—as lovers and friends—were strained, that remained. In that bond, Abigail dwelled.

"You're not real," he said. "I'm losing it."

It was the cold, right? Hallucinations as hypothermia set in? Abigail just smiled.

"Finley," Rainer said, his own voice sounding wobbly and scared. But Finley was in her own world, lost to him.

"Fin," he said again, louder still. "Will you *wake up*?"

Then he was following Abigail, because there was just no way *not* to follow. She danced like a sprite through the trees, and he found himself running to keep up. He'd see a flash of red, a starburst of white, hear the bells of her laughter. Even though he knew that she was leading him away from Finley, he followed anyway. Even though he knew that Abigail was a bad girl and not to be trusted, he found that he couldn't help but play her little game.

He'd had a friend like that when he was growing up, Scott from three doors down. Rainer's folks weren't always around. His dad worked nights, slept days. His mom worked days and wasn't usually home until right before dinner. But there were rules and chores, and he knew his parents loved him. Scott, on the other hand, was a stray dog. He never seemed to have to answer for where he was, skinny, rangy, dirt under his nails. He was smoking by the time they were ten, got Rainer his first beer when they were twelve. He was the kind of kid who said, "Hey, let's go set these bottle rockets off in that abandoned warehouse." And even though you knew it was a bad idea, you did it. With Scott, Rainer shoplifted, drank, smoked, explored a condemned building, and nearly got stuck inside an old refrigerator. Scott was dangerous; Rainer knew there was no bungee attached to that kid, nothing to pull him back from the hard landing of ugly consequences. Still, Rainer followed. *There are always going to be people like that, Rain,* warned his dad. *They open dark doorways and invite you to walk inside. Just remember that you don't have to go.*

But that was the problem. Rainer wanted to go. He wanted to

find the edge and push it, see how far you could go before you broke the seal and fell through. He always believed that he could pull himself back—just in time. And so far he had. He eventually graduated from high school, though several of the kids he hung with did not. He wasn't dead like Jeb or in a wheelchair like Raife, who got into an accident drag racing. He wasn't in jail like Scott, who was serving time for grand theft auto. It was like Finley always said about The Three Sisters, that she suspected they couldn't get her to do anything that on some deep, dark level, she didn't want to do herself. Rainer didn't want to go all the way down. He just wanted to peer over the edge and see what was waiting below.

But this time, as he chased Abigail through the woods, the ground beneath his feet gave way. And he fell and fell, knocking against protruding objects on his way down and landing hard. He could barely comprehend anything but the surprise of it at first, his stomach lurching as he knew he was falling, calling out for Finley, who he knew couldn't hear him. The pain, the fear came later.

And now, here he was in the darkness. He could hear the dripping of water somewhere, but that was it. And his own breathing. The ground around him was cold and wet, and he thought that if he died here no one would ever find him. Maybe a few years from now, some kid out in the woods with his friend would fall as he had and find Rainer's broken bones down here far beneath the ground, the rest of him long ago eaten away.

Shit. No way. In spite of the rockets of pain shooting up his leg, so bad he had to cling to consciousness and breathe deep to keep himself from hurling. One hard push and he was sitting up unsteadily, sick, but not flat on his back. He forced himself to run a hand down his leg. Warm, slick and sticky with blood, but there was nothing sticking out, like a bone. He hadn't impaled himself on anything. All good things.

That girl doesn't want you, Rainer. His mother always knew how to cut right to the quick. *If you follow her to that place, you're just asking for heartache.*

But his heart was already aching. It never stopped aching for Finley. From the minute he saw her, he was hopeless.

If you want her, if you love her, go get her, his dad said. *If it doesn't work out, at least you'll know it wasn't for lack of trying. Otherwise, you'll always wonder.* That's why he'd followed her from Seattle to The Hollows, because he never wanted to wonder. Now he was wondering what would have happened if he'd just stayed in Seattle. At least he wouldn't be down whatever hole he'd just fallen in.

Rainer felt on the wall for something to hold on to and found a grip. What was it? Wood, like a two-by-four. He knew where he was then, in one of those abandoned mine tunnels that Finley was talking about. He'd looked at the maps, marveled at how vast was the network, how deep and far the tunnels stretched. Finley had said that a kid falls into one nearly every summer, in spite of repeated warnings not to veer off park trails, in spite of the rangers' attempts to find and cordon off weak areas. She said that a man hid down there for months while the police hunted for him. Did she say if they ever got him? Was he still down here? Surely not.

His heart was pumping—with fear, with effort—he tried to slow his breathing. He'd heard Jake talk about the mines, too, hadn't he? Jake was some kind of history expert about The Hollows, was a total geek for the place, a lifelong member of The Hollows Historical Society. He said that there were climb-outs, places where ladders had been placed and led to openings, many of which had been sealed off by the park rangers.

Was it better to stay near the opening into which he'd fallen? Or feel his way deeper into the tunnel, hoping for a climb-out? He thought of the maps he'd looked at. There was a major mine head that Finley had circled, somewhere near the trail that he had been on. Had it been North? Rainer wasn't great with directions.

"*Finley*," he called, hearing his voice bounce around. "Finley, are you out there?"

His phone. Where was it? He patted at his pockets and found them empty. It must have fallen from his pocket when he fell. He reached around on the ground for it, finding only the damp and bumpy surfaces, not the slick, flat one he wanted.

"Come on," he said. "Where are you?"

He kept feeling around. *Please, please, please. Come on.* Then, as if in answer to a prayer, the phone started to ring, just out of his reach to the right. It vibrated, filling the small space around him with its light. He reached, straining, and with effort and a nauseating wave of pain, he grabbed it. Finley's face smiled out at him, a picture he'd snapped when she first loved him. Every time she called, he got to see the look that he didn't get to see on her face in real time anymore.

He slid the answer bar. "Finley," he said. "Hello?"

But there was only static and then the click of the line going dead. He had no signal bars at all. Then one flashed, tantalizingly, but then was gone. He tried to call back. "Calling Finley's Mobile" it read, teasing him with an expectant line of ellipses. But it hung there. Call failed. He tried again, and again, and finally slumped back against the dirt wall.

He'd watched that movie about the kid who'd gone out in the desert, fallen into a gap between rocks, got pinned, and wound up cutting off his own foot to survive. Or was it his hand? Either way, Rainer knew that he was not that kind of guy, not that he had any call to cut off a limb at the moment. But if it came to that, he knew he was not going to be the guy who did "whatever it took to survive." He just didn't have that kind of energy, the "belly of fire," as his father liked to call it. In fact, if Rainer had a light for the joint in his pocket, he'd be smoking right now to take the edge off his fear. Then he'd probably pass out, wake up too dopey to even think about how he might get out of this. Generally that's what he liked about pot; it softened the sharp edges of anxiety and fear and worry. You didn't *forget* about any of the things that nagged at you; you just stopped caring about them. When he was high, he was less angry, too. *Yeah, but all of that energy?* Finley countered during an argument about his pot smoking. *That's what keeps people from just lying around all day, eating Doritos and playing* Call of Duty.

He dialed the phone again, lifting it high into the air, as high as he could to try to get the signal. Nothing. He let his arm drop to his belly.

He remembered thinking, too, what kind of an idiot went out into the desert alone to begin with, not telling anyone where he was going? That was just plain hubris. And what was so great about being "a survivor"? Why was that such an admirable quality? It wasn't like that guy was risking his ass for someone else. He just didn't *want to die*. What was so unique about that? *No one* wanted to die. At least Rainer had an excuse for being out here alone; he was taking care of Finley, which is the only thing that had ever gotten him off his ass to do anything. If it weren't for Finley, he wouldn't have graduated high school. He wouldn't have driven across country. He wouldn't have opened his own tattoo shop. He did all of those things just to be worthy of her. On the other hand, he wouldn't have fallen down this hole either.

The phone rang again, sending an electric startle of hope through his body.

"Finley," he said. "Christ."

"Rainer?" She sounded young and panicked. "Rainer?"

"I fell down one of those mine tunnels. I'm down here. I'm okay, but I can't get out."

"Where are you?" she said before the line started to crackle and buzz.

"Fin?" he said. "Can you hear me? *Finley!*"

Silence was the only answer. He let out a cry of frustration, tried to call back. The call failed and he tried again. Nothing. Then he took a few more deep breaths, tried to calm himself down.

He used the light from the flashlight app to illuminate the area and realized he was sitting beside a narrow set of tracks. Looking up, he could just make out the place through which he'd fallen, a thin mouth where some ambient light stole in.

He rallied, using all his strength, pulling himself to his feet with a roar of pain. Then he was standing, looking around for one of those ladders, for a place where he could get a signal on his phone. He had to get out of here. He couldn't die in an abandoned mineshaft while Finley was in trouble above.

He heard something then. Was it laughter? Or was it the sound of someone crying? It was too far, too faint, but when it sounded again he started moving toward it. Was it a birdsong? No, it was the voice of a girl—or was it? Something about it filled him with hope and gave him a new rush of energy, the pain in his leg fading. Maybe he had an instinct to survive, after all. It was a damn good thing he didn't have a lighter.

He used the compass app to find his way north.

TWENTY-EIGHT

Merri pulled on the jeans she'd left over the chair and dug her sweater out of the bag, hastily getting dressed. She was pulling her coat on when she stopped and sank down onto the bed. The snow was falling heavily outside her window, and clouds above were glowing from the light of the hidden moon. Doubt whispered in her ear. This was crazy. What was she going to do? Plug those co-ordinates into her phone and drive there?

And yet every nerve ending in her body tingled with that intent. The instinct was powerful, compulsive. How many times had she ignored her instincts, done the opposite of what she knew was right? Like the day Abbey disappeared, wasn't there something inside her that knew, just as Jackson had claimed, just like Abbey's dreams, that she should go with them. The pills had quieted that voice, and all the other voices inside her. Not quieted exactly but muffled. She could hear the sound, but not make out the words—the worry, the self-criticism, the anxiety, the catalog of complaints and not-good-enoughs. Her mood had improved. Hell, her marriage had improved. In some ways, she was a better mother—less short-tempered and stressed. But she was not *herself*.

"Maybe that was a good thing," she told one of her shrinks. "Maybe in some cases it's not always such a great thing to 'be yourself.'"

"Unfortunately, there aren't any other options," he'd said mildly. "We can only hide or anesthetize our true nature for so long. We *can* strive to alter negative thought patterns. But we can't hide behind addiction and call that positive change."

Merri didn't buy it. Plenty of people were taking antidepressants, antianxiety meds. What made her self-medication so different?

"Antidepressants are prescribed to address chemical imbalance in the brain. Vicodin is prescribed for short-term pain relief," her shrink informed her very cogently. "The way you're taking it—in high doses, procured through illegitimate channels—is illegal."

It sounded like shrink-speak to her. Anyway, she'd been off the pills since her breakdown. But she still thought about them every day, those little white keys that opened the door to the mental cloud, that silent, mellow place that she'd never once visited before or since. But it was true that she'd been less aware, less present— there but not there for her kids. If she hadn't had three Vicodins that morning, she'd have gone on that hike or suggested that they go to the museum just outside of town. She was reasonably sure that nothing that happened would have happened, if she'd been *herself*.

Tonight, she *was* wide-awake, alert, so in tune, she was practically vibrating. She could listen to those other voices, as she often did, the ones that told her to stay put, let the police do their jobs, wait for the phone to ring. Or she could listen to that other voice, the voice that wasn't a voice but something so deep, so indivisible from her own consciousness that it didn't have sound. It told her to get dressed and go out there.

So she finished dressing and headed out the door as quietly as she could. She didn't want to wake Miss Lovely and have to explain where she was going on a night when one should obviously not be going anywhere. She felt like a teenager sneaking out of the house, which was precisely why Wolf hated B and Bs.

When she stepped outside into the snow, she almost shrieked. A man, tall, just a dark shadow stood on the sidewalk by the low gate. She backed toward the door as he moved into the light. Wolf. At the sight of him, there was such a blast, a rush of emotion that she put her hand to her heart. Anger, happiness, annoyance, love.

"You're here," she said.

"I told you I was on my way," he said. Snowflakes were gathering in his dark hair. He looked so young, so much like when she'd first loved him. "Where are you going?"

She walked up the path and unlatched the gate, stepping outside onto the sidewalk.

"Let me be here for you," he said. His voice was thick, his eyes bruised with fatigue. "For Abbey."

She moved into his arms and let him hold on tight, found herself clinging to him. A door that had been closed in her heart for him opened just a bit. She told him about her call to Blake, showed him the numbers she'd scribbled on the ivory stationery that read Miss Lovely's Bed & Breakfast.

"You were going up there alone?" he asked.

"I have to go," she said. "I know it's crazy and it doesn't make any sense. But I have to go up there."

Was he going to try to talk her out of it, talk sense into her? Was he going to say her most hated phrase: *I'm just trying to help you, Merri*.

"All right," he said. "Let's go."

Relief and gratitude mingled as she let him take her hand. They shuffled through the slick snow in the lot and climbed into the Range Rover, plugged the coordinates into an app she'd down-loaded on the phone.

"Merri," he said.

"Don't," she stopped him. She didn't want to prepare herself for what happened when Abbey wasn't up there, or make promises about what she'd do when she realized that they were on a fool's errand. She didn't want to live inside of near-future failures. She wanted to live in the now, when hope was strong, when she was following the true voice of herself no matter how much she often didn't want to hear it.

"No matter what happens," he said. "I'm here for you, for our family. I swear to you. From now on, come what may, I'm here."

His face was different, solemn, tired but set in some new way. He *had* been there, always, for the kids. And Merri always knew he loved her, even though she also knew he screwed around.

At first, she hadn't cared so much about that for some reason. She knew what he was the first night they were together, a player, a boy always looking for the next thrill, the next piece of candy. *I've never been faithful to anyone*, he said the night he told her that he loved her. *But I want to be faithful to you.* She believed him, that it was what he wanted.

She also knew that he wouldn't be faithful, that he *couldn't*. Merri was a smart woman; she knew that people didn't change. With Wolf, there would always be some girl when he was on assignment, some hookup after a press party, flirtations, one-night stands. Why didn't she care? It was a bad habit he had, like smoking or drinking too much. It had almost nothing to do with her. She could live with it, or so she thought. But, silently, like so many other things, it gnawed at the cord that tethered them, fraying it so that when it was pulled tight in stress it nearly snapped. Nearly.

She didn't even care about the mess with work. She understood him—his fears, his desires, that he was dishonest because he was afraid. She knew him in a way that you can only know someone you love totally. Daily, she forgave his flaws, just as she knew he forgave hers. Maybe that alone was the foundation of a good marriage, an endless willingness to forgive and to love in spite of ourselves, an ability to ride the highs and endure the lows, the decision to always go home.

She took Wolf's hand now. She'd always loved his hands, how big and solid they were, how warm they were on her body, how strong. He folded his grip around her thin fingers easily. In that moment, she knew they were both there, deeply flawed but *true*.

"I know," she said, her voice just a whisper. "I promise that, too. I'll be here. All of me."

The heat blew hot, warming them. Then Wolf pulled out of the lot and headed north out of town, following her directions. They turned onto Main Street and then onto the small road that led toward The Hollows Wood.

"That point looks like it's in the trees," she said, looking at the satellite map. "How close is it to the house we rented?"

She held it up to him and he glanced at it, then back at the road. "Not far," he said. "Ten miles maybe."

He'd always been the navigator in their relationship, the one at the wheel, so sure of where they were headed. Without him, she'd never go where she couldn't take the train, bus, or a taxi. He was the one who never minded going off road. It used to seem like a good thing.

"We'll take the car as far as we can," he said. "And then we'll get out and walk if we have to. Are you wearing boots?"

She was. She wore her thick Merrells and her heavy coat, a sweater under that. She even had a pair of gloves. For once, she was properly outfitted for what lay before them. The snowfall was growing heavier, accumulating on the road as they wound out of town, leaving the lights behind them. A star field of flakes battered the windshield; they were driving into oblivion.

"She's out there," she said, peering through the black. She didn't mean to say it. She'd learned not to say things like that to Wolf. He felt compelled to counter with something like: *You don't know that.*

But it was true, one way or another. Their girl was out there, not with them, someplace they couldn't reach. Were they headed toward her or away from her? Was she already beyond their reach?

"It's my fault," he said. "I failed her. I didn't protect her."

It was true in a sense; she knew that. But she had never blamed him, even though others had. He'd been careless, thoughtless. He'd been on the phone with his girlfriend and had let the kids go on ahead of him. But in another place and time, it wouldn't have mattered. The consequences were not appropriate to his actions. Even with his mistakes, he didn't deserve this pain.

"You didn't do this," she said. "Someone took her. That person is to blame and no one else."

"I brought her to this place," he said. He seemed to want to say more, but he didn't.

"We both failed her," she said. It felt good to acknowledge that out loud, not in some shrink's office, but out in the world where it was real. "I wasn't myself. If I had been, I would have gone with you, or we would have gone somewhere else—maybe. Maybe, *maybe,* things would have been different. All that matters is what we do now."

The blue blip on the screen moved closer to the red, the thin purple line of the road snaked along the edge of a black space. Wolf glanced over at the screen.

"When the dots are parallel, we'll stop the car and walk through the woods the rest of the way."

But as they approached that point, they saw the flashing lights of a police cruiser parked along the side of the road. As they grew closer, Merri saw that there were several vehicles, two other prowlers and a car she recognized as Detective Ferrigno's. Wolf pulled in front of it and got out, walking over to them as Merri climbed out after him.

"They're empty," he said. A scattering of footprints led from the cars into the woods.

They didn't have to go far, walking as quickly as they could through the trees, tripping over roots and avoiding branches tugging at their coats. Her throat was thick and dry. Soon, they saw more lights, an eerie silent red-and-white flash, through trees. Merri broke into a run with Wolf right behind her.

When they came into the clearing, she saw two police SUVs with lights flashing, a collection of uniformed officers. Apparently there was another way here, one in which vehicles could pass. In the center of the group, she saw Chuck Ferrigno. Wearing a thick black coat and hat, he somehow looked like a priest.

"Detective Ferrigno!" she called.

He looked up, his face registering surprise and annoyance.

"Mrs. Gleason," he said. He moved toward her and held up her hand. "What are you doing up here? This is a crime scene."

"Does this have something to do with Abbey?"

Something on his face. He didn't say no, dismiss her, or act like she was a fool. He just looked confused.

"Mrs. Gleason," he said. His voice was suddenly stern and unyielding. "You need to go back to Miss Lovely's and we will call you if this has any connection to Abbey."

She felt herself backing away, a rising creep of shame. She was becoming one of those people, like the ones they'd met in group, pushing themselves in where they didn't belong, their desperation for answers making them a nuisance to the police who had moved on to other cases, cases that *could* be solved. She was a fool to let something so random give her hope. That's how lost she was; she was listening to her grief-stricken, borderline OCD, teenage son. She was about to apologize.

"So you're saying it might?" asked Wolf. He had come up behind her, and he was wearing his reporter's attitude. The I-have-a-right-to-be-here-whether-you-like-it-or-not thing he did. Often she found it embarrassing and annoying. Not tonight. "Look, we just need to know if there's even a remote possibility."

Some of the hardness melted on Detective Ferrigno's face; he lifted a placating palm.

"All we know at the moment is that the vehicle of a missing man has been located in the barn in this clearing," he said. "That is all the information I have. How did *you* find out about this?"

Merri took her phone out of her pocket and dialed Jones Cooper, but he didn't answer. Wolf was arguing with Detective Ferrigno when something caught Merri's eye, a flash of white over by the trees. She moved through the snow, which was about an inch thick on the ground.

"Mrs. Gleason," said the detective. Getting angry, getting official. "I need you to stop or I will have you arrested. You are contaminating a crime scene."

She really didn't care, which was selfish and wrong. She did come to a stop, though, at the forest edge where there was a dark path leading in. On the ground was a tattered old doll made from rags with broken buttons for eyes and stitches for nose and mouth and a single child's riding boot. There was nothing about either object that connected to Abbey, and yet Merri felt a surge so powerful that it forced Abbey's name from her mouth in a shout. She used her phone as a flashlight, hearing Detective Ferrigno coming closer. She saw the brush was broken along the path, the marks of big boots in the snow—a chaos, pointing every which way. Something glittered on the branches, glittering gossamer in the snow. She stood, shining her light on blonde hairs tangled in the broken branches, wrapped around, binding two icy shoots together.

When Wolf came up behind her, she showed him. Even Detective Ferrigno stopped urging her to leave. Merri heard him say something into his phone. But she didn't hear what. She was running up the path, calling her daughter's name.

Finley ran from the barn in time to watch Jones step out onto the porch from inside the house, gun in hand. The snowfall was slowing.

"Did you see him?" he asked, looking out into the trees. His voice rang out, echoing.

"Who?" said Finley. She glanced around, peering into the dark spaces and shadows all around them. She felt like they were in a snow globe, held in an unseen hand, watched by some giant eye.

"The boy," he said. Jones's bearing was odd, his face slightly pale. "Not really a boy. A young man with a boyish face."

Finley shook her head. She didn't see anyone but the girl in the barn, and she wasn't sure she could tell Jones about that. How much could he take? What would he believe? "I heard a gunshot."

"He came out of the shadows," said Jones, shaking his head and moving down the steps toward her. "I thought he was armed."

"Was he?"

"He had something in his hand," said Jones. She remembered the flashlight she'd seen in her vision, a large metal object that might easily be confused for a gun.

Finley went to meet him, concerned. He didn't look right; someone so strong and sure of himself shouldn't look so wobbly. "Are you hurt?"

"No," he said. He brought his eyes back from the woods to Finley. "I opened fire. I shouldn't have, but I did. When the gun went off, though, there was no one there. He *was* there. And then he wasn't."

282

"He must have run," said Finley. She wasn't sure what Jones had experienced, but she sensed he needed a real-world explanation to pull himself together, whether one existed or not. In Jones's case, it probably did. He wasn't a Seer or a Listener. The chances of him being open enough to have an experience were slim.

"Right," said Jones. "It was dark."

Finley nodded toward the barn.

"They kept her back here," Finley said. "There's a hidden room."

She hadn't allowed herself to dwell on the horror of it. Abbey and how many others? Where were they, those "other girls like Finley." Eloise always said that there were more people "on the spectrum" than anyone supposed. Finley hadn't quite believed her; Finley had never met anyone with abilities except her grandmother. "There's a cot and chains." She felt her throat close up with sorrow.

"We were up here," he said. His despair was obvious in the lines on his forehead and around his eyes. "This property was searched."

"They must have been hiding her in that room," she said. "Or maybe he kept her somewhere else like the mines until the search was over. The room is empty now. She's gone."

"There's no one else in the house," he said, looking back at it as if he couldn't be sure who or what might be inside. In the light, he looked older, so sad. Fear had a way of aging people, making them look vulnerable.

"We're too late," said Finley. "He took her."

"Who took her?" Jones asked.

She noticed the truck then, a green, beat-up old Ford. There was a white sign on the door: POPPA'S LANDSCAPING. In that instant, Finley remembered the man in the wide-brimmed hat, looking at her as he trimmed the hedges by the school. She remembered the strange heat of his gaze.

"The man who drives this truck," she said. "He sees everything. But no one sees him."

"Crawley," said Jones, walking over to the truck. He rested his hand on the hood. "Abel Crawley."

"You know him?" Finley asked.

"He does most of the landscaping in The Hollows," said Jones. "Or a lot of it."

"With a son?"

Jones seemed to consider. "There was a fire up here—a long time ago. A girl was killed, his daughter. But, yes, I think there was a child who survived. The boy's name is—let me think—Arthur."

"They call him Bobo," said Finley.

"The family has been up here forever," said Jones.

"Could that have been his wife, back in the woods?" asked Finley. "The woman who died tonight?"

"I don't know. Could be," he said. "She worked part time at The Egg and Yolk. In fact, I just saw her the other day when I was meeting with Merri Gleason."

All this time, they were moving around The Hollows, landscaping, waitressing, while holding Abbey and other children back up in their barn. Everybody knows everybody in The Hollows; that was the famous phrase. Sometimes it's when you think you know that you stop seeing.

There were sirens then and flashing lights as two police cars pulled in through the gate. Her body should have flooded with relief. The good guys were here. She'd done her job, hadn't she? Using information and abilities that no one else had, she'd led the police to the people who had taken Abbey and maybe other lost children as well. That was her job. It was *their* job now, wasn't it, to finally find Abbey and the others that might be buried there? She had to turn her attention to finding Rainer. *Where* was he?

He took us because we're like you.

But no, that wasn't all. *You'll know when you're done*, Eloise said. *There's an unmistakable sense of release, like letting go of a breath you didn't know you were holding*. Finley didn't have that feeling. Not at all.

She pulled those pages from her pocket. If the maps were right, there was a mine head directly north of where she stood. As Jones walked off to greet the police, Finley walked in the other direction.

The wind was whipping through the trees, howling in that sad, angry way, as if no one could understand its sorrow. The snowflakes were no longer thick and fat. They had grown small and icy, hitting Finley's face like tiny shards of glass. She wrapped her arms tight around her body, but everything was raw and painful—her exposed throat, her hands without gloves. Her thighs were numb and she couldn't even feel her toes. She now understood how people died from exposure, how systems overwhelmed just started to slow down, then stopped altogether. The body freezes like every other thing left out too long. She needed to get warm, or at least dry, and soon.

There was a persistent, clinging smell of rot. It was a normal smell in the woods in summer, the scent of vegetation on the forest floor decomposing, returning to the earth. It was a warm smell, something for the months when things were green and alive. But now that the air and the ground was cold, the odor seemed odd, out of place to the point of being unsettling.

She didn't see the opening at first, almost walked right past it. But there it was, obscured by trees that had grown around it, by snow-covered debris. It was the trail in the snow that she saw, a long, thick gully, as if something had been dragged. When she got to the crooked opening of the mineshaft, she saw a bent nail, red with fresh blood, the wooden slats tossed to the side. A vein started to throb in her throat. Not fear, but an urgency that was beyond fear.

There was a kind of warmth inside the shaft, a breath blown from the darkness. At least she was blocked from the wind. Finley followed the sound she heard emanating from deep inside the darkness. She should be afraid; anyone would be. And her heart *was* an engine in her chest, pulse pounding. But it was as if that fear dwelled on another level of her awareness. What her body knew to fear, her mind did not. For better or for worse, she was exactly where she needed to be. She used the light from her phone to guide her way.

TWENTY-NINE

She'd never heard a man cry before. It was a strange sound—ugly and hopeless. Sometimes her dad got a little watery in his eyes when he told her that he loved her, or that he was very proud of her. But sobbing, moaning? No. Not even when he'd been shot had he cried. Then, he'd just been yelling for her to get away.

So the sound was weird in her dream. In it, there was a bear, a great snorting bear, wobbling toward her. She could smell it, a musty, sweet-foul odor that climbed up her nose and stayed there tickling. She felt bad for it. The way it was wobbling, she could see that it was unwell. But she knew, too, that it was dangerous, that one swipe of his great paw would slice her open. It was coming on fast, and there was nowhere for her to run.

"Go back!" she yelled. "Go away, bear!"

Then she was awake and it was dark. So dark that, for a long moment, she couldn't tell whether her eyes were open or not. The wailing was nearby, echoing all around her. Where was she? She struggled to remember what had happened and slowly it came back—Real Penny, Momma, the voices in the woods. Her head was heavy with pain, and she felt so leaden and sick. Once she'd had the flu and her mother wanted to take her to the doctor, and she wailed, begging to stay in bed. She was so tired then, couldn't imagine rousing herself. Her daddy had to carry her, and even that was hard. She felt like that. Worse.

The crying seemed to come from above her, from the right, from the left. Where was she? The ground beneath her was dirt, the air heavy, thick with a scent she couldn't name. She never thought she'd wish she were in her barn room on the hard cot. But she did wish that now. Even that was better than this.

"Mommamommamomma."

Bobo. The sound he made, it was horrible. Once she'd heard a dog howling, a mournful, desperate sound. She and her daddy had been walking up Eighty-Sixth Street. He'd taken her for frozen yogurt at the deli, and they were licking big creamy towers and laughing about something when they saw the small, tawny dog shut inside a beat-up yellow hatchback. It was hot, the kind of day in the city where heat rose up off the blacktop and shimmered, and everyone was cranky and flushed. The driver's side window was open, but just a crack. When they approached the car, the little dog came to the window and tried to push his nose out. She'd felt so bad for him that she gave him some of her frozen yogurt, his pink tongue slurping out the window crack.

"Don't do that honey," said her daddy.

Her father had called the police on his cell phone, and they'd waited as the dog continued to bark and howl, then went quiet. A man finally came out of a brownstone and yelled at them to get away from his car.

"You shouldn't leave your dog in the car like that," her father said. "I called the police."

"You should mind your own business," said the man, who wore a tank top and had so many tattoos on his arms that she couldn't see any skin. He had an earring in his lip, too. A thin mouth and a long, mean nose. He climbed into his ugly car and drove off, the dog perking up instantly. But that sound, it stayed with her, the sound of something trapped, calling for help.

"Bobo?" she said.

"She's dead," he wailed. "Momma's dead."

She couldn't see him, which she didn't like. She forced herself up from where she was lying and pushed against the wall. Slowly she started to see shapes, light draining from an opening to her right. Was that him? That lumpy object on the ground? She started to move away, toward the light. That must be the way out.

And she had to get back, back the way she came in, back toward the lights and the voices of the men in the clearing. She stood and started edging along the wall. Where was she? In a tunnel? Something in the air tickled her throat. But then the flashlight came on and there was Bobo, face streaked with blood, eyes bloodshot from crying. She shrieked, a loud echoing sound that seemed to go on forever. She backed away from him.

Then she heard another voice, Poppa's distant growl off in the distance toward the light. And something else, a scraping, dragging sound as if something large were being moved.

"He's going to put you with the others," Bobo said.

"No, he isn't," she said. She gritted her teeth. "No. He. Isn't."

When Bobo moved toward her, she drew her fist back and punched him hard in the face. Her fist landed with a hard crack on something that didn't feel like a face, sending a blaze of pain up her arm. A warm sluice of blood splashed back at her. She wiped it from her eyes and saw that her own hands were caked with blood. So much of it, dried and caked under her nails. Where had it come from? There was a picture in her mind then, of Momma beneath her, and her own arm coming down again and again, smashing, breaking.

"You killed her," said Bobo, standing to her right now.

"No," she said. There was a notch in her throat. "You did."

"No," said Bobo sadly. "It was you. You were *inside* me. I *felt* you. You made me do it."

She didn't know if it was true or not. Once when she'd been very angry, so angry—what had she been angry about? She couldn't even remember now—but the feeling had been so big, it didn't fit inside her body.

"Sweetie," her mother had said calmly. "You need to calm down and then we can talk about this."

She had wanted something—what had it been? Then, it had seemed like the most important thing in the world. She *couldn't* calm down. The feeling grew and grew, tumbled around inside her getting bigger, and she started shaking.

"Sweetie, relax," said her mother. "You're turning red. This is ridiculous."

When the lights flickered, then went dark, then came up again, it had scared the anger right out of her. Startled, she'd looked to her mother, whose eyes were wide, lips parted with surprise.

She knew she had done that; that her rage had leapt from her like an electric current and caused something to happen. Maybe it was like that with Bobo. Maybe she had made him do what he did. She didn't know and didn't care. She was glad Momma was dead, and she wished Bobo was dead, too.

Should she move toward the light, or back into the darkness? She opted for the dark, since she suspected that Poppa was up ahead. The light flickered and danced like a flame. She knew now that Bobo wouldn't stop her, that he couldn't.

"Momma's gone now," she said. "Penny's gone. You can go, too."

"I can't," he whispered fiercely. "I have to stay until—"

Poppa loped out of the darkness, a ghoul, a breathing skeleton, and knocked her down hard; she fell like a rag doll. No muscle, no bone. The manacle of Poppa's hand clamped around her ankle. And then Poppa was dragging her, pulling her toward the light.

She started screaming then, a squeal of rage and fear, the loudest sound she'd ever made. She clawed at the ground, looking for a hold.

Scream, make as much noise as you can. And whatever you do, don't let him take you. Don't let him.

"Bobo!" she cried. "Help me!"

But Bobo was gone, as if he'd never been there at all.

THIRTY

The boy with the trains knelt over the wooden tracks and moved the engine back and forth clumsily.

Choo-choo, he said, as happy and content with his toy as any child had ever been. Finley sat beside him, but he didn't look up at her, kept moving his train along the imaginary track on the ground. *Choo-choo*. Of all of them—Faith Good, Abigail, the *squeak-clink*, he'd been the quiet one, the least demanding.

"Where is she?" Finley asked.

The boy looked up at her, his face a pale, grim mask. "Penny's gone."

"Not Penny. Abbey," she said gently. She reached out to touch his golden hair. Of course, there was nothing there, but still he lifted his eyes from the train on the ground. Old eyes, a fathomless mineral green. Once she started staring, she found she couldn't look away.

"They're the same." He did not speak like a little boy.

"No," she said.

"We're all the same," he said. "Lost, broken, the victims of our parents' evils and mistakes. The Three Sisters, Penny, Bobo, Abbey, Elsie, even Momma . . ."

He went on listing names, and Finley listened until finally he stopped. The dark around them seemed to expand.

The last time she'd been with Agatha, Finley had asked, *What is this place?*

A vortex, Agatha had answered, *an energy center certainly*.

But it was more than that. It had intelligence, didn't it? It was running some kind of agenda.

What does it want? What does The Hollows want?

It's too soon to tell.

"What does it want?" she asked the boy with the trains, now. Joshua, she realized now. She recognized him from the photos in his mother's house. He appeared older now than when she had first seen him.

The boy cocked his head at her and frowned. "Don't you know?"

"I don't," she said. "I'm sorry."

"It wants all its children to come home."

A wind whipped around Finley, lifting her to her feet, and she saw them all, the faces of the lost ones. The Three Sisters, the victims of hatred and jealousy. A girl Finley knew as The Burning Girl and her sister, abused by their stepfather, then murdered by their own mother. Elsie, another little girl, drowned by her mother.

Finley staggered under the weight of a terrible sadness, pushing herself up against the wall for support. She saw, *lived* each horrible moment of abuse, neglect, and murder, flashing before her eyes like a stuttering horror reel. Not just those, but more, so many more. The gravity of each event sucked all the air from her lungs. And when it was over, the boy with the trains was gone, and Finley lay weak on the ground, shaking. She turned on her side and curled up and began to weep. Not for just the lost girls and all their sorrow, but for herself, the one who had to bear witness. She didn't want to watch. She didn't want to see how broken was the world, how flawed were its denizens. She didn't want to see.

But then there was a horrible screaming. It filled the tunnel, the sound of a little girl in pure terror. Finley pulled herself together, got up, and started to run deeper into the tunnel toward the sound. She felt like she had been running forever when she turned a hard corner, and was nearly blinded by the sudden light.

The scene revealed itself in pieces. A lantern lit on the wall, its light weirdly bright. There was a wide dark hole in the ground, a gaping emptiness that seemed to pull at the energy in the room. A towering ghoul of a man struggled with a little girl who was fighting like a berserker as he tried to drag her toward the hole.

"Stop!" Finley screamed.

Her voice was a bolt of lightning, shocking and powerful, moving everything else to stillness and silence. The man stared at her a moment, stunned. She knew him, the gardener who cared for the grounds at her school. She remembered his searing, haunting stare. Now those eyes filled her with cold terror.

She lunged at him, her shoulder connecting with his skeletal middle and sending them both crashing back against the hard wall. The girl was knocked to the side, where she lay motionless. Finley scrambled to her feet, and when he tried to get up, she used the sole of her thick motorcycle boot to kick him in the face. She saw the girl stir.

"Run, Abbey," she said. "Run!"

But the girl didn't move. Abel Crawley tried to lift himself, then quickly lunged at Finley's legs, knocking her to the ground hard. The hole yawned to her right. Rising from it was a foul odor, the breath of death so strong that Finley gagged.

"What is that?" she screamed at him. The horrible possibilities took shape in her mind. "What's down there?"

He had a strong grip on her ankle, impossibly strong, and pulled her closer to the edge of the hole. But she flipped herself and sat up quickly to punch him in the face as hard as she could. Pain traveled white hot up her arm. She'd forgotten how much it hurt to hit someone. Her early years had been spent wrestling and play fighting with Alfie and all his stupid friends. They were afraid of her, not because she was strong but because she was so ferocious. When you were small, you learned to claw and bite and pinch to get away. It always ended up with one of the boys crying. Even if she had been hurt, she'd never let them see her cry.

She had developed a good right hook, and she used it now to bash Crawley in the face again, eliciting a roar of pain and a spray of blood. But then he was on top of her, his strength, his weight too much. She was pinned. Never let them pin you, never let it be a match of strength alone. That was the first rule of being a girl in a group of boys. His mouth twisted into a cruel bloody smile, and struggle as she could, she couldn't get away.

"You can kill me," she said. "But they know who you are and where you are. And they'll find you. You'll never hurt anyone again."

The girl was a bullet shot from a gun. She flew over them screeching, dive-bombing into Crawley, knocking him back and off Finley. She heard the unsettling crack of skull against rock. He slumped against the wall. The girl went tumbling, and Finley dove for her, catching her by the arm just as her body went flying over the edge into the hole. Using all her strength, Finley pulled the girl back onto the ground. Both of them lay spent, panting with effort. Crawley started moving.

Finley pulled the girl to her feet. It was then that she saw her face for the first time and drew in a ragged breath of surprise. The girl blinked, her gaze glassy and confused.

"Is he dead?" she asked. "Did I kill him?"

Finley could feel the girl's shine, but it was just a candle flicker, something she might outgrow. She'd grow up to be an intuitive person, might even have a few dreams, or see shades and shadows that others never saw. Her rational mind, her intelligence would rule her, though. Those moments would be easily explained away. She wouldn't be like Finley. Lucky girl.

"Don't let him take you," the girl whispered as she drew closer. "Don't let him."

Finley grabbed her by the shoulders, pulled her close.

"Run," she said, through teeth gritted in fear. "Don't stop for anything. Turn right out of this tunnel and *run*."

The girl gave her a tight nod. And then she broke free, disappearing into the darkness. In her place, a form appeared, slim, not much taller than Finley. She knew him, not by face, but by his sad, angry, lost energy. When he moved into the light, she saw that he was a youngish man, maybe in his thirties, though it was hard to say. He seemed young and older at the same time. Lines of blood creased his face like warrior stripes, his breathing ragged and shallow.

"Put her with the others, Bobo," the old man growled to him, getting to his feet.

"No, Poppa," said Bobo.

His face wobbled between a frown and a strangled smile, as if he were straining under a terrible weight. A long moment passed between Finley and Bobo, a flicker of recognition in his otherwise blank eyes. Finley held up her hands, offered him a smile.

"You don't have to do what he tells you," she said. "Not anymore. The police are coming, yes. But they'll understand what he made you do, that you helped when you could. You saved her from Momma. I was there. I saw you save her."

"They'll take you from me," said the old man more loudly. "You killed your Momma, boy. They're going to lock you away forever."

Bobo looked between Finley and Poppa, the sound of his breathing filling the cavern in which they all stood. There were other sounds coming now, wafting like distant music on the cold still air.

"They're coming for you," said Poppa.

Finley inched closer to Bobo, away from the dark, empty hole. What was down there? The energy, a cold breath inhaling and exhaling, tugged at her and repelled her. She wanted to get away, and yet a part of her *didn't* want to. There was something, a hypnotic hum, something dark that lured and pulled. She'd felt it before, on her bike when she drove too fast, when she explored that abandoned warehouse with Rainer, when she played chicken on the train tracks with her friends watching that moon of light growing closer, hearing the wailing of the horn. When she was under Rainer's needle, feeling the heat and the pain, the metal in her flesh. How deep could he go? Her bones vibrated with the pain of it. She wanted it to stop—*How much longer, Rain?*—and yet she didn't. She wanted it, the pain, to swallow her, the ink to leak into her soul and color her blue-black so that she disappeared. Because she was tired, tired of being what she was, tired of trying to alternately hide it and understand it. It was always there in her, that desire to surrender to the dark.

It was so close to the skin, that hunger for the darkness, that when Bobo tackled her, knocking her back, she didn't even try to keep herself from falling. She let it rise up and swallow her whole.

THIRTY-ONE

Penny was on her knees, crawling, her leg throbbing, her body so heavy, her energy so *used up*. She was free from them, but she couldn't go.

She could hardly move, as if there were still a tether to her ankle. Too much was asked of her and she could not perform, like sometimes in math class where the numbers on the board floated, frustratingly incomprehensible. Sometimes she'd get so angry over her homework that she'd cry. *Oh, honey, don't cry*, her mom would say. *I don't get it either.*

She let the ground take her, falling from her hands and knees with a sigh to her belly. She felt the earth rising up and embracing her, the dirt and blood in her mouth. She wasn't sad or afraid as much as she was tired.

The tunnel was alive with sound, voices behind, voices ahead. She could hear some kind of song that was eerie and somehow beautiful. *Little flowers in the garden, yellow, orange, violet, blue.* The echo of it was like a lullaby. That's what she was, a flower in the garden, attached to the ground beneath her, rooted, one with the black earth. She couldn't leave this place. She belonged here.

She was about to close her eyes when she saw a point of light ahead, a tiny burst of white and red, a flicker of inky blue-black. And the birdsong, the song of the bird she heard the day Poppa took her. She remembered looking and looking for him, knowing that he must be as pretty as his voice and so he was. He flew toward her, then perched above singing, fat and puffy, reveling in his own prettiness. How could she see him in this dark? But she did. Maybe she was dreaming? His song was so sweet. Little Bird. Her daddy's nickname for her. And his song reminded her that her family was waiting for her; she knew they were. But then the little bird was gone, disappearing like ink into ink. The sound of his song turned into something else, notes so beautiful and familiar that she almost couldn't let herself believe that they might be real.

Abbey! Abbey Gleason!

"Mommy?" She could barely whisper, her voice cracked and dry.

A white glow approached, the sound of steps and voices yelling. And then a light, causing her to blink. She heard the sharp intake of a breath, a shocked pause, and then yelling.

"*Abbeyabbeyabbeyohmygodabbey!*"

Arms warm and strong lifted her. She was dreaming. Dreaming those soft arms, and the scent of her hair, and the notes of her mother's voice pulled taut with fear and worry and joy. And her daddy taking her and holding her close, carrying her like he used to do before he said, *You're a big girl. You're too old to carry now.* Which was no less sad because she knew it was true.

"Oh my God, she's so thin," he said. "There's nothing to her."

"My baby," she said, holding tight. "My little girl."

And if it was a dream, so be it. It would be her last, and she would dwell in that moment of enveloping love and blissful relief from pain and fear forever. But there was something wrong. Something not right. The woman wasn't her mother. And the man wasn't her daddy.

Before the world went black again, she managed to tell them: "My name's not Abbey. It's Eliza."

THIRTY-TWO

Rainer was obsessed with survival stories, those people who had found themselves in extreme circumstances and through will, luck, or accident had emerged from scenarios in which others had perished. *The Worst-Case Scenario Survival Handbook* was his Bible—what to do if you're caught in a flash flood, attacked by a shark, wrestling an alligator, have to jump off a building and land in a Dumpster. According to Rainer, one of the biggest factors that determined survival—other than a positive attitude—was hand strength, the ability to hang your body weight from your fingers.

Of course, this didn't motivate him to strengthen his fingers or exercise in any way. He just thought it was notable. Finley, as she hung from her fingertips over a dark abyss, was praying she'd have the opportunity to tell him that he was right.

She gazed up into the eyes of the boy who pushed her, his feet next to her fingers. She saw a helpless regret on his face, a kind of sad mystification.

"Please," she whispered. "You don't have to do this."

Then she was standing in the corner of his bedroom while he slept. The room was filled with smoke, and orange licked under the door. The house seemed to creak and groan, and the floor was hot beneath her feet. She was there and not there.

The door slammed open and a younger version of Poppa stood in the frame, a black shadow against a backdrop of swirling orange, red, and white. An intense blast of heat filled the room.

"*Bobo!*" he called. He moved into the room. There was nothing in him yet of the ghoul he would become. Still Finley could see what he was, a bad man with dark appetites. But it hadn't started to waste him. He was young and strong, handsome in a wiry, lanky way. "Fire!"

But Bobo couldn't be roused. The smoke, the poison of it had already leaked into him. He was small, not even six. Poppa lifted him easily and carried him from the room. Finley followed as he started down the hall toward another bedroom, but the flames were wild and there was no way through, a wall of heat driving him back.

As the man ran down the stairs, there was a horrible crash above. He burst through the front door before a great explosion blew him out the rest of the way. He fell to the ground with the lifeless child in his arms. On the ground, a woman wailed staring at the house, her eyes wild and wide with grief and pain.

"*Penny! My baby! Penny!*"

She never even glanced at the boy, didn't reach for him or check if he was breathing. She could only scream her daughter's name, a blade of sound cutting the night. Finley was the watcher; she saw everything. The abuse, the neglect, the desperate act of a girl who'd had enough.

When Finley came back, she was still hanging, her fingers slipping a sliver at a time, dirt giving way beneath them.

"She set the fire so he wouldn't come for her anymore," Bobo whispered. "Penny tried to kill us all. But Momma still loved her best."

"Help me, Bobo," said Finley.

"Bobo." Poppa's distant voice. "Is she gone?"

"Yes, Poppa," he said, holding her eyes. "I put her with the others."

She thought he'd step on her hands and that she'd fall to her death. How deep was the hole? What *was* it? What was down there? Instead, he stepped back disappearing from her view. She wanted to scream for him, but she'd just alert the old man. She heard Bobo blow out the candle, and a total darkness fell.

She tried to find purchase with her foot, but the wall was slick, nothing to put her toe on. Fingers slipping. Darkness calling. Her mother had tried so hard to keep Finley from this place. Amanda knew all along that something horrible would happen to Finley here, hadn't she? Some deep mother's instinct, or maybe she was more like Eloise than she let on. And all Finley could do was rail against her and rebel, do exactly everything her mother didn't want her to do. As her fingers lost their grip, she was sorry, truly sorry for being such a little brat. She hoped on the other side, she could find a way to go back and tell her mom that she'd been right all along. Amanda deserved that.

She couldn't hold on anymore, not with the dark pulling her and her strength waning, fingers cramping. She was going to fall. How far down? What was down there? She closed her eyes and prayed.

Voices and light broke into her awareness.

"I heard her." Rainer's voice was strident with worry. "I heard her voice."

"The tunnels play tricks," said someone else. "It's hard to know where sounds are coming from."

"Yeah," said Rainer. "The tunnels play tricks. But I *heard* her."

"I'm here," she called, her voice strangled with effort. "Hurry, I can't hold on!"

"Finley!" Rainer called. "Where are you?"

"In the hole!" she said. "Here!"

"Oh my God—*where*?" She saw a light bouncing on the ceiling. It gave her strength. She gripped her fingers, worked her feet, still struggling to find someplace to dig her toes in.

"Here," she said again to give them the sound of her voice. She wasn't going to make it; her fingers slipped another millimeter, the dirt soft, breaking away.

"Rainer," she managed, her voice strangled with effort, with fear. "I'm sorry I brought us here. Tell my mom I'm sorry."

"Tell her yourself," he said.

There were strong hands on her wrists then and she was looking up at Rainer, into his beautiful dirty face.

"Hold on," he said, gripping hard on her arms, taking her weight. She felt blessed relief, started to weep with it. "We are so going back to Seattle. This place is fucked."

She laughed a little, more a choking sound as he pulled her. But even then she knew it wasn't true. She *was* sorry that she hadn't listened to her mother, that she'd come to The Hollows. But she also knew that this was where she belonged.

Jones caught up to them then, and he and Rainer lifted Finley out of the hole. When she was safe on the ground, she started to cry, dropping into Rainer, who held on to her tight. She let him, clung to him hard. She didn't even think to ask him what the hell he was doing in the mines.

"The girl," she said to Jones. "It wasn't Abbey Gleason. It was Eliza Fitzpatrick. Did they find her? Do you have her?"

"The police have her," said Jones. "She's going to be okay. But the Gleasons—"

He let the sentence trail with a sad shake of his head. "Eliza's mother has been called. At least we're bringing one little girl home."

The signs were all there, Finley just hadn't understood them completely. The Little Bird, the boy with the train turning out to be Eliza's brother. She tried to stop the downward spiral of self-recrimination, but she could feel its tug. If she'd been more, better, more open—if she'd focused more on understanding, rather than setting boundaries, would the messages have been clearer?

"Poppa and Bobo," said Finley. "They're gone."

"The police are searching for them," said Jones. He peered off into the darkness with a squint. "There's nowhere to hide down here."

Finley knew he was wrong. There were a million places for them to hide; they belonged to these tunnels, in these woods. The Hollows would hide them until she was ready to give them up. Finley tamped down the tickle of unease. *We're not done here*, she thought.

"How did you get down here?" she asked Rainer as she helped him stand. He was hurt, his leg stiff and bloody, his face pale and strained. Jones stood and dusted himself off, and headed in the direction of lights and voices.

Rainer told her what happened, how he followed Abigail, then fell into the mine. How he followed the sound of her laughter until he heard Finley's voice.

It surprised her; Finley wouldn't have thought of Abigail as her ally. Abigail was always running her own agenda, like with the wedding rings, willing to use Finley and consider her collateral damage. Abigail liked drama and trouble, not rescue.

"Let's get you some medical attention, son," said Jones, returning to them. He took Rainer's other arm, and the two of them helped him out down the long tunnel and out of the mine. Even as they left, Finley felt an energetic tug at her back.

Eloise Montgomery had seen a good many things. Too many, she thought, as she pulled her car to the side of the road and donned her red wool hat, pulled on her gloves. She couldn't bear the cold anymore; it tightened her joints and seemed to burrow under her skin, causing her very bones to shiver inside her flesh.

The full rainbow of human suffering had revealed itself to her and she'd been asked to bear witness to all the violence men and women could do, all the havoc they could wreak through their neglect or ignorance or evil intentions. And the truth was, the honest truth was that she was tired.

She is ready, said the voice that wasn't a voice.

It grieved her that Finley might be asked to live the kind of life Eloise had lived. But it was beyond her control. Eloise was old enough to know that. Only the young think they have something to say about how their lives turn out. *We don't choose; we are chosen.*

Before she left the house, she'd phoned Ray, just to say that she was sorry, that she loved him in the way that she could. He didn't answer, which wasn't like him, and his voicemail picked up instead. But, actually, she supposed it was a good thing. They fought the last time they'd spoken.

"You're not coming," he'd said. "Are you?"

"Not yet."

He'd been quiet, his disappointment filling the line between him. Then, "You're not coming at all, are you?"

She didn't answer at first. She'd been promising for so long to come out to San Francisco, to spend a weekend at least just having fun. *You know, dinner and a show, a cable car ride, a walk along the beach. Like normal people.*

It sounded nice, but Eloise had given up trying to be like normal people long ago. The fact that he didn't realize she couldn't just switch off what she was troubled her. He was trying to move away from "the work," as they called it. He didn't seem to understand that she didn't have that choice.

"Finley needs me right now," she said weakly. "Maybe when she's more settled."

"It's time to put yourself first, El," he said. Didn't he really mean that it was time she put *him* first? His voice was flat, distant on the line. "Finley's a grown woman."

Of course, there were other reasons she couldn't come to San Francisco. She just didn't want to get into it.

"If I could have loved anyone else again," she said to his voice-mail. "It would have been you."

She stepped out of the car and into the weather. She'd worn her boots and warmest coat, and still the cold snaked up her sleeves and down her collar. She headed into the trees to a place she'd visited many times—in visions, to find Finley, to help a lost boy, and once to find a burning girl. She thought that the place had everything it needed. But she realized now that she'd been wrong.

In fact, now that she understood what was really needed, she felt like an old fool. She should have known long ago. It was obvious.

She'd heard the activity on her police scanner at home that the car belonging to the missing man had been found. She knew that he'd be found dead, but that because of the beacon in his car Eliza Fitzpatrick would be found alive. She'd return to her mother and go on to live a happy life. In fact, the horrors she'd endured would cause her to honor her gifts and know her own strengths in a way she never would have otherwise. Was it a fair trade? No. But nothing about this life had ever been fair.

You can make a trade, the voice said.

She also knew that Finley was in trouble, that she had a choice to make. The girl had been flirting with it for a while. Would she let the darkness take her? Or would she claw her way back to the light? Eloise wasn't worried. She knew Finley in a way she knew few others, even her own daughter Amanda. She knew Finley because she was so much like Eloise. Finley felt the tug of destruction, but she always came back from the edge. The girl knew that people loved her and needed her. That knowledge was the cord that pulled her back.

For Eloise, however, the scales had tipped. There were more that needed her on the other side now than here.

She crunched through the snow, The Whispers louder than the wind. Those million voices all around her, telling her their stories of sorrow and loss, of love and joy, of birth and death, and lives lived well or otherwise. It was the chorus of humanity in all its beauty and discord. Sometimes lovely, other times painful to hear. Eloise had been listening for so long. And she was very tired, tired to her bones, as if they didn't have the strength to hold her anymore.

She pushed through the clearing. The roof of the old church was covered in snow, caps of white resting on the gravestones, heavy frosting on the branches of the trees. She heard the voice of a woman she used to know, singing.

> Little flowers in the garden.
> Yellow, orange, violet, blue.

Eloise could see the lights off in the distance, the klieg of red and white shining up into the sky like a display of aurora borealis. She'd seen the Northern Lights once, eerie green dancers in the sky, the stroke of a cosmic paintbrush on the night. There were so many beautiful and mysterious things about this world. It almost made up for all the rest of it. Almost.

"Abel Crawley, what have you done?"

He stood at the low wall of the graveyard, weeping. Eloise was not one who believed in evil, per se, though she'd witnessed many evil acts. As far as Eloise was concerned, there were only two ways of being in the world. You either walked through life acting out of love, or you acted out of fear. But Abel Crawley made her wonder.

She'd known some black spots on the fabric of the universe, and he was certainly one. Like an ink stain on a wedding dress, they spread their blackness, and it worked its way into the delicate weave, damaging it, and leaving an indelible mark.

He'd been a terrible boy—a bully, an animal sadist, an arsonist. He got smart and learned to hide himself, and then he was more dangerous still. He liked young flesh, he liked fear, he liked misery and pain. And yet he moved among the people of The Hollows invisible, mowing lawns and trimming shrubs, and peering in windows for that special light, the shine of the Dreamers.

"I can't get them to be qu-qu-quiet," he sobbed. "They w-w-won't leave me a-a-alone."

She saw them all around him. They looked like angels in the snow. Abigail, Patience, Sarah, Priscilla—and others, so many others. The lost girls, the broken, abused, neglected, and murdered. All those Eloise had tried to help or save over the years but couldn't, and some she'd never seen before. They were restless, angry, and oh so tired, just like Eloise.

"You don't deserve silence, Abel," she said.

Eloise released a series of shuddering coughs then. Her last visit with Dr. Apple hadn't been a pleasant one.

"There's still hope, Eloise," he said, exasperated with her again. "But not without the treatment. Without the treatment, the way this is progressing, you don't even have six months."

"The cure is worse than the disease, Ben," she said.

"Until the cure takes hold," he said. "And then you live well again."

Live well again. The truth was, she hadn't lived well since Alfie and Emily died, since the accident that took their lives gave her these abilities. She'd tried to see what she did as a gift. She knew that she'd helped many people, that the world was a better place because of the things she had done. But it hadn't been a better place for her.

"I want you to understand that I view your refusal of treatment as a form of suicide." He was a serious young man about Amanda's age.

"Don't be so grim, doctor," she said. "It doesn't suit you."

He'd released a frustrated breath. Outside, the day had been bright and blue. She watched the wind blow the white clouds. They shifted and changed shape—a puppy, a dragon, a couple dancing.

"But there could hardly be a more grim situation," he said, taking off his glasses and rubbing his eyes. "Surely you see that."

Perhaps only doctors knew what Eloise and people like her knew, that life was a closed unit, a sphere you might hold in the palm of your hand, contained and finite. The body had its very unyielding limits, a thing youth never understands. But obviously the good doctor didn't comprehend that there was so much more than the life of the body. That, in fact, that was the least of it.

"I can see that's how you feel," she said. "And I'm sorry."

"Mrs. Montgomery," he said. "Eloise. Please don't do this."

Now, the snow had stopped falling and the air had taken on an icy stillness. The boy was there, too, standing behind his father. He was broken, damaged, but not a stain like his father.

"Arthur," she said gently.

He stepped into view, his head bowed. "I never wanted to hurt anyone."

"Arthur, walk yourself through those trees and find a man named Jones Cooper. Tell him who you are and what you and your father have done. Tell him where to find the girls."

"They'll lock me away."

"That's what you must do," she said. "You must make amends for the wrongs you've done."

He sat on the ground and cried. "I can't."

She shook her head. "They'll find help for you," she said. "You'll be all right."

She wasn't entirely sure this was true. Some things were beyond the reach of her sight. Some things were not for her to see. She had grown to accept this, as she had grown to accept so many things.

"Go now, Bobo," she said. He stood, staring at her as she moved closer to Abel.

"Show me where you've put them," she said. She was not angry with him; she did not hate him or judge him. She did not even fear him. That was for others to do. Eloise neither condemned the

307

wicked nor praised the good, because they were just two sides of the same coin. They were all one, all the same, even though so few ever seemed to realize that, would rail with fury at the very thought.

Sobbing, Abel Crawley turned and began to walk toward a path that led back into the woods.

They passed out of sight along the edge of the clearing where Eloise paused to watch Finley help Rainer into a police cruiser. Jones Cooper stood staring in her direction, though she was reasonably sure he couldn't see her, back as she was in the safety of darkness. She saw Wolf and Merri Gleason, holding each other, oblivious to everything around them, grief was wrapped around them like a curtain. How cruelly Merri Gleason had been treated to think she was close to finding her daughter, only to have everything snatched away. Abbey Gleason was gone. Merri had to find a way to let go, or lose herself.

Eloise saw a light around Finley, something bright and good and strong. She was different from Eloise, a natural. She had a big ego, a strong spirit. She was ready. The girl wouldn't let it rule her; she wouldn't let it take everything. Eloise spent a long moment taking in the youthful beauty of Finley's solid flesh, strong and flushed with life. *I'll stop when my outer self looks like my inner self*, she'd said when Eloise had expressed distress over the girl's myriad tattoos. Eloise still didn't like it, but she understood now that Finley was exerting some kind of control over her body, making it what she wanted it to be. Part of her wanted to call to Finley, to hold her in her arms and try to explain. But there was no explaining anything to youth. And there was no such thing as good-bye. She knew that better than anyone. She kept after Abel Crawley.

She followed him deeper and deeper into the woods, away from the mine opening that was now crawling with police and to another one a bit farther north. When they reached it, she followed him into the opening that was so well hidden that most would pass right by without seeing it. Just as she plunged into darkness, she heard Finley's voice.

Mimi? Mimi! Is that you?

"Faster, Abel," said Eloise. "They're coming."

THIRTY-THREE

Finley didn't know what made her turn in time to see Eloise and Abel Crawley move through the trees. In fact, she couldn't even say she *saw* them exactly. There was a tickle, something that made her turn away from Rainer. She had been standing there, leaning against a police cruiser, trying to get her head around the fact that the girl she'd saved was Eliza and not Abbey. How could she have been so wrong?

She'd watched Wolf Gleason collapse, weeping. "It's not Abbey. It's not Abbey."

And Merri had stood over him, gray faced and catatonic, broken.

Finley's throat was closed from crying, the blood rushing in her ears. Eliza had been carried from the scene, her mother called. There would be a joyful reunion tonight, just not the one Finley imagined. It was all so complicated, so fraught, wasn't it? No joy without sorrow, no sorrow without joy. It was then that she saw them, but maybe it was just a shadow, a shifting of light, something.

"Mimi?" she called. She didn't even know why. Finley moved quickly toward the trees, a sudden feeling of urgency making her pulse quicken.

Jones Cooper moved into step beside her. "What did you see?"

"I saw my grandmother," she said. The sky had cleared, a wide high moon hung silver in the blue-black sky. "With Abel Crawley."

Had she seen that? Surely not.

"Up here?" said Jones. "I don't think so."

The wind howled, and Jones frowned as they came to the edge.

"Mimi!" she called again. "Is that you?"

Finley and Jones exchanged a look, a worried energy passing between them. They both knew that Eloise turned up when she was least expected. Some people were always just where you thought they would be. But Eloise was exactly where she needed to be—wherever that was. Jones put the beam of his flashlight to the ground, and it wasn't long before it fell on two sets of tracks, one large, one small. Finley recognized the snowflake tread of her grandmother's boots.

"Those are her boot tracks," said Finley, a rush of fear making her hands shake.

"What would she be doing up here with him?" asked Jones, sounding in equal parts mystified and annoyed. "Your grandmother has to be more careful with herself." There was a note in his voice, the deep concern of friendship. And something else.

"Why did you say it like that?" Finley asked.

His glance told her that he knew something that Finley didn't— or rather hadn't wanted to know.

"She's an old woman," he said. "She should be at home knitting blankets."

"Oh, please," said Finley, picking up her pace, following the tracks.

Another voice. Another flashlight beam. "Where are you two going?"

Detective Chuck Ferrigno trailed up behind them, panting. He was not sure-footed in the woods, looked out of place even in his parka and heavy boots. Finley had a new jacket too, given to her from the trunk of a prowler. Thick and navy blue, hanging down to her thighs. Jones told them what they saw, and Chuck Ferrigno took out his walkie.

"It looks like they're headed for the north entrance to the mine," said Jones. "Have your guys block the head we already discovered."

"We have Arthur Crawley," said Chuck. "He turned himself in. But he was looking for you, Jones. He said: 'Eloise said Jones would take care of me. That he'd make them understand.' Freaky-looking kid, covered with blood, blank in the eyes."

"He asked for me?" said Jones.

"He said 'Eloise'?" asked Finley.

Finley didn't wait for Detective Ferrigno to answer; she just burst into a run, following her grandmother's tracks, calling after her.

For the first time as she ran, she heard The Whispers, as Eloise referred to them. *It's the sound of all the voices of this place and others, telling their stories to anyone who will listen,* Eloise had explained to her. *Some of them are sad, some joyful, some horrifying, some uplifting. It's the full rainbow of human experience.* Finley had been glad to never hear them; she had enough unwanted visitors.

Do they ever stop? Finley had asked Eloise.

No, said Eloise, as if considering for the first time. *I don't suppose they do. Sometimes they're quiet, sometimes loud. But, no, I don't believe they're ever completely silent.*

What do they want? Finley had asked.

Eloise regarded Finley with a bemused squint. *They just want to be heard. They just want us to listen to their stories.*

Are you sure that's all they want? Finley had asked. *Why would you be able to hear them if they didn't want something from you?*

If they want more, she told Finley, *I have no idea what it is.*

Hearing them now, Finley knew that Eloise had been wrong. It wasn't just a radio broadcast for those few who were able and willing to tune in. There was something more, something selfish and grasping.

The mouth of the tunnel was up ahead, Jones and Chuck lagging behind.

"Finley," she heard Jones say faintly. "Don't go in there alone."

But she did, she had to. There was no time, no time at all. Even though she was blind heading into the dark, she heard sounds. Movement, breath, a distant calling, her own heartbeat banging out the uneven rhythm of exertion and fear.

"Mimi," she called, reverting to the name she used as a child. "*Mimi!*"

The darkness, the tunnel seemed to grow and expand. Her hands touched the hard walls, the crown of her head skimming the ceiling, the wetness, the closeness all around her. Her breathing was labored and jagged. She felt the world wobble and tip, and it dropped her to her knees. And then she wasn't in the tunnel anymore; she was back in the graveyard.

It was a beautiful day, Finley's favorite kind. When the air was newly warm, and the sky was bright blue with high white clouds. The trees were lush with green, and the wildflowers a chaos all around. Eloise sat on the steps of the church, looking as Finley had never seen her. Once in an old photo album, Finley had found images of a beautiful woman with a dark pixie haircut and glittering black eyes. She had heavy lashes and high cheekbones, and she glowed. Her tiny frame was poured into a white lace shift, her tiny veil like a halo, pearl slippers, a bouquet of white roses.

"Mimi," little Finley had asked. "Is that a princess?"

"No, sweetie," Eloise had said with a laugh. "That's your Mimi and your grandpa Alfie."

"That's *you*?" she said with childish carelessness. "But you're so—"

"Young? Pretty? Not old and wrinkly," said Eloise, laughing. Her grandmother was never a vain woman, never quick to be insulted.

"You're still beautiful," said Finley. She'd been raised by a very vain mother, so she knew how to dole out a compliment—quickly when need be.

"I was very young," said Eloise. "In my twenties."

"That's not young!" said Finley. "That's old!"

"You think so?" said Eloise, pretending surprise. "Well, I suppose it must seem that way to an eight-year-old."

"You were so happy," said Finley.

"I was," said Eloise. "I loved your grandfather very much. So, so much."

"Where is he?"

"He's gone from this place," she said. "But he's all around us. In you, in your mommy and little Alfie, in my heart and dreams."

"Do you still see him?"

"I do," she said. "He seems to turn up whenever I need him most."

Even at eight, Finley didn't need that explained to her. "He has glittery eyes and such a nice smile. He looks just like *our* Alfie."

"He does, doesn't he?"

The Eloise who sat on the church steps looked like the girl in the picture, youthful and full of joy, everything ahead of her. The golden light that emanated off of her was warm, magnetic. Finley realized that she was lying on her belly on the ground among the gravestones.

Towering oaks shadowed the white church with its small steeple and bright red doors. A dappling light danced, sunlight fingering through the trees.

"It's a lovely spot to rest, isn't it?" said Eloise. "The Three Sisters deserve their place here, don't you think?"

Finley pulled herself to her feet and basked in the warmth of the air. She looked down at her wet and blood-soaked clothes, which were suddenly dry. The parka she'd been wearing was gone. She walked over to her grandmother, and Eloise patted the spot beside her, looking at her with a loving smile.

"Just the grave markers will be enough," said Eloise. "All they want is a remembrance. They just wanted to be known. All that youthful energy, combined with the injustice of their murders—it creates such chaos when trapped."

Finley didn't have a voice. Emotion was a ball of cotton in her chest.

"We hold on so tightly to it all," said Eloise. "All those negative emotions. We just cling to them. Or maybe it's that they cling to us."

"Or a little of both," managed Finley, her voice just a whisper.

"Yes," said Eloise. "Like a haunting. Places cling, too."

"He took them because they were 'Dreamers,'" said Finley. "Like me and like you. All those girls were somewhere on the spectrum. Why did he want them?"

"Abel Crawley had his own agendas," said Eloise darkly. "He

was a pain giver, a misery maker. As a child, he was content to hurt animals. As he grew older, his appetites changed. Even his own wife Millie didn't know what he was, or at least that's what she told herself."

Finley watched as Eloise deftly linked wildflowers into a chain—yellow, orange, violet, blue.

"But his daughter Penny knew what he was. She tried to kill him but killed herself instead trying to escape him. But Millie clung to her, blaming herself for not knowing what her husband did when she was gone working."

The chain of flowers grew longer and longer in Eloise's thin fingers.

"That clinging love kept poor Penny in these woods. And Abel brought the Dreamers, the ones who could see her—for his shattered wife and to fulfill his own dark needs. Abel Crawley is a bad, bad man."

Eloise shook her head, slow and sad.

"How could she stay with him?" asked Finley. "After everything he did."

Eloise looked up at the sky, as if the answer might be there, then back at Finley. "Millie Crawley was quite undone by the loss of her daughter Penny. And she wasn't all there to begin with, had a touch of what her son Arthur has, a slowness. She stayed because she had nowhere else to go, because she couldn't leave Penny alone in the woods."

Finley knew that it was so. She understood in that moment that it was Arthur she'd inhabited, his childish mind so confused, angry, and afraid. He was trapped here too with Abel.

"And then when Abel was done with them? Or Millie was? Or they became too much trouble? Then he just killed them?"

Eloise nodded grimly, her mouth pressed into a tight line of anger.

"He was also a Listener. He couldn't stand the sound of The Whispers. He knew, like you guessed long ago, that they wanted something, all those voices."

"*What* did they want?" asked Finley.

"They want to go home," said Eloise.

"So," Finley said, struggling to understand. "He thought the girls could quiet The Whispers, give them what they wanted—or needed?"

"Yes," said Eloise. "Among other darker, more hateful things. He thought because they were Dreamers that they could show the lost ones home. But they were far too young. And their passing was as wrong and ugly as the others'. Even you wouldn't have been able to help them, Finley. You would have just wound up trapped here, another voice in the trees, calling."

"Calling who?"

Eloise lifted the flowers, which she'd turned into a necklace, and hung them around Finley's neck. "Calling me. All this time, and I had no idea."

"No," said Finley, a sob nearly taking the word.

"Everything has its time and its season."

"I'm not ready," said Finley. She knew it was selfish, but she didn't care. "I don't want to stay here without you."

"You were born ready, my girl," said Eloise. "You are electric with power. It comes off you in waves. And you're smart, and stubborn, and have an iron will like your mother. You were more ready at eight than I have ever been."

"But I don't want this," said Finley. Tears fell, big and wet, an embarrassing flow, impossible to stop. Finley's shoulders shook with her choking sobs.

The young and pretty Eloise leaned in close and kissed Finley's tears away, pulled her close and then released her, rising.

"We don't choose, Finley," she said, her voice warm with loving kindness, but also somehow distant with resignation and understanding. "We are chosen."

"Mimi," cried Finley. "Mimi, *please*."

Eloise opened the door to the church, and Finley found herself backing away from the energy that seemed to flow out of it, the same glittering black pull that emanated from the hole in the mine.

It wasn't tugging at her anymore, it was pushing her away, farther and farther until she stood on the other side of the stone wall that surrounded the graveyard. She was just an observer here, allowed to bear witness.

"Why do they need *you*?" Finley yelled. "Why do you have to be the one?"

"It's my time," said Eloise, as if she were talking about an appointment she'd made. She gave a wry smile. "It's on my way."

At the door, Eloise opened her arms, and Finley watched them. Abigail, Patience, and Sarah danced and tugged at one another. Faith corralled them toward the doorway, giving a fleeting glance back at Finley. Then The Burning Girl dimmed her fire and she was just Priscilla Miller, another victim of violence and neglect. She skipped through the open door. Abbey and the other Snow Angels, as Finley had come to think of them, moved uncertainly, and Eloise extended her hand. And there were others, faces Finley had never seen, so many others. They, too, moved into the luring darkness. But it was not dark at all, not really. It was the presence of all color, a great twist of all the shades and hues of this life and the next. It was the most beautiful and terrible thing Finley had ever seen.

When the parade had concluded, Eloise stood for a moment in the doorway and glanced back at Finley with the very face of love and compassion. But then she, too, was swallowed.

And then the church was just a church, a quiet little place nestled deep in The Hollows Wood. And there was silence, a blessed, perfect silence, except for the singing of the rose-breasted grosbeak, its pretty notes filling the warm spring air. Finley dropped to her knees and let out a wail that was the single dark note of all her sadness and anger and loss.

When she came back to herself, she was on the edge of the hole in the mine, her torso hanging over the abyss with Jones Cooper holding on to her ankles, and a pale and shaken Chuck Ferrigno with a gun in his hand, the shot he'd just fired ringing in Finley's head.

THIRTY-FOUR

The smell of coffee, the hum of the espresso machine woke her. Bacon, cinnamon, eggs, a culinary symphony of aroma enticed Finley to pull the pillow from her head. But then it all came crashing back, as it did every morning since she lost Eloise. And Finley stayed in bed, pulling the covers tight around her, turning away from the idea of breakfast, even though her stomach was growling and she couldn't afford to lose any more weight. She looked like a ghoul, haunted and wasting.

Then came the pounding on the door. She put the pillow back over her head and clung to it, even as he tried to tug it away from her. He finally succeeded.

"Today's the day, sis," said Alfie, loudly snapping the shade open. The light was blinding. What time was it? "You've done enough wallowing. This morning, you rejoin the living."

"Go away, Alfie," she said.

"No," he said. "Enough's enough."

He gleefully stripped the covers off her bed, leaving her in only a tank top and underpants in the harsh cold of an old house in the morning.

"Go away," she roared. He ran off laughing, clutching at her blankets. She felt the energy of a laugh, but she tamped it down hard.

"Kids," said Amanda mildly, walking into the room. Finley's mother offered the soft chenille robe that was hanging over the chair. Finley took it grudgingly, got up, then sank into the chair by

317

the window, looking out at the oak tree in Eloise's yard. It was the oldest oak tree in The Hollows. Today, the branches were bare and black, a stark relief against the blue-gray sky.

"I think you should try to go back to class today," said Amanda. Her straw-colored hair pulled back into a ponytail, she wore no makeup. She looked as pale and young as the pictures hanging on the wall downstairs. She was small like Eloise, careful in her movements.

Alfie had returned with the covers, and Amanda busied herself making the bed. Then she moved to the dresser, neatly arranging everything there—the phone Finley wouldn't turn on, the brush she refused to pull through her hair, her wallet with no money, keys she hadn't touched since Eloise's memorial.

"I'll drive you," said Alfie.

"I'm not ready," she said.

"You're never going to be ready," said Amanda, sitting on the edge of the bed. She folded her hands in her lap, seemed to steel herself. "You have to ready yourself to return to life. Trust me. There's no magic doorway through grief. Sometimes you just have to bust out."

Any anger Finley usually had for her mother had drained the night Eloise left. That's how Finley saw it. Eloise made a choice and left her. Anger and sadness were one ugly mass in her stomach.

"I can't."

Amanda didn't say anything for a moment, just regarded Finley with eyes ringed with fatigue. Finley got a glimpse of her own selfishness; Eloise had been Amanda's mother. Amanda had been here within twenty-four hours and handled everything from phone calls, to funeral arrangements, to reception details. She handled it all with her usual steely panache. She cried at night when she thought everyone else was sleeping.

Your mother is a stoic, Eloise had said. *She holds everything in. I don't think she trusts anyone to take care of her when she's vulnerable.*

"Let's at least try for breakfast at the table."

When Finley had come home that first night, alone except for

Jones, who slept on the couch and stayed until Amanda arrived, they'd found the letters on the kitchen table. One for Jones, for Finley, for Amanda, Alfie, and Ray. Finley's sat unopened on her dresser. Everyone else had read his, but no one but Ray had talked about it. It seemed that everyone knew Eloise was sick, except for Finley. It was a big secret that everyone kept.

"It's what she wanted," Amanda had said when Finley confronted her. "A person has a right to choose how she lives."

"And how she dies?" asked Finley bitterly.

"Well, yes," said Amanda, her face going tight with sadness. "Don't you agree that we deserve that dignity if we can have it?"

"How the hell should I know what we deserve?"

Finley had wished that her father were here. But as usual when he was needed, he was nowhere to be found. He'd called, of course. But when it came to getting on a plane and dealing with the reality of everyone's grief—that was more than he could do. He'd made excuses about work, his new girlfriend, sent flowers.

"Okay," said Amanda, lifting her palms. "Okay."

"She was the only one who understood what I am," said Finley. Amanda hung her head. "I know," she said. "I'm sorry."

"I didn't mean—" started Finley.

"No, I get it," she said. "I screwed up and I'm sorry. Just know, please know, that I was just trying to keep you from having the kind of life she had. That's all. I'm so sorry."

A rare embrace had followed, one which went on for hours and in which Finley got her first good sleep since Eloise left.

Now, in the kitchen, Finley ate. She started off refusing, then nibbling, then scarfing down everything on her plate. Amanda and Alfie ate, too. Alfie was going home soon. Amanda was going to stay on for a while, so Finley could decide what to do.

"I never thought I'd be back in this house for any period of time," said Amanda, clearing the dishes. "But I guess The Hollows gets what it wants."

After breakfast, Finley took a shower, letting the near-scalding hot water turn her skin pink and fill the shower with steam. What was notable was the silence. For the first time in her life, Finley was alone. Everyone was gone—even Faith and The Three Sisters. The Whispers had been completely quiet. Eloise was right; they finally got what they wanted. There was nothing left to say.

Finley had managed to dress herself when the doorbell rang. It had been nearly a month since the service for Eloise, which was held at the little old church in the woods and attended by hundreds of people from all over the world, even though most of them had to stand outside. It had been simple, and brief, just the way Eloise had specified in her notes to Amanda and Ray.

"There shouldn't be any grief for me," she wrote in her note to Ray. "Just know I loved you in my way. And let me go."

"She had no idea how much I loved her," Ray had told Finley after the reception when she'd walked him out to his car. "I didn't even care that she'd never love anyone but Alfie. I just wanted to be with her, to show her some of the happiness of this world."

"I think she'd have let you if she could," said Finley. "She wanted to come and be with you. She told me so."

Eloise had been fighting cancer for the better part of seven years, Finley had learned. It had been in remission until very recently. When it returned, she refused treatment. It was a decision that she'd shared with no one, except her doctor.

Now, Finley stood at the landing, hearing the sound of an unfamiliar voice. Curious, she climbed down the stairs and was surprised to see Eliza and Betty Fitzpatrick in the foyer. She paused on the stairway and tried not to stare at Eliza, who looked pink and healthy, if a little haunted around the eyes.

"I'm sorry," said Betty, when she saw Finley. "I know your family is grieving a loss. But Eliza wanted so badly to come, to thank you."

"I'm sorry," Eliza said. "I'm sorry you lost your grandmother."

She was a sliver of a girl, with a Dreamer's eyes, a bright shine.

What else would Eliza see with those eyes? Finley hoped nothing but love and light and laughter. But that wasn't the way of things, was it?

"She said that it was her time to go," said Finley, happy to be able to talk about it with someone who could understand. "You couldn't have done it. And neither could I. It wasn't our time. Neither of us could have showed them the way home."

"Real Penny wanted me to do it."

"She was as lost as any of them," said Finley. She told Eliza about the fire, how Penny had killed herself to escape the father who abused her and the mother who didn't believe her. But the girl already knew.

"She didn't know what she was asking," Finley said. "They don't always know."

Eliza nodded grimly, and Finley led her over to the couch and took her hands.

"My grandmother told me that you would not be scarred by what's happened to you," said Finley. "That you will move through the pain and trauma in time, and learn to honor the strength and specialness inside you. Can you feel that?"

Eliza looked toward where her mother had stood and nodded uncertainly.

"I have nightmares," she said, starting to shake. "I still see him."

"He's gone," she said. "Detective Ferrigno shot him and he fell down the hole."

"They never found him."

"He's gone," said Finley. She squeezed Eliza's hands hard. "I swear he'll never hurt you or anyone ever again."

"And Bobo?"

"He's in the hospital," said Finley. "He won't be coming out. Not anytime soon."

The girl's mouth was just a thin line, her eyes a gray field of sadness. But she'd be happy again one day. Eloise had promised that, and she had never been wrong once.

"I'm sorry you lost her," said Eliza again.

"She's with me," Finley said, just to make the girl feel better. But as the words passed her lips, she knew it was true. She felt stronger than she had in weeks.

"You gave me my daughter back," Betty said at the door when they left. Her eyes brimmed wet with happiness. "I don't know how you did it, but you found her. We've lost so much—but there are no words for my gratitude."

"Just honor her," said Finley. "Honor who she is and what she is. Listen to her, so that she can learn to listen to herself."

"I will," said Betty, the words clearly resonating. "I will."

Finley didn't make it to class. Instead, Alfie, Amanda, and Finley tended Eloise's garden. They cleared the overgrowth and trimmed the healthy perennials. Eloise had neglected to clear the annuals, which Finley took to mean that she hadn't had the energy to do it. Why hadn't she asked Finley? Because if she had, then Finley would have known that Eloise was sick. And Eloise hadn't wanted her to know that.

Dear Finley,

Don't be angry. I know you are. You're just like your Aunt Emily that way. You'd rather be angry than sad. There's so much more power in that, or so it seems. Remember it's okay to be sad, to feel it and then move through.

Their breath came out in clouds as they raked the beds and pulled the weeds, which were withered and brown from the cold. It hadn't snowed again since that first snowfall, but the ground was hard and the sky was a persistent gray.

"This is what I hate about the Northeast," said Amanda, who also hated gardening. "You don't see the goddamn sky from November through March."

"It's not that bad," said Finley, seeking just one patch of blue to point at. But there was nothing. Amanda blew out a breath but didn't argue. She still had that hollowed look that grief gave a person, that sinking under the eyes, that thinness to the mouth. It had made her quieter, less eager to take up an argument.

"I'm going in to make some hot chocolate," Amanda said after a while. She leaned her shovel against the house and peeled off her gloves.

"Sweet," said Alfie. He dropped his rake and rubbed his hands together. It was his last weekend. On Monday, he was going back to Seattle. "I'll help."

"You coming?" said Amanda to Finley, who was still raking.

"Call me when it's ready," she said with a smile. "I'm going to bag up the mess."

We all have our time and season in this life. And I have had mine. Now I can do what I think has been expected of me all along. I just wasn't ready to let go until now.

Finley bagged up the clippings and the weeds. She liked the work, just like Eloise had, the tending, the cutting and clearing away of dead things, making room for the fresh green buds of new life. Finley trimmed away a few brown branches on the Devil's Walking Stick.

For years Eloise had tried to get rid of the plant, she'd told Finley, only to find it coming back year after year. Finally, she just let be the native plant that she had thought was just a weed. She discovered that its flowers and berries were a valuable nutrition source for butterflies, wasps, and bees. That its fruit drew robins, bluebirds, towhees, thrushes, and rusty blackbirds to her yard. It wasn't a plant that she had chosen for her garden, but there it was nonetheless. Ralph Waldo Emerson thought of weeds as plants "whose virtues had not yet been discovered." Eloise decided that she would take the same position. She let the plant grow, only to discover that it flowered in autumn, enjoying a final color show before winter fell.

You have been a joy to me, Finley. You are so much more native, so much more in charge of your gifts than I ever was. The road you walk will be easier and more fulfilling than mine, I'm sure. And I will always be here for you. My great love for you does not end with my passing. You, better than anyone, must know that. So hold that love in your heart and let me go.

Finley heard her mother calling, but she wasn't ready to go inside, even though the sun was dropping and the air growing colder. When the bag was full, she tied it and sat on the little bench, spent. Her body ached from the work, reminding her that she was horribly out of shape. She took a deep breath and surveyed her work, as the sun dropped lower.

"Finley!" Her mother's voice carried on the air, faint and beckoning.

"Coming, Mom!"

She was about to go inside when something caught her eye, a glitter, a rush of shadow. When she turned back, Eloise and her grandfather Alfie stood over by the garden gate, looking as bright and giddy as a pair of lovebirds. Finley half expected to see a robin come down and land on Eloise's finger as they approached.

Finley wanted to be angry, to rage, to cling to her sadness, but instead she felt the energy of a smile. Finley never realized how much she looked like Eloise when her grandmother was younger and happier with everything before her.

"Are you ready to let me go?" asked Eloise.

Eloise told Finley long ago that a haunting was a relationship, that the dead clung to the living only as much as the living clung to the dead.

Finley felt a fresh wash of tears, a desire to run toward Eloise, to cling and to hold on. But she didn't. She had already learned the most important lesson Eloise had to teach, though it still hurt like hell: Fear holds on. Love lets go.

"Yes, Mimi," said Finley. "I'm ready."

Eloise offered that slow, considering nod, that warm, loving smile Finley so adored. Then she looped her arm through Alfie's, and together they walked through the gate and disappeared into the gloaming as if they'd never been there at all.

"Who were you talking to?" Amanda had come to sit beside Finley.

Finley thought about lying. That was her instinct, to pretend for Amanda that she was something other than what she was.

"I was talking to Mimi," said Finley. "She's with Grandpa, and she's happy. She wants me to let her go."

A rainbow of micro-expressions flashed across Amanda's face—fear, sadness, worry. She put a strong arm around Finley's shoulder and squeezed.

"Can you do that?" asked Amanda.

Finley stood and reached out a hand to her mother, helping her up off the bench.

"Do I have a choice?"

"I don't suppose you do," said Amanda, sounding very much like Eloise.

THIRTY-FIVE

The next day, Alfie offered to drive her to school, but Finley wanted to take her bike. She needed the air, the roar, the vibration of the engine. When she took off down the road, it felt like she had wings.

She arrived late at class, earning an understanding nod from her professor who was talking about Jung's break from Freud.

"Rumors abound from hints of homosexual tension, to Jung's disagreement with Freud's theories that sex was at the root of all human behavior. But most people agree that it was Jung's *Psychology of the Unconscious* published in 1912 that was the final nail in the coffin. Jung's fascination with the paranormal and his beliefs that psychic phenomenon could be brought into the purview of psychology were unacceptable to Freud."

But almost as soon as she sat, Finley tuned out, spent the rest of the class doodling only to find after the hour had passed that she'd drawn the church and graveyard, overrun with wildflowers.

"Not much of a note taker."

She looked up to see Jason standing beside her and the rest of the classroom empty.

"Hey," she said.

"Don't mind me saying," he said. "But you look a little worse for wear. You okay?"

"Death in the family," she said.

He lifted his chin and nodded. "Sorry to hear that," he said. "My condolences."

She stood and gathered up her things, wondering why she'd even bothered to come to class and if she would ever really return to the living. When she turned to leave, Jason was still there looking at her with concern.

"Can I walk you to your bike?"

"Sure," she said. There was something about him, something calming. They walked down the hall and exited the building. The air had grown colder, and the sky had taken on a flat black-gray color again. The blue of earlier was gone.

"I've lost people, too," he said. "I feel you."

"Need a ride?" she said when they got to her bike.

"No. I'm good." He nodded over toward a beat-up Toyota. "Another time."

"Hey," she said, digging into her bag for her phone. "Can I get your email? Would you mind sharing your notes from the last couple of weeks?"

But when she looked up, he was gone. Not walking off to his car, not heading back to class. Gone. The Toyota he'd nodded at was likewise not there. Other people from class were lingering in front of the building, climbing into their vehicles. But Jason was not among them. It took her a second to get it. He'd never been there at all.

Finley rode her bike from Sacred Heart College back into town. She drove past the precious town square, and turned off Main Street onto Jones Cooper's block. She parked on the street and walked up his driveway, turning onto the path that led to his office. She knocked on the door, and he opened it for her as if he'd been expecting her.

He offered her coffee, which she accepted, and then sat on his couch while he lowered himself into the chair behind his desk.

"How are you holding up, kiddo?" he asked gently.

"Eh," she said. "You?"

"I miss her," he said, looking down at his nails. "She was a special lady. I learned things from her—which she would have been surprised to hear me admit."

He laughed a little.

"She respected you and considered you a friend," said Finley.

"A high compliment indeed," he said. "Not necessarily deserved."

They sat a moment, each lost in thought. Then, "I have a check for you."

"I don't want it," she said. She assumed it was from the Gleason case.

"I refused payment from the Gleasons," he said. "But Mr. Gleason sent money anyway, said we spared them a lifetime of wondering and waiting. I want you to have it."

She shook her head. "No."

"Well, it's yours," he said, tone brooking no further discussion. "You earned it. Lord knows I was no help."

He took an envelope from the drawer and put it on the corner of his desk. Her name was written in a careful printed hand. She let it sit there. Anyway, she hadn't come to talk about that.

"You know, Mr. Cooper," she said. "I don't remember what happened that night. I mean, what really happened after we followed Mimi into the tunnel."

"It's kind of a blur," he said, rubbing his eyes. "And it was dark."

"But you made a statement," she said.

"I did," he said. "Best I could."

He had a habit of running his hand over the top of his head, of looking at you when he was listening—looking through you. He also tended to turn his eyes away when he was talking about himself, as if he wasn't as interested in your reaction as he was in choosing the right words.

"Could you share it with me?"

He also had this way of releasing a breath before doing something he didn't want to do but thought he should.

"Are you sure? Because maybe you remember just exactly what you need to remember. Maybe what you saw is all you want to see."

She'd told him about the graveyard and the doorway, the things

Eloise had said and how she'd looked. She did so not because she expected him to believe her, or because she needed him to. She did so to give him comfort when he'd broken down driving Finley home that night, when he'd pulled the car over and began to weep, big unapologetic sobs. She'd sat stone still for a time, afraid to move, not wanting to touch him, big tears falling down her own face. It was good to see an oak like Jones Cooper bend with sorrow; he'd been dealt a hard blow, they both had. *Bend or break in the storm of this life*, Eloise always said.

Now, in the light of Jones's office, she felt stronger. Not strong. But strong enough to hear what really happened the night she lost Eloise.

"I followed you into the tunnel, with Chuck right behind me. We had our flashlights, but you were quickly out of sight. Running in the dark. I could hear you up ahead, feeling your way, yelling for your grandmother. I kept calling for you, asking you to slow down. But you were in your own zone, not hearing me or ignoring me."

He cleared his throat, leaned forward in his chair.

"For a little while we lost you altogether, but then Chuck heard the sound of your voice, and we found our way back to the cavern, the seat of that mine shaft, or whatever it is. The hole where they—" He paused a moment, folded his hands, and looked down. "Found all the bodies."

Put her with the others, Bobo. She could still hear Poppa's voice, that unearthly growl. The horror of what he did was almost too much for Finley; she felt herself shutting it away, turning from it.

"Crawley had her at the edge. There was already a standoff underway because the tunnels were full of cops. It was a crime scene. A young officer had his gun drawn, pointing it at Crawley, who had your grandmother across the chest, holding her in front of him. And you were standing there, screaming at him to let her go."

He stopped a minute and stared up the ceiling.

"She looked at me with that expression she always wore. You know what I mean, right? That sad half smile like she already knew how everything was going to be and she was just waiting for me to figure out."

"Yeah," said Finley. "I know what you mean."

"I knew she was sick," Jones said. "She was sick when we first met. But she got better. She never told me about it; I could just tell. Just like I could tell when she wasn't well again. I asked her about it, but she waved me off—you know how she is."

Outside, Finley heard a woodpecker tapping on the oak tree, cars going by, a school bus letting out a pack of laughing boys.

"But that night when I locked eyes with her, I felt this tremendous wash of peace. I can't explain it. She gave me something, some kind of gift. That's Eloise, always giving but never allowing you to give back."

Jones was stringing more words together than Finley had ever heard him utter. *He's one of the few who only talk when absolutely necessary. Jones Cooper does not rush to fill a silence.*

"Then he just—jumped, taking Eloise with him." His eyes took on an unfocused quality, like he was staring at something he didn't want to see. "It was just like that. One minute she was there, all Eloise. The next minute she was gone. She never even uttered a sound."

She wondered if he'd cry again, but he stayed steely eyed. She figured he only cried about once a decade, if that. He'd probably used up his supply of tears.

"Chuck fired his gun, just as you dove for them. *I* dove to grab hold of you and caught you by the ankles before you went in after them."

"You should have let me go," she said blackly.

He shook his head grimly.

"Are you kidding? And have your grandmother haunting me for all eternity, complaining about how I didn't save you. No."

She smiled a little, just a little.

"All the best things are before you, Finley," he said softly. "Don't let that darkness lure you away from that. It's a false promise. Stay in the light as long as you can."

He sounded old and tired, and she wondered not for the first time what kind of dark secrets Jones Cooper had.

"Have you been up there?" she asked. "Since that night."

"A couple times," he said. "So far only one body has been recovered. They think it's Abbey Gleason, but DNA matching is underway."

He rubbed at his eyes. "We went through the cold cases, to see if we could connect other missing persons to Abel Crawley. There are two more missing girls—Jessie Holmes since 1995, Annie Taylor from 2003. They were local, girls from the hills. Jessie was not even reported missing until a year after she'd been gone; her mother died about ten years ago. And there's no other family. Annie was an assumed runaway. Her father still runs a farm outside The Hollows now. I had the feeling he'd rather have kept thinking she ran away."

He put a hand on files on his desk, kept his eyes there a minute, flicked at the oak tag with his thumb. Finley wanted to stop thinking about the girls, imagining their pain and fear. But she couldn't so she didn't stop him from going on.

"How long he had them up there, what he did to them, and when he finally killed them we may never know. His son Arthur, the only one who might have some idea, is virtually catatonic, can barely even feed himself at this point."

"He was as much Abel Crawley's victim as anyone," said Finley. Inhabiting him, she'd felt all his anger and sadness, his pain. She couldn't see him as an accomplice, though, of course, he was.

Jones dipped his head to the side. "Maybe."

"Then Eliza, and eighteen months later Abbey Gleason," she said. "If not for Abbey, we would never have found Eliza. If not for them, who knows how many others."

She wanted to be like Eloise, who let go of anger, who didn't judge. But she wasn't there, might never be.

"It's a horror show," said Jones. "And there's another whole network of tunnels down there. If they're down there, we may never find any remains."

Finley stood and paced the office a little. She tried to push it back, the horror of it, the terrible sadness. But it wrapped itself around her, a cloak she feared she'd have to carry. She'd seen them, those angels in the snow. The only comfort she had was that Eloise had helped them find their way home.

Finley looked around the office, noticing that Jones had hung some more pictures—his swearing in as a police officer, his wedding, being given an award by the mayor, his son's graduation. There were even some white throw pillows on the couch.

"Why haven't they found her?" Finley asked. "My grandmother."

Amanda had insisted after three weeks that there be a service for Eloise, that a headstone be erected for her in the small graveyard. They had done the same for The Three Sisters. Joy Martin, the librarian from The Hollows Historical Society had helped Finley make that happen. They would all be at rest together, finally.

"Or Crawley," he said. "I don't know. I'll admit it's odd. They say that the water table was high this year, and that some of the tunnels fill. Bodies could—wash away."

Finley dried her tears with the sleeve of her shirt and turned back to Jones.

"They'll find her," he said, rising to hand her a tissue from the box on his desk.

Finley wasn't sure why, but she had a feeling that he was wrong. It didn't matter, not really. She wasn't clinging to some hope that maybe Eloise was down there alive. Her grandmother was gone. And Finley was alone, though people whom she loved and who loved her were all around. Eloise was the only one who ever truly understood her. She still had Agatha, of course, but it wasn't the same.

"I had a call today," said Jones. He lifted a piece of paper from his desk and put on his glasses. "An older couple looking for their missing adult son. He served in Afghanistan, came back with PTSD in 2012. He was home for a while, then said he wanted to take a road trip, find himself kind of a thing. They haven't heard from him in over a year."

"What's his name?" asked Finley as Jones handed her a photograph he'd printed from the internet. She wasn't surprised to see the face of the guy she'd met at the school, though he was very different. In the photograph, he was clean cut and erect in his uniform, not slouchy and high with a three-day beard growth.

"Jason," said Jones, looking down at his notes. "Jason Birch."

Finley put down the paper. "Help them," she said.

Something flickered across his face, a mingle of amusement and relief. "You're in?"

"I suppose I am."

And there it was, beneath the riot of all her other emotions, that calm, that rightness, that absolute certainty that she was doing the right thing. It was something.

Later that night, Finley rode her bike to Hollows Ink. Rainer was waiting for her. There was a lot of work to be done, and they both knew it couldn't wait. She stripped off her shirt, lay down on the table, and while he worked, they talked about everything and nothing.

He shaded in the boy with the trains, Joshua, the mineral green of his eyes, the white gold of his hair, the navy blue of his tee-shirt. He'd been quiet, so unobtrusive that Finley almost missed him. Finley believed that he'd been there to make sure she knew that it was Eliza who needed her, not Abbey. But Finley hadn't understood until she looked Eliza in the face. It was Finley's fault, of course. If she hadn't been so focused on getting rid of her visitors, she might not have missed what Joshua was trying to tell her.

The needle hummed, and the pain was hot and bright.

"How are you doing, Fin?" Rainer kept asking.

"I'm fine," she said, even when it wasn't true. Pain was a reminder that she was alive, that she drew breath into her lungs and was tied to the world of the living. Even when it moved through her like a wave, bringing tears to her eyes, there was a part of her that relished it.

Then it was on to Abigail—the auburn of her hair, the blue of her eyes, the tattered hem of her dress. Abigail, Finley's enemy and ally, the one who connected her to the worst part of herself, but who had also made sure Rainer was there when Finley needed him. Abigail was there to remind her that most people, no matter how badly they behave, just want to be known. And that even bad girls can sometimes be good, and good girls can sometimes be bad.

"How're you feeling?" asked Rainer. "Need a break?"

She shook her head, watching him in the mirror, bent over her, her skin a wild rainbow of his work and hers.

Finley's body was a living canvas of ink and bone. It would grow and change, evolve. It would age and fade, it would grow softer, get bigger, shrink and shrivel, as bodies will. Maybe what she was on the outside could never truly reflect what she was on the inside, but when she looked in the mirror she saw herself in all her true colors.

EPILOGUE

Abbey loved the ocean. The gray churning waters of the Atlantic, where it lapped against the shores of Rockaway Beach. The hot lazy days they'd spent there with toes buried down to the damp cold layer of sand beneath the hot, and the blue cooler sweating underneath the shade of their wide umbrella, a kaleidoscope of rainbow colors, were among the happiest they'd spent as a family.

"Be careful of the riptide," Wolf always felt compelled to warn.

"What's a riptide?" asked Abbey.

"It's a current that can pull you under and yank you out to sea."

They both glanced out at the water, then back at him. Jackson looked worried.

"What do I do if that happens?" he asked.

"Don't panic," Wolf told them. "Swim sideways along the shoreline. I'll come for you. I'll be watching. Every minute."

"Okay," Abbey had said, unconcerned. She was using a plastic cup to build a tilting sand castle.

"How many people die in riptides every year?" Jackson wanted to know. "I mean, statistically, is it common?"

"Just be careful," Wolf had answered. He didn't know. "It happens often enough."

The music coming from their portable Bluetooth speaker was tinny. What was it that they'd been listening to that last day? He wanted that detail. Something alternative and slow, something old. Grace Jones. That was it. "I've Seen That Face Before."

They'd played in the shallows, Abbey with her bucket, Jackson with his net. Jackson, little brainiac that he was, kept walking back to the umbrella for his iPad to try to identify the shells he found. Wolf wanted to tell him not to worry about what they were. Just collecting them was enough. But he didn't bother nagging. The gulls called, always complaining in their funny way.

"It's always good here," Merri said sleepily from her low lounger. She wore a red bikini. She was beautiful; her body toned and caramel, but soft, yielding. There was a wiggle to her ass that was pretty just because it was *her* wiggle. His wife, the mother of his children; no one and nothing could be more special than that. And yet Wolf had been secretly sexting with an editorial assistant at *Outside* magazine all afternoon. Nothing had ever happened in the flesh. But he was flirting with it.

That day, so beautiful, so perfect. He'd missed it. His memory of it was more vivid than his awareness had been at the time. And he only remembered it now because Abbey was gone. He *hadn't* been watching her every minute, not then, not ever. And the riptide, the dark current that runs under every life, had carried her off.

Today they gathered on the beach in overcoats, hats and gloves, a mean winter sun painting the world a harsh white. Merri held Jackson, who leaned against her, an arm wrapped around her waist. Wolf's parents stood back, wearing the same stunned expression they'd worn since they learned that Abbey's body had been among those found up in The Hollows. Merri's mother, the same auburn-haired, hazel-eyed beauty as Merri, stood behind her daughter, a steadying hand on her shoulder. She wouldn't even look at Wolf.

They'd tried to keep the church service small, but it had been packed with friends, colleagues, parents of children from Abbey's school, some of the kids, too. Their friend Bryce who was a singer-songwriter, sang Abbey's favorite, "Somewhere Over the Rainbow." Everyone wept.

The ceremony was short and tasteful, the chapel air rich with the smell of stargazer lilies. They considered themselves lucky that Abbey had been returned to them. Two other families' parents were still waiting; one girl had been missing since the early nineties, another since 2003. At least for Wolf and Merri the waiting was over.

Blake delivered the eulogy.

Our Abbey, our angel, gone too soon.

You'll live in us always.

And more, so many more eloquent words about her light and her joy and her kindness, a beautiful blur of sincere sentiment that Wolf could barely hear, Merri clinging to him, blank and glassy eyed. It was a tragically beautiful affair after which everyone but they went back to intact lives, a program with Abbey's shining face folded into pockets or stuffed into purses to be later discarded. Not a keepsake.

But on the beach, it was just those of them with the long stretch of grief and rebuilding ahead.

"My darling girl," Wolf said. "You will always be with us."

It was a crock wasn't it? She was gone, so far away. He couldn't feel her. The sound of every little girl's voice reminded him of hers. What had her voice sounded like? Sweet and smoky, full of laughter. He could describe it, but not hear it. His girl was gone.

"But today," said Merri, rock solid. "Today we let you go."

And they watched as the wind took her away into the waves and the gray sky.

He'd never seen Merri stronger. The knowing had ripped her to pieces, but she'd reassembled herself stronger than she was before. He laid his hand on her belly, which was already starting to swell just a little—or was it his imagination? Their saving grace. A child was conceived in The Hollows the night they realized that Abbey wasn't coming home to them.

Their sad and desperate lovemaking, the ultimate act of comfort in an abyss of grief and sorrow, had yielded this gift. In his wife's eyes now he still saw the depth of her pain and the bright glint of the future, and also her forgiveness. The fact that he didn't deserve her wouldn't keep him from accepting her love.

Would he ever tell her that he planned to leave her that weekend that they went to The Hollows? About the dark and ill-defined plan he'd hatched with Kristi, that she'd meet him up there and together they'd break his family apart?

No. Because he was weak, and they'd all lost too much. He'd take this second chance he'd been given. And if there was no such thing as a redemptive narrative, not truly, well, then he'd write one anyway.

ACKNOWLEDGMENTS

It's a myth that the life of the writer is a solitary one. Certainly, there are many hours spent alone at the keyboard. But when that work is done, it takes the efforts and talents of a passionate team of professionals to get those words out into the world. I am grateful beyond measure for the long list of people who support and bolster me, without whom I wouldn't be able to do what I do.

Thanks to my editor Sally Kim who, as usual, brought her wisdom, keen insight, and passion to the manuscript, pushing me to make this book the best it could be, and encouraging me to go someplace I wasn't sure I could go. Every book we have worked on together is better than it would have been without you.

My agent, Amy Berkower of Writers House, is a superstar. I am so grateful for her insight, support, and direction. I want to be just like her when I grow up.

The folks at Simon & Schuster, Touchstone, and Pocket are an absolutely stellar group. Each and every person brings their own special gifts and talents to the table. My heartfelt thanks to: Carolyn Reidy, Susan Moldow, Michael Selleck, Liz Perl, Louise Burke, Jennifer Long, Liz Psaltis, David Falk, Brian Belfiglio, Jessica Roth, Cherlynne Li, Wendy Sheanin, Paula Amendolara, Teresa Brumm, Colin Shields, Chrissy Festa, Charlotte Gill, Gary Urda, Gregory Hruska, Michelle Fadlalla, Meredith Vilarello, Laura Flavin, Paul O'Halloran, Etinosa Agbonlahor, Irene Lipsky, and Miya Kumangai. And I can never heap enough praise on the top-notch sales team, out there on the front lines in this super-competitive, ever-changing business, getting books in every format into as many hands as possible. It's everything; thank you.

I have an amazing network of family and friends who cheer me through the good days and carry me through the challenging ones. I am so grateful for my parents, Joseph and Virginia Miscione, and my brother, Joe, who have supported me in every way possible all my life and are unstoppable as a PR team doing everything from facing out books on the shelves, to carting me to and attending book events, and endless bragging. Thanks to Heather Mikesell for being one of my first and most important readers. She also takes pictures of people she sees reading my books—which is always a boost! Shaye Areheart, former editor and forever friend, remains a wellspring of wisdom and good advice and I lean on her more than I should. Thanks to Tara Popick and Marion Chartoff for their unfailing friendship. Even though way too much time passes between visits, they've been with me every step of the way.

My husband, Jeffrey, and our daughter, Ocean Rae, are the foundation upon which my entire life is built. I would be a lesser person and a lesser writer without the love, support, friendship, and laughter that fills our days together. I am so blessed in so many ways, but nowhere more so than at home with my two favorite people in the world, and our kooky Labradoodle, Jak Jak.

ABOUT THE AUTHOR

Lisa Unger is an award-winning *New York Times* and internationally bestselling author. Her novels have sold more than two million copies and have been translated into twenty-six languages. She lives in Florida. Visit LisaUnger.com.